Deception's
PLAYGROUND
1, 2, & 3

Deception's
PLAYGROUND
1, 2, & 3

By

Kush Lamma

Felony Books, a division of Olive Group, LLC,
P.O. Box 1577, Belton, MO 64012

ISBN-13: 978-1545169483

Felony Books 1st edition April 2017

10 9 8 7 6 5 4 3 2 1

Manufactured in the United States of America

For information regarding special discounts for bulk purchases, please contact Felony Books at felonybooks@gmail.com.

www.felonybooks.com

Text JORDAN to 77948
And stay updated on all of Jordan Belcher Presents' **newest releases, free giveaways,** *and* **special promotions!**

ACKNOWLEDGMENTS

First and foremost, all praise is due to Allah. I seek his help and ask for his mercy for my shortcomings.

I would like to thank my mother for her nurturing and motherly wisdom. I thank her for staying in my corner through all my ups and downs. I love you. I would also like to thank my pops. Even though our relationship is rocky, I thank you. Through your coldness and inconsistency I was compelled to emerge into manhood young. And although I've made many mistakes on this ongoing journey, I'm still solid. It's good, big dog. I still love you. I would also like to thank my baby sister, Kali. Your heart is my heart, and mine is yours. I got you pimpin', I love you. I would also like to thank my grandparents, all my uncles, aunties, cousins, nieces, and my nephew. A special thank you to my son, li'l Baby Kev, you keep me focused young papi.

I also want to thank Mr. Jordan Belcher. Right on for giving me a platform to express my literary talent. Insha'Allah the brand will flower accordingly.

Thank you to everybody that looked out during my iron vacation. My family, Yola the Guru what's good big cuzz, Shemond, Shila, Marco, The Hitters, FA, Li'l Noodles, Diamond, Big Baby, Silly Tay, D2, Li'l Juno, Ms. Jessy,

Cheeze, The Popper, Shanese, Garfield, Moose, Reshena, Emma, Mario, PJ, Jazzy, 2we, Boogy, Corrie, Li'l Greedy, Nayna, Lisa, Mac, Nisha, Ashley, Deron, Milisha, Mexican Dave and TEO. Right on for everything.

Shout out to my comrades behind the wall: Sun-Tzu, Spud, Gramps, C-man, Li'l Kwaty, Knot-Head, Bubbles, Steve-O, Li'l Reecy, Mandy, Uncle Denver (Forward Progress), Li'l Chris, Tonka, LB, Cheeze, D-Loc da Chop, Li'l Larry, Poppa, Le Le, Zuk, Fat Dev, TJ, D (megatron), Stink, and the Ummah. Anybody I missed my fault, it's still love.

To my readers, thank you for your support and I hope I don't disappoint. Enjoy!

Deception's
PLAYGROUND

PROLOGUE

I was heating up my hot pot, getting ready to make a meal with my celly, when I was briefly interrupted.

"Wright, inmate number!" the pale-faced C.O. shouted.

"1067238," I replied.

After she slid my mail under the cell door, the bitch rolled her eyes and took all three-hundred pounds she was carrying on her frame down the walk. I bent down to get the precious cargo and noticed the name "Casey Thomas" on the front of the envelope. *Goofy ass bitch*, I thought.

As I dwelled on the stranger who decided to send me a scribe, I laughed in disbelief and caught my celly's attention with my laughter.

"Who wrote you, cuzz?"

"This silly ass bitch Casey, bro," I said.

"She must've heard you 'bout to touch, my nigga."

"No good. I forgot her ass even existed. You know how these hoes do. Out of sight, out of mind. As soon as they hear a nigga 'bout to touch, they reappear like a magic trick."

"Fuck that shit. Let's finish dis meal."

And we did just that. We made our special—tuna with broccoli cheddar rice pizza. Ingredients: normal Ramen noodle soups, crackers and refried beans for the dough; layered with the broccoli cheddar rice and tuna, topped off with melted cheese, ranch dressing, picante sauce and crunched up hot chips. Pretty decent eating considering the circumstances.

We finished that off, shot the shit for a hot second and went to our individual routines. My celly was reading while I was taking some power notes, putting my game plan down for my return to the blacktop.

I'd been locked up for seven years. I came down when I was eighteen years old. I was twenty-five now and I had a new perspective on life.

I realized the game I loved so much … didn't love me in return.

It's funny because during my teenage years I thought I knew it all. I thought my niggas was solid and my main chick, Casey, was as loyal as they came. The seven I'd spent in the D.O.C. told me I was the smartest fool around. My so-called niggas showed me the least amount of support. And Casey didn't support me financially or emotionally.

My nigga, Duece, had been the only homey in my corner. Real stand-up nigga. Him and random females had kept a nigga cool on this iron vacation.

I had two weeks before I was going to be released from this hell hole, and I couldn't wait. The apex was my destination.

CHAPTER 1

Five years later ...

I was laying in the bed at my temporary abode at Embassy Suites, watching a wonderful show being performed on the part of my body that had a mind of its own. Then my phone rang.

"Yeah?"

"What's good, cuzz?" Duece said. "We on the way to the spot. It's gravy."

"You like that, papi?" the Spanish mami asked me, as she was feeding on my meat.

Duece heard her. "Nigga, you stay wit' a bitch."

"She's not a bitch, she's my bitch. And I'ma be there in a hot second," I told him before I hung up.

The wonderful creature before me continued doing wonders with her mouth. Speaking Spanish periodically as she came up for air, kissing the head. She knew from my phone call I wouldn't be fucking her at this hour. So she wanted to spend as much time as she could tasting me.

Deception's PLAYGROUND

She eased her mouth back down my shaft as I held the back of her head, navigating her direction on that orientation. She knew I was about to cum because this wasn't her first time being up close and personal with the rebellious part of my anatomy. Soon I felt the lion trying to escape the cage. The beast in front of me was ready to swallow him whole. And she did just that, "*mmmm*ing" and "*awww*ing" as she digested my unborn child.

She did her signature kiss to the head of my dick afterwards, telling him she'll miss him and she'll see him soon. Then she sashayed to the bathroom to get herself together.

Damn, she's a fool, I thought.

I followed behind her shortly after, grabbed a face towel and lathered it with soap to wash her saliva off my dick.

"Let me do it, Spade," Maria said after spitting the mouthwash in the sink.

"Yeah, let you do it and next you'll be trying to suck the life out a nigga. No good, baby."

She rolled her eyes and jumped in the shower. I watched as the Mexican goddess got herself sudsy with the sponge. She was five-two, hair down to the middle of her back, hour glass figure—and she was sexy as hell. Aside from my name permanently inked across the small of her back, her skin was flawless.

"A'ight, lil' mama," I yelled over the running shower water. "I'm 'bout to bust this move. I'll be back in a hot one."

19

"Okay, Daddy. I love you. Don't keep me waiting too long."

I went back to the bed area and got dressed. I grabbed my keys, phone, and my life insurance policy. Then I was out the door.

***

I pulled up to Duece's spot at about 10:15 p.m. He stayed in Belton, Missouri, in a quiet neighborhood. He always said Kansas City was too hot for niggas like us to lay our heads. And I couldn't agree more. Don't get me wrong, I love my town. But at thirty years old, I refused to have my primary residence in the city.

Had too many demons.

I noticed Ace's car parked behind Duece's when I bent the block. I called Duece and told him to unlock the door. I parked, jumped out the whip and headed in.

"What's good, big homie?" Ace greeted as I walked in.

"Hopefully this package yall got from Kutz," I replied. We embraced in a hug.

"This shit is right, Spade. I had my lil' chick put some up the vacuum, butter baby."

"Is that right? What chick?"

"My lil' whore. She's straight."

I wanted to chew his ass out for putting a bitch in our mix, but this wasn't the time. I noticed Ace looking at me like he agreed with my unspoken logic. Ace was the lil' homie, only nineteen. He probably thought if he said something to Duece about the bitch testing it, Duece would blow him down.

"I can't believe yo plug lettin' 'em go for ten a kick, cuzz," Duece said.

I'm hip, I thought to myself. I met Kutz one year after I got out of prison, through my OG partna, OG Casa. He started off fronting me a few bricks. I got back with him asap, and it's been rotating ever since. I stacked my peanuts and started copping straight up. I've always had hustle so getting it off wasn't a problem.

I eventually brought Duece in; and shortly after that my lil' nigga Ace. Duece has been in my corner since we were kids. And I saw how determined Ace was when I used to throw him four-ways when he was about sixteen. I also saw myself in young Ace, so I kind of took to him.

When Kutz told me I could start paying ten grand a kick six months ago, I was a little skeptical. *What can I say; I have trust issues with muhfuckas.* But Kutz had always kept it one-hunid wit' me. Once we agreed on the ten grand a brick, it was on.

Now we were sitting on ten yickens. Kutz had his hundred grand up front. I didn't need anyone breathing down my neck for currency. I could have paid the whole one hundred grand myself, but I believe in letting my niggas eat with me. So I put in fifty for five bricks, Duece put in thirty grand for three bricks, and Ace put in twenty grand for two bricks.

I only had two customers that I fucked with period. Duece had a handful of people he dealt with. And Ace supplied the hood with zips, four-ways and even broke down a few zips for his piece serves.

"Yo, five right there, bro," Ace told me, pointing to a black backpack on Duece's leather couch. I opened it to make sure my issue was in there. Like I said, I have trust issues.

"So what you 'bout to do, Duece?" I asked, interrupting his phone call.

He told the person on the line to hold on before he took it from his ear. "Shit, I'm 'bout to bend a couple corners."

I asked Ace if he was about to hit the turf and he gave me a knowing smile. "A'ight, I'm 'bout to shake," I said to them. "I'll get wit' you niggas in a minute. Pleasure doin' business wit' you gentlemen."

I gave them both dap and was about to head out the door when Duece stopped me.

"Aw yeah, cuzz, Sonya called and said she ain't talk to you all day. She want you to call."

"A'ight," I said simply and left.

I got in the Yukon and dipped off.

Damn, she gon' be hot, I thought to myself. I turned my Ron Isley CD up and headed to my woman's house.

***

I met Sonya two years after I got out of prison. Duece made that happen. He told me he met Sonya at June-Teenth about a year before I got out of prison. Duece told me he used to dig her but she only liked him as a friend. So they were just cool. I didn't want to fuck with her at first. I thought she was the typical chick from the hood, trying to get on any nigga that's winning.

But after she and her best friend, Nicole, and a couple of their homegirls came out to kick it with us a few times, I started digging her. Nicole was digging a nigga, but she had all body, no brains. Sonya was the total package—intelligent, sexy, bad body, the whole nine.

My kind of bitch.

I pulled up to her spot in Grandview, Missouri, about fifteen to twenty minutes away from Belton. I parked in her driveway behind her new-booty Monte Carlo. Grabbing my backpack out the backseat, I got out and headed to the front door.

I should have put the yandy in the stash spot. *Fuckin' rushing.*

My phone rang and I picked up.

"Spade, I been at this room waiting for almost two hours," an upset Maria said.

"Baby, I'm bustin' this move and then I'm on my way," I lied.

"Hurry, papi. My pussy is so wet right now, *mmm*," she purred. "I want you, Daddy."

"Keep it wet for me, baby. In a minute."

I used my key to enter the townhouse. I noticed an angry Sonya sitting on her sofa, leg bouncing over the other.

"What's good, baby?" I walked over to her to give her a kiss.

"Where you been, Spade?" she asked while our lips were still touching.

"I been doin' my two-step." I was standing over her. "You know how intense my schedule is."

"I bet you made time for that bitch," she fished.

"You the only bitch in my life," I joked. She laughed a little.

"I know you be busy, but can't you at least call?"

"I hit yo phone but got the voicemail, baby," I lied.

"So why you didn't call back?"

"We gon' have this conversation all night?"

She got up off her sofa with a frustrated look on her face and stomped her way to the kitchen—after she pushed me out the way, of course. I headed upstairs to one of the extra bedrooms that I used for one of my offices. I took the bricks out the backpack and placed them in my small safe behind the bookshelf.

I knew two of them would be gone the next morning. The other three would disappear two days later. I sold my bricks like I got them—bricks. No need to bust them down and zip them out. I got them for ten grand, sold them for eighteen. Easy flip.

My phone went off again.

"Yeah?" I answered.

"Spade, what's good, young man?" OG Casa said. He was from my set. He watched me grow up, always hit me with words of wisdom every time I lent my ear to him.

Aside from him being an old school playa, real slick nigga with the women, he was one of the smartest men I knew.

"OG Casa, what's the deal?" I said back.

"Ah, man, I'm down here in the ATL right now, shoppin' for real estate wit' a lady friend," he said. "Listen. I know you go yo underworld thang goin', and that's coo'. But don't forget about that lil' vacation you was on. You been out for about five years and you're livin' well. But you're not bein' smart wit' yo money. You gotta—"

I interrupted him. "You know I'm 'bout to start my entertainment company."

"About to start it ain't good enough, nephew. Legitimize yo hustle, baby."

He hung up on me.

I hated when that nigga did that.

I went back downstairs and headed to the kitchen. Sonya was at the table drinking Grey Goose, talking on the phone.

"Girl, that bitch got me fucked up!" she exclaimed into her phone. I was opening the fridge to get my bottle of Remy. I grabbed a glass out the cabinet and poured my poison. I felt her looking at me. "I don't care how long that trifling bitch knew him … And …? Girl, let me call you back."

"Who was that?" I asked calmly.

She was pissed. "That was Nicole. She said her cousin told her Casey keep tellin' people she gon' get you back. And will do whatever she has to, even if it means killin' me."

"That bitch just blowin' smoke, baby. Come here." I held my arms out to her, gave her the puppy-dog face.

I loved it when she wore just a bra and boy shorts. And she was sexier when she was mad. I knew all she needed was some dick. She came over to me.

"What?" she said, still trying to act mad.

I didn't respond verbally. I grabbed her small waist and pulled her to me, giving her my tongue, and she gave me hers; it tasted like Grey Goose. I know mine tasted like Remy. Under any other circumstances I wouldn't mix clear with brown, but I was willing to make an exception.

She moaned while our tongues slow danced. I grabbed her ass. She pulled my shirt over my head and started kissing on the physique the Missouri Department of Corrections gave me. Then she squatted in front of me, unfastening my belt and pants. They fell to my ankles.

"I miss you, baby, *mmm.*"

I didn't know if she was talking to me or my dick. She took me in her mouth slow and methodical, knowing how I liked it. She played childish games with the tip, using her tongue ring.

"Suck that muhfucka, bitch," I demanded. She loved when I talked dirty to her.

She proceeded, using a little more saliva. Taking it out her mouth, she slapped herself in the face with it. Then she hummed and tongued my balls. Not too rough, not too gentle—I taught her well.

Before I came, I stopped her. Standing her up, I unsnapped her bra, letting her C-cups sit at attention like two soldiers. I let my tongue and soft kisses spend time with both of her erect nipples. I wiggled my pants off my ankles, pulling her boy shorts down at the same time.

I leaned her against the kitchen counter, hurried and grabbed a chair, sat down and kissed her pussy.

"*Aww, mmm,*" she moaned. I explored her pussy with my tongue. Her button at the top of her fleshy entrance winked at me. I kissed and played with it. Her knees buckled.

"Damn, I'm 'bout to cum, Spade. Shit!"

After she came, I stood up, moving the chair from behind me with my leg. I turned her chocolate frame around and entered her from behind aggressively. I fucked her good and hard.

"Shiiit!" she shouted. Then she whispered, "Damn, Spade."

My phone rang but I ignored it.

"Fuck me harder, baby," she said. I did just that. And she came again. Shortly after, I exploded inside her.

***

After I got out the shower, I applied my hygiene and threw on my Coogi sweat suit. I had four missed calls on my phone. Two from Maria, one from Ace, and one from a number I didn't recognize. I called Ace.

"What's good, big bro?" he answered. He sounded tipsy.

"What's the deal?"

"Big bro, I'm just out bendin' corners, you know? Off this yak, in my box, my nigga. Just callin' to let you know I love you, my nigga. And that's on da third letter. Anybody can get it behind this bond we got, cuzz."

Ace was always good for an emotional moment. *I love that lil' nigga.*

"I already know lil' bro. You know what it is my way. Where you headed?"

"My lil' lollipop's house," he said.

"A'ight, lil' nigga. C-safe. I'll get wit' you in a hot one."

"Okay, bro."

We hung up. My conversation woke Sonya up.

"You leavin' this late?" she asked.

"I'm on my way to the spot. Gotta be ready for my dude in the mornin'," I told her. I had already took two of the bricks out the safe and stashed them in my truck when she was in the shower.

"It's twelve in the morning, Spade," she said with frustration.

"You know how it go, baby. I appreciate yo concern, though. Daddy'a drive safe," I joked. She smiled after I gently kissed her lips. "I'll call you first thing tomorrow."

I left. Jumped in my Yukon and pulled out the driveway. I couldn't help but notice a new butt yellow Impala sitting a few houses down.

CHAPTER 2

I entered the room at Embassy Suites, and the room was empty. I called Maria but didn't get an answer.

"Where da fuck is this bitch," I whispered to myself. I called her again.

"Hello!" she yelled over loud music.

"Where yo hot ass at?" I asked.

"Hold on, baby," she said. I knew she was at the club. "Sorry, baby. I had to come to the ladies room so I can hear you. I'm at Expressions, me and my friend Selena."

"I need you to handle somethin' in the a.m.," I told her. I had already stopped by her house off of Southwest Boulevard and put treats in the stash spot I had installed in her Benz.

"Ok, papi, we're goin to be leavin' here soon. Be there in no time."

It was getting late and I was tired as fuck. I stripped down to my boxers, laid down in bed and I was gone.

Deception's PLAYGROUND

***

Two sets of lips kissed my dick, two sets of hands touched my body, and it woke me up out of my sleep. Maria and a stranger were licking and sucking me, in between kissing each other.

"Damn, papi. Me like," the stranger said. I noticed the sun peeking through the curtains. It was morning. Maria gently moved the stranger aside and jumped on my dick. Her pussy was wet, but I was ready to throw her off me because I didn't have on a condom. It felt too good to do that.

I grabbed her hips and directed her motions.

"Yes … Aw … Oh God!" Maria moaned. The stranger hunched behind Maria and licked her ass, then started licking my balls.

"Aw, Selena, you so nasty, mami .. *Aww*," said Maria.

So this is Selena, I thought.

I would have got up and fucked the dog shit out of both of them but I was too tired for that shit. I let them fuck me.

When I felt myself on the verge of exploding, I told Maria, "Get up and put yo mouth back on this muhfucka," I ordered. She eased up off my shit, and she and Selena licked her pussy juices off my dick, fighting over who was going to swallow my babies. I squirted mostly on Maria's tongue. She won.

I got up and headed to the shower. I glanced at Maria and Selena, and they looked damn near identical. Selena just looked a few years younger than Maria's thirty-one, and Selena had a little more meat on her bones.

After I washed my sins away, I got myself together. I checked my phone and it was 9:30.

"Baby, this is Selena," Maria said, grabbing Selena's hand.

Fine time to introduce this bitch, I thought.

"I see," I replied with a devilish grin.

"We're 'bout to get in the shower, then she's gon' take me to get my car," Maria said.

I gave her a look. "Make sure you handle that."

"I know daddy," she said, a little irritated. This wouldn't be her first run. In fact, she did all of my runs. She never crossed me and I loved her for that. I was big on not making any drug transactions. I wasn't around when they were purchased or sold.

"A'ight. I'm 'bout to bust this move. I'll call you later," I told her.

"Okay, papi."

"Nice to meet you, Selena." I smiled.

"You too," she replied, licking her lips and batting her eyes.

I pulled Maria to the side.

She knew what I was about to ask her. "She's coo', Spade. She's like my sister. She just got back in town."

"That don't mean shit," I retorted.

"Trust me, Spade. She's coo'."

"How long do yo pops got this room for?"

"Two weeks."

I'd never met her dad because he was always busy. I just knew his name was Carlos. And he spoiled the shit out of his daughter. I didn't know how he got his money, but he got it.

"I'm gone," I said. "In a minute."

I left the room, jumped on the elevator and headed down. When I got in traffic, I called Duece.

"What that is?" he greeted me.

"Where you at, fool?"

"Leavin' Jub's. Had to stop and holla at Ace for a second."

"Meet me at my house in forty-five minutes."

"Okay, cuzz."

I made a quick stop at a gas station on Broadway. I filled up, then headed toward the highway and shot to my spot. I lived in Lee's Summit, Missouri.

In the cuts.

I pulled up and hit the garage door opener. As I backed my truck in and the garage door was closing, I saw Duece's new Camaro pulling up.

In the house, I turned the alarm system off. There were security monitors in my living room, kitchen, bedroom, and my office. My home had three bedrooms, two baths.

Bachelor pad, no doubt. I opened the door for Duece and headed to the kitchen.

"Yo, Spade, guess who I fucked last night."

"Who, nigga?"

"You remember that thick ass white bitch, Jamie?"

"You talkin' 'bout redhead Jamie?" I asked.

"Nigga, that bitch go!" Duece said excitedly.

"She ain't shit, my nigga. She knocked me down in the whip on her lunch break one time. Silly wit' the face game," I told him.

"Straight up, huh?" Duece looked away. I thought I saw a little envy in his eyes. Not my nigga Duece.

I changed the subject. "So what's up wit' Ace?"

"Yeah, I had to pull up on lil' cuzz and give him another wetter. He had to yank on some suckas last night, threw the pep."

"I just talked to that nigga last night," I said, mostly to myself.

"He coo', cuzz, said he gon' let you know."

I started to call Ace but decided against it. I'd wait till he told me. I told Duece that I would be getting with Kutz on Monday, that I was going to get ten bricks for myself, so he needed to decide how many he wanted. I would holla at Ace on his end also.

It was a Friday and I had a feeling it was going to be a long weekend. I discussed a few legitimate avenues for income with Duece. The shit O.G. Casa talked about was sinking in. I was thinking bigger and wanted my brother in on it. But Duece wasn't feeling it.

After we talked, he left. Then I got a text from Maria shortly after. It read: *I love you papi.* That meant the transaction went smooth.

***

Over the phone, I tried to encourage Sonya to get into college for accounting. She didn't agree with me, said she was cool at the beauty salon she worked at. I admit she was good at doing hair and made decent money, but she wasn't smart with the money she made.

She had a little in her savings account but managed it poorly. I told her if we were going to build something substantial, she should go to college. That convo didn't go anywhere.

Changing the subject, we decided we would step out later that night. She was going to bring Nicole and a few other home girls. Me and the squad were going to meet them down there. We were hitting the Westport area.

I called Ace after I talked to Sonya and he was cool. In code I told him what was up on the re-up Monday. He said he'd meet us down at the Westport. He was bringing out his new toy, a '72 Cutlass—all white, pearl candy with a gold base. I was going to ride with Duece, so I called him and told him to pick me up around ten. Then I hit Maria to make sure she put that thirty-six grand in her safe.

Phone calls done, I stuffed my cell in my pocket.

CHAPTER 3

The Westport was packed. I was riding with Duece in his all black Chevy Suburban with black and chrome 26-inch Davons, peanut butter interior. Ace was trailing in his Cutlass, and Sonya, Nicole, and their friends were behind him. A few of my homies were in the line also. The bitches were out and the city was on fire.

Duece had his four eighteen subwoofers sounding like a marching band. He had Re da Hog pumping through his speakers, preaching the truth.

"Turn that down real quick, cuzz," I said. He twisted his face at me and turned it down. I'd seen it was the same number that I didn't recognize.

I picked up. "Yeah?"

"Hi, Spade. You don't know how to answer yo phone?" It was Casey. I knew her raunchy voice.

But I asked anyway. "Who dis?"

"This Casey."

"Who gave you this number, man?"

"Don't trip. You know I been missin—"

I hung up on her and turned the music back up.

We hit a few corners and eventually parked. We stepped in a club called Karma; it was brimming with women, a few hustlers, a few suckas too. Ace had to bust a couple moves but he said he'd be back. Duece was at the bar macking on some girl. She looked like she was loving what she was hearing. He noticed me looking and raised his glass to acknowledge his newfound victim.

That's my nigga.

Sonya and Nicole were on the dance floor getting it. I sipped on some Remy, observing the scene. Nicole kept eyeing me down. *This bitch a fool, I thought.* Then her and Sonya made their way to me.

"You enjoyin' yo'self baby?" Sonya asked.

"You know I'm straight, baby." I smacked her ass.

"You always think you too coo' to dance," Nicole chimed in.

Sonya wrapped her arm around mine. "Girl, you know he think he too fly for this shit."

They both laughed.

"Why don't yall take yall hot asses on the dance floor wit' all that energy," I joked. They both rolled their eyes and left my presence. Nicole looked back at me, biting her bottom lip, before disappearing in the crowd.

We left the club tipsy, headed to our cars. We always parked together when we went out.

"A'ight, take yall drunk asses home," I said to the girls.

"It's too early to go home," Nicole said.

"Yeah, baby, we 'bout to go to Denny's," Sonya said.

I shrugged. "A'ight. In a minute."

"You ain't comin'?" Sonya asked, holding on to me.

"Not tonight. I got moves," I lied. She unwrapped her arms from around me.

"Okay, baby," she said, sounding disappointed. "Come on, Nicole."

I noticed the same Impala I seen down the street from Sonya's in the parking spot right next to Duece's truck. I looked for Duece and spotted him talking to some women in a red Dodge Charger.

"Come here, bro!" he yelled. I walked over to him to see what was good. Two fine ladies were smiling at me. I was still worried about the Impala.

"Hi, Spade," said the driver.

"What's good, lil' mama," I said. I was a little disappointed Duece told her my name.

"Tamika, Spade. Spade, Tamika." Duece pulled me to the side and told me the passenger was trying to shake with him. And the driver wanted to get at me. Jump-offs off the flip. Tamika looked tasty tonight too.

I checked my phone and saw it was about three in the morning. I called Ace to let him know not to slide back through. Then I grabbed my life insurance policy from Duece's truck and switched places with Tamika's friend.

I was doing it for Duece, because I wasn't going to fuck Tamika that night. I had her drop me off at the room. We exchanged numbers and I went up to my suite. When I got in I decided to check on Sonya.

"Hello?" Nicole answered.

"What the fuck you answerin' the phone for?"

"She went to the bathroom, Spade."

"Yall still at Denny's?" I asked.

"Yeah, we just now ordering our food."

"A'ight, tell her I called and call me when she make it home."

"We going to my house so we don't have to do all that driving," she said.

"Just tell her I called."

"Okay, Daddy," she said.

"Yo lil' hot ass need to quit playing," I told her.

"Sonya's my bitch, but you know I been diggin' you, Spade." Her voice was seductive.

"Ain't that sweet," I said sarcastically.

"I'm serious, baby. I just want to fuck … mmm … you just don't know."

I hung up on her.

She had me curious, I can't lie. I felt my dick waking up. But I had to get some sleep. There was a lot of shit to do tomorrow.

After I took a shower, I jumped in the bed. Maria laid next to me, sound asleep.

***

I pulled up to Sonya's house. It was late and the neighborhood was quiet. All the lights in Sonya's house were out. I got out of my truck and approached her door, using my key. I went in and shut the door behind me.

The living room was dark as fuck so I went for the light switch on the wall. As soon as the light came on, I saw four men masked down sitting in the living room, armed. One of them stood up and pointed his steel at me.

"Sit down, nigga," he said. I just stood there. I thought about reaching for my cannon but I left it in the truck. "Sit the fuck down!"

"What the fuck yall niggas want?" I asked, heading towards the couch.

I heard someone coming down the stairs. It was Sonya.

"What's the code to the safe, Spade?" she asked. I looked at her in disbelief.

"Bitch, is you crazy?" I flared.

41

A different nigga smacked me upside my head with his pistol. Blood leaked down my face.

"What's the code, nigga?" my first friend asked.

"Man, I don't know what the fuck yall talking about," I said, holding the side of my head as it throbbed. I couldn't believe Sonya was in on it. She was supposed to be my bitch.

"Oh, you don't know?" the fourth gentleman spoke up. He got off the couch and approached me. He put his pistol to my kneecap and pulled the trigger.

Bang!

I screamed as I collapsed to the floor. "Aw, fuuuck!"

Sonya smiled.

The first nigga grabbed my throat. He put his gun to my forehead. I saw murder in his eyes.

"The code or yo life, nigga," he spit in my face. I didn't respond.

So he pulled the trigger.

Then my phone rang, waking me up from my sleep.

CHAPTER 4

Still tired, I said into the phone, "Momma, I called the nig-ga."

"Samuel Lendall Wright," she started, "what did I tell you about using the N-word?"

Sometimes I felt like she forgot I was thirty, not thirteen.

"Come on now, Momma," I pleaded. "You know me and pops don't see eye to eye."

"Today is his birthday, and he's still yo daddy. Now call him and tell him happy birthday."

"A'ight, Moms. I gotta go. I'll call him."

"Okay, boy, I love you. And be careful out there."

"Love you too."

Maria was still fast asleep. That dream I had felt too real. I wanted to tell Maria about it but decided against it. I had ordered room service for us and she was sleeping so peace-fully. She even looked good in her sleep.

Her and Sonya were the two women I spent the most time with. I loved them both for different reasons. Maria was hungrier, eager to learn. She listened and was willing to do whatever for a nigga. Sonya was sexy and smart, but she got too content and was stubborn at times. She had a loving heart, though.

Room service knocked at the door. I wheeled the cart in and saw that the knock woke Maria up. She sat up and I served her breakfast. Then my phone rang. It was O.G. Casa.

"Spade, what's good, baby boy?" he asked.

"Same ol' two step. You still in the A?"

"I'm on my way to the airport. Headed back that way."

"That's what's up. Hit me when you land. We'll meet up," I said.

"Will do, nephew."

Maria rubbed my arm. "Thanks for the breakfast, papi."

"Anything for you, mami," I joked.

She smiled. "You so silly."

"I gotta bust a couple of moves in a minute. I might be busy all day."

"You need me to do anything?"

I talked to her about getting into some legitimate businesses. That was the plan when I got out the joint anyway. It was time to start acting on it. I'd told myself I'd fuck around with the underworld until I was secure enough to start my own business. I was more than secure.

I told her I wanted her to go to school for business management. She said she'd inquire about it the following week. That's what I loved about her. She was a real team player. Those type of bitches were rare. She said her dad would pay for her to go. When I asked her why her father was never around, she simply said that he was always busy.

Getting a legitimate business off the ground was something I was serious about. I had $150,000 in my home safe, about $86,000 in Maria's safe, and three bricks and $40,000 in the safe I had at Sonya's. It was time for me to start investing in something legitimate.

"In a minute, baby," I said to Maria.

I left the room, heading to Sonya's.

***

When I arrived, Sonya was running a mop across the kitchen floor, as Nicole crouched to wipe dust of the running boards. They both wore boyshorts and bras. I couldn't help but notice how amazing Nicole's body was. She was a yellow bone—not ugly, but not a beauty queen. She had lots of tattoos too.

I approached Sonya. ""What's good, baby?"

"Nothing. Just doing a little straightening up."

"Why you didn't call me back last night?"

"I'm sorry, babe. Nicole told me you called but it slipped my mind," she said sincerely.

"A'ight, slipped my mind," I uttered with hints of sarcasm.

I figured I'd act like I was upset with her. I knew she would question my whereabouts, so I beat her to the punch.

"It did slip my mind, baby. You don't have to worry, we came straight here last night. We was gon' go to Nicole's but since we was gon' have to come here today anyway to get her car, we just came here," she said.

Nicole came into the kitchen. "Girl, you ain't gotta explain nothin' to him."

"Mind yo damn business," I said.

"Whateva, Spade."

"Yall crazy." Sonya flicked her wrist and smiled. "I'm 'bout to get in the shower. You comin'?"

"I was just stoppin' by, baby. I gotta run, you know how it go," I said.

"Whatever, boy."

"Last time I checked, you didn't have no kids so watch yo mouth," I told her. "I'm 'bout to grab somethin' to snack on, and I'm gone."

Nicole rolled her eyes and went back in the living room.

"Baby, just call me later. I'm getting' in the shower," she said. She gave me a kiss and went upstairs. Then she yelled down the steps and told Nicole to put her shirt on while I was there. Like she just noticed her shirt was off.

I opened the fridge and found a snack. Then I opened the freezer to grab my Remy. I heard Nicole come in the kitchen as I was grabbing a glass out of the cabinet. While I poured my issue, Nicole was acting like she was wiping the kitchen table. Bending over, letting the bottom of her ass peek at me. I loved the view but I couldn't go that route.

She came over to the kitchen counter where I was standing and started wiping it down, her D-cups damn near busting out her bra. *This bitch silly*, I thought.

"Why you drinkin' this early?" she asked.

"Because I'm grown."

"You always gettin' smart." She put her hand on her hip—it made her titties bounce.

"That's because I am," I said.

"Whatever, Spade."

It was something about the way she said my name that turned me on. I was wondering how she would say it if I had my dick in her throat. I had to leave before I got into some shit. I finished my drink and went to the sink to rinse my glass out.

"Let me do it," she said.

Rubbing her ass on my dick instantly got it hard. I pressed up against her, then whispered in her ear, "You're not ready."

CHAPTER 5

I pulled up to the Cheesecake Factory on the Plaza. O.G. Casa met me there. We got our table and had general conversation about the streets first. O.G. Casa was fifty years old. He flipped houses and had a used car lot on Truman Road, milked bitches for a living, and he still had connections that allowed him to flip a bird or two every now and then.

"You got you a business attorney?" he asked.

I already had a criminal attorney on retainer, but O.G. Casa said I needed a business attorney for my business endeavors. I told him I would get on it. He asked me how business was going with Kutz. I told him everything was good. But he reminded me that one couldn't make a career out of my dealings.

"In and out," he said.

We finished our meal and split. When I got in my whip, an unfamiliar number called my phone.

"Yeah?" I answered.

"Hi, Spade," the feminine voice said.

"What's good? Who dis?"

"It's Tamika."

She told me she was at her house and wanted me to stop by. I did the normal run-down on her, found out she was 23, no kids, and she worked at H&R Block.

I normally didn't just slide over a female's house without a thorough background check. But she seemed cool. She a little younger but it seemed like she had a head on her shoulders. She stayed off Hillcrest with the friend Duece slid off with. I told her I'd be through there in a hot one.

After I ended that call, I called Duece. He was out busting moves as usual. He told me Ace dropped off twenty grand for two bricks. He said he was putting in fifty grand for five. I told him I was grabbing ten. I tried to slide in my ideas about the legitimate shit, but he wasn't feeling it.

He told me the game was treating him good and he couldn't turn his back on it. He was a real stubborn nigga. I ended that call and checked on Maria. I know I did a lot of checking, but it's a habit of mine to know what's going on with my family circle. She said she was at the mall with Selena. I went to my house to get in the shower, and get dressed.

I had a young bitch waiting on me.

***

I made a stop at a gas station before I went to Tamika's house. Had to get some condoms—I knew what was in store for me. When I pulled up to an empty pump, I noticed a car similar to Nicole's.

I went in and stood in line. Then Nicole approached me.

"What's up, baby?" she said, tugging on my pants pocket.

"What's good?"

"'Bout to go to yo girls house," she said.

The line moved. One more person ahead of me. I had to admit, Nicole was looking right. Thick as ever.

"Where you headed?" she asked.

"Bust this move," I said. Then the customer in front of me left the counter. I approached the overweight cashier. "Let me get twenty on four, and a pack of magnums." I handed her the money.

"Bust this move, huh?" Nicole said, in a suspicious—yet seductive—tone.

I told the cashier to keep the change and pushed past Nicole, even though I wanted to push *in* her. At my truck, I started pumping gas and clicked it to automatic as I sat in my driver's seat and waited. Nicole's thick-ass switched my way.

"Man, what do yo hot-ass want?"

"This." She reached and grabbed my dick. I was turned on but couldn't go there.

I moved her hand. "Man, take yo big-head ass to Sonya's. You trippin'."

"You 'bout to go see some bitch?"

"I'm grown, lil' mama."

"Whatever, Spade. You don't know what you missing."

And with that, she left my truck, her ass shaking all the way to her car.

***

I pulled up to Tamika's about eight-thirty. I called her to let her know I was outside, then grabbed my life insurance policy and headed to her front door. She was opening it as I approached, wearing a satin chemise over a lace bralette.

"You're late," she said as I entered her house.

I did a quick assessment—it was fully furnished, clean, well-decorated, nice sent. So far, so good.

"I'm here, ain't I?"

She looked me up and down, then she extended her arm to the couch. "Have a seat. Drink? All I have is vodka and Remy."

"Remy," I requested smoothly, as I plopped down on the couch. *Damn, lil' mama got the drink of my preference,* I thought.

As she walked to get the drinks, I did a quick appraisal of the goods. Nice caramel complexion, little bubble butt, petite with a handful of titties. I also noticed her tongue ring when she offered drinks.

When she returned with the glasses, we talked for a hot second. We both knew what I was there for. I told her a little about me, she told me a lot about her. She was single, her favorite color was red, she used to strip in college to get by. Typical shit. She wanted to get married one day and have kids. A bunch of shit I didn't give a fuck about right now.

"Let's hit the bedroom, baby."

"Okay," she said softly.

As soon as I took a seat on her queen-size bed, she started undressing in front of me. Then my fucking phone rang. It was Sonya.

"Yeah," I answered. I put my index finger to my lips to tell the young freak to stay quiet for a minute.

"Let's go out to eat tonight," said Sonya.

Tamika was down to her thong, gyrating her hips.

"Baby, I'm in St. Joe right now. I won't be yo way until another hour or so," I said into the phone.

Coming out her thong, Tamika showed me a fat, hairy pussy. She laid down on the floor, spread-eagle. She put two fingers in her meaty pussy and my dick got rock hard.

"You always fuckin' busy, pussy. I'm tired of this sh—"

I hung up.

"Everything okay, baby?" Tamika asked.

"I'm good."

She got up from the floor and sashayed to her stereo. She put on a slow mix. *Young bitches*, I thought. *Wasn't shit romantic about this situation.* She came back to me and pushed me back on the bed. She got on her knees and unbuckled my belt.

"Hold up, lil' mama." I got up and put my cannon on the nightstand. I took my shirt off and laid back down. As she was pulling my pants down, I was kicking my shoes off.

My boxers came down next and she slid her mouth down my dick. She moaned like I was penetrating her pussy. Her warm mouth slid on my shit like a pro—using her tongue ring on the tip, kissing it and playing with my nuts at the same time.

"Mmm. Damn, you taste good. You like that, daddy?" she purred.

No answer was required. I grabbed the back of her head and shoved it down my dick. I let her taste if for a while longer and put her in the doggy-style position. I hurried and got my helmets out of my pants and rolled one on, then slammed my dick into the young tender. Her pussy was *tight*.

"Oh shit!" she screamed. I fucked her harder. "Yes! Yes! Yes! Mmmm ... hit this pussy, hit this pussy!"

I pushed my thumb in her asshole while I hit her from the back. Her pussy was dripping wet, making the inside of her thighs *and* mine moist.

"Oh shit, I'm cumin', baby, *ooooohhh!*" She came hard, more juices running down her legs. *She's a squirter,* I thought.

"You like that, bitch?" I spat.

"Yes, daddy … put it in my ass," she demanded. And I did. She started playing with her pussy while I fucked her in her ass. She came three more times before I was about to come.

I pulled out and yanked the condom off. She turned around, ready to catch my nut in her mouth. I busted in her face and she rubbed it in and put her mouth back on my dick, welcoming any more cum I had left in me.

***

I pulled away from Tamika's house around ten. I left her stretched out on her bed asleep. That young hoe was a piece of work.

I noticed I had a few missed calls. I returned the one I got from Kutz.

"Ay, my man."

"What's good? You call?" I countered.

"Meet me at the bar."

"Okay, playa."

Every time Kutz called, it was about business. We never had a discussion longer than thirty seconds on the phone. He was real careful, very meticulous. I liked that about him.

We always met at *Kelly's* on the Westport. It was always a mixed crowd there. I called Sonya back on the way there.

"What, Spade?" She was pissed.

"Girl, I don't know why you even bother," Nicole said in the background.

"What's yo problem, man?" I asked.

"My problem is you don't *never* have time for me."

"Don't start this shit."

"So you too busy for me, Spade?"

"Girl, fuck Spade!" Nicole's voice again.

"Man, tell that bitch to shut the fuck up," I said.

"I know you fuckin' around on me, Spade."

I regretted calling her ass. "I'll be over there in a few hours."

"What, you wit' yo lil' Mexican bitch?"

I hung up on her. *How in the fuck she know about Maria?*

***

I walked in Kelly's shortly after. The place was packed. A few drunk women were giving me the eye. I spotted Kutz accompanied by two Latin women at a table in a corner, and they were beautiful. I grabbed a seat across from him and gave both girls a look and they left our presence.

Kutz was about fifty-two years old, but he looked a lot younger. He always wore Armani suits and fancy shoes. I never seen him wear jewelry, though. "It's a waste of money," he'd always say. He was real low-key, kept his private life concealed, never discussed anything personal. I've only hear him mention his only daughter once about eight months prior. He didn't even mention her name. This Mexican nigga was a mystery.

"Spade, how's it going, my friend?" He smiled.

"Everything's good. I'ma do seventeen Monday."

"Okay. I see business is good."

"I can't complain."

"How's Duece?"

"He straight," I said flatly. Kutz *never* asked about Duece.

"Duece brings a lot of unwanted attention, Spade. He'll bring you down."

I looked at him like he lost his fucking mind. But I listened, didn't act off emotions because I'm a thinker.

"A couple of my people said they seen him in a club last night, downtown," he went on. "Throwing money everywhere, highly intoxicated. Said he got into it with a few gentlemen over a white young lady with red hair …"

Jamie, I thought.

"He's hot, Spade. And this isn't the first time I've heard his name in some foolishness."

Why in the fuck Duece didn't tell me? I knew sometimes Duece could be a lil' outrageous; he's been like that since we were kids. I just didn't expect him to jump out the window for a jump-off. And I definitely didn't expect him to be drunk, slipping in a fucking club.

"I'll talk to him," was all I could say.

"Good, good."

We went our separate ways shortly after that. It kind of bothered me that Kutz knew about the altercation and I didn't. I had to talk to Duece.

***

It was late when I walked in Sonya's house. Her and Nicole were watching TV and drinking.

"Don't you ever go home?" I asked Nicole's drunk ass. She just rolled her eyes at me as I walked straight to the kitchen to get my issue. I knew it was about to be a long night. Sonya came stomping in the kitchen right on time.

"So who the fuck is this Mexican bitch I'm hearing about?" Sonya was standing on the opposite side of the kitchen counter.

I played stupid. "What the fuck are you talkin' about?"

"So you gon' stand in my fuckin' kitchen and lie to me?" She started walking toward me. She was so sexy when she got mad.

I smiled. "Man, calm yo ass down."

"It ain't funny, Spade. Somebody texted my phone and said they seen you wit' her." She showed me the text at the same time the volume in the living room went down. Nicole was a nosy bitch. I looked at the number; it was the same number Casey called me from.

"And whose number is this?" I asked.

"I don't know." She looked embarrassed. I laughed and told her somebody was fucking with her head. I told her they wanted what she had and not to worry about it. She finally agreed with my reasoning.

I knew I had to do something about Casey's ass. And fast.

I took Sonya up to the bedroom. I had to give her some necessary loving. After I fucked her I apologized for not being available like I should. I went and jumped in the shower. When I got out, Sonya was sleeping like a baby. I threw on some boxers and some sweatpants to wear around the house.

In the other bedroom, I called Maria and told her about the move for the bricks tomorrow. When I hung up with her I called Duece and let him know the money for the move would be in the trash can in his garage for the re-up Monday. I wanted to discuss what Kutz told me, but I would wait till I saw him.

Afterwards, I went downstairs to put something on my stomach. When I made it down, Nicole was laying on the couch ass naked, playing with her pussy.

"I heard yall upstairs." She moaned. "It just turned me on, *ahhh* ..." I couldn't take my eyes away. "I see you like what you see," she said, staring at my dick as it hardened through the sweats.

Damn, it's been a long day, I thought.

I left her there and walked in the kitchen. That little bitch was too much. Sonya was right upstairs. As I was searching the fridge, I heard her walk into the kitchen.

CHAPTER 6

"What time you tryna drop yo car off at the paint shop?" I asked Sonya, who was in the bathroom mirror combing her long silky hair.

"Eight o'clock, and I need you to drop me off at the salon," she said.

"Well, hurry yo big head ass up," I joked. "I got shit to do."

"I'll be ready in a minute, baby."

For some reason she wanted to get her car painted exactly like mine. She'd been talking about it for the last two months. I was footing the bill. My Yukon had a simple navy blue paint job on it, not too flashy. She wanted her Monte the same color.

Half an hour later, I followed her to the paint shop to drop it off. After that, we pulled up at her job and she told me Nicole was going to pick her up. She gave me a kiss and went in the salon.

I headed to Maria's house. I had dropped off the other three bricks the previous day. Everything went smooth with the transaction so I was going over to spend a little time with her. Show her I appreciated everything she did for a nigga.

***

"I know you fuck other bitches, Spade. As long as you keep it real with me, papi, I'll always be here for you."

We'd been in her living room talking since I walked in the door.

"I'ma always keep it a hunid wit' you, baby," I said.

"I just want you to know I love you. I don't have to do any of this, Spade. My father will give me anything I want. I do these things because I love you." She was in her feelings. "He'd kill me if he knew I was doin' these things. He hasn't seen this tattoo on my back. He—"

"Damn, slow down, baby. I feel you but it sounds like pops got some control issues."

"He's just protective, that's all. I'm his only daughter."

"So why haven't I met him?" I asked. She looked like she wanted to say something, but was afraid to. "Speak on it, baby."

She avoided eye contact. "He thinks I should date inside my race."

"So he's racist?" I lifted her chin up and turned her face so we were eye to eye.

"He just …" She paused, looking for the right thing to say. "He just has his ways. But he can't control what I do."

We talked for a little while longer. She told me she had been inquiring about some college courses. We also went over our game plan for future underworld business. After she made that last move, I had $140,000 in her safe. I took $100,000 out, secured it in her Benz, and I followed close behind her as we went to my spot.

***

Maria was in the shower cleaning off the magic we just performed. During the performance, my phone had rang like crazy. I had missed calls from Casey, Ace, and Tamika.

When I called Ace back, he said he was just seeing what was good. I didn't call Casey back, but I did call Tamika. I walked downstairs to my living room because I didn't want Maria hearing my conversation. All that "keep it real" shit would of went out the window if she heard me talking to another bitch right after I fucked her.

"Hi, Spade," Tamika answered.

"What's good?"

"Boy, you know what's good."

"I didn't know you had kids, lil' mama," I said.

"I don't," she countered.

"Well, act like it. I ain't cha boy," I quipped.

"Okay, whatever. Can I see you soon?"

I tested her. "I'm wit' my chick right now. I'ma call you later."

"Oh, so you have a chick?"

"Is that a problem?"

After a long pause, she said, "Uh-uh, just call me later."

We hung up. It was about six-thirty in the evening. Duece and Ace had to meet Kutz's people at eight. I knew Nicole was going to pick up Sonya so that end was covered. Maria eventually came downstairs to join me in the living room. I told her to go to her house and wait for my call. I was taking five of the ten bricks over there.

My shit was running smooth. I had $230,000 put up in cash. After Duece made that move, I'd have and additional $180,000 liquid. The five bricks I was taking to Maria's were going to be gone Wednesday. The other five would be gone by Friday morning.

My plan was to re-up two more times for ten bricks each. I'd have a little over a half a ticket. I would let Duece and Ace run the drug shit and I was going to focus on my legitimate business.

Kush Lamma

***

When I walked in Duece's spot, him and Ace were separating the bricks. As I made my way to the couch, I noticed Jamie going from the bathroom to his bedroom down the hallway. *This nigga got this bitch here while we gettin' this shit together?*

I tried to hide my frustration. "What's good, fellas?"

"You already know," Duece said, unusually excited.

"Yo ten in the duffle bag," Ace told me.

"Right on, lil' bro. You 'bout to bust a move?" I asked. It was more of a hint than a question. He knew I wanted to holla at Duece.

"Yeah, bro. I'm up." He left the house.

My nigga Duece was a grown ass man but he was slipping. I couldn't let his foolish decisions interfere with my op.

"So what's the deal, cuzz?" I asked.

"Tryna keep this money rotating," he said.

"That's what's up. So what happened at the club Friday?"

He looked surprised. And his tone bothered me. "Nothing I couldn't handle, nigga."

"That ain't what I asked, bro."

"And who the fuck is you? My pops or somethin'!"

"Calm down, cuzz. I'm tryna make sure you on yo toes."

"I stay on my toes, nigga!"

I got irritated, and just as loud. "I can't tell, nigga! We don't fonk over hoes, nigga."

Jamie walked in to see what was going on. The bitch was out of pocket. She looked my way, smiled, and sat next to Duece.

"Give us a minute, lil' mama," I said.

She started to rise to her feet.

"Nah." Duece grabbed her leg. "We done talkin'."

Something else was on that nigga's mind. I just didn't know what. We grew up together, I broke bread with him—I was winning, he was winning. He was on some other shit right now.

I left the house without another word.

After I secured the bricks in my truck, I dropped five off at Maria's. The other five would go to Sonya's.

***

I pulled up to Sonya's pissed. That shit Duece was on had me hot. I know he wasn't stunting for Jamie.

I'd deal with that shit at a later time. Nicole's car was parked behind Sonya's car. That bitch was stopping by a lot.

Grabbing the backpack, I headed in. As usual, they were in their night attire watching TV with cups in their hands. They were some vodka-drinking bitches, I swear. Straight up.

I nodded my head to acknowledge both of them, then headed upstairs. I put the bricks in the safe and headed back downstairs. I went to the kitchen to fetch my Remy. My bottle was kind of light in the ass. I went back in the living room and sat on the opposite couch from Sonya and Nicole.

Nicole smiled and spoke before me. "Who drunk all my shit?" she teased.

"You know I don't drink that shit," Sonya said to me.

"I'll buy you some more, damn." Nicole rolled her eyes.

I scrutinized Sonya with my eyes. "What is she doing over here? Again?"

"Oh," Sonya said as if she just realized something. "She's going to be staying with me for a little while. Her and her cousin wasn't gettin' along."

"Is that right?"

"Is that okay wit' you?" Nicole smirked.

"That's on Sonya, man," I said.

I left it alone and started watching TV with them. I'm glad my phone was on vibrate because Tamika was blowing it up. While Sonya was tipsy, laughing at a Katt Williams stand-up, I crept to the kitchen to call Tamika back. I told her I'd call her tomorrow. She sounded upset, but it was what it was. I went back to the living room.

"What you cook?" I asked Sonya.

"You betta get a slice of pizza out the oven," she said.

When I went back to the kitchen I heard Sonya run upstairs. As I expected, Nicole came in the kitchen. She bit her bottom lip and batted her eyes.

This bitch, I thought.

"You been thinking 'bout me?" Her voice was husky.

"Gone somewhere," I said.

"You wasn't saying that when I was sucking yo dick right in this kitchen the other night."

Sonya was coming back downstairs. Nicole was already back in the living room, and Sonya handed her some Kush and some backwoods to roll up.

I went upstairs to get in the shower, and while I let stream of water soak my skin I thought about that night I came downstairs and saw Nicole playing with that pussy. My desires got the best of me. I let that bitch suck me dry. *"It's between us, baby,"* she had said while sucking me up.

Stepping out the shower, I walked in the bedroom—where Sonya was naked in the bed waiting on me.

"Come here, daddy," she said, motioning me in her direction with her index finger. I dropped my towel, went over to her and shoved my dick in her.

"Yes! … Fuck me! Fuck me!" She wrapped her legs around my waist as I went deeper.

After fucking her missionary style for a little bit, I turned her over doggy-style. I eased back in, gripping both of her ass cheeks.

67

"Damn, baby," she cried. "*Oooouuu*, this is yo pussy, daddy."

She came on my dick.

"You like that, bitch?"

"*Mmm-hmmm.*"

I continued my attack on her wetness, smacking her ass, talking dirty to her. Then—*BOOM!*

Nicole busted in the room. "Spade! Ace got shot, he's in the hospital!"

My mind started racing. I pulled out of Sonya, my rod instantly going soft. Anger filled my whole being. *Not Ace.* I got dressed and grabbed my heat. We jumped in Nicole's new booty Mustang and smashed to the hospital.

On the way there, Nicole told me Duece called her and told her some niggas caught Ace leaving one of his females' house. Ace got hit in his chest, shoulder and leg. Nicole and Sonya were crying the whole ride. I was just gripping my steel, looking out the car window, hoping Ace would pull through.

***

When we walked in Truman Medical, Duece—along with a small crowd of family and friends—were in the emergency entrance lobby. They were crying like my lil' nigga was dead. I spotted Ace's auntie that he lived with and went over to her. Sonya and Nicole joined the small crowd.

"Is he alright?" I hugged his auntie.

"They say he's stable." She squeezed me. "Take care of this, Spade."

She didn't have to tell me that; I was going to handle it. She told me all of the shots were exit wounds except the one in his thigh. It would have to be surgically removed. I wanted to see him but she said I'd have to wait until morning.

I went over to Duece. "Step outside wit' me." We went out and walked up the sidewalk. I could tell he was pissed off, just like I was. "What the fuck happened?"

"Man, I got a call from this bitch." He wiped his eyes. "Said lil' cuzz got hit up."

"What bitch? Where the fuck was he at!"

"His lil' bitch Ashley's, bro. The one in the lobby wit' the tattoo on her face. She stay in Hidden Valley."

"Did she see who it was?"

"Man, I don't know." He looked away and frowned. "I don't trust no bitch! Fuck that bitch, she probably set him up."

I stood there and thought for a second. I couldn't get emotional or I might have done something sloppy. I decided to leave the hospital since I couldn't see Ace anyway. I had some shit to figure out. One thing was for sure; whoever shot Ace laid on him. I told Duece I was leaving, went in and said goodbye to Ace's auntie, and me, Sonya, and Nicole left.

CHAPTER 7

I couldn't sleep since Ace got shot. It was the following morning and I was on my way to see him. When I walked in his room he was laying down watching TV.

He cracked a smile. "Big bro, what's good?"

"I'm chillin'. You good?" I knew damn well he wasn't. I took a seat.

"Suckas caught me slippin'. I'm straight, though." He sat up a little bit in the hospital bed. "They was gon' do surgery on my thigh. They say the bullet ain't gon' move though, so I'm good."

"Did you see them niggas?"

"It was dark, bro. I was on my way to the whip. They dropped their windows on some weak shit. Ain't have the heart to bounce out."

He told me Ashley was a stand-up girl. He said he couldn't see her setting him up, but he would look into it. He said he'd talked to Duece earlier that night too. We talked a little longer, then I told him I'd be back later.

I walked out of the hospital pissed. Even though Ace was a strong little nigga, I didn't like the fact that someone that close to me was touched in that fashion. I called Duece to see if he heard anything. He said he hadn't. I checked with Maria to see if she was on point for the move the next day. She was at work. I had a lot on my mind so I stopped by the nearest liquor store, had to get my issue.

Intoxicated, I drove through the city in my Yukon Denali, just me and my thoughts. Casey's number kept popping up but I didn't answer. She kept calling so I finally picked up.

"What's up, man?" I answered. I wasn't in the mood for her bullshit.

"I think I know who shot Ace."

She had my attention then. But how did she know? It *just* happened.

"And how in the fuck you know?" I asked.

"Not over the phone. Meet me somewhere."

She was pushing it. I really didn't want to meet the bitch, but I wanted to know what she knew. I told her to meet me at *Chubby's* on Broadway.

We were pulling in the parking lot at the same time. She was in the same yellow Impala I had seen down the street from Sonya's.

I parked my truck and got out. She parked right next to me and got out also. She looked good. She had on a form-fitting Rocawear outfit with the right amount of

71

accessories—faux wood earrings, a tiny diamond chain and a ring on her thumb. We headed in and grabbed a table.

"So how you been?" she asked as we sat down.

"I'm straight. What about you?"

"Missing you," she said seriously. "Spade, I just want to tell you that I'm sorry for not being there for you when you was locked up. I was young and I was used to you being there." She dropped her head, then looked back up into my eyes. "I wasn't strong without you."

"It's all good," I stated simply. I felt her, though. "What's wit' this textin' Sonya shit?"

She grabbed my hand. "Love will make you do some crazy things, Spade."

"Well, that shit need to stop. I still got love for you but we know what it is." I pulled my hand back. She looked disappointed but her feelings were the least of my concerns. I needed to know what she knew about Ace. I told her to get to it.

She told me her cousin stayed two doors down form Ashley. When her cousin heard the shots, she hurried to her window to look out. She saw a new Camaro similar to Duece's leaving, being followed by a Ford Taurus. She said the Taurus had three niggas in it, but the Camaro had tints.

The way she said Duece's name, and the expression on her face when she mentioned him, told me she was implying that it was him. I couldn't believe it. *Duece wouldn't do no shit like that.*

Me and Casey ordered our food and ate. She told me again how sorry she was for not being there for me. And she promised to stop texting Sonya's phone. I asked her about the rumors I heard about her being loose and she denied it. I believed her too. I knew her like a pimp knows pussy, knew when she was lying.

And she *didn't* get pregnant while I was gone.

And I sort of missed her.

We finished our meal and she offered to pay. I let her. When we made it to our vehicles, she came over to me.

"I'm sorry again, Spade," she said sincerely. She leaned in and softly kissed my lips. Then she slowly wiped her lipstick off my lips with her thumb, biting her bottom lip at the same time. "Call me, baby. And give Ace my condolences."

She sashayed to her car.

CHAPTER 8

I left Chubby's a little confused. That bitch Casey had me thinking about Duece. He wasn't acting like himself either. I thought about Casey too. Maybe I was a little selfish and inconsiderate. Maybe riding a bit out with me was too much for her to handle. I couldn't help but think about how good she looked also.

I shook those thoughts and headed to Verizon on Main Street. I had been meaning to upgrade one of my phones. I pulled up to the cellular store and put my biscuit on my hip and headed in. I walked towards the display in the middle of the floor, looking at the new model phones. I was quickly interrupted.

"Excuse me," a woman said.

When I turned to see who it was I was instantly attracted. She looked like she was about thirty-eight, maybe forty. Chocolate complexion, nice body, and she sported her hair short. She had full lips and a nice smile.

"Excuse *me*," I flirted.

"You silly. I was wondering if you knew if the Droid phones get good service." She smiled.

"I'm not sure, baby. But if you wanted to spark a conversation with me you could've came wit' somethin' better." I smiled back at her.

"I just thought maybe you would know, sweetie." She put her hand on her hip, slightly tilting her head to the right.

"Sounds good," I said, grabbing her hand. "I love a woman who goes for what she wants. And if this is your way of doing that, it's fine wit' me."

"Are you always this cocky?"

"Most of the time," I joked. She laughed but kept her hand in mines.

"Hmm … I guess. What's your name?" She squeezed my hand a little. "If you don't mind me asking."

"I'm Spade."

"I know yo mama didn't name you Spade. But I'll find out soon. My name is Lisa."

"So I'm assuming we'll see each other *soon*, Lisa."

"We'll see." She took her hand away.

We exchanged numbers and talked for another few minutes. She was forty-five, had a son in college, and she'd been divorced for eight years. She was single, lived alone and owned a beauty salon. We both purchased the phones we wanted and went our separate ways with a promise to see each other soon.

I called Maria and told her to meet me at my house. I planned on chilling for the rest of the day.

***

"I start my business courses next month, baby," Maria said.

"That's what's up. Make sure you're mentally ready," I told her.

We were in the living room chilling. We went from talking about her college courses to fucking the day away. It was night time now, and we were laying in bed watching *Paid in Full*. I thought, *That clown nigga Rico fucks me up*. I was just thinking about the game in general and how niggas turn snake in a split second. I had to reassess some shit.

"What you thinkin' about, papi?" Maria asked. She was laying next to me, rubbing my bare chest, looking at me with worry in her eyes. She knew when something was wrong.

"I'm chillin', baby. It ain't nothin'."

"Okay, papi." She kissed my lips.

Eventually she fell asleep, while I sat up thinking about my situation. I had to find out who was behind that shit with Ace, and eliminate them.

***

"Let me get two wings, one breast, some bombers, and two rolls," I said to the speaker at the Church's Chicken Drive-Thru. I figured I'd stop through the 'hood to see what I could see. I felt refreshed when I woke up, so I was out and about.

"What kind of drink would you like, sir?" the woman asked.

"Strawberry pop," I said.

"Pull to the window for your total," she replied.

I pulled to the window and got my free meal and went to my little homie's house on 26th and Denver. He said he heard some niggas that Ace shot at a month ago did it. I left after that. He didn't sound too convinced, and neither was I.

While I was pushing down Van Brunt, my phone rang several times. I ignored the calls. It was Tamika and I didn't feel like talking to her. Then OG Casa called to give his condolences, said if he heard anything he'd let me know.

I shot out to Duece's to see what was up with him. I didn't call to let him know I was on my way. I pulled up at his house and hopped out my truck. I heard him yelling when I approached his door.

"I already told you … Fuck that! … look, Sonya … A'ight, whatever man, call me later," he said.

I knocked on the door a few seconds later. He opened the door looking surprised.

"Spade, what's good?" He embraced me.

I walked in and spotted some powder on a tray, sitting on his living room table. *This nigga trippin'*, I thought. "What's good, my nigga?" I said.

He quickly grabbed the cocaine off the table and took it back to his room. He came back in, rubbing his nose, and sat down. I sat down too.

"So you fuckin' wit' that shit, I see."

"I ain't gon' stunt." He gave me a weak smile. "Every now and then. That shit wit' Ace got me on edge."

"Man, that shit for street punks," I said, and he frowned at me. "It'll have you all off schedule, my nigga. I been there, done that."

"Cuzz, I really don't need you tellin' me what the fuck to do," he said in a calm but serious tone.

"You my nigga and I love you. I'ma always keep it a hunid wit' you."

"I'm coo', cuzz."

I talked to him for a minute longer, just to see where his head was at. He seemed like he was hiding something but I didn't want to assume. I didn't mention the argument he had with my bitch on the phone. I told him to be easy with that coke and I left.

Deception's PLAYGROUND

I got a text from Ashley and she told me they were letting Ace leave the hospital in a couple of hours. She was taking him to his auntie's. Her text was followed by Maria's text—the move went smooth. Tamika kept calling my phone also. I really didn't dig young females because they were too clingy. And seeing how Tamika kept calling made me regret fucking her. I called her back to stop the excessive calling.

"You don't know how to pick up yo phone?"

"I'm busy, what's good?"

"I need to talk to you. Can you come over?"

"In a couple days. It's a lot goin' on right now," I said.

"Whatever. I just wanted you to know I'm pregnant, Spade."

"Congratulations."

She was insulted. "By *you!*"

"Quit playin' wit' me, man."

"I'm serious, Spade. It's yours, daddy."

"I'ma hit right back," I said. And I hung up.

***

I pulled up to Ace's auntie's house to pick him up. I told him he could stay with me. His room was already furnished. And I was barely there anyway, so he would get all the privacy he needed. I figured I'd get him out of his auntie's so he wouldn't draw any heat there.

He was on the porch smoking a blunt. When he saw me pull up, he got his crutches and stood up. It fucked me up to see my little nigga like that. But I knew he was strong. He had the heart of a lion.

Ashley came out with a few suitcases and sat them on the porch. I got out of my truck and went up to grab them.

"What's good, bro?" I embraced Ace.

"Same-o, same-o," he said. I grabbed the suitcases and headed back to my truck with them. "You need some help, cuzz?" he joked. It was good to see his sense of humor didn't go anywhere.

"I got it, nigga. Is this it?"

"Yeah, bro."

His chick helped him down the steps and in the truck, and he told her goodbye.

"That nigga didn't need no help," I said to her.

"Whatever, Spade," she said. "Bye, babe." She kissed Ace hard.

"A'ight, lil' mama," he said to her.

***

"You call?" I asked.

"Yeah, I called. I was just seeing what was up wit' you," Casey said.

"Out bustin' moves. What's good?"

"I was just wondering, if you weren't busy later, could you stop by?"

"I'll see. Let me call you in a minute. Text me the address."

"A'ight, Spade," she said excitedly.

I ain't gon' front, I missed her. I sort of felt her when she told me why she wasn't there for me. She couldn't handle riding a bit. She was too young.

I was on my way to Sonya's house. Ace was at my crib; I told him he could invite Ashley over if he wanted to. I really didn't want her to know where I stayed, but I trusted Ace's judgment. She had been by his side since he got shot, obeying his every command. She seemed like a real stomp-down.

It was getting kind of late and I needed to purchase some Remy before I made it to Sonya's. I stopped at 7-Eleven on 107th Street. As I was walking into the store, a red Monte Carlo pulled up blasting Messy Marv's "You Gotta Pay Me."

"Let me get a pint of Remy," I told the cashier.

Two young brothas walked in sporting black hoodies. I noticed red ropes in their shoes, and they both mugged me. The cashier looked nervous. *These lil' niggas is silly,* I thought.

The cashier set the bottle on the counter. "Will that be all, sir?"

"Yeah." I paid him and headed out.

Curly and Moe came out behind me. And I noticed they didn't buy anything.

Kush Lamma

When I got in my truck I popped the standard clip out of my Glock and slapped the thirty-rounder in. I started my engine and backed out. As I exited the parking lot and headed up Blue Ridge, the Monte followed me.

I took the first left into a residential area. So did they. I slammed on my brakes, parked and hopped out on them, started firing immediately.

BANG! BANG! BANG! BANG!

The driver tried to reverse his whip. I kept firing.

BANG! BANG! BANG! BANG!

He smacked a parked car. *Pussies*, I thought to myself.

I jumped in my truck and drove off, headed to Sonya's. Them little niggas had to be jack-boys, I assumed.

I had to wake they game up, though.

CHAPTER 9

I made it to her house, where she and Nicole were stretched out ass naked on the bed. The room smelled like pussy and purp.

They were still sleeping when I jumped out the shower. I quickly got dressed because I had to meet up with Maria to discuss some business.

I left and jumped on 435 North. On the way there, Maria called my phone.

"I was just on the way to yo house," I said.

"No, Spade." Her voice was shaky. "Don't come here."

"What's wrong, baby?"

"My father knows about us. He said he's going to kill you."

"Stop playin' wit' me, man. Pops better sit his ass down."

"You don't understand, baby," she said just above a whisper. "He's well connected. I gotta go."

She hung up.

I looked at my phone screen in disbelief. Me and that bitch were like Clyde and Bonnie. She said her pops only wanted her to fuck with Mexicans, but damn. The man was threatening my life. I had to find out who he was.

I re-routed and headed to my spot. When I walked in, Ace and Ashley were watching TV, smoking something tropical. I greeted them both and headed to the kitchen. I grabbed a bottle of Remy and sat my ass down. I had to think.

Maria made all my moves. Her pops was fucking with my timetable. Maybe it was a sign to go legit. I just sat there, weighing my options. Casey called my phone but I ignored it. She called again.

"What's good?" I answered. I really didn't feel like talking.

"I'm chilling, wanting some company."

Hearing her voice made me want her.

"You sure your man won't mind?" I asked.

"I'm single, baby."

"Sounds good."

"You get my text?" she asked, referring to her address.

"I got it."

"Well come see me. We need to talk." She sounded like she wanted to do something else.

"Give me a minute," I said.

"Okay."

I called Ace into the kitchen. I told him what was up with Maria and her pops. He didn't take the threat her pops made too lightly either. We had to re-group, so I told him to call Duece and put him on game. I also gave him the address to Casey's house.

"Yall back jamming, huh?" he joked.

I told him to just do what I asked and left. Casey stayed in Independence, Missouri.

***

"So that's why I wasn't there," she said for the hundredth time.

"I know," I replied. "You told me already."

"I just want you to believe me, Spade."

I had arrived at her house thirty minutes prior. She had dinner ready when I got here, and we were just catching up. She lived in a nice two-bedroom home. Her grandfather owned a restaurant when we were young. I guess they expanded the family business. Casey was the co-owner of one of them. I was impressed to say the least.

"I believe you, man," I said back.

"Man?" She frowned.

"Chill out, lil' homie. Where yo bathroom at?"

"Down the hall, to the right."

I made my way to the bathroom. As soon as I closed the door, I retrieved my phone that had been vibrating. It was Tamika.

"What's up?" I asked.

"This baby's what's up," she spat.

"Bitch, you know that ain't mine. Now quit callin' my phone."

"I got yo bitch, pussy." She hung up.

I shook my head in disbelief. The nerve of these dumb ass hoes. I opened the door and there was Casey, standing with her hands on her hips. She still looked sexy when she was pissed.

"Who was that?" she asked.

"Nobody," I said, looking down at her.

"I know we ain't together, but I still love you," she said. "Don't be callin' no bitches in my house, Spade."

"Yeah, a'ight."

I tried to walk past her to go back to the living room. She grabbed my arm, shoved me against the wall and stuck her tongue in my mouth. I grabbed her ass through the silk night gown, as she grinded her pussy on my erection. Her body was still tight—just like it was before I went to the joint.

"Mmm, I been waitin' for this," she said, pulling my shirt over my head. She tugged at my pants. "Take these off."

What seemed like a second later, we were both naked in the hallway. She licked me from my ears down to my waist. My dick was jumping like it had a mind of its own. She caught it with her mouth.

"*Mmm*, damn." She was in her own world.

She sucked me for what seemed like forever, then started licking my balls and playing with her pussy at the same time. She did it so well that my knees damn near buckled. Then she put her mouth back on my dick, *mmm*-ing and *aah*-ing while she orally pleased me. Shortly after that she grabbed both of my ass cheeks and tried to shove my dick down her throat. I let her stay in control for about another ten minutes or so. Then I jumped in the driver's seat.

We ended up on her queen size bed. I was face deep in her pussy. Licking every inch.

"Damn, Spade … I … miss you … yes, yes! I'm … cu … cumin'!" she cried.

I started licking her clit while I moved my finger in and out of her asshole, which was lubricated by the constant stream of cum and pussy juices.

She then got my face out her pussy. "Let me ride it," she said in a husky voice. She straddled me and went to work. Her pussy was so tight and moist. I gripped her hips and controlled her movement. She grabbed my wrist and put my arms back over my head, got on the heels of her feet and bounced up and down on my dick like she was possessed.

Kush Lamma

***

Back at my house, I was wondering who I could get to move my dope. It had to be someone trustworthy, preferably a woman. Niggas went on too many ego trips for me. I considered Sonya initially, but decided against it. Sometimes she could be too smart for her own good. Plus, all my moves were in the mornings, and she worked the mornings.

Me and Casey just started talking again. I didn't know if I could trust her yet. I even considered Nicole's hot ass. I was tripping. I couldn't believe I was in this position. I had to figure out something fast.

As I was sitting there pondering, my phone went off. I picked up.

"I'm sorry for makin' you mad earlier," Tamika said.

"Look, man, I got some shit I'm dealin' wit' right now. Let me—"

"Hold on, baby. Before you finish, let me say somethin'. I swear to God this yo baby. I wouldn't lie to you, Spade."

I barely knew the bitch and she was talking about she wouldn't lie to me. She was crazy.

"I strapped up." I laughed a little. "I know it ain't mines."

"What? I'm not good enough to have a baby with?"

"I didn't say that. I said I strapped up," I retorted.

"Spade, I like you. And I know you like me. We can make this work, baby. We can get married and be a happy family."

"I'm gone, man," I said, and hung up.

I'd gotten myself in some bullshit by fucking with that chick. After I got a drink of Remy, I went and popped in a Kevin Hart DVD, tried to lighten my mood. Tamika called my phone about ten times after I hung up on her but I didn't answer. Still, she kept calling. I came to the realization that she would be the last young bitch I would ever fuck.

She eventually figured out I wasn't going to answer my phone, so she sent me a text and I read it.

Tamika: *Ok Spade. U wanna play wit me. I'll see you around pussy. Watch yo back. Love yo baby momma.*

CHAPTER 10

I was leaving OG Casa's spot in North Kansas City. I had to fill him in on the latest. I was on the highway headed to Sonya's, when my hotline went off.

It was Casey. "Look, I ain't tryna be in yo business or nothin', but I seen yo boy Duece pickin' up yo lil' bitch from work. And they was lookin' mighty friendly." She sounded pleased to be the one to tell me.

"Yeah?" I said.

"Just thought you should know. I knew that hoe couldn't be trusted."

I thought maybe she was overreacting. I didn't give a fuck about Duece picking up Sonya. They were friends before she was my bitch. I doubted he was trying to push up on her.

As soon as Casey hung up, Maria sent me a text telling me to come pick my money up from her house. I put my foot to the gas and got there.

***

"Spade, I love you," Maria said as I was putting the duffle bag in my trunk.

"I love you, too, lil' mama." I gave her a hug and a kiss. She told me she was scared for me and that once she convinced her father to accept our relationship she would call.

"I promise I'll make this work," she said seriously.

"Just hit me," I said.

***

I walked in Sonya's house and she was cooking a meal.

"What you makin'?" I asked, walking up behind her, kissing her neck. She smelled good.

"Grilled fish, green beans, and Rice-A-Roni." She shook the pot, loosening the greens.

"So how was work?" I wanted to see if it was some truth behind Casey's claim.

"Same ol', same ol'."

"That's what's up. Nicole came and got you?"

"Yeah, she was late as usual, but she came," Sonya lied. "She went to her auntie's house after she dropped me off."

I knew her like the back of my hand. I knew when she was being deceptive. But why lie about Duece coming to get her?

"That's what's up," I said.

She brought my plate to the table and we ate. We was shooting-the-shit for a minute, but I could tell she was uneasy about something. I acted like I didn't notice.

We drank, headed to the bedroom and sucked and fucked like normal. After we showered, we went down to the living room to watch some television—and Nicole came in. She greeted us both, then her and Sonya started talking like they hadn't seen each other all day.

I left out the house shortly after that and was about to head back to my spot. I had been by there to drop the money off I got from Maria's. Ace was gone then. I hoped he was there when I arrived.

When I approached my truck, I saw the word "pussy" keyed in my paint. I looked around for any signs of the culprit. I was pissed. It had to be that bitch Tamika. But how the fuck did she know where Sonya stayed?

CHAPTER 11

"Who you think did it, cuzz?" Ace asked. We were chilling in the living room.

"I think it was that bitch Tamika," I said, fuming. "But I ain't sure."

"You need to get yo women in line, bro." He smiled.

"Yeah, that hoe was out of pocket."

Ace changed the subject to an even serious matter. He said Duece had been acting funny. He said he called Duece and said he was gon' stop by and holler at him, but Duece said he was too busy. Duece was never too busy for Ace.

I started thinking about how strange Duece was acting also. Little things I normally would overlook were things I was focusing on. My thoughts were interrupted by my horn.

"Yeah?" I answered.

"Yeah, nothing, pussy," Tamika replied. "Did you get my message?"

"Bitch, what message?"

"On yo truck." She laughed and hung up the phone.

I looked at Ace. "It *was* Tamika," I told him.

"You need to slap that bitch up," he said.

Without a doubt, she was getting too far ahead of herself. She was fucking with the wrong one. *I knew I shouldn't have fucked her young ass*, I thought. Not that other chicks didn't do dumb shit too; it's just younger females are quicker on the trigger.

I didn't need any extra problems on my plate. Ace had gotten shot, Maria was off the team, and her dad supposedly wanted me knocked. And my right-hand man was slipping off that "Tony." It seemed like shit was falling apart. Fuck that, shit *was* falling apart. I needed to make some adjustments, and fast. I got another phone call. But I didn't recognize the number.

I picked up.

A woman said, "Spade, this is Jamie."

"Who?" I was confused.

"Jamie. You don't remember me?" She sounded disappointed. "From Macy's."

The girl Duece been playing house wit', I remembered.

"Yeah, yeah what's up?"

"I'm worried about Duece," she pleaded.

"Why is that?"

"He's been getting high, gambling all his money away. He's not the same, Spade. I know I shouldn't be telling you this, but sometimes he talks down on you and Ace. He—"

"Where's he at?" I heard enough from her ass.

"He's at the house sleep. I ran to the store real quick," she said.

He had to be off that shit. Duece was never sleep at this hour.

"Just tell him to call me when he gets up."

I filled Ace in on the details and he just shook his head disgusted at the thought of Duece on some sucka shit. I knew Jamie wasn't lying about Duece either. He loved to gamble since we were teenagers. But he never fell off behind it. The Tony had him off schedule.

Whatever the case, he was slipping. And pillow talking with a bitch was a no-no. Last time I tried to holler at Duece it didn't go so well. So I had been falling back on him. But that was my nigga and I loved him so I had to figure something out. Just not at this moment.

I needed to get my mind off of all the bullshit so I called Lisa and asked her to meet me for dinner.

***

Me and Lisa met at The Cheesecake Factory around seven-thirty.

"So what do you do, Spade?" she asked across the table.

She wore a white knit shirt and slacks, with strappy sandals. I had on a plain gray button-up, comfortable denims—fitted, not baggy—and a pair of gray Air Jordans. I wasn't dressed like a lowdown thug. I was casual.

"I'm tryna get my entertainment company off the ground," I answered, leaving my underworld dealings out.

"That's fine boo. But how are you bringing income in?"

"A few investments."

"Not to be in your business, baby, but I know you playin' wit' a nice amount of money. I can tell, but I know it's not legitimate."

"And how do you know that?" I countered.

"I checked on you." She smiled. "And I like you. I can help you get your entertainment company off the ground. And I can help you clean some of that money up."

"Is that right?" I was all ears.

"That's right, baby." She exposed that beautiful smile again. "I'm tryna open another beauty salon next year. I'm lookin' at locations right now. I would love to bring you aboard."

"Sounds interesting and lucrative."

"I'm interesting and lucrative," she said back.

Over the course of the dinner, I found Lisa really intriguing. She was independent, sexy, educated, and a good conversationalist. Making some legitimate moves only made sense. The short time I spent with her made me realize we had chemistry. It reminded me of the chemistry me and Maria had. I had to see where it led me.

***

I told Lisa I would call her soon. I was on my way to the club. I needed to be around some fresh energy. It was going on eleven-thirty and I was still in my truck with the keyed-in message on it. I thought about pulling out my old school I barely drove. But I was cool.

My hotline went off as I was pulling up to the club.

"Yeah," I said after I turned my music down.

"Touchdown, bro," Army Tank said. He was letting me know they got the niggas that shot Ace.

"Everything everything?" I asked.

"You too ugly, cuzz, you know how we do," he said.

"Ok, lil' bro. I'ma hit you first thing."

I felt good after that call. Them suckas were eradicated, so that's one problem solved.

***

"Remy on the rocks," I told the sexy bartender.

"Ok, boo," she replied with a smile.

The club was packed. I didn't notice any threats in the building so I was straight. It was a few niggas in the building that I knew was going to push if shit got fonky.

"So yo bitches is keying yo shit up, Spade?" a voice asked from behind me. I turned around and it was Casey. She looked good.

"I'ma handle that. Who you here wit'?"

"My cousins. You?"

"Solo."

"You comin' over tonight?" She put her hand on her hip.

"I'll see," I said.

"Let me know." She sashayed off.

I was enjoying myself, talking to a few females that caught my eye, just chilling. Then I saw Selena from a distance, walking my way. She was looking sexy as hell in a black mesh dress, the neckline exposed to reveal a black brassiere and a gold-glittered chest. She strutted over with leggings underneath—can't go wrong with leggings, especially with taut thighs like hers—topped off with a pair of open-toe heels.

But even more than how she was dressed, I knew she "went" too. I thought about that ménage-a-morning with Maria.

"Hi, Spade," she said.

"How you doin', baby?" I looked her up and down.

"Just enjoying the night."

"You want a drink?" I asked.

"Sure," she said. She got a little closer to me and I smelled Chanel perfume.

"Bartender." I put my hand up to get her attention. "One shot of Patron."

"Did I ask for Patron?" she joked, close enough to my face to kiss me.

"I offered," I said to her, putting the money on the bar. I handed her the drink and we spent the next few minutes flirting and touching on each other. Casey walked by rolling her eyes, but she kept it moving.

"Let's go outside and talk." Selena grabbed my hand and led me out of the club.

We went to my truck that was parked right next to the club. Once we got in, the Mexican goddess stuck her tongue down my throat. She reached down, unzipped my pants and pulled my dick out. Real aggressive.

"I miss you, papi." She started bobbing on my shaft like a true professional.

"Damn. Suck that muhfucka, bitch," I demanded.

"*Mmm*, papi." She came up for air, then went back to work. She yanked the top of her dress and bra down while she sucked my dick, revealing her round breasts. Her knees were in my passenger seat, ass facing my passenger window, her face in my lap.

I fingered her pussy while she continued to knock me down. She was hot and wet.

"Damn that pussy wet," I said.

She got off my dick and straddled me. I hit the button to slide my seat all the way back. People were walking by and all that. But she didn't care and neither did I. My dark tint concealed us. Her tight, wet pussy gripped my dick as she went up and down my manhood.

"Damn, papi," she moaned. "*Mmm* … yes, papi .. Oh God …"

I gripped her ass while she rode me. Her plump breasts sat in my face so I played with them with my tongue.

"I'm comin', Spade! *Aaah*, yes!"

I grabbed her hips and slammed her down on my dick. I knew I was about to nut soon. This little Mexican bitch was riding the shit out of a nigga!

"I'm comin' again, Spade!" she screamed. I exploded also, and she collapsed on top of me. She started sucking my neck while she sat on me, her pussy juices running down my thighs.

When she finally got off my dick, she sat in my passenger seat and pulled the visor down. She straightened herself up in the mirror. She glanced over at me, biting her bottom lip. Still looking sexy as hell.

"Let me see your phone," she said.

I handed it to her. She put her number in my phone and I gave her mine. She kissed me on the cheek and reached for my door handle.

She said, "See you soon, baby."

CHAPTER 12

I was stepping out the bathroom of Casey's house. I had to wash Selena's juices off me. I sat down on the bed and Casey started applying lotion to my back.

"So who keyed yo truck, Spade?"

"This lil' bitch named Tamika," I said.

"Wit' the red Charger?" She sounded disappointed.

"Yeah."

"You sho' know how to pick 'em." She stood up. "That lil' hoe just lookin' for a nigga to save her."

"I only hit her one time, strapped up and all." I looked at Casey seriously. "And she swore I got her knocked up."

"Huh, that lil' bitch." She laughed.

"I'm hip," I said.

Casey left the room. I finished applying my hygiene. It was getting late so I laid back and relaxed. The movie that was on the tube—some AMC drama starring Morgan Freeman—slightly had my attention, but I was tired. Casey came back in the room and laid next to me wearing a tank top and thong. I was watching the tube; she wanted to play, started kissing on my torso. She came up to look me in my eyes.

"I love you, Spade," she said sincerely. "And I'm sorry."

"It's coo'. And I love you too," I said.

She grabbed a condom from her dresser.

***

I was sleep on Sonya's living room couch. I woke up when I heard noises coming from the stairs. I sat up and looked around, didn't see anyone. As I walked up the stairs, the noises got louder.

"Oh! Oh! Oh!"

The familiar moan got even louder. I made it to the bedroom door; it was cracked open a little. Sonya was riding some nigga, but I couldn't see him.

"Ah, shit, Duece!" she screamed.

What the fuck?!

"You like that, bitch?" he asked.

I couldn't move from the door.

"Yes, baby … *Oooo!*" she cried.

I finally walked in.

"What the fuck yall doin'?" I asked. They didn't answer me. Sonya got off of Duece, then got on her knees so Duece could fuck her from the back.

"Damn this pussy wet," he said. Nicole came in the room ass naked and joined them. The bitch didn't even acknowledge me. She got under Sonya, and Sonya started eating her pussy.

"Keep fuckin' me Duece," Sonya demanded, lifting her ass so he could see her wet pussy from behind. Duece looked at me with a devilish grin.

"I see why you been keepin' this bitch around, cuzz," he said.

I looked at him like he was crazy, then walked out of the room and went downstairs. Grabbing my Glock 23 from under the sofa cushion, I ran back upstairs and entered the room. Sonya and Nicole were both sucking Duece's dick.

In a rage, I aimed and emptied my clip in all three of them, loving the fire that jumped out the barrel.

They were all still now. Dead and naked …

… then I woke up in the middle of the night.

CHAPTER 13

The next morning Casey was cooking breakfast in the nude. Her body was still flawless. The scarf she had on her head revealed the back of her neck; it was the first time I saw the tattoo—she had my government name inked on her. *Samuel Wright.*

"When did you get that?" I asked.

"Get what?"

"That on yo neck."

"Oh." She rubbed it. "About a year after you got locked up."

"Is that right?" I was surprised.

"That's right. You're the only one for—"

My phone rang and she stopped talking. It was Sonya.

"Yeah," I answered.

"Spade, somebody broke in my house!" she said angrily.

"What?!" I was pissed. I stood up and paced the kitchen.

"They did it last night. When me and Nicole came here this morning my shit was trashed!"

"What's up wit' the shit?" I asked, referring to the cocaine. I didn't give a fuck about her place being trashed.

"Gone," she said.

I hung up on her. I had to get there.

"What's wrong, baby?" Casey had heard everything.

"This bitch just told me somebody broke in her shit and took my stash that was over there."

"Before you get too emotional and react foolishly, evaluate the situation."

She made perfect sense. But I wasn't trying to hear that shit. I looked at her like she was crazy.

"I'll be back," I said.

I went and got dressed, then headed out the door.

"Be careful, Spade!" Casey yelled behind me.

CHAPTER 14

Before I headed to Sonya's house, I decided to stop at Duece's. When I got to the front door, he was opening it.

"Sonya called me and told me what happened," he said.

"I knew I should of put cameras on that muhfucka." I walked in.

"We gon' find the niggas that did this shit, bro."

We both sat on his sofa. His house was a little filthier than usual. And he didn't look too good.

"Man, they got four bricks and forty thousand," I said, looking at him upside his head.

"Damn," he replied.

"We gotta get up wit' Kutz later on. You in?"

"Not on this run, bro." He rubbed his face. "I'm kinda fucked up."

I didn't feel like asking why he wasn't ready. "A'ight, cuzz, I'ma shake. Call me if you hear somethin'."

I got up and left. In my truck, on the way to Sonya's, I called OG Casa. He told me the bitch was behind it with no hesitation. He never really liked Sonya.

***

Sonya and Nicole were cleaning up when I walked in. I walked straight to the room that my safe was in. The safe was ripped out of the wall. Someone knew it was there. No doubt about that.

There was never heavy traffic over Sonya's. No flashy cars parked outside, nothing. Someone had to put somebody on it. I walked back downstairs.

"What time you get here?" I asked Sonya.

"Like a hour ago." She looked frustrated.

"Yo neighbors ain't see nothin'?"

"Nothin', baby. I'm scared, I have to move, Spade." She hugged me tight. I felt sorry for her because her house was ransacked. But I didn't trust her. I noticed there was no forced entry. No broken windows. Nicole was cleaning up, on hush-mouth. She kept looking at me like she had something to tell me.

I told Sonya not to call the police, then I walked out of the house. I had to get to the bottom of this shit.

***

"I'm ready to rock, big bro," Ace said.

"We gon' take care of it, lil' bro. Keep yo ears to the streets and eyes open. It'll surface," I said. We were in my living room talking. My nerves had calmed down. "We gotta get up wit' Kutz and re-up. You in?"

"Yeah, I'ma get a few."

"A'ight. I'ma get ten of 'em. Get yo change together. I'ma try to call Kutz."

"Duece gon' bring his change through?" he asked.

"He said it's all bad."

Ace couldn't believe it. "That nigga on some funny shit, bro."

"I'm hip."

I walked upstairs to my room to think. Maria called me as soon as I sat on my bed.

"How are you doin'?"

"I'm straight," I said curtly. I didn't feel like informing her about the recent events.

"Somebody's been followin' me, Spade."

"Like who?" I really didn't give a fuck.

"I don't know. I think they work for my dad."

"Yeah?"

"Spade, be careful," she said, and hung up.

That was the second or third time that bitch told me to be careful. Her pops must have been a dangerous man.

Maria never acted that emotional. I shook those thoughts and called Kutz.

"Spade, my man," he answered.

"What's good?"

"House shopping."

"I need to holla at you," I said.

"No time soon, my man. Have to take my lady to Denver tomorrow. I'll let you know when I return, my friend."

He was letting me know it was all bad. We hung up. *This some bullshit,* I thought.

Back downstairs, I told Ace what was going on. I didn't tell him about my suspicions. Kutz never ran out of dope. Maybe I was just on edge.

Me and Ace popped a bottle of XO to ease the tension. He put in a Kevin Hart DVD—that nigga Kevin had us rolling; the laughter was much needed. Twenty minutes in Lisa hit me.

I was happy she called.

"How are you?" I asked.

"I'm fine, sweety. Are you busy?"

"I'm just chillin', watchin' this comedy shit."

"I know this might sound a little cheesy, but I miss you," she said.

And I temporarily forgot about the madness around me. "Well, I guess we gon' have to do somethin' about that."

"I guess so," she said seductively.

"So what do you have in—" My line clicked. It was Nicole. She never called, so it had to be important. "Can I call you right back, Lisa?"

"Make sure you call back, baby."

"Will do." I clicked over. "What's good, Nicole?"

She whispered, "It's about Sonya and Duece."

"I'm listening."

"Well, first of all, they been fuckin' wit' each other since you was in prison. They—"

I cut her off. "Is that right?"

"Yeah, that's right. That's my homegirl and I love her, but you a solid nigga and I been diggin' you since I first saw you. I don't know what it is about you, Spade. I—"

"Get to it, Nicole," I told her.

"I want to tell you everything, but she's right upstairs. Meet me tomorrow and I'll tell you everything."

I called Lisa back and she invited me to her home. She stayed in The Vineyards. I told Ace I was heading out. A part of me wanted to tell him about the call I got from Nicole, but I decided to wait until I got the whole scoop. I wondered about Nicole's motives. We already fucked so it had to be some truth behind her statements.

I gave Ace Lisa's address and left. I was at Lisa's in no time.

Deception's PLAYGROUND

***

Lisa had Gerald Levert's "Pop, Goes My Mind" playing at a low, soothing volume. We sat at her kitchen table, eating an Italian meal she prepared before I arrived. She had her lights low and she was looking stunning in her night attire—a simple crème, backless cotton dress, and her hair was trimmed short with glints of sheen to accentuate her high gloss shellac earrings. She didn't know how much I needed her company. I had to escape the madness around me.

"You seem like a busy man. Do you get to do this often?" she asked.

"Do what?" I replied, really not sure what she was implying.

"Have a queen prepare a home cooked meal." Arrogance was in her tone. A sexy arrogance, though.

I smiled. "Not that often."

"Hmm, so where's Mrs. Spade?"

"There is no Mrs. Spade," I said. "I know you've been divorced for a while, but I know there's somebody. Where's *he?*"

"There is no 'he.' I have friends but no one special." She smiled.

We chatted a little longer. She was even more intelligent and interesting than I assumed. We talked about everything

111

from our favorite dishes to investment opportunities. Twenty minutes later we were in her bedroom.

We undressed each other, kissing slow and methodical like we were life-long lovers. Her level of maturity showed in the bed. I let her take control initially. She liked kissing because she acted like she couldn't get enough of my tongue. Eventually she kissed my chest, laying over top of me so my dick was poking her in her stomach.

Then she went down to my stomach, her tongue tasting my skin. Her mouth was warm. She let out a few soft moans before she took me in her mouth.

"You taste good, baby," she said. She moved slowly up and down my shaft using just enough saliva. She played with her clit, making herself cum as she sucked. "Talk dirty to me, baby," she said when she came up for air.

I grabbed the back of her head and tried to lose my dick in her jaws. Shortly after that I was ready to taste her.

"Turn around," I demanded.

We sixty-nined it. Her hairless, meaty pussy tasted good too. She moaned, I grunted, as Levert sang to us. It was magic.

She got up off my face and slipped down my torso. She eased down my dick, reverse cowgirl. She did her *thang*! And the view of her fit body and bouncing ass was just right!

"*Ahh*, shit, baby," she cried, slamming up and down on my dick. She felt good, her pussy gripped me like a glove—it didn't seem like a human being came out of here. I gripped both of her ass cheeks and navigated the ride.

Then I flipped her on her back. I went in hard. She screamed and made a lot of ugly faces.

"You like that, bitch?" I asked.

"Yes, baby! I'm 'bout … 'bout to cum!" she cried.

"Yeah?" I was fucking her like I was possessed.

"Oooh … shit !" She came.

Then I turned her over doggy style, made a slow entry, very slow. Teasing her. She looked back at my package to watch what was bringing her so much pleasure. I sped up, beast-fucking her again. I smacked her ass repetitiously, and fucked her like I had something to prove.

CHAPTER 15

It was the next morning and the smell of breakfast woke me up. Last night, me and Lisa showered after sex fell asleep. I usually didn't spend the night over women's houses on the first night. Old habit, I guess. But I had felt comfortable.

I went to her bathroom and helped myself to a spare toothbrush. I got myself together and headed toward the kitchen. No shirt, just pants and shoes.

Lisa stood over the stove in a Victoria's Secret embroidered apron number. It stopped right below her ass, showing off her strong legs.

"Hey, sleepy," she shot.

"What's up, baby?" I sat down at the kitchen table, phone in hand.

I had a few missed calls from OG Casa, Nicole, and Duece. I planned on calling them later. I enjoyed my night with Lisa and it looked like it was going to be a good morning also. Had to enjoy this moment of serenity.

"I'm fixing you pancakes, turkey bacon, and eggs," she said.

Looking at the food and her amazing frame, I replied, "I see."

"It'll be ready in a minute. Can you get the orange juice out the fridge?"

I got the juice out, grabbed a couple glasses too. As we ate, we engaged in small talk. Then the conversation got interesting. She admitted to seeing me prior to the Verizon run-in. She told me that the beauty salon she owned was the same one Sonya worked at. She saw me pick Sonya up a few times, and she told me somebody else picked her up too. That "somebody" drove a black suburban.

Duece, I thought.

Lisa said Sonya didn't deserve a nigga like me. According to her, Sonya had loose lips, bragging about her control over me. Which was bullshit.

I had mixed feelings at the moment. I understood Lisa going after what she wanted; I even admired it. But I also felt vulnerable, not knowing what business of mine Sonya may have put out there.

But for some odd reason I felt like I could trust Lisa. I filled her in on a fraction of the recent events. I told her to keep her eyes and ears open. She was more than willing. Shortly after, I left with a promise to call her soon.

***

I was pulling up to my house thirty minutes later. I noticed two Mexicans sitting a few houses down, in a gray Cadillac with light tints. I opened my garage and pulled in.

When I got in the house I went straight to the window. The 'Lac had Arizona plates on it. I noticed Ace was gone too. I watched the idle Cadillac for about five minutes. They just sat there. I left the window and returned OG Casa's call.

"Spade, what's goin' on?" he answered.

"Tryna figure it out."

"I'm just letting you know Duece has been lookin' at some houses."

Code for: *Deuce has been looking for customers to sell some bricks to.*

"Ah yeah?" I was pissed.

"Be meticulous wit' it," he said, then hung up. I hated when he did that shit.

I had a strong feeling Duece hit my safe. I had to be sure before I acted. I went and looked out my window again.

The 'Lac was gone.

I had a lot of shit to square off. Find out who was behind taking my bricks, find somebody *with* some bricks on deck, *and* a new runner. I had to get that bitch Tamika off my heels. Maria's pops wanted me knocked ...

Too much was going on.

Deception's PLAYGROUND

***

Casey wanted me to meet her at The Cheese Cake Factory. I had to run to Macy's in Independence first. Some new Coogi had hit the racks and I had to have it.

Only in the store about twenty minutes, I already had what I wanted in hand.

"Did you get my message?"

I turned around and it was Tamika. She had a funny ass smirk on her face. I felt like slapping this bitch for keying my truck.

"What the fuck you doin', bitch? Followin' me?"

"As a matter of fact, I am." She smiled.

I headed toward the cashier.

"Don't walk away from me, Spade!"

Customers in the store started looking at her. Then at me. I kept walking. Lucky for me, a lane was open. I made it to the cashier.

"Will this be all sir?" the feminine male asked.

"Yeah, man."

"Pussy, you can't run from this." Tamika got in my face. I shoved her ass back. "Oh, so you gon' hit me?"

The cashier told me my price nervously. I handed him eleven hundred and grabbed my bags and left, leaving the receipt and the change.

That bitch followed me out. She didn't even buy shit. She had to be nuts, I thought, as she trailed behind me in the parking lot.

"Baby, I'm sorry for causin' a scene in there. Please forgive me."

We were by my truck. She was a different person then. She had to be bipolar.

"You good?" I said. I decided to take a subtle approach.

She smiled, forced a hug and kissed my cheek. Then, oddly, she turned and ran to her car. "Bye, baby!" she yelled as she trucked it the other way.

***

"That's all you eatin'?" I asked Casey.

"Yes. Thank you," she said sarcastically.

"A'ight, lil' mama. I was just askin'."

"So, did you find out anything?"

My phone rang. "Not yet, hold up," I said, putting the cell to my ear. "What's good?"

"I got a room at the Red Roof Inn on Noland. Meet me there later; I'll tell you everything," Nicole said.

"A'ight." I hung up on her.

"Who was that?" Casey was slightly irritated.

"Nobody. So, how's the restaurant comin'?"

"It's doin' okay. The profit margin could be better. But it's cool."

As we talked, Casey had a few emotional moments, but the dinner was cool. We exited the spot hand-in-hand, heading to our cars, which were parked next to each other. I loved Casey. We had history.

When we made it to our cars, our happy faces turned into angry faces. All four of my tires were flat. And another message was written in my paint—keyed in, I should say. It read: "Tamika." I looked around for the red Charger. I didn't see one.

"That bitch Tamika did this?" Casey asked.

"Dumb ass bitch," I thought out loud.

"Don't worry, baby. I'll have it towed to my uncle's shop and I'll take you to Enterprise to get a rental." She rubbed my back.

"I'ma kill that bitch."

"Don't trip, baby. I got you."

***

An hour and a half later I was in a Chrysler 300M. Casey said her uncle would be done with my truck by tomorrow. I rented the 300 for two weeks anyway. I felt secure in something different.

When I talked to Ace while I was at Enterprise, he said him and his chick were out shopping. They were also stepping out later. It felt like Ace was the only person I could trust at this moment in my life. My young nigga.

I called Nicole and she was already at Red Roof Inn. I told her I'd be there shortly. On the way there I saw a car just like Sonya's. Same paint as my truck, but it had rims and tinted windows on it. *Couldn't have been her,* I thought.

I pulled up to the Red Roof and parked in front of the room Nicole said she was in.

"New car?" She opened the door.

"Somethin' like that." I walked past her and entered the room. She shut the door. "Why you got this room?" I took a seat in the chair by the window.

"Needed to be alone. Sonya's on some different shit." Nicole sat on the bed and fired up a backwood. She went right in.

She told me Sonya and Duece had been fucking with each other for seven years. They met two years before I was released. She told me she knew for a fact that Duece intentionally hooked me and Sonya up. He knew my type. I still doubted what she was saying. She tried to pass the "wood," but I declined.

Nicole knew all about my case. When I was seventeen, a situation near Central High School I was involved in got out of hand, and before I knew it I was leaving a shoot-out. Speeding as I left the scene, I smacked a car—I tried to swerve but it was too late—on 27th and Indiana. I killed the passenger of the vehicle I hit, left the scene on foot and got rid of the gun. I ran all the way to my homeboy's house on 24th and Brighton. Nicole told me the innocent passenger was Duece's step-brother. I never knew; Nicole did. I felt like slapping this bitch.

Apparently Duece had a hidden agenda. It turns out him and this mysterious brother of his were quite close. She told me Sonya told her that Duece knew I would get out and bubble. He wanted to keep me close, *and* in the dark. Sonya was his pawn, not my bitch.

I wanted to kill Sonya, Duece, and Nicole. But there was more.

"Duece hit yo safe," Nicole said. "I know it for a fact. I was in on the overall scheme at first, but once I got to know you, I fell back."

She went on to tell me that Sonya and Duece had been off that "soft." Getting their nose dirty. They came up with a plan to fake an abduction and have me pay a ransom for Sonya. But Duece was falling off so he hit my safe. Supposedly, Duece paid some niggas to kill Ace but they failed. She even said Duece had a plan for my permanent demise.

Death was in Duece's future for sure.

"Where's Sonya at?" I asked her.

"I don't know. But Sonya got her car out the paint shop, and she put some rims on it."

"Why you tellin' me this shit?" I asked, trying to keep my emotions in check.

"I'm not scandalous, Spade. And I like you."

"Is that right?"

She looked down at her feet. "I just think this shit is gettin' out of hand."

"It's all good," I told her. "We never had this conversation." I looked at her, waiting for her to reply.

She finally did. "Right, right. We never had this conversation."

I saw fear in her eyes. "A'ight," I said, then got up to leave. But she tried to stop me, tears welling in her eyes.

"Spade, tell me you're not going to hurt Sonya."

"Nah, I ain't gon' do nothin' to that bitch."

"Please don't. She don't know no better," Nicole pled.

"I know."

"Thank you, Spade." She hugged me.

"It ain't shit."

She kissed my neck and my dick got hard. I think it was her kisses and her good-smelling hair. She felt my erection and dropped to her knees, as I stood against the door. She tugged my sweatpants down and took me in her mouth. *The nerve of this bitch.*

I grabbed the back of her head, loving the warmth of her mouth. She sucked my dick like her life depended on it. She looked up at me and winked. *Silly bitch, I'm not flattered.*

I couldn't stop thinking about the level of deception they tried to play on me.

I pulled my dick out of her mouth … and I smacked the shit out of her.

She held her sore jaw as I left.

"Spade, what's wrong?!" I heard her yell.

CHAPTER 16

It was Sunday morning. Last night I found out my nigga was an insect, a parasite. He had to be crushed. Nicole and Sonya would also be victims.

I sat at my kitchen table eating Frosted Flakes. Pissed. My phone rang.

"Yeah?" I answered.

"What's up, baby?" Casey said.

For some reason I felt relieved every time I talked to her. "Chillin'. What's good?"

"Nothin'. You're truck will be ready tomorrow."

"That's what's up. Tell him I'll call tomorrow afternoon."

"Okay. I'ma be goin' to Miami today, too," she slid in.

"Vacation?"

"Somethin' like that."

Her shortness bothered me. "Somethin' like that?" I echoed.

"My cousin Sparkle had been askin' me to come down there. So I'ma go chill wit' her for a couple weeks."

"That's what's up. Enjoy yo'self, and call me when you land."

"Will do. I love you."

"I love you too."

Ace walked in shortly after I hung up. He came to the kitchen table and sat down.

"What's goo, big bro?" he asked.

"Talked to Nicole last night," I said seriously.

His demeanor changed with mine. "What she on?"

I gave him the rundown. Told him everything, damn near verbatim. He was beyond pissed, ready to kill something. I wanted to kill Duece but Ace insisted he do it. It was personal for the both of us.

My phone rang again. It was OG Casa.

"What's goin' on, OG?"

"I gotta holla at you," he said.

"Come through. I'm at the house."

"I'm pulling up. Open the door."

Ace opened the door for him. I took a seat in my living room, as OG Casa walked in. His full beard nearly masked his dark-skinned face, bringing attention to his sleek bald head. He wore a two-button Salvatore Ferragamo suit and his boots were Ferragamo too. Sharp as always. He sat down, looking like he had something on his mind. Ace sat next to him.

"Now don't overreact." He looked at me. "But I know for a fact Kutz put a hit on you."

"Get the fuck outta here. Kutz?" I couldn't believe it.

"Yeah. He said he didn't want you bringin' his organization down."

"What the fuck he mean 'bring his organization down'?"

"I don't know. But I'm on it. Got a couple of my people ready," he said.

"I been fuckin' wit' Kutz for years. Never crossed him. And he tryna rock like that?" I was boiling with anger. Too much was going on.

"We gotta be smart about this," said OG Casa. "Dude ain't a joke. But he bleeds like we bleed."

Ace was quiet, very attentive.

We talked about different ways to eliminate Kutz. I included Duece, Sonya, and Nicole in that process of elimination. Shit needed to get handled. I'd been out of prison for five years, had a nice amount of money, ready to legitimize my hustle. And here I was conspiring to kill.

But it was necessary. No question.

***

I called Jamie. I told her I had someone trying to get a couple of bricks. She was a simple woman. I told her that me and Duece were not talking but I still had love for him and wanted to see him eating. I told her she couldn't tell Duece that I had the move for him. His ego would get in the way.

"Okay, okay," an excited Jamie said. "I promise I won't tell him."

I guess she assumed more money for Duece meant more money for her. I gave her a number to a burnout phone Ace had. Duece didn't know the number. I told her to call that number at eight.

***

Ace and OG Casa had been gone for a while. I was still at the house and had made plans to meet Lisa at her house at seven. It was five-thirty. I was chilling, sipping Remy.

I was startled by a loud knock at my door.

Looking out the peephole, I saw two detectives. One of them looked familiar. I opened the door.

"Spade, long time no see," the pale-faced officer said. He had a devilish grin on his face. One that was too familiar.

It was Detective Kremensky. The other one I'd never seen before. He looked younger than Kremensky, the asshole cop who used to harass me every chance he got back in the day. And he was the one who apprehended me when I went to the slammer.

"What the fuck you want?" I asked.

127

"You know this woman?" Kremensky held up a picture of Tamika.

"Do *you*?" I retorted.

"Same funny Spade." He smiled.

I returned his smile. "It's Mr. Wright."

"I see you're doin' well for yo'self, Spade."

He kept saying my street name, trying to fuck with me. It was working.

"Good day, gentlemen." I tried to shut the door. He stopped it with his hand.

"This woman is Tamika Daniels." Kremensky shoved the picture in my face; I shoved it back. "She was found dead behind the wheel of her car last night. Brakes went out. She hit a light pole head-on. Going sixty miles an hour."

"And?" I said.

"Her roommate brought your name up. Said you might have had something to do with it. Said Tamika was pregnant with your child. You weren't happy about that."

"You chargin' me wit' somethin'?" I asked.

"Just want to ask a few questions," the other detective finally spoke up.

"Contact my attorney." I slammed the door.

I looked through the peephole again and saw them leaving.

I didn't know what to feel. I was happy and sad at the same time. Tamika was a cool chick at first. Until she falsely claimed I got her pregnant. Then that bitch was a pain in the ass. But she met her maker behind the wheel of the car I met her in. One thing I did know was that I didn't have shit to do with it. I called my attorney, Antonio Puzzo.

The secretary picked up. "Puzzo, Ortiz, and Brown."

"Yes, may I speak with Mr. Antonio Puzzo please?"

"He's in a meeting. May I ask who's calling?" she asked.

"Have him call Mr. Samuel Wright, please."

"Sure thing, Mr. Wright."

CHAPTER 17

Antonio Puzzo called an hour later at six-thirty. I was relieved.

"Sam. What's up?"

"Kremensky and his sidekick popped up at my house," I
said, "talkin' 'bout I had somethin' to do with a car accident
last night. The bitch died."

"Details?" Puzzo asked.

"Her name is Tamika Daniels. Brakes went out on her
car and she hit a light pole."

"Your whereabouts?"

"Red Roof Inn on Noland. I got there at about ten. I left
at about eleven or so. Went straight home."

"Okay. Let me look into this. I'll see what time the accident occurred. See if I can get the footage from the hotel
also. I'm assuming they don't have enough evidence to
charge you. So don't worry, and don't say shit to the cops."

"A'ight man, get this shit taken care of," I stated.

I felt a little better after talking to Puzzo. I knew he would handle his business. There was another knock at my door. It was OG Casa again. I let him in and we sat at my kitchen table.

"I talked to my people, Spade. They said Kutz definitely has a couple of hitmen on you."

"So how do we eliminate Kutz?" I couldn't believe what was happening. "We still haven't come to a conclusion."

"I know, I know. It has to be well thought out." He rubbed his beard. "Kutz is a very careful man. But I'm workin' on somethin'."

"So what's up wit' these so-called hitmen?" I asked.

"Not 'so-called.' Real deal. Two Mexicans from Arizona."

"Arizona?" I said out loud.

"Yeah. So keep yo eyes open." He gave me a serious look.

"I seen a couple Mexicans sittin' two houses down the other day. Arizona plates."

"What were they drivin'?" OG Casa asked.

"Gray 'Lac," I told him.

"Okay. Let me run that by my people, get the four-one-one."

The "people" OG Casa spoke of were Russians he did business with, a relationship he'd had for over twenty years. He had a lot of connections.

"Just get back wit' me and let me know," I said. "I'll tell Ace the latest when I see him."

"Okay, nephew. I'ma go. Be careful."

Then he got up and left. I felt nervous, prepared, and under-prepared at the same time. OG Casa's lady friend was meeting Ace while he was over. She dropped off some hardware to him. A gift from the Russians. I called Casey and told her I needed to use her spot while she was out of town. I had to lay low until this shit blew over.

I told Ace to meet me there. Casey didn't stay that far from me. I was there in a hot one. Ace pulled up shortly after. He put the hardware up, grabbed what he needed and was right back out the door.

***

"So where you wanna go eat, baby?" Lisa asked. We were in her front room.

"It don't matter. Let's go where you wanna go," I said, admiring her body.

"Okay, come on. I'm driving."

We headed out of her front door and jumped in her black BMW. It was a nice two-door. Sexy, like her. She decided to go to Applebee's on 63rd Street. It didn't matter to me.

At about eight-forty-five we arrived there. I knew Ace would be meeting Duece at nine. I had to be somewhere that had cameras. Lisa probably thought it was just a nice night out. It was far from it.

A chubby-cheeked hostess with a warm smile led us to a table, where we ordered our food and had small talk. Lisa joked about me buying Sonya some rims for her car. She said Sonya came in the shop bragging about her man buying her some rims. I had to let Lisa know I wasn't the man Sonya was talking about.

An hour and a half passed, and I found out something new about Lisa tonight. She loved to talk. I didn't even have to keep the conversation alive—as I had planned to do, to stall and waste time—because she did most of the talking. When I looked at my phone, it was after ten.

I helped her out of her chair and we finally left, heading back to Lisa's place.

It felt like we were both walking fast to get into the house. We went right at it as soon as we walked in her door, didn't even make it to her bedroom. Somehow we ended up on her couch, ass naked. She was on top of me, riding me like a true professional, her sweaty breast slapping my face.

"Damn this pussy wet." I looked her in her eyes and saw confusion, pleasure and pain.

"I'm cum … cumin' again … *shiiit!*" she cried.

CHAPTER 18

Sunrays whispered through her bedroom window and woke me up. I looked over and Lisa was still fast asleep, still just as naked as I was. My phone rang loud as hell.

"Yeah?" I answered. Lisa moved in her sleep.

"Hi, Spade," Selena said.

Lisa stirred again, wiping sleep from her eyes.

"What's up? What time is it?" I was still tired. I felt Lisa grab my meat, and then she bent down and kissed the head.

"It's nine-thirty in the morning, Spade. I'm on my first break at work, figured I'd call."

Lisa took me in her mouth and started playing with my balls. I jerked a little.

"What's going on?" I asked Selena, trying to stay focused.

"I'm pregnant," she said. I got Lisa off my shit and sat up. "That night at the club we were caught in the moment. You came in me."

Lisa looked at me sideways as I hurriedly put my boxers and pants on.

"Spade?" said Selena.

"Yeah, I'm here. Where you at?"

"I told you I'm at work." She sounded frustrated. "Are you busy?"

"Nah, nah," I lied. "It's just early. Can I call you in a minute?"

"Yes, Spade."

After I hung up, Lisa asked, "Everything alright?"

"Yeah," I told her. "I gotta bust this move in a minute. I'ma hit the shower."

"Okay, babe." She laid back down.

I didn't know what to think. I knew the pregnancy was a possibility. I did hit her raw. Slipping.

You gon' get enough of playin' all them women, my mother always told me. I wasn't ready for no kids. And the baby probably wasn't mine anyway. I'd find out soon. Either way, I'd put something in her hand and get it taken care of. I knew her fine ass wasn't ready for kids either.

I showered and got myself together. I called Selena when I was pulling away from Lisa's house, told her we'd meet on her lunch break. I didn't know what to think or what to make out of what Selena was claiming. But I was going to find out.

CHAPTER 19

Me and Selena met at Taco Bell on Front Street. She worked at a telecommunication company nearby.

"So you're sayin' you're pregnant?" I asked. We were sitting near a window. There were a few other people in here as well.

"Yes, Spade. And you may not believe me when I tell you this. But you are the only man I've been with." She looked like she was ready to cry.

"The only man?" I didn't believe her.

"The *only* man," she stated again. She grabbed my hand. "To be more specific, you're the second man I've ever been with in my entire life. The first was ten years ago. I've been with women. That morning me, you, and Maria …" She paused and licked her lips. "I, I enjoyed it. When I seen you at the club I wanted more."

I was turned on because she said I was the second nigga to touch that pussy. *Some good pussy*, I might add. I was turned off, for one, because I wasn't ready for kids. For two, this bitch could be lying.

"We barely know each other, baby. I gotta lot goin' on. I know you ain't tryin' to keep this baby," I said.

She looked offended and pulled her hands away. "I don't believe in abortions, Spade." She was serious.

"What does your family think?" I asked, with thoughts of Maria's dad on my brain.

"They want me to keep it. They want to meet you."

I was uncomfortable then. "They wanna meet me?"

"Yes. My parents are nice people. My mother is a Latina, my father is Black and Latino. Race is not an issue, Spade," she said, reading my mind.

"Damn, you gettin' ahead of yo'self, ain't you?"

"Look, I know you didn't ask for this. Neither did I. And neither did this child." She rubbed her stomach like the baby was already developed. "But I know we can handle this situation like adults."

My phone went off. It was Sonya. I ignored it.

"A'ight, I'll let you know when I get back wit' you," I said, standing up. She gave me a look that said we weren't finished talking. But I was.

"You're leavin'?" she whispered, and stared out the window. Her eyes had puddles in them.

"I gotta bust this move. I'll call you later."

It was too much for me to handle.

***

I was back at Casey's house, in the living room watching the news. Ace was on his way over.

On screen, the reporter straightened her paperwork. "A Black male who looked to be about thirty to thirty-five and a white female who looked to be about twenty-five to thirty were found dead this morning. Both were shot in the head. A witness said she saw them slumped inside of a newer model Chevy Suburban while walking her dog—"

Ace walked in and I hit the mute button. He headed to the kitchen. Sonya kept calling my damn phone. I finally answered.

"Spade! Somebody killed Duece!" She was panic-stricken.

"What!" I played the part.

"Yeah. They found him this mornin'."

I could hear her crying. Ace came in and sat on the couch.

"Fuck nah!" I paused. "Don't trip, baby. Where you at?"

"At work. Can you come by the house later?"

"Yeah, baby. Damn, I can't believe this shit. Not Duece. Fuck!"

I might have went a little overboard. I hung up. Ace was smiling.

"What you smiling for, lil' nigga?" I asked with a grin of my own.

"Yo silly ass, nigga."

"She sounded hurt," I said.

"It is what it is."

Ace started explaining the previous nights' events to me. He told me he had Duece meet him at a park in the 40's. He said he changed his voice when Duece had called, told Duece he wanted four bricks. Ace, donning a dreadlock wig and a red KC ballcap over it, was sitting at the park waiting on Duece to pull up.

He said when Duece arrived, he had Jamie in the passenger seat. He knew better. The bitch should have been driving, with Duece in the backseat. He was slipping hard. You should never let a move get in the backseat. And when Ace got in the back, he pulled his heat out, took his wig off and put his metal to Duece's head. He asked Duece why he crossed game but killed him before he could answer. Then he shot Jamie. After executing both of them, he took the bricks and left.

"Well, that eliminates one problem," I said.

"We gotta get Nicole and Sonya," Ace said seriously.

CHAPTER 20

I was on my way to Lisa's house, for one reason only: to see what Sonya said while she was at work. I was pushing down 70 West when I noticed the same gray 'Lac two cars behind me. Two Mexicans in it.

I moved to the far right lane. So did they. I got off on the Van Brunt exit; they did also. Instead of turning left to go to Lisa's, I turned right and headed to my 'hood. They were still behind me. My Desert Eagle was on my lap.

I got on my phone and called my young niggas, told them to drive to 19th and Lister and sit at the top of Lister behind East Elementary. The hitmen were riding me kind of close. I proceeded down Van Brunt, passing up Van Brunt Liquors. When I got to 24th Street I took a left—and the Cadillac followed. I made a quick right on Denver. When I approached 23rd and Denver, I had to stop at a stop sign. Too much traffic going up and down 23rd Street.

I thought they were going to hop out on me. I was ready, my "Desi" in hand, trigger finger itching. But they didn't hop out. Traffic cleared and I proceeded; they did too. I took Denver to 19th and made a left.

They were still behind me.

When I got to Lister, I took a slow right. Had to make sure the lil' homeboys were at the top of the block. They were. I went up the street slow, honked my horn twice to let the homeboys know it was me in the Chrysler 300M. They knew the trouble was behind me. When I got to the top of the block, I turned left. The Mexicans couldn't.

The lil' homies ran up on their car firing. My rearview look like an action film.

***

"She was trippin'," Lisa said.

I had been here at her house for about twenty minutes. "Straight up?" I was listening close.

"She said she made a mistake. She kept sayin' she shouldn't have done it."

"Done what?" I asked.

"I don't know, Spade. She just kept sayin' it to herself."

"Was she cryin' at work?"

"All day," Lisa said. "I let her take the day off for today. Did you know him?"

"Somewhat."

She looked at me sideways. "Well, I hope you didn't have anything to do wit' it."

"I was wit' you, baby. All night," I joked, grabbing her thigh.

She smiled, then playfully hit my shoulder with her fist.

***

I was on the way to Sonya's house. I took 71 Highway. I noticed a detective car behind me. Then I saw the cherries. I pulled over to the right shoulder.

Kremensky stepped out.

I let my window down, license and insurance in hand. He made it to my window.

"Spade, what's goin' on?" he asked with a devilish grin on his face.

I wasn't in the mood for bullshit. "Was I speedin'?"

"Who knows," he said. His sarcasm annoyed me. "Step out of the car." He opened my door.

"This some bullshit," I said, stepping out. I headed towards the back of my car.

"I know you had something to do with Tamika's murder." He was close to my face. His breath smelled like cigarettes and coffee.

"Charge me." I smiled.

"Oh, I will. You Black son of a bitch."

142

I smiled harder. "Yeah?"

"Your friend Duece was found dead this morning."

"I heard."

"Know anything about that?" He backed up and put his hands on his hip, pushing his suit jacket back, exposing his cannon.

"Man, if you ain't arrestin' me, I'm gone." I tried to walk past him.

He bumped me with his shoulder. "See you around," he said.

I got back in my car. Kremensky jumped in his, burned rubber and streaked down the road. I wanted to kill that muthafucka. I cooled down while I drove to Sonya's house. Had to control my emotions. I finally pulled up to Sonya's house. I noticed her car and Nicole's.

I used my key to enter. Sonya and Nicole were sitting in the living room drinking. And smoking. Sonya looked like she lost her mother. She tried to get her emotions in check when she noticed my presence. Nicole looked scared.

"What's up?" I said, as I sat down between them.

"Hey," they said in unison.

"Don't trip yall." I rubbed their backs. "We gon' find out who did this shit."

"I hope so, Spade," Sonya said painfully.

"Me and Ace on top of it, baby," I told her. Casey called my phone but I ignored it.

"Who was that chick he was wit'?" Nicole inquired.

I gave an Oscar performance. "I don't know."

"It's too much goin' on, Spade," Sonya said.

"I'm hip." I got up and went to the kitchen. I opened the freezer and got my Remy. Sonya ran upstairs, and Nicole came in the kitchen.

"Spade, I didn't tell Sonya about our conversation," she said right above a whisper.

"Yeah?"

"I came clean, Spade. Leave me out of this, please."

The bitch was trying to save her own ass. Self-preservation is a muthafucka. Then she bit her bottom lip and smiled.

"Can you meet me at the room tonight?"

I couldn't believe she was thinking about dick. "I'll call you," I said.

"Please call me."

"I will, baby. Let me go upstairs and check on Sonya."

I walked off. These little hoes were terrified. To my understanding, Sonya didn't know I knew her and Duece tried to play me. Nicole was more dangerous to me than Sonya was. Because after she exposed her hand, Duece was killed. So I had decided to keep it on the up-and-up with her and Sonya until I figured something out.

When I got upstairs to the main bedroom, I heard the shower water running. I opened the bathroom door and startled a naked Sonya. She was just about to open the polished-edge shower door.

"Hey," she said, looking sad as ever.

"You okay?" I approached her and hugged her.

"I guess. First someone breaks into my house. Now this."

"I know, baby. I'ma figure it out." I grabbed her ass and kissed her hard. She gave me her tongue, and I sat her on the bathroom sink and fucked her with hateful fire in my veins.

CHAPTER 21

I headed back to Casey's house. On the way there OG Casa called and told me not to worry about Kutz. He had a plan for him. As I turned on Casey's block I saw a police car near her house. I wanted to turn around, but it would look too obvious. So I proceeded down the block.

As I got closer to her house, I noticed the police car was parked two houses down. I pulled in her driveway and the officers were coming out of a home with an old white lady. I was relieved. Stepping inside the house, I went straight to Casey's landline and called her.

"What's up, baby?" she answered.

"Chillin', what's good?"

"Just left the beach."

"Must be nice." I was dealing with chaos and she was fiddling her toes in the sand.

"It is. We should come down here together."

"Sounds like a plan," I replied.

"So what's wrong? I can tell something's botherin' you."
She knew me too well.

"Shit. Bitches tried to set me up for the okey-doke."

"Who? Sonya and her sidekick?"

"Congratulations."

"Hmm, well well." She changed the subject. "You know me and Sparkle are comin' back early."

I had remembered Sparkle vaguely. We were kids then. I think her parents were killed and she had to go into foster care. I wasn't sure.

"That's what's up. When?" I asked.

"Tomorrow night. Can you pick us up from the airport?"

"Yeah. I can do that. What time?"

"We should be landing at about nine."

"Okay, baby."

I called Ace. He told me he was with his girl Ashley. They were in Kansas at her mother's house. I let Ace know that OG Casa said he had the Kutz situation under control. Ace said he'd be in Kansas for a while. He wanted to lay low. I told him to be safe.

I went for the freezer to get my issue. Before I could sit down and get comfortable, Nicole was calling my phone. I didn't answer. And she called back. I still didn't answer, but when my phone rang again, I finally picked up. Had to play it cool.

"Yeah?"

***

"Damn, daddy!" Nicole screamed.

I had been at the Embassy Suites for about twenty minutes. When I got here, Nicole was naked on the bed, playing with her pussy. She had a dildo in her hand, putting it in every hole. I watched for a hot second and enjoyed the show. But I had eventually joined.

"You like that, bitch?" I was fucking her from behind.

"Yes, yes ... daddy ... I ... I'm cumin' again."

Nicole was on the edge of the bed with her ass in the air, while I stood. She started pushing her ass back toward me, fucking me back, moving her hips and ass while I stood still. Every time she came back on my dick I smacked her ass.

My hand print had branded her ass cheeks, and her pussy dripped all over the place. I let her fuck me that way for a hot second, then I started beast-fucking her again. I figured I might as well, since it would probably be the last time. I turned her over on her back and pounded her.

"Grab those handcuffs ... out of my purse," she moaned.

"What?" I asked, sweat dripping down my face.

"Handcuff me to the bed."

I eased out, grabbed the handcuffs and cuffed her to the bed. I had her right back on her knees, ass up, arms spread, each wrist cuffed to the opposite end of the headboard.

I went into her hard—and she screamed, I mean really *screamed*. She looked like she wanted to get free from the cuffs, but she couldn't.

"I'm cumin again!" she cried out.

I started playing with her clit while I fucked her in her ass. She came again. We fucked like for a minute, then I uncuffed her. She got on top and rode me like a thorough-bred. Then she eased off of my dick and put her mouth on it. And swallowed my babies.

She thought shit was sweet.

A while later, as we laid in bed post-sex, Nicole said, "Spade ..." She paused. "I think I love you."

She was delusional, straight up. If she only knew ...

"Yeah?" I said.

"I'm serious, baby. If you want me to ..." She paused again. "I can take care of Sonya for you."

"You'd do that for me?" This shit was entertaining.

"Yes," she said adamantly.

"Nah. You ain't gotta do that lil' mama. I don't want nothin' to happen to you *or* her. I care about both of yall too much," I lied.

"You do?" She smiled.

"Yes. I do."

CHAPTER 22

After I left the hotel, I went straight to Casey's and passed out. I woke up around 2:00 p.m. the next day. I had a couple messages on my phone from Casey and my attorney. Casey was letting me know her flight was still on schedule. My attorney wanted me to give him a call. I did.

He sounded like he was in a good mood when he answered. That put me at ease. He told me he had the tape from Red Roof Inn. It showed I was there from 9:45 p.m. until 11:20 p.m. Tamika's car hit the light pole at 10:24 p.m. I was relieved. He also told me Tamika was never pregnant. *Bitch!*

Despite all that, my attorney said Kremensky was still investigating me. He said they didn't have any evidence to charge me, and if Kremensky continued to harass me, he'd file a lawsuit.

I thanked him and hung up. I went and showered, got myself together and chilled after that. I stayed at Casey's until it was time to go her and Sparkle from the airport.

Deception's PLAYGROUND

***

I'd been waiting for Casey and Sparkle to exit the airport. They finally did. Casey was looking sexy as ever in a cowl neck halter dress, but Sparkle looked even sexier in a metallic bustier and a tight—*real tight*—miniskirt. I had forgotten Sparkle was mixed with something. Her hair was long and her walk was strong. She had a compact body to kill for. I hopped out to help them with their bags.

"Hey, baby," Casey said, giving me a hug.

"What's good?" I said.

Sparkle stood to the side, waiting to be introduced.

"You remember Sparkle, don't you?" Casey looked in Sparkle's direction.

"How can I forget?" I flirted, extending my hand, smiling.

Casey smacked my shoulder. "Boy, quit playin'."

"How are you doin', Spade?" Sparkle said, letting her hand slip away from mine.

"I'm good. So how was it in the M.I.A.?" I asked them both, as I hoisted their bags up and into the trunk.

"It was coo'," Casey said.

"Yeah. We had a ball," Sparkle added.

Soon we were on the move, headed to Casey's. We got there an hour later. They unloaded their bags and I got comfortable in the living room and watched TV. Sparkle was the first downstairs.

151

"So, Mr. Spade, how have you been?" she asked, sitting on the couch.

"I'm maintaining," I said. "How 'bout yourself?"

"I'm doin' well for myself. I've been living in Miami for about seven years. But I'm always in and out of Kansas City."

"When was the last time you was in the town?" I was trying to avoid looking at her sexy frame.

"A few days ago. Before me and Casey went back to Miami."

Casey didn't mention that. I was lost.

"Straight up?" I changed the subject. "If you don't mind me asking, Where did you go when we were kids?"

She didn't mind telling me. She went right in, told me her mother was Russian and her father was Black. I remembered her mother was a different nationality, just didn't know what. And I used to see her pops in the 'hood from time to time. Him and OG Casa were real close. They damn near looked like brothers.

Sparkle said one day she was at school some niggas from another 'hood—niggas her father sold dope to—broke in their house. They robbed her pops, then killed him. And her moms. She said after that she moved to Russia with her mother's side of the family. She said her Russian uncles were who her father got his guns and drugs from. They murdered everybody who was involved in her parent's death.

She also said while she stayed with them, they taught her how to kill in many ways. I didn't believe her, but the look on her face—and her body language—convinced me. Casey walked downstairs.

"What yall talkin' 'bout?" Casey sat next to me. I could smell her bodywash.

"I'm just catchin' up wit' Spade," said Sparkle.

I was intrigued by Sparkle. She seemed strong and confident. Not affected by her parents death. A kind of calmness only revenge would give someone.

"Is that a'ight wit' you?" I joked with Casey.

"Sure. So, how's Tamika?" Casey asked out of left field.

"Damn. I forgot to tell you. The lil' bitch hit a light pole. Died behind the wheel. Brakes went out or some shit."

"Told you that would do it," Sparkle told Casey.

At first I was confused. I looked at Casey, then at Sparkle. They smiled, and I put two-and-two together. Casey must have called Sparkle and told her about Tamika. Sparkle flew into town, cut the bitch's brake line and they both went to Miami.

"Keep that under your hat," Sparkle said with a wicked grin on her face.

"That ain't a thang," I said.

These hoes is something else.

"I hope so," Sparkle said. "I did it for Casey. I mean, you coo'. But I don't trust you. So I hope you will keep this info to yourself. If not, it could get ugly."

153

Is this bitch threatening me? I thought.

"You good, lil' mama," I said. I figured she had to say that. Maybe she meant it, I wasn't sure. But Sparkle was on thin ice.

"So, baby …" Casey eased the tension. "I told her about Sonya and Nicole."

"And?" I looked Casey upside her head.

"They need to be taken care of," Sparkle asserted.

They were ready to kill. And I dug it. They were really willing to assist, and I was willing to allow them. Sparkle went upstairs to get something, and when she came back down she had a white substance—concealed in a glass jar—in her hand.

She held it up. "This is what I'm gonna use."

"What's that?" I asked.

"One of my favorite tools. Put this on the rim of a glass they're drinking out of. They'll be dead within minutes." Sparkle grinned.

Then Casey joined in on the plot. She knew Sonya and Nicole loved to go out so she insisted I find out when and where. Whichever club they were going to, Sparkle would already be there—ready, her favorite tool in hand.

"So it's that simple, cousin," Sparkle said.

Now we're cousins, I thought.

CHAPTER 23

I told Sonya I was going to stop by. When I got there, she and Nicole were in the kitchen eating. I sat at the table with them.

"What's up, ladies?"

"Nothin', baby," Sonya said.

Nicole smiled. "Yeah, nothin'. Just chillin'."

"Where's my plate?" I tried to be sarcastic.

"It's in the microwave," Nicole said. "I'll get it." She got her thick ass up and got my plate.

We had small talk over dinner. The last meal I planned on having with these hoes. Sonya told me Duece's mother called and told her his funeral was the weekend coming up. She said his moms also told her to tell me thanks for the flowers I sent. That had to be Ace's doing. I didn't send flowers. Didn't plan to either.

I told Sonya and Nicole we should all go out tomorrow. I told them Duece wouldn't want us to be down. He'd want us to celebrate. Sonya agreed, no problem. Nicole looked a little skeptical, but she eventually came around.

I popped a bottle of Remy and encouraged them to have a drink with me. They grabbed their glasses and we just chilled and got tipsy. I felt sort of bad for them. Really, I did. *Poor bitches, they had their whole lives ahead of them.*

We were shooting-the-shit in the living room. Nicole had put on some music, and then they were having a ball. My phone rang. It was Selena. I stepped outside for some privacy, then I answered.

"Yeah?"

"Hello, Spade." Her voice was sweet as ever.

"How are you doin', baby?"

"I guess I'm fine. Look, Spade, I know you don't want this child but I'm going to have him, or her," she stumbled. "If you want to help me and be there, that's fine. If not, that's too bad for you. I don't want your money, and I don't want to cause any friction in your life. I—"

"Slow down, baby. Look … I just gotta lot goin' on right now …" I tried to sound sincere. "When I handle this business, we can sit down and figure this shit out."

Then Sonya's door swung open. Her and Nicole were naked in the doorway.

"You comin' in?" they both asked.

Dumb-ass hoes. I shoved them back in the house, shut the door with me on the opposite side.

"Okay, Spade. I'll be waiting," Selena said.

"Another thing. No offense, but we need to get a blood test."

"That's fine. I know you have your doubts."

With that phone call wrapped up, I headed toward my car. I left Sonya and Nicole to deal with their sexual desires by themselves. I was on my way to Casey's.

***

Casey and Sparkle were in their pajamas, full top and pants sets. We were all in the living room talking.

"So what club are they going to?" Sparkle asked.

"American Pub on the Westport," I said.

"And they'll be there when?"

"They'll probably be there around ten. Trying to make an entrance."

Casey smiled. "Well, they'll definitely be makin' an exit."

CHAPTER 24

The next day, me and OG Casa met at The Cheese Cake Factory.

"So, Spade, Kutz should be taken care of in a couple of days."

"Sounds like a party. Am I invited?" I asked.

"Do you want to be?" he asked.

"Hell yeah. That muhfucka had people at my house."

"Say no more, son." He paused. "So how's Casey doin'?"

"She coo'," I stated, wondering where the fuck that came from.

"So are you two back together?"

I broke off a piece of one of my hand-battered onions and dipped it in the ranch, then ate it. "Why you ask, OG? How'd you know we were back talkin'?"

"I asked because I care about you two. I watched you both grow up." He smiled. "And I know everything that's goin' on."

OG Casa was a muhfucka. This slick-ass old nigga didn't miss a beat. But I never cared if he was in my business. I knew he had my best interest at heart.

"Yeah, I guess we coo'," I said. "We ain't together or nothin'. I got too much goin' on right now."

"That comes wit' the game," he said. "But you gotta know how to keep your affairs away from home and in their proper perspective."

We chatted for another twenty minutes, told him about Selena and he looked a little disappointed. He told me to handle it like a man, and that was that.

***

"Where you at?" I asked Sonya. I was driving on 70 East, leaving Kansas. I had to stop and talk to Ace.

"We're about to be on the Westport," Sonya said.

"Where *you* at?" Nicole said from the background. "While you askin' all these questions."

"Forty minutes away." I was happy that this night would be the last night these bitches breathed.

"Well, we'll be in the club waitin' on you, baby," said Sonya.

"A'ight, I'll see yall in a minute."

I called Sparkle. She answered on the second ring.

"Talk to me," she said. I heard music in the background.

"What's good?"

"At the club. Lookin' for somethin' hot," she joked.

"I'm sure you'll find somethin'."

"I hope so."

"I'll see you soon," I said.

"No, you won't." She hung up.

I pulled up to the Westport area. About thirty minutes later it was jammed packed. There were cops—or *pigs*, as I liked to call them—everywhere, as usual. I parked on Pennsylvania Avenue and walked to Kelly's, a live music venue. I ordered a few shots of Remy and flirted with a few women.

Damn near an hour had passed and I didn't hear an ambulance. I didn't hear any rumors about two females dropping dead in American Pub. Then my phone rang. It was Sparkle.

"Meet me at Conoco now!" she exclaimed and hung up.

I hurried out of Kelly's and got in my rental. I was at Conoco in no time, spotted Sparkle in her rental—a black Impala. I pulled up next to her.

"Them bitches didn't show up," she said, as she got in my whip. Frustration covered her sex appeal.

"What? Man, let me see what's up." I dialed Sonya's number. No answer. I called Nicole.

She answered on the fifth ring. "What's up, baby?"

"Where the fuck yall at?" I asked.

"Karma."

"Yall got me all in American Pub lookin' for yall hot asses."

"Sorry, sorry. Sonya tried to call and tell you."

"So when yall leavin'?"

Sparkle smacked her lips, irritated.

"In a minute," Nicole said. "Sonya drunk as fuck. I'ma have to drive her car."

So they in Sonya's whip, I thought.

"A'ight, just call me later." I hung up and told Sparkle, "They're at Karma."

"Damn!" She paused. "You lucky I brought a plan B." She held up her Ruger, a 9mm. She held it like it was her lover. I told her what kind of car they were in and she was out of my car with the quickness.

It was going on two in the morning when I checked my phone. I was driving slow down Pennsylvania, music low, trying to spot Sonya's car. I heard gunshots.

Boom! Boom! Boom! Boom!

The sound came from where BP's gas station was. I headed that way, cars heading in the opposite direction. It was so much traffic. Too much! Police cars were closing in.

I took a right on 39th, and when I got to Broadway I took another right. I drove slow and BP came into view, so did Sonya's Monte Carlo. The front windshield had four bullet holes in it. Two bodies were slumped in the front of the car.

Police cars surrounded the vehicle and an ambulance was on the way.

I went to the spot.

Sparkle went back to Miami.

CHAPTER 25

Me and Casey were laying in her bed talking the next morning. Sparkle was probably forty thousand feet in the air on her flight back. Sonya and Nicole were in a morgue.

"Spade, we should go to Miami for a while," Casey said.

"That's cool," I replied, rubbing her back. "But I got some shit I gotta handle first."

"Like what?" she asked, and I sensed irritation.

I didn't feel like talking about it. "Some shit," I said flatly.

"Whatever." She got out of bed. "What, you gotta check wit' yo bitches first?"

"That's funny. What I look like checkin' wit a bitch?"

"Spade, you ain't gon' miss shit." She put her hands on her hips, looking good just waking up. "It's a lot of opportunities in Miami."

"I'ma let you know, I just—"

Lisa called my phone, but I ignored it.

"You can answer it," Casey said.

"I know I can. I'll call her back," I countered.

She left the bedroom. I guess she had an attitude. She always was emotional when it came to me. I jumped in the shower to freshen up. Then I heard the bathroom door open and close. Casey slid the shower door open and joined me.

***

"How much do you need on the investment?" I asked.

"Well, the property is about sixty-thousand," Lisa said. "Renovations will probably run about fifteen thousand. So about thirty-seven-five initially."

"So we're goin' down the middle?"

"Yes. And even though I'm going to be more hands-on than you, I'm willing to split the profits down the middle."

"Even though I'm not going to be *that* hands-on, I still will play a part in tracking business income, expenses, and tax issues. I have to know the inner workings of the business."

"Fine wit' me." She smiled. "I suggest you get an account solely for business income. And look for an accountant to get on your team."

"I'm on top of it. Anything else?" I asked.

"Yes. I'll have my attorney draw up the written agreements."

"Coo'. But I have to hire an attorney for my business affairs. I'll have one by the end of the week."

"Okay, Mr. Spade." She paused. "Trust me, this is a positive move. Get you off the block and eventually in the boardroom." She smiled again.

"I can dig it."

Lisa gave me referrals for reputable tax advisors, accountants, insurance agents, and attorneys. I had $280,000 to my name. All dirty money. But that would change soon. I would invest $37,000 in the beauty salon with Lisa, and I felt good about it. OG Casa had been telling me to invest in real estate. But I still had one problem I had to take care of. After that, I'd be ready for that legitimate paper.

***

I was pushing down Cleaver Blvd, headed to grab something to eat. Casey had called me and told me she went and got my truck from her uncle's shop. I told her I'd be at her house shortly.

My music was up and I was feeling kind of good. My last problem would soon be taken care of. Then I could focus on my money. I felt my phone vibrating, indicating I had some missed calls. I didn't hear it because of my music. Checking it, I saw I had two missed calls from OG Casa. I turned my music down and called him back.

"Nephew," he said. "I been callin'. You busy or somethin'?"

I frowned. Something was up. "Nah, I'm good."

"Meet me off 40 Highway. The lil' village," he said, referring to the trailer park homes.

"I'm on my way."

***

I drove through the trailer park homes until I spotted OG Casa's car. Parked next his car was a black SUV. Both vehicles were empty. I drove in and parked behind OG Casa and my phone rang.

"Come on in," OG Casa said and hung up.

When I walked through the doorway of the trailer home, I saw Kutz tied to a chair, bloody as fuck.

"Spade … my man," Kutz said weakly.

I smiled, as I approached him. "What's good, Kutz?"

"You … betray me," he said.

His Armani suit didn't look too good. Neither did his face. I barely recognized him. Two Russians came from the back room, sleeves rolled up, blood on their hands.

"They're wit' me," OG Casa said. He nodded to the Russians and they left. I pulled up a chair and sat down in front of Kutz.

"You tried to kill me?" I asked.

He spit blood in my face.

I smacked him twice with the back of my hand. Then I grabbed my life insurance policy and smacked him with that.

He smiled—smiled like I just told him a joke. Inside I knew he knew the joke was on him. I smacked him again with my pistol.

OG Casa grabbed my shoulder. "We don't have much time," he said. "Get this over with. My people will burn this trailer down when we're done."

I turned back to Kutz. "Why did you try to kill me, muthafucka?"

"You ... broke ... my heart," he said.

OG Casa gave me a 9 millimeter with a silencer on it. I put it to Kutz's forehead. He smiled again. And I shot him twice in the head, his dead weight slumping forward. He would have fallen out the chair if he wasn't tied to it.

"Let's go, son," said OG Casa.

"Yeah, let's shake."

We walked out of the trailer and the Russians got out of the black SUV. OG Casa nodded again. They got some gasoline out of their backseat and decorated the trailer.

"I'll meet you at yo spot in twenty minutes," OG Casa said.

I jumped in my Chrysler and I was gone.

CHAPTER 26

"Spade, it might be a good idea to head outta town for a while," OG Casa said, as he shared the evening with me at my house.

"Yeah, I might."

He gave me a frustrated look. "It wouldn't hurt, go take a lil' vacation."

"After I secure this investment, I'll shake for a while."

"Investment?" he questioned.

"Yeah. My lady friend, Lisa, wants to open another beauty salon. Need a partner."

"Yo lady friend, huh?" He smiled.

"She's coo'. She owns the beauty salon on 39th Street," I said.

"You talkin' 'bout fine-ass Lisa? Nice body, short hair cut?"

Ain't that a bitch, OG done hit her? I wondered.

"You know her?" I asked.

"I been trying to get to know her." He paused. "You hittin' that?"

I smiled. "Somethin' like that."

"Hmm. I been tryna sink my teeth in her forever. As long as you got her, I'm good"

"We just coo'," I told him. I took a swig of my Remy that was sitting on my living room table.

"So when's the last time you spoke to Casey?" he asked.

"Earlier today. She wanna go to Miami."

"You might as well. Go on down there and enjoy yo'self. And you know Casey's got yo back."

"You think so?"

"I know so," he stated.

"And how you know, OG?" I wanted to know.

He smiled. "I know everything."

He left shortly after that. I called Lisa and asked her when she needed the money. She said her attorney was drawing up the contract. My criminal attorney, Antonio Puzzo, recommended a business attorney for me. So I was good.

I told Lisa to have her attorney e-mail a copy of the paperwork to my attorney. And we would go from there. She invited me over for dinner. I was reluctant to go, but she kept insisting so I finally got my ass off my couch.

***

I had been at Lisa's for about forty minutes or so. We laid in her bed talking.

"So when can I come to your place?" she asked.

"I don't know. Soon, I guess."

"You guess?"

"I got trust issues," I said, smiling.

"Whatever, Sam."

I looked her upside her head. "Sam?"

"Told you I'd find out." Her tone was seductive. She rubbed my dick.

"Since we're goin' to be business partners, we shouldn't be doin' this. Could be bad for business," I said, but didn't mean it.

She unbuckled my belt and unzipped my pants. Had my dick in her hand, and it was standing at attention.

"Really?" she said. And slowly she started sucking me. She did this until I came. I didn't have the energy to fuck her tonight.

Plus, my mind was on my next move. Would I go out of town for a hot second? Would I stay in the town? I really didn't want to go to another state. It made me feel like I was running from something.

CHAPTER 27

About a week had passed and I was still in the town. OG Casa plugged me with a new connect. I decided to let Ace handle that. I told Ace he could keep the four bricks he got back from Duece also. I had my mind on things that were more legitimate. But I still planned on keeping an eye on Ace. I called him.

"I'm leavin' Kansas, bro," he said. "I been thinking about shootin' to Columbia for a second."

"You and yo lil' female?" I asked.

"She's a stomp-down bitch, bro. You know I gotta take bonnie." He was charismatic as always.

"You holla at OG Casa?"

"I did, bro. I'll be ready right after I get this lil' spot out the way."

My line clicked. It was Casey.

"A'ight, cuzz. C-safe," I told him. "I gotta take this call."

"Yep."

I clicked over and greeted Casey. She went into that Miami shit again. I told her I had a few more things to handle. But I really was stalling. I felt like I would be leaving my life.

"You really don't wanna go, do you?" She sounded bothered.

"Did I say that?"

"Okay, look. I see you have an attitude so just call me later." She hung up.

I thought about calling her right back, but I didn't. I called OG Casa and told him to let me in on his real estate moves. He insisted that I take some real estate classes first. He said one should never just jump into an investment without doing the proper research. I agreed.

I continued to chill at my house, brainstorming. I had already made the beauty salon investment. After our attorneys made sure both of our interests were protected, we had signed the agreement. The salon would be up and running in two months.

I was going to let Ace get my brick serves. But in return he would have to give me two thousand dollars of each brick he sold to them. They were good for at least seven bricks a month. So that would be fourteen thousand a month in dirty money.

I did my research on properly setting up my entertainment company. I just had to get up with an entertainment attorney, which I planned on doing next week. My thoughts were then interrupted by a loud knock at my door.

When I went to the door, no one was there. I stepped out to see if anyone was around. No one was. I saw a detective car bending the corner at the end of my block. *What the fuck*, I thought.

I started to head back inside when I noticed an envelope on my front steps. I picked it up and went in my house, sat down and opened it. Inside were pictures of Tamika, Duece, Sonya and Nicole. None of Jamie. The pictures weren't happy pictures. They were images after their little accidents. There was also a letter inside. It read:

> *Mr. Spade,*
>
> *I know these people were close to you. Your best friend, your woman and her friend, and your sex toy. I know you had something to do with these murders. I won't rest until you're in prison doing life. I'll get you, you black son of a bitch.*
>
> *K,*

It was Detective Kremensky. *Fuckin' pig.* I thought about Miami. Maybe it was a good idea. I called my attorney to inform him about this shit. The secretary put me straight through.

"Sam," he answered.

"This muthafucka just dropped an envelope off at my fuckin' door step. Threatening a nigga," I said hotly.

"Kremensky?"

"Yeah."

"Bring it by the office in the morning," he said.

There was a hard knock at my door.

"What time?" I asked, walking toward the door.

"About nine."

"That's coo'."

"Okay, Sam," he said, and we ended the call.

There was another hard knock before I made it to my entrance hall. I opened the door and Casey stormed inside. After I shut my door, I turned to her. She looked like she had something on her mind. She sat on one of my couches.

"What's up?" I asked, sitting on a different couch.

"You tell me." She moved to the couch I was on. She was upset, clearly. She wore a strapless sundress that stopped above the knees. Sexy, as always, and even more so because she was mad.

"I'm chillin', man. What's the deal?" I smiled.

"Man?" She turned her face up.

I laughed at her frustration. "Man, what's up?"

"I don't see nothin' funny, Spade."

Then she suppressed her anger. She told me our plane tickets were already purchased. I wondered why she insisted we go to Miami. Like she knew something I didn't. She told me our flight was in a couple of days.

"Let's just get away for minute," she said.

Maybe that's what I needed. To get away for a hot second.

I finally agreed. "A'ight, man," I said.

She smiled, not tripping on me calling her a man. Then she straddled me. "Our flight leaves at ten in the mornin', Wednesday." She gave me a peck on the lips. "So be ready." Another peck. I grabbed her soft ass.

She put her tongue in my mouth and I lifted her sundress up, exposing her ass. She didn't have any panties on. I lifted my waist and pulled my sweatpants down, then eased her down on my shaft.

"Mmmm," she moaned. She started riding me slow at first. I smacked her ass. "Ah shit," she hissed. Her pussy started gushing, and she sped up. I grabbed her hips, navigating the rollercoaster. *"Shiiiit,* Spade … I … love you."

Then there was another knock at my door. Casey hurried and jumped up off me. She started straightening her dress and her hair. I pulled my sweatpants up, pissed, dick hard. After Casey got herself together I checked my peephole. It was OG Casa.

I opened the door and he came in.

"Am I interrupting somethin'?" He looked at me, then at Casey.

"Nah, you good."

He went over and gave Casey a hug. "Hey, baby girl," he said.

"Hey," she replied with a nervousness that probably stemmed from my dick just being inside her.

After they embraced, Casey excused herself and went upstairs. To the bathroom, I thought.

OG Casa took a seat. I lit an incent before I joined him.

"I just thought I'd stop by," he said.

"I'm straight. I'ma go ahead and shoot to Miami for a couple weeks."

Casey came back downstairs and sat next to me.

"That's what's up," he replied.

"I really don't want to go," I said.

Casey rolled her eyes. "Tell him it's coo' down there, daddy," she said to OG Casa.

Daddy, I thought. I gave them both a confused look. Casey looked at me like I was crazy. OG Casa did too.

"Daddy?" I questioned aloud.

"Make sure my daughter is safe down there, Spade." He smiled.

I was even more confused. Casey seen it in my face so she decided to help me understand. She told me OG Casa had too many women back in the day. So him and her mother split up. She stayed with her mother, but she saw OG Casa in the 'hood every day, so it was cool.

Then OG Casa said he didn't want to tell me because

he didn't want to come in between me and Casey. Or me and him. He'd rather Casey fuck with me instead of some street punk he didn't know or respect. I was still tripping, though, wondering why I didn't know OG Casa was Casey's father. OG Casa was cool with the kids in the 'hood. When I thought about it, he did give special attention to Casey. I never thought anything of it.

"So you wasn't ever gon' tell me, OG?" I asked.

"I thought you would've knew by now," he countered.

"What about you?" I said to Casey.

She smiled. "Daddy didn't want me to tell you."

This shit was crazy. OG Casa knew about the bitches I fucked and all that. I guess he knew that came with the game. He even laced me when it came to women. Casanova, OG Casa for short.

"Is that right?" I said to both of them. We sat silent for a second. Then we all had a good laugh. "So, OG, let me guess … You and Sparkles' Pops …?"

"Brothers," he said.

"The Russians?" I wanted to know.

"In-laws." He smiled.

Slick-ass OG Casa. My nigga, my mentor. He always had looked out for me. We talked for a little longer, and then he gave me a firm hug and left. Casey ended up spending the night.

CHAPTER 28

I was leaving my attorney's office, had to drop off that precious cargo Kremensky left me. It was going on ten in the morning. I told Ace to meet me at my spot. When I got there, I saw Ace's car. I walked in my house and him and Casey were in the living room talking.

"So you shootin' to Miami, big bro?" Ace asked.

"Yeah, in the morning. Casey, let me holla at Ace."

She rolled her eyes and went upstairs.

I took a seat next to Ace. "I'ma be gone for about two weeks."

"Must be nice." He grinned.

"I'ma go clear my head. Me and Casey big-head ass."

She came stomping down the stairs, purse over her shoulder. "I'm 'bout to go to the house real quick and pack," she said.

"A'ight," I replied. And she walked out the door.

I told Ace that OG Casa was ready when he was ready. I also told him to stop by and check on my house. After that—and a few other instructions I had for him—we embraced and Ace left.

Deception's PLAYGROUND

***

I had just left Lisa's house. It was going on about six in the evening. I thought I saw Selena parked a few houses down from Lisa's. I probably was tripping.

My stomach started fucking with me. I had to put some food on it. I decided to go to the Peachtree Buffet off Eastwood Trafficway. I got there about twenty minutes later. I hopped out my car and went in.

Once I got a table, I ordered my food. Then I looked up and Maria walked in. She looked good as fuck too, wearing a sorrel one-shoulder mini dress and a pair of round-toe pumps. I assumed she would go to another table since her father didn't want her around me. To my surprise, she came to my table and had a seat.

"Hi, Spade." She smiled. Smelling good.

I hit her with it. "What's good?"

"Lookin' for you." She grabbed my hand. "I miss you."

"Yeah?"

I knew she would come back, I thought.

"Mmm hmm." She leaned over the table and kissed me hard.

"How did you know I was here?" I asked after our lips unlocked.

"I been followin' you, baby," she said.

"Quit playin' wit' me, man."

Her expression was still the same. "My father was Carlos. Also known as Kutz."

I looked at her, baffled.

"You killed him!"

Maria pulled a gun out of her purse—and pulled the trigger. *BANG! BANG! BANG!* I heard screaming, felt sharp pains in my chest and stomach. I was blacking out.

Then she stood over me. "The mother of your seed. Selena. She's next. See you in hell," she said.

I lost consciousness.

EPILOGUE
One Year Later

I was in Miami chilling. I recovered from the almost fatal shots I got a year prior. An ambulance had showed up just in time to assist me. I heard the police apprehended Maria one week after the shooting and that she got charged with attempted murder.

I came to the conclusion that Kutz wanted to kill me because I was fucking his daughter. I had no idea that bitch was his daughter. She was the reason I had one good lung and fucked up nerves in my left hand.

The salon me and Lisa invested in was doing well. We still communicated on the regular. I had been in Miami for six months. Me and Casey were staying at Sparkle's beach house.

I was on the patio of the beach house leaning against the bannister when Casey walked out with her phone in hand.

"Telephone, baby," she said, giving me the phone. "It's Ace."

"What's good, bro?"

"Chillin', my nigga. I got some news for you."

"Yeah?"

"Maria got out. I'm tryin' to get a location on the bitch," he said.

"Is that right? I'm bookin' a flight in the morning."

"Okay, cuzz. I'll pick you up when you land."

I went in the house. Casey and Sparkle were in the guest room, drinking some tropical shit.

"Maria got out," I told them. "I'm headin' back to the town."

"We're comin' too," Casey said.

Sparkle chimed in. "Yeah, we'll catch a flight first thing."

"A'ight," I said, and walked to the bedroom me and Casey shared. I heard her walking behind me.

"Spade," she said.

"What's up?"

I noticed she had *my* phone in her hand.

"Somebody just sent you this picture," she said. "Whose baby is this?"

I grabbed the phone and looked at the image. It was from Selena. I was happy she was alive. It was a picture of her child, a little girl. She had my eyebrows and nose. She looked like I did as a child.

Then a text came.

Deception's PLAYGROUND

This is your daughter. Samantha Dasia Wright. She was born on February 10th. Nine pounds, seven ounces. Call me when you're ready to meet her. Love, Selena.

I guess I had more than one reason to go back to Kansas City, Missouri. To kill a beautiful woman, and meet my beautiful baby girl.

Deception's
PLAYGROUND
2

An individual must never wait for outside evaluation to correct something in themselves. Never look for external affirmation when you possess all the elements to peace, happiness, and success internally.

—Kush Lamma

CHAPTER 1

"Nigga, you wanna make music or fuck off on the black-top?" I asked.

Coach Kid twisted his face up at me. "I'm tryna get this money."

This lil' nigga is too tough, I thought.

I stood up and paced my office. "Do I not keep money in yo pocket, nigga? Yo mixtape is almost done. I got shows lined up for you, *and* Young Dice." I leaned on my desk and gave him the once-over. "Shit's movin' along. You gotta stay levelheaded."

"A'ight, Spade."

"A'ight, bro, holla at you later."

He got up and left my office.

I had been back in Kansas City for about a year and a half. Still no sign of Maria yet, but we'd been keeping our eyes open.

Since I'd been back I had started my entertainment company. Me and Lisa's beauty salon was booming so much we were thinking about investing in another location. And I was still getting my underworld cut from Ace. So money was good. My personal life had been okay. Still wasn't committed to anybody. Just jamming with Casey, Lisa, and baby moms. I was kind of cool on fucking with a gang of chicks. I had one good lung behind a bitch—the same bitch I couldn't wait to bump into.

***

"I'm outside."

"Okay," she said, a little snappy. "You're not coming in?"

"I gotta run, baby," I countered.

"Whatever, Spade."

"A'ight, man." I hung up and headed for her front door. She owned a house by the Plaza. I used my key to enter.

"In here!" In the kitchen, I assumed. I made my way to her. "Hey," she greeted me.

I gave her a kiss. "Where my baby?"

"She's in her crib, sleep," said Selena. She stood at the sleek island shredding cheese. I saw a few tortilla bowls off to the side, along with lettuce, grilled chicken, onions, the works.

It smelled good in here.

"I'm 'bout to go wake her up." I pretended I was walking toward little Samantha's room.

"Spade, no!" Selena grabbed my arm. "She just went to sleep."

189

"I'm just playin'." I gave her another kiss, then sat an envelope on the counter. "Two grand."

She smiled. "Where's mine?"

"You don't need shit," I said, tapping her nose twice with my forefinger. "Make sure you get her them J's too."

"Whatever, Spade."

"I'll be back later." I headed for the door.

"Yeah right," I heard her say.

***

I was on my way to Ace's house. Him and Ashley found a cool three-bedroom home a few blocks from my spot in Lee's Summit. I couldn't believe my lil' nigga was engaged. I guess he learned from the troubles I went through with the women in my life.

I had him on the phone when I pulled up to his house. "Open the door."

"A'ight, bro."

As soon as I walked in, the tropical smell hit me. The aroma was coming from half of a Backwood burning in the ashtray. I embraced Ace and took a seat. He had the movie *Heat* playing on his sixty-two-inch flatscreen.

"Where Ashley?"

"At her momma's house."

"Everything on the up and up?"

"Smooth sailing, baby." He smiled. "'Bout to start clean-ing the money through OG Casa's dealership."

"Smart move. So when's the wedding?" I grinned.

"Six months, best man," he said, returning the grin.

I still couldn't believe this shit. Here I was, thirty-two, and didn't have a marriage idea. Ace was brave enough to go through with it.

"You ready?" I knew he was. I just wanted to hear it.

"Come on, bro." He smiled again. "These hoes out here can't do shit for the kid. Ash is the one. She keep *papi* happy."

"Sound good, lil' nigga. You better be sure before it's too late. She might flip the script on yo ass."

"Not in a million, big bro."

***

I walked in my house about an hour later. My phone rang as soon as I walked through the door.

"Yeah?" I answered.

"Hey, babe," said Lisa.

"What's good?" I threw my keys on the couch.

"Oh nothing. Just seeing what you was up to. Dinner?"

"What's on the menu?"

She laughed at my inquiry. "Pussy," she said right above a whisper.

"Is that right?" I was amused.

191

"That's right, baby."

"Sounds like a plan. Let me get back wit' you."

"I'll be waiting."

I hung up, tossed my phone on my couch and headed to my kitchen. Opening the freezer, I snatched my green bottle. My day had been so busy, I needed a drink. I hit it a few times and put the poison back in the freezer and headed upstairs to my bedroom.

I had to jump in the shower. Lisa's freaky ass was waiting on a nigga, and I planned on seeing what the she was hollering about. I opened my bedroom door and—to my surprise—I found a fine specimen laying in my king-size bed.

"What's up, baby?" Casey was naked in my bed. Her meaty pussy taunted me.

I stood there for a minute. Just admiring. "What's good, baby?"

"You." She spread her legs and stuck two fingers in and out of her pussy, slow. Then she sucked her pussy juices off her fingers. "Come here."

I took my shirt off and approached her.

CHAPTER 2

The next morning I was sitting on my back patio, checking my messages. I had a few of them. Lisa and Selena both gave me a piece of their minds. The only call I returned was OG Casa's.

"Nephew," he answered.

"What's good, OG?"

"Meet me on the Plaza."

"What time?" I sat up in my chair. He must've had some news for me.

"I'll be there in forty-five minutes."

"A'ight, I'll meet you there."

I hoped he had some info on Maria. I couldn't wait to get my hands on that bitch. Straight up. I should've ran a thorough background check on that ho. She caught me slipping, and it damn near cost me my life. The game is a bitch, I swear. A nigga always in some shit behind one of these bighead hoes.

Pussy is dangerous, serious "bidness."

"Spade, you want some breakfast?!" Casey yelled from the kitchen.

I got up and walked through the sliding doors. "Nah, I'm good. I gotta bust a move," I said, heading to my room.

"Yeah, whatever," she said to herself.

I hurried and got dressed, jumped in my Benz and shot to the Cheesecake Factory. I was there in a hot one. I located OG Casa and sat down at his table, observing the people around us.

"What's good, OG?"

"Got some info on Maria."

I shifted in my seat. I needed to find that whore. "What's new?"

"I got word that she's been in and out of town." He sipped his water. "She just got back from Texas a couple weeks ago. I think she's stayin' with a family member."

"Where at?"

"On the westside. Haven't got the exact address yet, but I'm on it."

A couple of young, shapely ladies passing our table spoke. "Hi, Spade," they said in unison.

"How yall doin'," I said to them, then turned my attention back to OG Casa. "Let me know when you here somethin'."

"It'll be soon, I hope," he said.

***

All the ladies in the beauty salon that knew me—which was just about all of them—spoke when I walked in. I offered back a "What's good" and headed for Lisa's office.

This salon me and Lisa opened was located on Noland Road. Perfect location, and the stylists were top of the line. I couldn't have thanked Lisa enough for letting me invest in the business. *This muthafucka was checkin' like clockwork.* This and my entertainment business kept me away from the dope game.

"I enjoyed your company last night," Lisa said, still looking at her computer screen. She was purposely not making eye contact with a nigga.

"I got tied up." I sat behind my desk. "I'll make it up to you, baby."

She looked me in my eyes. I guess she was looking for the truth. *Women*, I thought.

"After I take this paperwork to the tax advisor, I'll be at home."

"That's coo', I'll be by later," I said. "So how's the day been?"

"Same ol' gossip and sex talk."

I shook my head and smiled. "Bitches."

"Can't live with them, can't live without 'em."

I detected more sarcasm in her tone.

195

So I gave a smile. "Whatever, man. I just came to see what was good." I stood up and went over to kiss her.

"This is what's good." She grabbed my dick. "You better be over tonight."

"I will." I gave her one more peck on the lips and I left the office.

As I was walking toward the door, Shantel looked me up and down, biting her bottom lip. Like I was her prey.

"Be careful, Spade," she said.

Shantel was just eighteen. She had trouble staying in a kids place. I knew she wanted to fuck but I was good on that young bitch.

"I'll try," I replied.

"Girl, don't let Lisa find out you flirtin' and shit," I heard somebody say as I walked out the door.

I made it to my Benz and my hip vibrated. It was Sparkle.

"Yeah?" I answered.

"Any word on chica?"

Chica was what she called Maria.

"Not yet." I opened my car door and got in.

"Let me know, cuz." She hung up.

I didn't know where Sparkle was. She could've been anywhere in the country. She could've been laying on a target for all I knew. That's what she did for a living. A damn good living I might add. I'm glad that ho was on my team.

CHAPTER 3

I had another nightmare about Maria. She was telling me how much she missed her father, Carlos, otherwise known as Kutz, the man I murdered. When she pulled a pistol out her purse and pulled the trigger, I jumped out of my sleep.

I was sitting up in my bed now, the last vestiges of the dream slowly fading. Looking at the clock, I saw it was three in the morning. Lisa was stretched out beside me, ass naked, still sound asleep. I got out of bed and headed to the kitchen. I had been having that fucking dream since it happened.

I needed my poison.

After I retrieved the green bottle from the freezer, I sat at the kitchen table in the dark, thinking about Maria. My right thumb started moving on its own due to damaged nerves from the shots I received from her. I couldn't wait to get that big head whore.

Kush Lamma

***

Later that day I was at the studio. Young Dice was in the booth doing his thing. I sat next to the engineer. I had a keen ear for music so I knew talent when I heard it. My nigga Young Dice had skills. He was only nineteen but he was mature for his age. He wasn't in a bunch of bullshit, and he was a team player.

He only had a couple more tracks to finish up for his album. He already had a gang of mixtapes out. It was time to hit the people with some of that oil. Crack raps. And we had it for them.

"Spade, what's up, cuzz?" Young Dice said after coming out the booth.

"Just stoppin' by, seein' what's good."

"In here knockin' this shit out." He sat down on a sofa across from the mixing board. "Baby mom's blowin' a nigga up." He smiled.

"Yeah?"

Him mentioning his baby momma made me think of Selena—and lil' Samantha.

"How much longer you gon' be here?" I asked him.

"Gotta put a hook on one track and I'm gone," he said, extracting a baggie filled with some tropical shit. He grabbed a chocolate Philly off the table, dumped the tobacco from the cigar and rolled him a stogey.

"Coach Kid been by?"

"He came through yesterday," Justin said. He did all the mixing and mastering for my label. "He knocked out a few tracks and shook it."

Young Dice stood up. "He 'sposed to come put a couple sixteens on some of my shit," he said, then he stepped outside to smoke his blunt.

Smoking was allowed in the lab, just not around me. Had to keep my one good lung good.

***

"You think the ho will show up?" Ace asked.

We were at the bar out south. We had been here for about thirty minutes, and there was a small, Thursday night crowd.

"OG Casa should have the full scoop soon." I hit my Remy and leaned back into the booth seat by the window.

"I sho' hope so, bro. That bitch—"

"Bitch, why you lookin' at my man?!" a young lady shouted at another.

"James, you better get yo ho!" the second female said to the nigga at the bar. They were about teen feet away from where me and Ace were sitting.

"Homie got his hands full," I said.

Ace nodded. "I'm hip. But yeah, bro, Maria gotta go." He looked at his phone, checking the time.

"Close to curfew?" I joked.

"That's funny, nigga. Imagine a fly guy like myself witta curfew." He rubbed his chin, smiling.

"Okay, fly guy. Yo woman is gonna—"

"Bitch!" the accused screamed, smacking the accuser with a bottle.

There were a few "damns" and "oh shits" coming from the crowd. The big guy behind the bar jumped the counter to break up the fight. A few more big guys headed that way too.

Me and Ace made our exit. Wasn't our problem, and we didn't give a fuck about a show. We headed to my car.

"Man, them hoes outta control," Ace said.

"Did you see lil' mama in the orange dress?"

We both laughed. As we made it to my Benz, a figure emerged from the darkness.

"Spade," Kremensky said. He leaned on the hood of my car. Me and Ace stopped in front of him. Ace had his blammy on his waist but he kept his cool. My wetter was in the stash spot in my car.

"What the fuck do you want?" I asked.

"Well ..." He pulled out a cigarette from a silver case. "... the question is, What do you want?" He exposed his rotten teeth when he smiled.

"Dis muhfucka," Ace said to himself.

"You got somethin' on me, charge me. Come on, cuzz." I motioned Ace to get in the car and I opened my door to get in. Kremensky was still sitting on my hood. I got in and started my engine.

"See you around," I heard the detective say. Before he got up he put his cigarette out on the hood of my car.

"Muthafucka." I reached for my door handle to get out but Ace grabbed my arm.

"Come on, bro. Let's shake."

I pulled out the parking lot pissed. It was about to be death on a cop tonight. Straight up. I headed towards Ace's house to drop him off.

"That nigga on some other shit, cuzz," Ace said.

"I gotta do somethin' about that nigga."

I was getting my emotions in check. *Wu-sa*, I thought to myself.

Ace's phone started ringing and he picked up. "What's goin' on, baby?"

I smiled. I couldn't believe my lil' dude was getting married.

"I'm on my way. It ain't shit but eleven-thirty." I saw him shaking his head out of my peripheral.

"Ashley, sit yo big head ass down somewhere!" I yelled.

"A'ight." Ace smiled and handed me the phone. "She wanna holla at you."

"Yeah?" I said into the phone.

"Are you aware that Ace is engaged?" she asked.

"Nah, when this happen?" I joked.

"Boy, you better stop playing. Bring my baby home."

"Yes, ma'am. Be there in a jiffy." I hung up on her and tossed the phone to Ace. We both laughed as I turned up my *Kush Lamma* CD.

***

"How was your day, baby?" Selena asked. She was giving me a massage while I sat on the edge of our bed.

"Long," I simply stated.

"Any luck on her whereabouts?" She was referring to Maria.

"Not yet. Something will come through, though."

She stopped rubbing my shoulders and walked to the dresser. "I can see if my father knows something." She stripped down to just her thong. Body flawless, skin smooth, legs firm, and that ass was just right. Her 5'3" frame was my playground.

"You ain't gotta put yo pops in this."

"He won't mind." She grabbed her night attire out of the top dresser drawer. She was getting ready to get in the shower. I appreciated her wanting to ask her pops. But I just wasn't sure if I wanted to get him involved.

Her pops owned real estate all over the country. The nigga was caked-up. Him and her mother owned some land in California, Missouri. That was their primary residence. Selena didn't have to work if she didn't want to. I guess she wanted to prove her independence or some shit.

"I'm sure he wouldn't mind," I said, "but I think I got it under control." I got up off the bed and went to her. I kissed the back of her neck and walked out the room.

I headed to my daughter's room down the hall. She was asleep in her little bed. *Daddy's little girl*, I thought. I kneeled down beside her and kissed her on her fat cheeks. I said a prayer for her and I headed out her room. Snoop Dogg was right—having a daughter will bring all the baby powder out a nigga.

I went back to me and Selena's room and undressed. The shower water was running so I knew she was already in there. I went in to join her.

"I knew you'd come in," she said as I slid the shower door open.

"I'm just trying to take a shower."

The hot water felt good.

"Yeah right," she said, rubbing her pussy with a soapy luffa ball.

"I'm good tonight. But I'll wash you up." I grabbed the luffa ball from her hand and started going over her body with it. When I got to her pussy she opened her legs a little. I rubbed her mound gently and she let out soft moans.

"Let me do you." She took the ball back and started tracing my frame with it. "Turn around."

When I did, she started washing my back and then made her way down to my calves. I turned around to face her. My dick was in her face. She kissed the head.

"I told you I'm coo', baby." I brought her to her feet.

She let out a sigh. She was tired of me playing with her. We rinsed off and got out the shower. I grabbed my dry towel and walked in the bedroom to dry off. She stayed in the bathroom to rub down.

"Let me put some lotion on your back, baby." She came out of the bathroom naked. She got the lotion off the nightstand and came to me. She applied it methodically. Kissing my neck and shoulders as well. My dick got hard instantly. I tossed my towel to the side and I laid back on the bed. She took me in her mouth.

"Damn, baby."

Her mouth was warm. I reached over to bring her pussy to my face. Her mouth was still on my package as she positioned herself over me. We were in the sixty-nine position. I started tasting her meaty and bald pussy. She was wet as hell, as usual.

"*Ayi, papi,*" she moaned after she came up off my shaft.

We sixty-nined for another ten minutes or so and I got behind her. She was in the doggy-style position on the bed, gyrating her hips, silently begging me to enter.

I slammed in her like a mad man.

"Aah!" she let out. She started fucking me back. "*Ayi, papi. Ayi, papi.*"

I loved it when she talked that Spanish shit. I grabbed her hips and sped up my penetration. She ran to the headboard but didn't get far. I kept slamming in her.

"*¡Duro!*" she yelled. "*¡Duro!*"

I obliged.

CHAPTER 4

My phone ringing woke me up from my sleep. Selena was still out cold. The morning sun was coming through the curtains.

"Yeah?" I answered.

It was Justin, the music pro. "What's up, Spade?"

"Shit, chillin'. What's good?" I got out of the bed and walked to the dresser to get some boxers to put on.

"Just letting you know I've started the mixing and mastering for Young Dice's disc."

"That's what's up." I was excited. I couldn't wait to drop Young Dice's disc. "How long we talkin'?"

"It'll be ready in two weeks."

"A'ight, let me know."

"Okay, bro."

I'd made it down to the kitchen, opened the refrigerator and pulled out a jug of orange juice and hit it straight from the jug. I looked at the clock on the wall and it read ten-thirty in the A.M. I got dressed and headed out. Had to make a couple moves.

***

Later in the evening I was sitting in OG Casa's office at his dealership on Truman Road. I had been there for about fifteen minutes.

"Got an address where chica might be," he said.

"Yeah?" I was all ears.

"It's on the west side," he said, reaching in his desk to grab the info. "Here you go. Have somebody lay on it for a while."

"I'm on top of it."

I was eager. I had to get that whore. Maybe that fucking dream would cease after I knocked that bitch's top off.

"So, how's Lisa?"

OG always asked about her. I knew he wanted to fuck her. He wanted to before I even met her.

I smiled at him. "She's good," I said.

He rubbed his chin. The diamonds on his timepiece winked at me. "*Mmm*," was all he uttered.

"You'a fool, OG."

We both laughed, and after a little more conversation I got up to leave. As I was pulling out the parking lot, I called Army Tank.

"What's up, cuzzo?" he said, his east side swag coming through his tone.

"I need you one time, lil' bro."

"What's really good?"

"Need you to check on this spizzle for chica."

"I'm listening."

I ran down the address and told him to be safe and we hung up.

***

I was on my way to Ace's house. On the way there I called Sparkle.

"What's up, cousin?" she answered.

"Out bendin' corners. What's good?"

"Out here in L.A. shopping."

Shopping my ass, I thought.

"I'ma need you. I got an address," I said.

"Verity it," she said, then hung up.

I looked at my phone and uttered, "Just gon' hang up on a nigga ..."

Ten minutes later I was pulling up at Ace's house. As I was exiting my car, Ace was coming out the door.

"I gotta bust this move, bro," he said. "You rollin'?"

He was walking to his all black BMW. He had a tank top on, exposing all of his tattoos—and his pistol. *This nigga silly.*

"You just gon' stroll out the spot wit' yo' hand out?" I asked, walking to the passenger side of his car and plopping inside.

"Movin' too fuckin' fast," he replied.

He started his engine and backed out of the driveway with Nye' Usi playing on the stereo.

"Where we headed?" I asked, reclining in my seat.

"Gotta pull up on Ashley and give her this change to take to OG Casa."

"Where she at?"

"At her momma's house."

Her mother still stayed in Kansas.

***

"What time do I need to be there?" Ashley asked. She was leaning in the window on Ace's side.

"At nine," he said.

"And what time are you going to be home." She grabbed the hang time from his braids and started twirling it in her fingers.

"Later on."

He was trying to show out in front of me.

Ashley's cousin, Tanya, walked out on the porch and I licked my lips involuntarily. Baby was *thick*, almost unbelievably so. She'd been trying to get me to fuck but I was cool on little mama. I had restraint, believe it or not.

"Hi, Ace! Hi, Spade!" she yelled.

"What's good?" Ace said back.

I just hit her with the black power fist, acknowledging her.

"Boy, you better speak to my cousin." Ashley turned her face up.

"Damn, when you and Ace have some kids?" I asked.

"Funny," she said, knowing what was coming next.

"Funny my ass. Watch ya mouth, lil' mama." I smiled but was serious as hell.

"Yall silly, man," Ace cut in. "Well, we 'bout to push, baby."

"Hold on, my momma wanna talk to you."

Ace took a deep breath. "About what?"

I laughed.

"Go see." She got up out the window and put her hand on her hip.

"Damn, man," he said to himself, opening the door to get out. Ashley rolled her eyes at me before she turned around to follow him.

I stayed in the car. It was a beautiful evening. The sun was just starting to set. As I was sitting in the beamer waiting on Ace, my phone started vibrating.

"Yeah?" I answered.

"Hey, babe," said Lisa. I loved her voice.

"I'm in K-town. What's good, baby?"

"Just checkin' on you. I'm on my way to the house."

She wanted me to come through. I could tell her by her tone.

"A'ight, call me or text me when you touch, baby," I said, but I knew I wasn't pulling up on her tonight.

"All right. Love you."

"Love you, too."

Just as I hung up, Tanya got in Ace's car with me. The driver's seat, of all places. Smacking on some gum, she said, "Hey there, Spade."

Straight jump-off. I looked back at the house to see if Ace was coming out. I didn't have time to entertain her ass. But I gave her a reply. "Slow motion."

"Hmm." She looked down at my crotch area. She looked in the rearview mirror, stuck her tongue out and started fucking with her tongue ring. I guess she thought that shit would move me or something. "So what yall got up for tonight?"

"Bendin' corners," I said as I fiddled with my phone, showing her no attention.

Tanya was sexy as hell, granted. Chocolate, stayed fresh, hair stayed done. I just wasn't feeling her, though. Her intellect was nowhere.

"So when you gon' call me, Spade?" She rubbed my thigh.

"Got too much goin' on right now, lil' mama." I removed her hand. She rolled her eyes and smacked her lips.

"Well, I'm here when you're ready." She adjusted her bra, trying to get me to focus on her big ass titties. It worked. "I'm not goin' nowhere," she added.

"I can dig it," was all I gave her.

I heard the screen door to Ashley's momma's house shut. Ace was making his way to the car, as Tanya got out.

"Bye, baby," she said to me. Her G-string was exposed. I shook my head.

Ace got back in the car smiling. "Baby persistent, ain't she?"

"I'm good," I retorted.

CHAPTER 5

It was going on nine-thirty when I pulled up to Casey's soul food restaurant. Ace was somewhere busting his own moves, and I had to get here because the restaurant closed at nine.

I called Casey to tell her to open the door. I walked in and locked the door behind me.

"What's up, baby?" I asked when I walked into her office.

"Just goin' over some paperwork."

I took a seat in a chair opposite her desk. "How did today go?"

"It went well, baby." Then she let out a soft sigh. "Had a little rush around four but we handled it."

I went around the desk and stood her up, then sat down and placed her on my lap. She still smelled good after a hard day at work.

"Take these off." I tugged at the waistline of her business slacks.

"No." She laughed. "Last time was the *last* time."

"Straight up?" I reached up and grabbed her titties. My member woke up and she grinded on it a little before she got up.

"Straight up," she said back, placing her hands on her hips. "Now if you want some of this pussy ..." She pointed to it. "... Be at my house later on."

***

I was on my way to the crib when my phone rang. It was Cram, Ace's big cousin—and my label manager. I answered and he let me know about a show lined up for tonight. I was clueless.

"I know it's last minute," he said. "I already got the show disc from Justin for Young Dice and Coach Kid."

"Where at?" I was a little pissed. I hated last minute shit.

"Club Sphinx in Independence. I got Coach and Dice wit' me right now. We should be there in about twenty minutes."

"A'ight, let me get dressed and I'll be there. Ace on the way?"

"He's in route now."

"See yall in a hot second."

I was pulling up to my house by the time our conversation ended. I rushed inside and jumped in the shower. Afterwards, I applied my hygiene and threw on a brand new

Coogi outfit I'd been waiting to rock. As I was putting on my Franck Muller timepiece, my phone rang.

"Where you at, *papi*?" Selena asked.

"At the spot, 'bout to head out. Coach and Dice got a show tonight."

"Okay, call me later."

I loved that about her. When business was to be handled, she gave me my space.

In the full body mirror, I checked to make sure I was on point. The different colors in the Coogi looked good on my dark frame. I hit my all-even fade a few times with a brush and I was out the door.

***

I parked my whip and went to the back door of the club as music boomed from inside.

"What's good, Spade?" the bouncer said, opening the back door.

"Slow motion, what's poppin'?" I walked past him and headed up to the VIP section. The club was packed. All kinds of women wiggled through the building, dancing, drinking, enjoying their sexy. I spotted Ace, Cram, and Young Dice sitting a few feet away. A few women sat with them as well.

"What's good, fellas?" I embraced all of them before I took a seat. "Where's Coach Kid?"

"He 'bout to hit the stage!" Ace yelled from across the table.

They had a gallon of XO out, and I helped myself to a couple shots. Then we heard Coach Kid's first song off his show disc come on. We all got up and went to the edge of the bannister. The people below started going crazy when they heard his song come on.

Throughout his performance I noticed he wasn't up to par. He slurred his words *and* forgot a couple of bars. The partygoers probably didn't notice it but I did. Coach Kid was too drunk, and it showed. Me and him were going to have a talk.

When his last song started, Young Dice made his way down. He was next. And when he hit the stage the club went crazier! He was like the people's champ. His stage presence was superb. In the middle of his first song a young lady slid in front of me and started grinding her ass on my dick. I backed up a little. I was cool on dancing.

She turned around and spoke. "What's up, Spade?" It was Shantel's hot ass. She looked good too.

"What's poppin'?" I countered.

"You." She bit her bottom lip.

"That's funny. You too young, baby."

The crowd started chanting with Young Dice. "We jammin', swagged out daily! We jammin', swagged out daily!" He had them going!

Shantel said, "Too young means the pussy is still tight. But the mouth game is even better."

My dick started to rise but I had to chill.

"That's good to know," I said to her. Then I walked back to the sofa by our table and helped myself to some more XO. The young tender followed.

"What's the problem, baby?" she asked, sitting next to me. I glanced over at Ace. He shook his head, telling me don't go there with the young tender. I didn't plan on it anyway.

"You work for me, lil' mama," I said.

"Ain't nothing wrong with me tasting it, is it?" she asked seductively. "We can go to the ladies room real quick. Let you fuck my mouth until you feel I'm old enough to fuck this my pussy."

"I'm good," I told her. "Here, have a drink." I poured her a shot and joined Ace and Cram. I looked back and Shantel was still sitting there, looking disappointed. I guess she wasn't used to rejection.

Ace leaned in and asked, "What's up wit' baby girl?"

"She's in heat."

Me and him shared a laugh.

Out of my peripheral I noticed Coach Kid making his way to our table. He grabbed the XO and poured himself an issue. Shantel got lost in the crowd.

As I made my way over to him, a young lady bumped me as she was walking past. She apologized and kept it moving. "What's the deal, baby boy?" I said to Coach.

He hit his cup. "Bro, you see them hoes goin' crazy for the Kid?"

"You did yo thang," I said, slapping dap with him. I would discuss his inability to drink and perform at a later hour.

"Right on, bro." He wiped sweat from his forehead, as Ace and Cram made their way over to us.

"You killed 'em out there, baby!" Cram shook Coach Kid's hand.

"Yeah, good performance, bro." Ace embraced him too.

We all were sitting in our section just talking. Cram called a couple of whores over to our table. He always found fresh prey when we went out. I was cool on them hoes, though. Been there, done that.

Fifteen minutes later Young Dice approached the table with his baby momma following him. I didn't know she was there that night.

"How yall doing?" she said when they sat down. We all returned the greeting.

"If I'da known you was here, you could've came up here," I said to her.

"It's fine." She grabbed Young Dice's arm. "I like to watch my baby up close."

"That's what's up," I countered.

"And he did his damn thing!" Cram yelled out. We all laughed. Cram had an outgoing character. Real charismatic.

We chilled for another thirty minutes or so before we shook it. We made our way out of the back of the club. Ace jumped in his car by himself, said he was shooting to his soon-to-be wife's house. Cram, a couple of his groupies, and Coach Kid hopped in his Escalade and went to a room. Young Dice left with his baby moms.

I headed to Casey's house. All in all, it was a cool night. Job well done for my entertainment company.

CHAPTER 6

The next morning I was at Casey's house, sitting at the kitchen table having breakfast.

"So, how's Selena and the baby?" Casey asked.

I kept no secrets from Casey, Selena, or Lisa. They were well aware of the program.

"They coo'," I said. I cut into one of my pancakes and devoured it.

"That's good. I'ma buy her some shoes today." She got up from the table and made it to the sink with her plate and glass.

"Right on, baby." I took a swig from my orange juice, watching her. I knew she wanted a baby by me. But I wasn't with it. I admired her willingness to support lil' Samantha, though.

"No problem, Spade." She put the dishes she rinsed off into the dishwasher. "You done?"

"Yeah." I shoved the rest of the eggs I had on my plate in my mouth and took the dishes to her. I kissed her on her cheek before I dropped the dishes in the sink. "I'ma go get dressed, baby."

"Okay."

I made my way to the bedroom to get my clothes together. As I was laying out my clothes, I heard my phone beeping. I picked it up and noticed I had about twenty missed calls. From Ace, Cram, and Young Dice's baby momma. Most of them were from Young Dice's baby moms. I immediately called her back. First ring she picked it up.

"Spade! Oh my god … They … They …" She started crying. My heart dropped.

"Misha, Misha. Calm down, baby girl. What's goin' on?"

"They … They took him." She cried harder.

I started pacing the bedroom floor. *What the fuck?* Unconsciously, my fist clinched.

"Who took him?"

"They took Dice! Spade, they took Dice!"

"Misha, I'ma need you to calm down," I said. "Who took Young Dice?"

"What's goin' on?" Casey asked as she walked into the room. I held up a finger, telling her to hold on.

"Some guys took him," Misha said, trying to pull it together. "They … they left a number for you to call."

Want me *to call?*

"What's the number?" I asked.

"Hold on."

221

She must have put the phone down to retrieve the number. She was back on in seconds. She gave me the number and I told her I'd call her back.

"Who was that?" Casey was standing with her back to the dresser. Judging by her tone, I knew she knew something was wrong.

"Some niggas kidnapped Dice." I let out a sigh. "Left a number for me to call."

"I'm calling Sparkle." Casey left the room.

I was sitting on the edge of the bed. I got up and retrieved one of my burnout phones from the closet and called the number.

"This must be Spade," the person on the other end said. His Mexican accent was thick.

"Who is this?"

"My name is Santos, my friend."

"Do I know you?"

"Nooo, my friend." He chuckled a little. "But I know *you*."

Casey walked back in the room. I put my new friend on speaker.

"And how do you know me?" I asked.

"Well ..." He paused. "You did business with my brother Carlos."

Kutz' brother, I realized. Casey dialed a number on her phone and walked back out of the room.

"Where's my artist?"

"He's safe for now. You have five hours to bring me two hundred thousand or he will die. When you get the money, call me for the location." He hung up.

"Ain't this a bitch!" I said out loud.

I hurried and got dressed, headed to Selena's. I had the money in the safe over there.

CHAPTER 7

Walking in the door, I noticed Selena sitting on the couch with lil' Samantha watching TV. I walked right past them and headed to the safe.

"Really?" she huffed.

"What's up?" I came off a little aggressive and her nose flared up. I caught myself. "My fault," I said.

"What's the problem?" She got up off the couch and came over to me.

"Daddy, whadda *p'oblem?*" Lil' Samantha tried to ask as well.

"Nothing, baby." I smiled at my daughter, then said to Selena, "Kutz has a brother named Santos. He kidnapped one of my artists and wants two hundred thousand."

"Shit," she said. "If he is who I think he is, he's playing you. Young Dice is dead." She covered her mouth, trying to get control of her emotions.

"Who is he?"

"Maria used to tell me about him. He was like the enforcer for Carlos. He's fuckin' crazy." She hugged me tight.

"I gotta bust this move, baby." I got her off of me and I headed to the room with my safe in it.

As I walked in, my phone rang. It was OG Casa.

"OG," I answered.

"Me and Ace got fifty grand each. Meet us at your house." Casey must've called him.

"A'ight," I said.

***

As I was pulling up to my spot, OG Casa and Ace were sitting in my driveway. Ace was in his BMW and OG Casa was in a Dodge Ram pickup truck with an extended cab. I parked behind Ace and jumped out my whip with a backpack full of money. OG Casa and Ace hopped out too.

"Where did this nigga come from?" Ace asked when we made it inside my house.

"I don't fuckin' know." I sat on my couch, real frustrated and anxious. Young Dice had nothing to do with this fonk. I hoped he was alive. I hoped what Selena said wasn't true.

"Got my people lookin' in on this muhfucka," OG Casa said.

"I'm 'bout to call dis nigga." I picked up my burnout and dialed the number Misha gave me.

Santos came on. "I'm assuming you have the money, my friend."

I'ma kill this muthafucka, I thought to myself.

"I got it. Where's my artist?"

"He's safe." He laughed. "So how's business?" He was trying to fuck with me.

"Where's my artist?" I asked again. I didn't have time to play with this fucking clown.

"Okay, okay." I heard him say something to someone in the background. Then he gave me an address on the west side.

"Take the money there?" I inquired.

"Yes, take the money there."

The line went dead.

"Yall ready?" OG Casa said. "I got two AR's in the truck. I know yall got yall hand cannons."

"Let me call Misha real quick." I dialed her number and she spoke before me.

"Spade, tell me you got my baby," she said.

"We're about to go get him now."

"Please, please bring my baby home, Spade." She started to cry.

"Don't trip, Mish. I'll call you when I get him." I hung up.

OG Casa headed for the door. "Let's go." Me and Ace followed.

We hopped in the truck and OG pulled off. I was in the back seat with one of the AR-15s on my lap—I held it like a lover. Ace had the other one on his lap in the passenger seat. We rode in silence. No music, just our thoughts.

On the way there, Army Tank called me to tell me there was no sign of Maria. I told him to shake it. We had bigger shit to worry about at the moment.

CHAPTER 8

"Is this the spot?" Ace asked.

The house sat on top of a hill. It looked vacant.

"I think so. Let me call this nigga." I dialed the number for Santos and waited. "This muthafucka ain't answerin'."

"That's what the fuck I be talkin' about." Ace slapped one in the head of the AR. "Fuckin' *guala gualas* playin' too much."

I agreed and cocked my rifle back as well. I was looking up and down the street for any sign of trouble. Ace and OG Casa were working the mirrors. It was about seven in the evening.

"Call him back," OG Casa said.

I did, but there was still no answer.

"Fuck dis." I slid the length of the weapon down my pants leg and opened the door to get out. Ace came with me.

"I got it out here," OG Casa said.

Me and Ace headed up to the house. On the porch, Ace knocked on the door. There was an unusual silence at this muthafucka. I didn't feel good about the odds. Me and Ace simultaneously pulled our rifles out and signaled to OG Casa, telling him we were going in. I turned the door knob and the door came open.

"Dis muhfucka filthy," Ace said as we slowly entered.

"Young Dice!" I called out. I got no answer.

"You sure dis the spot, bro?"

I looked at him upside his head.

The living room had no furniture, just trash. The walls were covered with gang graffiti. There was a small hallway that led to a couple of bedrooms. Me and Ace headed to the first bedroom. When I opened it, my jaw clenched. Young Dice was tied to a chair—like the Russians tied Kutz to a chair. His shirt was off and there was bullet holes in his torso. He was dead to the world. His face looked like they beat him before they killed him.

"Fuck!" I yelled.

"Ain't this a bitch," Ace said.

"We gotta go, cuzz."

I told Ace and we jetted out the spot. We were back in the truck in no time. OG Casa gave us a raised eyebrow.

"They knocked him," Ace said.

I didn't reply. I was too pissed. OG Casa hurried and started the truck. We headed back to my spot. On the way there, Ace called one of his old serves to report the body. Couldn't just leave him there dead. But we damn sure wasn't reporting it ourselves.

**

"No! ... Nooooo!" Misa cried over the phone.

Me, OG Casa, and Ace were back at my spot. I decided to call Misha and give her the news.

"I know, I know," was all I could say at the time.

"Why, Spade?! Why?!"

"Misha, Misha," I said, trying to calm her down. After about another ten or fifteen minutes, she finally calmed down.

"I'm listenin' ..."

"We're goin' to take care of this," I told her. "Do you hear me?"

Ace walked in my bedroom where I was. I held up my finger, telling him to hold on. He walked back out.

"I hear you." She let out a long sigh of frustration. "But what are saying?"

I started pacing my bedroom floor.

"If the boys contact you to question you, you don't know shit."

"Spade, you—"

"Listen!" I cut her off. "You don't know shit. You gotta let us take care of this shit."

"Okay, okay," she finally said.

"I'ma shoot you some change every month for you and cuzz daughter."

She started crying again. Guilt rushed through me.

"Alright," she said and hung up the phone. I shook my head, walked out of my bedroom, and walked downstairs to join Ace and OG Casa.

"We gotta find out everything 'bout dis nigga, OG," Ace was saying as I walked into the dining room where they were at.

"I'm hip," OG Casa said.

I sat down at the kitchen table with them. "How soon can we get the scoop on this muthafucka?" I asked OG.

"Don't know, but I'm on it, though." He rubbed his beard.

"I'm ready to make some *isamadagotas* out of these muhfuckas," Ace said as he got up and headed to the kitchen.

"I can't believe this shit," I said to myself. My jaw clenched along with my fists. I felt responsible for Young Dice's murder. I thought about when I first met his mother. She told me to take care of her baby. And at this moment he was probably getting carted out on a stretcher, lifeless.

"A nigga can't just get money and live!" Ace said as he came back into the kitchen with a fifth of Remy in his hand. "I'm sayin', though …" He hit the bottle. "It's time to send the women away and do some layin'."

"Calm down, cuzz," I said.

"Calm down?! Calm down?! You saw lil' cuzz, off in a vaco, cut down!"

231

"Ace." I gave him a look that told him to chill the fuck out. I understood his frustration. But we needed to make our next move our best move. "This shit gon' get handled."

"Spade is right. Let's regroup in the a.m.," OG Casa said. He rose to his feet. "Be down at the dealership in the morning." And then he left.

"What time is it, bro?" Ace asked when he finally took a seat and calmed down.

"Eight-thirty," I said after I looked at my phone. "I'ma try and—" My phone rang, interrupting my sentence. It was Sparkle. "Yeah?" I answered.

"My flight will land tomorrow," she said and hung up.

"Who was that, bro?" Ace asked.

"Sparkle. She'll be here tomorrow."

"Let's get to making these isamadagotas then," Ace said with a devilish grin.

CHAPTER 9

I was in my whip headed to the salon to holler at Lisa. It was about nine-fifteen when I looked at my phone. I was solo, Ace had went to his spot when he left my house. I was about twenty minutes away from the salon when some cherries lit up my rearview mirror.

"Ain't this a bitch," I said as I pulled over to the side of the street. I turned my music down, grabbed my license and registration, and let my window down. The officer stepped out of the car. Working my rearview I noticed he had on plain clothes. It was a detect; it was Kremensky's bitch ass.

"Get the fuck outta the car," he said when he made it to my door. He yanked it open.

"Man, what the fuck do you want?" I threw my license and registration in my passenger seat. I knew he was on some bullshit.

"Out!"

I reluctantly exited my vehicle. I walked toward the back of my vehicle and leaned on my trunk.

"Turn the fuck around," he ordered. A few cars passed by, honking their horns.

"This some bullshit." I turned around, putting my hands on my trunk and spread my legs. The pig frisked me and found nothing. After he was done patting me down, I turned around to face him.

"You know …" He began, extracting a cancer stick and lighting it. "… you ride around in a 2012 Benz. You know what I drive?"

"I got shit to do," I said. I didn't have time for this shit. I had an artist that just got killed.

"I drive a Buick, you Black sonofabitch." He blew smoke in my face. I kept a cool head; he was trying to draw me out. I looked at the cars passing by, trying to keep my mind off of stealing on this bitch in his fucking mouth.

"Nice car." I smiled. He frowned. "You ain't got shit better to do? A wife? Girlfriend?" His expression was price-less. "I mean come on, homey. You pulled me over to talk? I got a bitch for you."

"Listen here, motherfucker!" He grabbed me by the collar after he tossed his cigarette to the side. "I'm bringing you down for murder. And when I do, I'll be fucking your bitch. Now get the fuck out of here." He walked back to his car and peeled out.

I'ma kill that muhfucka, I thought to myself as I watched his car disappear in traffic. I jumped in my whip and headed to the salon.

***

When I walked in the salon, Shantel was sweeping up. She was the only stylist here so far.

"Hi, Spade," she said.

"What's good? Where Lisa?"

"In the office, baby."

I ignored the flirtation and walked back to the office.

"Fine ass," I heard Shantel say.

I went over and gave Lisa a kiss. "What's good, baby?"

"What's wrong?" she asked as I took a seat behind my desk.

"Young Dice got killed."

"Damn, baby." She came over and sat on my lap and hugged me. "Sorry to hear that. Who did this?" She had a confused look on her face.

"I know who did it, baby. We gon' take care of it."

"I'm 'bout to go yall," Shantel said as she opened the door. She paused at the entrance, looking disappointed because Lisa was sitting on my lap.

"Okay, Shantel," Lisa said.

I didn't offer any response. I saw Shantel roll her eyes and close the door.

"Should I be worried?" Lisa got up from my lap and gave me a concerned look.

235

"I'm on top of it, baby, don't trip," I said. She didn't look too convinced.

"I hope so, Spade," she said.

"Trust me." I got up and grabbed her hands. "I got this."

CHAPTER 10

I pulled up to the studio about thirty minutes later. I noticed Coach Kids' car was parked outside. I was going over there to let Justin know what was up with Young Dice. Since Coach Kid was here too, that was even better.

I sat outside the studio parked in my whip. Had to get my thoughts together. Seeing my young nigga cut down like that was fucking with me. I pulled it together and called Justin.

"Hello?" he answered.

"Open the door, bro," I said and hung up the phone. I jumped out my car and headed to the door. "What's up, bro?" I embraced Justin when I walked in the studio.

"Shit, Coach Kid in the booth knockin' it out," he said as we walked toward the couch. I took a seat and Justin walked over to the mixing board.

"Tell Coach to come out here real quick."

"Coach, step out for a minute," he said through the mic. "Everything coo'?" he asked me.

"Nah, bro."

Coach Kid joined us in the lab. He smiled and came over and shook my hand. "Spade, what's good?"

"Slow motion. Sit down real quick, bro. Young Dice got killed today."

"What?!" Justin countered.

"Damn, straight up …?" Coach Kid rose to his feet.

"Straight up," I said back. "So yall niggas need to be on yall toes."

"When? Where was he at?" Justin asked.

"They found him on the West Side." I didn't want to tell them he got kidnapped. Didn't want to shake them up.

"That's fucked up, bro," Coach Kid said. "We gotta find out who did dis shit." He walked to the other side of the room.

"We on it, bro. I just wanted to fill yall in." I kept my eye on Coach Kid. He looked a little spooked. *Is this nigga really solid?* I asked myself.

"Damn, cuzz, the album is finished," Justine said. "Just had to mix a few more songs."

"We still gon' put it out," I said.

"Damn right." Justin nodded his head for emphasis.

"I already told his baby moms I'd look out for her every month." I stood up and walked toward the refrigerator. Coach Kid was still pacing back and forth, mumbling to himself. "Coach Kid," I said, snapping him out of his trance. "Have a seat, bro."

"I'm 'bout to step outside and hit dis stogey." He walked out of the studio.

I reached in the fridge and snatched out a bottle of XO. I took a swig from the bottle before I took it back over to the couch with me.

"How's Misha takin' it?" Justin inquired.

"Rough," I stated flatly. I hit the poison one more time and handed him the bottle.

"His moms?" he asked as he hit the bottle.

"Haven't talked to her yet."

"This shit is fucked up, bro."

Coach Kid stuck his head in the door. "Ay yall, I'm 'bout to bust a move."

"A'ight," me and Justin said in unison.

Me and Justin conversed for a few more minutes and I shook it. It felt like the world was on my shoulders.

***

I was on the way to my house. A million thoughts were running through my head. My thoughts were interrupted by my phone ringing.

"Yeah?"

"My people will be here in a couple of days," OG Casa said.

"That'll work." I was happy to hear that. The Russians were ready for war. "Heard anything else?"

"Nah, got my ears open, though."

"A'ight, I'll get wit' you in a minute."

"Okay, son."

I pulled up to my house about twenty minutes later. As I was pulling up, so was Casey. We both parked in the driveway and hopped out.

"Baby, I'm so sorry." She came over to me and gave me a hug.

"You heard?" I asked while we were embracing each other.

"Daddy told me." She let me go and we walked toward the front door of my house.

"Yeah, they fucked cuzz up," I told her as I unlocked the door and we headed in.

"We gotta do something about these muthafuckas, babe."
She was always ready to ride.

"I'm hip," I said to myself. I took a seat in the living room, grabbed the remote and turned the TV on.

"Sparkle will be here tomorrow," Casey said as she threw her purse on the couch and walked into the kitchen. She had a bottle of Ciroc in her right hand, and a shot glass in her left. She sat next to me on the couch.

"I know, she called me."

"You need me to do anything?"

"Just keep yo head down, baby. We'll handle it."

"He was so young …" She poured her issue and shook her head in disbelief.

I envisioned him tied to that chair. Face fat as a pumpkin, lifeless. I couldn't believe that shit. That pussy Santos had it coming, serious business.

CHAPTER 11

one week later

It was Saturday morning. The church on Emanuel Cleaver Blvd was packed. Niggas with "rest in peace Young Dice" shirts on stood in the back of the congregation. Family members and friends filled the rows. Young women cried uncontrollably. Young Dice's mother and grandmother sat in the front row, along with Misha and a few of his cousins. Me, Ace, Cram, Justin, and Coach were in the row behind them.

"DeAnthony Steward was a good young man," the pastor said. "Honest, vibrant, and determined. Loved by many." He eyeballed those in attendance. "But his life was cut short. Cut short by a demon so powerful, so elusive—"

"No! No!" Misha cried out. Young Dice's mother hugged her tight, allowing her to let all her pain out on her shoulder. A couple of niggas in the back walked out wiping tears from their faces.

"Bless yo heart, sista," the pastor said to Misha. "When will the violence stop?! When?! When?!" He came from behind the podium. "You guys in the back … I know you're products of the streets. But when will you make the streets better?! What will you do to stop this senseless killin'?"

The nigga hit a nerve; he was good. I looked back and noticed some of the brothas adjusting their pistols on their waist through their t-shirts, game faces on.

***

When we drove to the burial site, it looked like a parade. Car after car, after car. Filled with loved ones, fans, associates, gangstas, you name it. Me, Ace, Justin, and Coach Kid were riding in Cram's Escalade.

"We need to get them niggas that did that shit to Young Dice," Coach Kid said.

"And what you gon' do, nigga?" Ace asked him. I was sitting shotgun. I glanced over and saw the look on Ace's face; he wasn't joking.

"Nigga, rock-out. What you think I'm gon' do," Coach Kid retorted.

"Rock-out, huh?" Ace cracked a smile. I did too. *Ace was a fuckin' foo'.* "What you done rocked-out on, nigga?"

"Yall niggas chill out, man," Cram said.

"Nah, big cuzz. This nigga always runnin' his fuckin' mouth," Ace countered.

"I really do dis shit, nigga," Coach Kid said.

"Enough of the tough guy shit. You niggas handle that on a later date." Cram turned up the sounds. He had Yola the Guru playing on his stereo.

We proceeded to the burial site. By the time we got there, we were a little tipsy. That green bottle we were swigging had us cut. The burial site was off of Blue Ridge. Two of the police cars that escorted the motorcade were parked at the entrance. It had to have been fifty or more cars.

Let's get this shit over with, I thought to myself as we exited the truck.

CHAPTER 12

Two hours later I was in my whip solo, headed to OG Casa's dealership. He hated funerals so he didn't attend Young Dice's. He'd called my phone and told me to stop by. I'd finally pulled up. When I wheeled into the parking lot I spotted him talking to an older couple standing by a four-door Cadillac STS.

I parked next to his Cadillac and went into the office. Sitting in his office alone made me observe the pictures and other items around. On his desk he had a picture of Casey walking across the stage at her graduation back in the day. A major accomplishment if you were from the 'hood. He had a couple enlarge pictures of Bob Marley and Marcus Garvey hanging on his wall. As I continued to observe his office, my phone rang. It was Selena.

"What's up, baby?" I said.

"Hey, how was the funeral?" She was making sure there wasn't any casualties at that muthafucka. Something that was a strong possibility.

"It was coo', baby. Where's Samantha?"

"In there playin' with her toys," she said.

OG Casa walked in. "What's up, nephew?"

I nodded my head at him. He sat in his chair.

"That's what's up," I said into the phone. "Kiss her for me, baby. And I'll hit you in a minute."

"Alright," she said, and we hung up.

"What's good, OG?"

"Santos was the enforcer for Kutz." He gave me an intense look. "He's Kutz's older brother."

"Where did this pussy come from?" I sat on the edge of the seat.

"Don't know, but he's smart." He reached in the small refrigerator next to his desk and pulled out a Crown Royal bottle. He poured himself a shot and continued. "So I'ma need you to be on yo toes. Ranno and Stavi are put up in a loft downtown."

"Ranno and Stavi?" I inquired.

"The Russians." He hit his poison. That was the first time he mentioned their names. "Sparkle's uncles."

"That's what's up. When can we get a location on this nigga?"

"Workin' on it."

***

Heather Headley was singing her truth as I was pushing toward the salon. I love her; she can blow her ass off. When I was sitting at a stop light I glanced at my phone and seen I had a few missed calls. All from Casey. I immediately hit her back.

"Spade!" She was a little frantic. "This dirty muthafucka just pulled me over."

"Who?" I asked as my face formed a frown.

"Kremensky," she answered.

Ain't dis a bitch, I thought to myself. The light turned green and I proceeded to the salon.

"For what?"

"For nothing. He tore up my car, talkin' 'bout he had probable cause to search the vehicle, he—"

"Calm down, baby. His bitch ass is tryin' to fuck wit' us."

"Well it's workin', dammit."

"Don't let him get to you. His time will come. Where you headed?"

"To the house to meet Sparkle."

"A'ight, go ahead there, and I'll hit you in a minute."

Ten minutes later I pulled up to the salon. It was about six in the evening. We closed at five that day. When I walked in, Lisa and Shantel were sitting down in the stylist chairs talking.

247

"What's up yall?" I greeted them.

"Hi, Spade." Shantel smiled.

"Just sittin' here talkin'," said Lisa. "How are you feelin', baby?"

"I'm good." I headed back to me and Lisa's office. She got up and followed me.

"How was the funeral?" she asked, as we both took a seat at our desks.

"It went well. No nonsense went down." I rubbed my face with both of my hands. I was a little exhausted.

She came over and sat on my lap. "That's good. If it's worth anything, baby, you're handling this well." She kissed me on my neck.

"Thanks, baby." My hand went to her firm ass.

"You're wel—"

My phone rang. I hurried and answered it.

"What's up, baby?" I said. It was Selena. Lisa kept kissing my neck.

"Oh nothing. What time will you be home?" she asked.

"In a minute," I replied.

Lisa grabbed my dick through my pants.

"Okay, you know we have to go to my parents' house today."

I'd forgot we told her parents we were stopping by.

"Alright, baby," I said, then hung up on her.

"Selena?" Lisa asked as she licked my ear.

"Mmm-hmm."

My dick was hard as titanium steel. Lisa got up off my lap and pulled my tucked-in Ermenegildo Zegna shirt out of my pants. She unbuckled my belt, unzipped my pants and—along with my boxers—she pulled them down to my ankles.

"Just sit back and relax," she whispered. I didn't contest. First she kissed the head. Then swirled her tongue around the head.

"Straight up, huh?" I said, looking down at her with a smirk on my face.

She looked up at me and smiled. "Straight up."

I grabbed the back of her head and guided her down my dick. Her mouth was warm. And baby could suck a mean dick. She really started getting into it. Unconsciously, my head went back, and I briefly closed my eyes. And at that moment nothing was on my mind but getting a nut off. Not Santos, not Maria. Not the funeral. Just getting my nut off.

"You love this, don't you?" she asked.

"Damn right."

I looked back down at her. Out of my peripheral, I noticed someone standing in the doorway watching. It was Shantel, standing there licking her lips. We made eye contact, as Lisa sucked me behind my desk, which was directly across from the door entrance. Lisa's back was to the door; she couldn't see Shantel.

I just smirked at the bitch. She bit her bottom lip and slowly pulled the door closed.

"Let me see how that pussy feel," I said.

She got up off my shit, turned around so she could sit on my dick with her ass facing me. She slowly sat on my dick. Her pussy was warmer than her mouth.

"Ooh *shiiit*," she moaned as she methodically bounced up and down my dick. I gripped both of her ass cheeks. "I'm comin' already, baby."

She sped up the rhythm. White film poured on my shaft.

"Damn," I said to myself.

Baby was gettin' it!

***

"This is the last track I gotta mix, bro," Justin said.

I was at the studio. I planned on putting Young Dice's CD out. I also had hella tracks he recorded for some mixtapes. I planned on keeping him alive through his music.

"A'ight, I'ma call the graphic designer next week," I said. "See how long he'll be."

"That's what's up," Justin replied.

My phone rang. It was Ace.

"What's up, bro?" I answered.

"Chillin', what's the deal?"

"At the lab, wrappin' this shit up."

The door to the studio opened. I glanced over to see who it was, and it was Coach Kid. He came in and took a seat on the couch. He looked a little on edge.

"A'ight bro, I was just checkin' on you," he said.

In the background, I heard Ashley say, "Tell Spade I said what's up!"

"You hear Ashley's ass?"

"Yeah. Tell her I said what's good."

He relayed the message, we said we'd speak later and then we hung up.

I looked at Coach Kid. "What's good, lil' fella?"

He stood up and took his shirt off. He had a bulletproof vest on. He also had a Glock tucked in the waist of his Enyce jeans. "I'm ready for whateva," he said.

"I see." I smiled. I was amazed to say the least.

"Real talk." He started pacing the floor. "If them mutha-fuckas think they gon' come boo-bop me, they got another thing comin'."

"You been drinkin'?" I asked. Justin leaned back in his seat and shook his head at Coach Kid's dramatics.

"I keep a bottle of Hindu." He looked at me like I was crazy for asking him some shit like that. "You want some, bro?"

"I'm good." I hated Hennessy.

"A'ight, a'ight." He took a seat. His legs were bouncing uncontrollably.

"Bro, chill out. We got this under control," I assured him.

CHAPTER 13

"Look at her, back there knocked out," I told Selena from the passenger seat. She glanced in the rearview and smiled at the sight of our daughter in her car seat, sleeping like an angel. We were on way to California, Missouri. To her parents' house.

"She's going to be up all night," Selena said.

"Yeah well, you gon' have to deal wit' her." I smiled. "I'ma be knocked out."

"Whatever." She laughed.

"Straight up. *Shiiid.* I'm already tired."

We had about twenty miles to go before we made it to her parents'. They were coo' people. Her moms didn't speak English and her pops was bilingual. Some of the things her mother said I couldn't understand. That kind of fucked with a nigga.

My phone rang. I checked it, and when I saw it was Sparkle, I hurried and answered it.

"What's poppin'?" I said.

"His sister says hello," she said and hung up.

That's what's up, I thought. She was letting me know she killed Santos' sister. I planned on meeting with everybody when I got back to Kansas City to let them know shit was about to pop off.

"Who was that?" Selena asked.

"Ace." I hit the recline button on my seat.

We pulled up to her parents' property thirty minutes later. They had a nice piece of land. Her pops had a ranch for his horses. There were four Cadillac ATS's, different colors, and two Cadillac Escalades parked in the driveway. That nigga loved 'Lacs.

We parked and hopped out. I opened the back door and got my daughter out of her car seat, and she started tossing and turning her head.

"Is she woke?" Selena asked, walking over to get her from me.

"Not yet," I replied.

"Come to mommy," she said to Samantha, as she took her from my arms. She walked with our baby toward the front door, and I popped the trunk and got our bags out.

When I got through the door, her father was there waiting on me.

"Hello, young man." He smiled. I sat the bags down to shake his hand.

"Mr. Gomez," I said. "How are you, sir?"

"Fine, fine. Let me get those bags." He picked them up and walked down the hallway. I walked into the sitting area and Selena and Mrs. Gomez were sitting on the couch talking. When they noticed my presence, Mrs. Gomez looked up and greeted me.

"*¿Como estas, mijo?*" she said.

"Fine, how are you?" I replied.

She said something to Selena in Spanish.

"She said get ready for dinner," Selena told me.

"Which room are we stayin' in?"

"Second door to the right." She pointed. "Down the hall."

I went that way and found a spacious, fully furnished room. We had our own bathroom in here too. I went in the bathroom to freshen up. That long ass ride had me feeling a little salty.

When I came out of the bathroom Selena was coming in the bedroom.

"Mother says you're looking good." She smiled as she glopped on the bed.

"Is that right? Samantha still sleep?"

"Yep, she's in mommy's room."

"Good, let's get it in real quick." I walked over to her. For some reason I was feeling horny.

"Spade, no." She pushed me away from her and smiled. "You so nasty. Dinner will be ready in a minute."

"Well, gon' and knock dis muhfucka down real quick."

She looked at my crotch area like she was thinking about it. "No, now come on." She giggled and walked out of the room.

Just gon' leave a nigga hangin' like that, I thought as I followed her out.

Twenty minutes later we were at one end of the eight-foot long dinner table eating.

"So how's business?" Mr. Gomez asked me.

"It's coo'. Been having a nice quarter," I said. I thought about Young Dice getting put into the ground …

"That's good." He sipped his wine. "Let me know when you're ready to go in on some land."

"Will do."

I noticed an awkward silence between Selena and her mother. Then her mother finally said something to her.

"¿Cuando se va a casar?" she said to Selena. Her father looked at her as well, waiting for a reply.

"What she say?" I asked Selena.

"She wants to know when we're getting married," she said. "Ta no decidimos," she told her mother.

"Necesitas apurarte , mija."

"Cundo estamos listo," Selena retorted.

"¿Cuando estas listo?" Her mother frowned a little.

I hit my glass of water. I didn't know what the fuck was being said.

Her father finally intervened. "¿Podemos comer con placer?" he said, then grabbed his wife's hand and squeezed it.

"Thank you," Selena said to herself.

After that brief conversation, there was a silence that cloaked the whole table. I wiped my mouth with a napkin and excuses myself form the table.

"I gotta make a call," I lied as I stood up.

"Okay, son," Mr. Gomez said.

I walked toward the room we were occupying. I laid back on the bad and stared at the ceiling, thinking about my situation in the town. I had to figure this shit out.

"Sorry about that, babe," Selena said as she came in, interrupting my pondering.

"It's good." I was still laying back, staring at the ceiling.

"What's wrong?"

"Tryna figure dis shit out."

"I'm sorry. I thought maybe us getting away would ease your mind a little." She laid down on the bed next to me and kissed my ear.

"It's good," was all I offered.

"Well, maybe this will help."

She unzipped my pants.

CHAPTER 14

Then next afternoon I was back in the city, sitting in my office with Ace, OG Casa, Sparkle, and Casey. Selena and Samantha were back at home chilling.

"Ranno and Stavi are close to finding a location for Santos," OG Casa was saying. "In the meantime everybody—and I mean everybody—needs to be on their toes."

"Yeah, so Ace, make sure Ashley lays low for a minute." I looked in Ace's direction. "I already told Lisa and Selena this morning to chill." Casey rolled her eyes. "And you make sure you sit yo big-head ass down too." I smiled at her.

"Whatever," Casey said.

"I been working on his wife," Sparkled said. "I think I should have a location on her place of business by this evening."

"I'm just ready to burrito some'n," Ace said flatly.

"In due time," OG Casa said.

"A'ight, so is that it, OG?" I asked.

"Yeah, that's it. Just keep yall eyes open out there. This muthafucka is slick."

After that, everyone stood up to leave, except Ace. Casey gave me a hug and kiss before her and Sparkle left. OG Casa said he was going down to his dealership for a hot second. Me and Ace stayed behind.

"Can't wait till we nip this shit in the bud," Ace said after everyone else was gone.

"I'm hip." I walked toward the fridge I had in my office. "What you want, bro?"

"Grab the green bottle," he said. I went over and gave it to him. "Right on."

"My fault, bro. I know you 'sposed to be focusing on the wedding."

"That shit can wait. We gon' handle this nigga Santos off the flip." He took a swig from the bottle.

There was a loud knock on my office door that startled me and Ace. I stood up and felt my waist to make sure my life insurance policy was on my hip.

"Who the fuck is that?" Ace asked.

"I don't know." I walked over to the door and opened it. "Can I help you gentlemen?"

Four niggas stood in the hallway.

"Can you help us?" One nigga laughed at my question like I offended him. "You *betta* be able to help us."

"Chill out, nigga," the gentleman closest to the door said to the tough guy in the back. "We Young Dice's cousins. We wanted to holla at you."

"Come in." I backed up to let them inside. Me and the tough guy locked eyes. He kept tugging on his waist so I'd know he had his wetter on him. All of them probably did.

Ace got up out of his seat, sat the bottle down and stood by the wall closest to my desk. I walked behind my desk and took a seat.

"Yall can sit down." I motioned my arm to the leather couches I had in my office.

"Nah, we good," one gentleman said.

"Yeah, we good." The tough nigga screwed his face up. Out of my peripheral I noticed Ace smiled. He too must've found the tough guy hilarious.

"How can I help yall niggas?" I offered.

"Who killed my lil' cousin?" one guy asked. I assumed he was the leader of their cute little clique.

"Don't know yet, but I'm on it," I said.

"Man, that's some bullshit, nigga!" Tough Guy hollered.

I was getting tired of him. "Listen, homie ... I know yall niggas is frustrated. I am too. I know this hard for you niggas, but yall gotta let me find out what the deal is—"

"Dis nigga," the tough guy interrupted.

Ace tugged on his waist.

"Now it look like yall ready to rock," I continued as calm as I could be. I had too much going on to be fucking talking to these clowns. Since they were Young Dice's family I swallowed my pride. "But I'd advise yall to let me handle this situation."

"Now why in da fuck would we do that!" The tough guy acted like he was going to walk toward me.

"Fall back, cowboy," Ace said, taking a couple steps forward.

"Cowboy?" Sir-Tough-A-Lot looked at Ace like he was crazy.

"Gino, chill out," the leader told him.

Gino, huh?

"Yeah, chill out, Gino," Ace teased with a smile.

"Man, fuck this." Gino acted like he was reaching. Ace already had his Glock 23 pointed at the other three.

"Don't do it," I told one of the niggas that looked like he wanted to draw his cannon. "Now check game, you niggas gon' get the fuck outta here. This meeting is over with."

"A'ight, nigga," they kept saying as they backpedaled out of my office.

"Can you believe that shit?!" Ace said. "Homie was 'bout to get his noodle knocked, bro. That's what the fuck I be talkin' 'bout. I'm tired of being civilized with these muhfuckas."

260

***

Twenty minutes later I was riding with Ace. We were headed to OG Casa's dealership.

"You know what, bro, I been thinking." Ace turned his music down so I could hear him. "You done jumped out of the dope game. Started the label, the salon is boomin'. You got one good lung—"

I cut him off. "Where you goin' wit' this, bro?"

"I'm sayin', cuzz, fall on back and let us handle this." He gave me a sincere look. "Straight up. Because I'm good, bro. I'm not a felon, I have my health. I can wiggle, my nigga."

"You know I can't fall back on this shit. It's personal." I glanced out the passenger side window and looked into space. I thought about my health. My one good lung. Maria. "I'm all in, my nigga."

"Bring the tortillas then." He laughed and turned up the music.

We proceeded to OG Casa's dealership. It was a cool Sunday afternoon, not too hot, not too cold. We pulled up to the dealership about ten minutes later.

"That Yukon tough," Ace said as we were pulling in.

"You already got too many whips, nigga."

"I'm hip, but that muhfucka nice."

He parked and we hopped out and headed inside. There were a couple of white guys seated across from OG Casa.

They looked a little rough around the edges, but they were dressed in some expensive Giorgio Armani suits. *Who the fuck are these niggas?* I thought.

Then I remembered. They were the same niggas from the trailer park homes. The same gentlemen that had Kutz tied to a chair, bloody. *The Russians.*

"What's good, OG?" Me and Ace said before we took a seat.

"Nothin' much." He hit his glass of Crown Royal, then he introduced us. "Spade and Ace, Ranno and Stavi. Ranna and Stavi, Spade and Ace."

"What's good," I said.

"What's the deal," Ace said.

Ranno and Stavi didn't say a word in return. They just offered head nods. Maybe they were mutes or some shit.

"So, are the women laying low?" OG Casa asked.

"As far as I know," I replied.

"Bitch betta," Ace said.

"Good, good." He nodded his head. "Ranno and Stavi are good at fishing out insects. So we should be wrapping this shit up soon."

"Sounds like a plan," I replied.

"In my opinion," OG Casa continued. "I think he's trying to draw attention on his self, and take the attention off Maria."

I never considered that. "Makes sense."

"But that bitch will still have her day to see the judge," OG Casa said. He was just as pissed about her shooting me than I was.

Then my phone rang. It was Sparkle.

"Yeah?" I answered.

"I got the location, cousin," she said, and hung up.

"That was Sparkled," I said to the group. "She knows where his wife works."

Ranno and Stavi just smiled. Proud uncles, I guess.

"Good," OG Casa said.

"Damn right," Ace added.

"A'ight, but we need to find the location on Santos before we bust a move," I said.

"I agree," said OG Casa. "I'll call you as soon as we get the intel."

"A'ight, well we 'bout to shake."

Me and Ace rose to our feet. We shook Ranno's and Stavi's hands, and we embraced OG Casa before we left.

"Yall keep yall eyes open," OG Casa said to us.

***

Later that night I was back at my spot. Casey was already there. We were sitting in my living room watching the tube.

"Change the channel, baby," Casey said.

"I'm tryna see who the Chiefs might consider gettin'."

"You and this damn *SportsCenter*." She got up from the couch and walked to the kitchen.

"Bitch is crazy," I laughed to myself.

"I heard you, boy!" she yelled from the kitchen.

"What you talkin' 'bout?"

"Don't play wit' me?"

I heard her opening the freezer. My phone started beeping. It was laying on the marble table sitting in my living room. I retrieved it and seen I had a text from Justin telling me to call him. I did.

"Spade, what's poppin'," he answered.

"At the pad. What's good?"

"Coach Kid in jail. Got caught wit' a blammy and some twirks."

Stupid muhfucka, I thought.

"They charge him?"

"I'll know in the morning. Cram called me and told me."

"A'ight, let me know." I hung up.

CHAPTER 15

"*Goddamn,* baby …"

Casey was losing control. I had her up on my shoulders, while I stood up. Her back was supported by the wall in my bedroom. Her legs were wrapped around my neck while I was face deep in that pussy.

"*Ooooh shiiit!*" she moaned again.

My hands gripped her hips to prevent her from moving too much. My oral attack lasted for another ten minutes before I eased her down the wall. I slammed into her hard, missionary style. Her head was hitting the wall due to my aggressiveness, so I scooted her away from the wall a little bit. Then I continued slamming into her.

"Damn, daddy!" she screamed. Her eyes were watering up. "I'm 'bout … I'm 'bout to cum!"

"Yeah?"

"Yeeaah!"

I felt her left leg shake. She bit my sweaty shoulder, as I kept digging in that pussy. She was so wet, so tight. I was fuckin' her like I was fresh out the joint again.

Eventually I turned over, and brought her with me. I loved the way she rode dick. At first she rode me slow, real meticulous. She leaned down and stuck her tongue in my mouth. Kissing me hard, nibbling on my bottom lip while she rode me.

"Shit, daddy!" She sounded exhausted. She got on the bottom of her feet and started getting it like that. Bouncing up and down on my meat.

"Get it then," I said.

"Okay …"

She sped up her rhythm. Her shit was so juicy her pussy was farting.

***

When I jumped out the shower the next morning, Casey was still sleep. I applied my hygiene and got dressed. Justin texted my phone and said they charged Coach Kid. His bond was $75,000. So I had to shoot over to Justin's and give him ten percent to go grab the lil' nigga.

Coach Kid was starting to fuck up again. When I first met the lil' nigga he was at a crap house. I was there with Ace; he had to pick up some change from some nigga. The owner of that crap house was Coach Kid's uncle. When me and Ace approached the house, Coach kid and a few other thundercats were engaged in a cypher. And Coach Kid was getting off. I dug his swag. And his catchy vocals had me hooked.

266

I approached the young nigga and told him I was trying to get him in the studio. After that, it was on. I kept him close, but he'd always be in some bullshit in the streets. I thought he could be reformed. I told him if he'd calm down on the hot shit I'd sign him to my label. He eventually calmed down so I signed him.

I guess old habits do die hard because he was costing me money still.

I grabbed my car keys and I headed out of Casey's place. Although I didn't want to spend that Monday morning coming off seventy-five hundred, I wasn't going to just leave the nigga in there.

I pulled up to Justin's thirty minutes later. I called him to let him know I was outside. He came out and strutted to my car. *Freeway lookin'-ass-nigga,* I laughed to myself.

"What's good, bro?" he said, getting in my car.

"Slow motion." I handed him the money. "Talk to Cram?"

"Nah, not yet. I'ma—"

My phone rand and he stopped to let me answer it. "Yeah?" I answered.

"Hey, baby," Lisa said.

"Handlin' business. What's good?"

"Just walking in the shop. You stoppin' by my house later?"

"Yeah, baby." I let out a little chuckle.

267

"What's funny?"

"Nothin', baby. I'll be over there."

"Alright, don't be playin' wit' me."

"A'ight, I'll see you later."

"Okay." And we hung up.

"Selena?" Justin asked.

"Nah, Lisa," I told him. "So you 'bout to go gram him now?"

"Yeah."

"A'ight, I'ma bend a couple corners, bro." I shook his hand and he jumped out my whip.

***

I was pushing down Paseo later in the afternoon. I was headed south. As I was passing 39th Street, I noticed a black Yukon come into my rearview. They were riding me kind of close so I keyed-in on them. There were four Black dudes in the truck. I kept my cool as I grabbed my Ruger with the "extendo" from in between my seat and the floor panel.

Who the fuck is these nigga?

I passed Conoco and they were still behind me, but they weren't riding me as close as they were. I kept pushing south but I kept working my mirrors; they moved over to the next lane. They sped up a little and I slid my index finger across the trigger of my Ruger. But it was too late—I noticed someone hanging out the window with something stupid!

The shots sounded like percussion drums.

I leaned my head down and pressed the gas. My windows on the passenger side of my car were shot out. Both of my right tires were blown out. But I wasn't hit. It all happened so fast. The pussies responsible fled after that. They probably thought they hit me. Sparks flew from the two rims on my passenger side as I drove into the Gates barbeque parking lot.

I hurried and grabbed my phone, tucked my cannon in my waist, snatched my keys out of the ignition and rushed inside of Gates. I was dialing Ace's number as I entered the restaurant.

"What's up, bro?" he answered.

"Come get me, bro! I'm at Gates on Paseo!" I was pissed. The people in the restaurant looked at me like I was crazy. "I'ma kill them bitch-ass niggas!" I said more to myself than Ace. Then I hung up on him.

I couldn't believe I got pushed-up-on. I kept mumbling shit to myself as I made my way to a booth by a window. I was just sitting there scorching. Jaw clinched, looking out the window for any sign of Ace. The police could have pulled up at any minute.

"Spade, what's wrong?"

Shantel showed up out of nowhere with a drink in her hand. She must've already been here. I was happy to see the bitch.

"Shantel." I stood up. "Take me to the salon."

"Okay, okay, let's go," she said, sensing the urgency in my demeanor.

As we exited Gates, I followed her to her all black Challenger.

"What happened to your car?" she asked.

My Benz was parked scandalous in the corner of the parking lot.

"Got slid on," I told her. "Hurry up, let's get outta here."

She hurried and unlocked the doors and we got in. Baby girl peeled out of the parking lot like she had handles. Leaving the scene, I looked back at my Benz swiss-cheesed in the corner. I felt like I was leaving a piece of myself back there.

"You know who it was?" Shantel sounded like she was genuinely concerned.

"Nah." I dialed Ace's number and told him to meet me at the shop. After I got off the phone with him, I said to Shantel, "Not yet."

"Are you okay?"

"I'm straight." I turned up the stereo because I didn't feel like talking about the situation at the moment. She got the picture.

On the way to the salon I was trying to figure out who them niggas was. Then it hit me. Young Dice's cousins. *It had to be,* I figured. They came in my office a little too aggressive. And they left my office with their balls in their hands.

Me and Shantel finally pulled up to the salon. Ace was parked on the side of the building, leaning on the hood of his car.

"Right on, Shantel," I said, getting out of her car.

"It's coo', baby."

"What happened, cuzz?" Ace asked as I approached him.

"Some niggas slid on me. I think it was Young Dice's cousins."

"Let's go find these niggas." He made his way to his driver's door.

"Hold on, bro. We can't just move off emotions. Gotta find out fo' sho'."

"A'ight, a'ight. You coo'?"

"Yeah, I'm straight. Just wanted to let you know the play. I'ma jump in Lisa's whip and have Casey call and see if the boys got the Benz."

"Okay, bro." He leaned in and embraced me. "I'ma keep my eyes and ears open."

"Yep," I said, and we parted ways.

As Ace was leaving, Lisa stormed out of the salon. "Are you okay?" She hugged me tight. Shantel must've told her what happened.

"Yeah, I'm coo', baby," I said. She smelled good. "I'ma need to push yo whip."

"Alright." She broke our embrace. "I'll have one of the girls take me to the house."

"Coo'. I'll be over there later."

***

"So how long is the hold?" Casey was on the phone with the KCPD impound. I was sitting next to her on the couch. I had been at her house for about ten minutes. "Okay, thank you," she said before she hung up.

"What they say?"

"They're going to call when they release it." She let out a sigh. She looked frustrated. "How did you let them niggas get up on you?"

"Slippin'." I stood up and went over to look out the window. I was hot because I let them niggas get up on me. They could of DOA'd me."

"Well you can't afford to slip, baby." She walked over to me and stood behind me. She started rubbing my back. "Don't sweat it. I know you'll figure it out."

"ASAP," I said, as I turned and gave her a hug.

"I know that's right."

***

I was on the way to my spot. It was about four in the evening. When I got about fifteen minutes away from home, my phone rang. It was OG Casa. I knew what he wanted.

I turned my music down. "Yeah?"

"What's up, son? Heard you slippin' on yo' pimpin'." He sounded disappointed.

"Yeah, pussies caught me wit' my pants down."

"Find out who?"

"Not yet."

"Let me know if I can help." And he hung up on me.

Shortly after that call I pulled up to my spot. I jumped out my whip and headed in. Tossing my keys on the couch, I hit the kitchen and got my issue. Them niggas cheesing my whip had me *hot*. I rushed back in the living room and called Ace, but he still hadn't heard anything.

I threw my phone on my other couch out of frustration. I had to get control of my emotions before I made an irrational move. I grabbed my bottle and took a swig. Then there was a loud know at my door. *Who da fuck at my door?* I thought as I stood up to go see.

When I looked through the peephole I saw Kremensky and his partner. I opened it.

"What the fuck do yall want?" I said, standing in my doorway.

"Watch your fuckin' mouth," the other detective said.

"Fuck you," I retorted. "I can say what the fuck I want."

"Spade …" Kremensky smiled his devilish grin. "How are you doing?"

"I like women, Kremensky. Bitches. Coca-Cola bottle shapes. Titties, ass. Ever seen 'em?" I laughed at this nigga.

"Smalls, go to the car real quick. I got this," Kremensky said to his partner. His partner left, reluctantly. "Listen here, motherfucker." He leaned a little closer. His voice was right above a whisper. "I'll ruin your fucking life."

"I'm gone, man." I tried to shut me door. He stopped it with his arm.

"How would it look for your entertainment company if you were charged with the murder of Duece, Sonya, Nicole, *and* Jamie?"

"Get the fuck outta here." I was tired of playing with this nigga.

"Call this number." He handed me a card.

"For what?" I turned my nose up at the pig.

"You bring me five-hundred K within a week, or I'm bringing your Black ass down." He left me with that and walked to his car.

"Bitch-ass nigga," I said to myself as I closed my door.

I looked down at the card he gave me and tossed it on my living room table. That nigga had me in a jam. I couldn't afford to play with that clown. I started to call my lawyer but decided against it. Kremensky was playing a dirty game. I had to deal with his ass on another level.

Me going down for murder was definitely not an option. That would've fucked up my whole program. And I couldn't have that. I had to figure some shit out. In a hurry.

CHAPTER 16

I headed to Lisa's house. Had to take her car back to her. She'd probably want a nigga to spend some time with her but I had too much on my plate. In route there, my phone rang. It was Selena.

"What's up, baby?" I answered.

"Nothing. Where are you?" She sounded concerned.

"'Bout to take Lisa her whip. Then—"

"Are you okay? I seen your car on the five o'clock news."

"Yeah, I'm coo', baby. Some niggas caught me slippin'."

"You need to come home," said Selena.

"In a minute, baby. I gotta handle somethin'."

I didn't have time for her emotions. I knew she was concerned, but I had to stay focused.

"Your daughter needs you home." She started crying. "It's always—"

"Ay, I got this," I said. "I'll be over there tonight." Then I dunked on her. I wasn't ready for the verbal warfare.

I kept pushing towards Lisa's house. Just me and my thoughts. I had to get a grip on my situation. I had Santos to worry about, niggas sliding on me, Kremensky on my heels, and I still needed to get that bitch Maria. Not to mention managing my businesses and my personal life.

The game is a bitch.

I eventually pulled up to Lisa's at about six-thirty. I pulled in her driveway, parked and headed in her house. I inserted my key but the door was already unlocked. She must've seen me pull up.

When I walked in I didn't see her in the living room. She must've been in her bedroom. I headed that way.

"Baby, I need you to …"

When I opened the bedroom door my heart stopped.

"Fuck! Fuck! Fuuuuck!" I punched the door hard as a muthafucka.

Lisa was tied to a chair, naked. Her intestine sat on her bare thighs. Her lifeless facial expression looked horrifying. My heart told me to go untie her and hold her. My rationale told me to get the fuck outta there.

"I'ma kill that muthafucka!" I screamed as I punched the door again. She didn't deserve this.

I left the room because I couldn't look at her any longer. I called Ace.

"What's good, cuzz?" he answered on the third ring.

"Come over Lisa's and swoop me up."

"What's the deal?"

"Just drop what you doin' and come get me."

There was a knock at the door. *Who the fuck at the door?* I thought.

"I'm on my way, bro," Ace said, then we hung up.

I tiptoed to the window and tried to get a glance at who was at Lisa's door. I hoped it wasn't the boys. When I got to the window I peeked through the half-cracked blinds. It was Candace, Lisa's neighbor.

"Ain't this a bitch," I said to myself. I had to think of something quick. I finally walked to the door. "Who is it?"

"It's Candace," she said. I opened the door and she smiled. "Spade, hey."

"Come in." I grabbed her arm and pulled her in the house.

"What's goin' on? I been tryin' to call Lisa since five ..." She walked over to the couch and sat down. "... and when I seen the black Lincoln in the driveway I figured—"

"Black Lincoln?"

"Yeah, they were here for about twenty minutes and they left. Then you pulled up and—"

I cut her off again. "Candace, check game. You need to listen carefully." I took a seat next to her. She was a big chick, a cute one. "Whoever was in the Lincoln killed Lisa."

"What!" She tried to stand up but I pulled her back down on the couch. "No! This can't be."

278

"*Listen.*" I knew her and Lisa were good friends. I felt her pain. "I'm going to leave, and I need you to call the police and report this shit. But leave me out of it. Don't tell them you seen me pull up. None of that shit." I eyed her hard. Had to make sure she felt me.

"Why would they do this?" she asked herself as tears rolled down her chubby cheeks.

"I don't know …" I said, my voice trailing. Then my phone rang. It was Ace. "Yeah," I answered.

"I'm outside, bro." He must have already been in the area.

"Give me a second." I hung up the phone and turned my attention back to Candace. "Just tell them Lisa wasn't answering the phone so you let yo'self in. And you found her in her bedroom. Can you do that for me?"

I cupped her chunky chin and locked eyes with her. She cracked a sad smile and concurred with a head nod.

"Thank you," I said, then kissed her on the cheek and stood up to leave.

"Be careful," she said.

"Don't go in that room," I said back. "It ain't pretty."

***

"That nigga doin' his homework, bro," Ace said.

I was riding shotgun with him. We were headed to Casey's house.

"I'm hip. He probably got the scoop on all our spots. You need to tell Ashley to go to her mom's for a second, bro. Shit 'bout to get ugly."

"I'm on top of it."

We stopped at a red light. Some niggas pulled up beside us in a red Camaro. I clutched my cannon, index on the trigger. Ace did the same. They couldn't see us because Ace had limo tint on his BMW. But we could see them.

"Who the fuck is that?" Ace asked. The niggas kept looking our way. Trying to see through the tint.

"Let's find out." I started letting the window down but they turned right and skated off. "Get on 'em, cuzz."

"You trippin', bro. We got bigger shit to worry about." The light turned green and Ace kept going straight. "We don't even know who them niggas was."

He was right, though. I was tripping. I was letting my emotions cloud my judgment. I just wanted to down something because I was frustrated.

"I'ma call Shantel real quick," I said to myself. I dialed her number, and as it rang, Ace looked at me.

"Shantel?" he questioned.

"From the salon," I said.

He nodded. "Ah, yeah."

She answered on the second ring. "Hello?" It sounded like she was in her car. I noticed she turned her stereo down.

"Where you at?" I asked her.

"In traffic. What's up?"

"Somethin' happened to Lisa."

"She coo'?"

"Nah, I'ma need to holla at you, though."

"Let me know when and where," she said.

"A'ight, I'll call you." We hung up.

A few minutes later me and Ace were pulling up at Casey's. We hopped out and headed to her front door, and she had it open before we reached her front porch.

"What's goin' on, yall?" she said.

"You here by yo'self?" I asked, as me and Ace walked in the house.

"Yeah," she replied. "What's up, Ace?"

"What's good?" he said back.

I took a seat on the couch. Ace walked toward the kitchen. He was probably about to attack her snack cabinet.

"Is everything coo', baby?" Casey sat next to me.

"Lisa got knocked off today."

"Damn, that's fucked up."

"Damn right it's fucked up. These gualas ain't fuckin' around," Ace said as he came back in the living room munching on some Hot Cheetos. He took a seat in the lounge chair across from where we were sitting.

"I'ma need you to book a flight to Miami," I told Casey. "See if you can get one for tonight. I can't risk it."

"Miami? I'm not—"

"Casey. This ain't the time for that tough shit. Go to Sparkle's spot in Miami. I'ma see if Ranno or Stavi can take you there."

"Okay, okay."

"Shit 'bout to get real messy 'round this bitch," Ace added. "No place for a lady right now." He popped a few more Cheetos in his mouth.

CHAPTER 17

"You on the way there?" Ace said into in his phone. He was talking to Ashley, making sure she headed to her mom's like he told her. I was still riding with him; we were on the way to Selena's. "A'ight, call me when you make it."

I dialed OG Casa. Had to see if Casey and Selena could get some escorts.

"What's up, son?" he answered.

"OG, what's poppin'?"

"Brainstorming. I heard about what happened to Lisa, sorry to hear that."

"Right on," I said. "Check game, though. I need Ranno and Stavi to escort Casey and Selena for me."

"Where to?"

"Casey to the airport, Selena to her parent's house in California, Missouri."

"I'm on it," he said, and hung up on me.

I sat my phone on my lap and gazed out the window.

"Everything good?" Ace inquired.

"Should be."

"That's wussup."

He turned his music up and we kept pushing to Selena's house. The whole ride there I was thinking about Lisa. That shit hurt. I thought about all the shit that was going on—all this shit was popping off behind Maria. And we'd been so pre-occupied with Santos, that bitch hadn't even been the topic of discussion.

My phone vibrating on my hip took me out of my contemplation. It was Sparkle.

"What's good?" I answered.

"Heard the news. Got wifey on speed dial," she said.

"Hit her up." I hung up on her. *Damn right*, I thought.

"Who was that?" Ace asked as we finally pulled up to Selena's house.

"Sparkle. She 'bout to push up on Santos' wife."

We both opened our doors and started walking towards the house.

Ace said, "Tell her don't cut her down, bro. Have her hold the bitch so we can see if we can find out Santos' location."

We stopped walking and stood in the middle of Selena's driveway.

"You right, you right." I dialed Sparkle's number. When she picked up I told her the play. At first she was upset because she couldn't down the bitch. Then she finally agreed. "She wit' it," I told Ace after I hung up the phone.

We headed in Selena's spot. I used my key to get in. As soon as I opened the door, my daughter ran to me from the living room. She smiled the whole little run.

"Daddy, Daddy!"

"Hey, baby." I picked her little chubby butt up and kissed her fat cheeks.

Ace just stood next to me. He'd only been over Selena's a couple of times. So he wasn't as comfortable as he was over Casey's. I walked in the living room where Selena was. Ace followed behind me. I gave him the nigga-you-at-home look and he relaxed a little.

"What's up, baby?" Selena asked. She had *Glee* playing on the 62-inch flat screen. I sat next to her. Ace grabbed a seat across from us.

"Glee?" Ace laughed a little. "Straight up?"

"Yes, Glee. Samantha loves it. Ain't that right, mommy." She pinched our daughter's cheeks.

"Uh-uh," Lil' Samantha uttered, shaking her head no as she buried her face in my chest. Me and Ace laughed.

"I need you to do somethin' for me." I grabbed Selena's hand.

"What is it?" she countered.

"I need yall to go to yo parents' house for a minute." I sat Samantha down between us on the couch.

"Spade, what's going on?"

"I'm 'bout to step outside and choke, bro," Ace said, rising to his feet and heading outside. He hadn't tasted any chronic since he picked me up. It was about that time, I guess. Selena gave him an intense look as he left. I guess she was trying to understand the severity of the situation by reading his facial expression.

"Lisa got killed earlier," I told her.

"That's horrible," she gasped, covering her mouth with her hand.

"Yeah, that nigga Santos outta pocket, baby. I need you to take our daughter and shoot to yo people's spot."

"Okay, I'll pack some stuff."

"A'ight, I gotta bust this move real quick. I'ma have my peoples take you there."

"Who?" Her face turned into a frown.

"A friend. You'll be safe."

She grabbed our daughter off the couch and stormed off yelling, *"¡Esta mierda es aburrido!"*

"What you say?" I stood up, frustrated. I hated when she said that shit I couldn't understand.

"When will this shit be over with, Spade?!" She came back into view, empty handed. She must've put Samantha in her playpen.

"Soon," I said, walking toward her to give her a hug.

"Soon?" Her palm hit my chest, stopping me from getting any closer to her. I didn't move it; I just stood there. I knew she was frustrated too.

"We gon' handle this shit, baby." I grabbed her hand. "You'll be able to come back home before you know it."

"*Para de mentir mé*," she said, and disappeared back into the room.

"Just be ready when my people pull up!" I yelled as I walked away. I wasn't about to keep sitting here arguing with her.

"*¡Callate la boca!*" she yelled as I walked out the door.

***

Me and Ace were pushing to my spot. Selena was riding with Ranno, and Casey was riding with Stavi. I felt a little better because they were getting away from the madness. It was damn near ten o'clock at night. I'd been riding with my young nigga Ace the whole evening. That's what I loved about him. Whenever I needed him he was there. He'd drop everything and slide up on me.

As we were pushing, my phone rang. It was my lil' bro Army Tank. I turned the slaps down and answered.

"What's the deal?"

"Big bro, what's good, man?" he said. I heard some little bitches in the background. He must have been with some-thing hot.

"I'm riding wit' Ace," I said. "You got some lil' lollipops wit' you?"

"Yeah, yeah. Somethin' like that. They ready to do a couple backflips for a nigga."

"Sound good, nigga."

"Straight-out. Ay, tell Ace what's up wit' his fiancé's cousins."

Tank must have been zooming. He was always trying to get his dick wet when he was zooming.

"Man, sit yo hot-ass down, bro," I laughed.

"Yall too ugly, man," he returned with a laugh. "Ay, I'm gone though, bro. Hit me when you get the scoop on chica."

"A'ight, lil' bro. C-safe."

"Yep," I said, and he hung up.

"Who was that, cuzz?" Ace asked.

"Army."

"Where that fool at?"

"He wit' some little …" My phone rang. "… hold up, bro," I told Ace before I picked up my line. "What's good, Casey?"

"Spade … ! I'm not going to Miami." Her voice was cracking.

"What's goin' on?"

"That pussy Kremensky just … just pulled us over, and he …" She started crying.

What happened now? I thought.

"He what?"

"He violated me, Spade. He … he dug all in my pussy. Felt all on my titties."

"What the fuck did Stavi do?!" I was hot.

"He was told to stay in the car …"

I glanced over at Ace and shook my head. From the look on his face I knew he knew something was up.

"… he took me to the back of the truck and frisked me."

"Let me talk to Stavi."

He came on the line, his Russian accent thick. "Hello?"

"Take her to the airport, and make sure she gets on the plane. No matter what she says."

"Okay." He hung up.

"What happened?" Ace asked. We were finally pulling up to my spot.

"That nigga Kremensky molested Casey."

"Ah naw, my nigga. He gotta go."

We got out of the car and walked toward my front door. I glanced up and down my street as we were walking across my yard. Had to make sure we weren't getting laid on.

I opened my door and me and Ace slid in.

"What you got to snack on in this muhfucka?" Ace asked as he headed to my kitchen.

"Mm-mm," I said to myself, flopping down on my couch. That shit Kremensky pulled was beyond disrespectful. That nigga had to die. I just had to figure out how.

"You ain't got no Hot Cheetos in this muhfucka, cuzz?" Ace came into view, munching on some Pringles.

"It's all bad," I said to him. My phone started ringing. It was OG Casa so I picked up. "What's the deal?"

"What's this shit Casey's talkin' 'bout?"

"I'm on top of it."

"I hope so, son. It's your job to make sure she's safe." He was pissed. He didn't play when it came to his daughter.

"OG, I got it."

"You better."

I shook my head. That's all I could do.

"I got it," I said again.

"Okay," he said, finally. "Listen, some more of my friends are coming to town."

"That's what's up." I was glad the conversation took a turn.

"They'll be here in a couple of days. Real serious players. Compensation will be necessary."

"Alright, let me know."

"Okay, son." And he hung up.

"What OG talkin' 'bout?" Ace asked.

"More Russians are comin' in a couple days. Shit 'bout to get nasty."

"I'm ready my nigga." He cracked a devilish grin. I knew he was ready. But I didn't want him to be involved.

"I need you to fall back on this one, bro," I told him. He screwed his face up. I knew he wouldn't feel that shit.

"You got me fucked up." He hurried to his feet and started pacing the living room. "You know I been tryna get at the muhfuckas! They—"

"Bro ..." I cut him off. I had to get him to understand where I was coming from. "... I need you to make sure shit is straight at the salon, and the label. Plus you and lil' mama 'bout to get married. We got this shit."

Ace just stood there with an appalled look on his face. "I'm front line, bro. Fuck that." He reached in his pocket and pulled out his purp and Backwoods. "I'm rockin'," he said, then sat down and started unraveling the Backwood.

"No you're not, my nigga." I felt his passion but I needed him elsewhere.

"We'll see ..." he mumbled to himself.

CHAPTER 18

Two Days Later, Wednesday Morning

I was sitting in a hotbox parked in front of a vacant house, southbound of Kansas City. I picked up my phone and dialed the number on the card Kremensky gave me.

He picked up on the fourth ring. "Hello?"

I responded by giving him the address to the vacant property.

"Do you have all of it?" he asked.

"Five hundred K."

"Give me twenty minutes," he said and hung up.

I called Selena right after. I had to check on her. I'd been speaking with her and Casey frequently since they left.

"Hi, *papi,*" Selena answered.

"What's good, baby?"

"Nothing, 'bout to give Samantha a bath."

I missed seeing my daughter. And in a way, I hoped I'd see her again. I didn't know how the upcoming events would play out.

"That's what's up. Well, kiss her for me and I'll take to you in a minute."

"Okay."

After I hung up, I grabbed the duffle bag I had in my backseat. My Sig Sauer was already on my hip. I grabbed the duffle with the counterfeit money in it, stepped out of the hotbox and walked cautiously toward the vaco.

***

My phone rang.

"Yeah?"

It was Kremensky. "I'm outside," he said.

"Come in."

"Okay."

I walked to the window and peeked outside. Kremensky was getting out of a black Chevy Silverado pick-up truck. He was alone, and I noticed him coughing uncontrollably after he tossed his cancer stick on the sidewalk. He cautiously looked both ways before proceeding to the vaco. I backed up to a wall in the empty living room. I pulled my cannon out, picked up the duffle bag off the floor and stood there.

He finally made it to the door and knocked twice. My nerves were fucking with me but I pulled it together.

"Come in!"

The door knob turned slowly. He pushed the door open just as slow. "Spade," he called out.

"Come in, man," I said. My grip got tighter on my cannon.

Kremensky finally came into view. He had his police-issue .40 cal gripped tight in both of his hands.

I raised my cannon and pointed it at the door entrance.

Once he noticed me, he paused in the doorway. "Put the gun down, Spade," he said, easing further in the vaco. He pushed the door closed with his leg.

"Put yo shit down, nigga!" I aimed at his head. I wanted to just fire on his ass but it was too soon.

"Listen, I'ma put mine away. Just lower your weapon."

"Fuck I look like?"

"Alright, look …" He started lowering his cannon. "I'm putting it away." He secured it in his holster.

"How do I know after I pay you this money you'll quit fuckin' wit' me?"

"You don't know. You just have to trust me."

I noticed a few rats run from the empty living room to the used-to-be dining room.

"Trust you?" I echoed. I still had my biscuit pointed at him. "You gotta be fuckin' crazy." I cracked a devilish grin.

"Spade, listen, man." He offered a pitiful expression—one of exhaustion and frustration. "You won't even see me after today. I'm getting the fuck out of Kansas City. Missouri is too broke for me. Lousy pay, shitty benefits. Fuck Nixon, fuck Sly, fuck all of 'em."

I tossed the bag in the middle of the floor. "There you go." I lowered my cannon to make him feel a little better. Once I did that, he eagerly approached the duffle bag.

After he unzipped the duffle he smiled. "Is it all here?"

"Count it."

"Don't have time." He hurried and zipped the duffle bag up.

This desperate nigga stupid as fuck.

I pointed my cannon at his knee and fired.

BANG!

He dropped to the floor and grabbed his knee. "Fuuuuck!"

I rushed over to him and removed his .40 cal from his waist. "Why did you do that, you black son of a bitch?!"

"Shut the fuck up and sit up." I grabbed him by his collar and sat him up. I squatted down so I could be at eye level with him, and then I put my wetter in his face. "I been waitin' for this." I smacked him in the face with what would soon take his life.

"Aaagh!" He spit out some blood.

"This is for harassin' me when I was little."

SMACK!

"Come on, Sam. I'm sorry."

I smiled at that weak ass apology. "This is for puttin' yo cigarette out on the Benz." *SMACK!* "This is for molestin' my bitch." *SMACK! SMACK!*

His eyes rolled in the back of his head as I let him go. His head hit the hardwood floor with a thump. The barrel of my

Sig Sauer had his blood all over it. I rose to my feet and took a couple steps forward. I was standing by his bloody head, with my bloody barrel pointing down at his head.

"I'll probably see you there, bitch," I said before firing four shots in his face.

I dropped my cannon next to his body and left. I had my burners on so I wasn't tripping on the prints. I left the duffle bag with the counterfeit money there too. When his colleagues found him, they'd probably figure he was in some bullshit. Another dirty pig down.

CHAPTER 19

Stepping out my shower, I quickly applied my hygiene and got dressed. The hotbox I was in earlier was burned down to the frame on some train tracks on the northside of Kansas City. I had to hurry and meet Selena. She had Santos' wife held up at a location off St. John.

As I was walking out my front door my phone rang. It was OG Casa.

"Yeah?" I answered as I opened my car door. I had to pull out my Chevy Impala I bought a couple years ago since my Benz was still in the impound.

"They're here," he said, referring to the Russians.

"That's what's up." I started my engine.

"Get wit' me when you and Sparkle get finished." And he hung up.

That nigga don't miss a beep.

I pulled out my driveway and skated off. I couldn't wait to holla at Santos' wife. Once I slapped that bitch around a little bit, she'd tell me where Santos and Maria was.

***

When I pulled up to the address Sparkle gave me, it was eleven in the morning. I called Sparkle to let her know I was outside.

"Pull in the driveway," she said. "It wraps around to the back of the house."

"Yep." I hung up and did as she suggested. I was eager. That nigga Santos was doing too fucking much.

As I was stepping out my whip, I noticed Sparkle was standing in the back doorway, motioning for me to come in. I slammed my door shut and walked toward the house.

"What's good?" I asked Sparkle as I passed through the doorway.

"She's back there," she said, nodding her head toward a hallway leading to the front of the house.

I extended my arm toward the hallway. "After you."

Sparkle led the way and we stopped at a small bedroom about ten feet from the back door. Sparkle opened the door and I saw a beautiful Latina tied to a chair. Baby was fine.

I hurried to her and backhanded the taste out of her mouth. A tear rolled down her face as she looked up at me emotionless. *Damn, this bitch fine.*

"Where's Santos?" I asked her.

She just gave me a cold stare. No words.

"That's how she's been since I got her," Sparkle said with her hands on her hips. She had an irritated look on her face. "Should've just killed he bitch," she whispered to herself.

"Nah, she just a little stubborn."

I smiled at our captive. I pulled my Desert Eagle from my waist and smacked her in the face with it. She screamed as blood flew out of her mouth.

"What do you want!" she hollered.

I was glad I got a reaction out of her. "Santos," I said.

She laughed uncontrollably at that. "*Sobre mi cuerpo.*"

I looked back at Sparkle to see if she knew Spanish. "What this bitch just say?"

"Over my dead body," Sparkle translated.

I turned back to the tough cookie and smacked the shit out of her again. "Bitch, where is he?"

"*¡No te voy a decir ni madre!*"

I looked back at Sparkle.

"She said she's not telling you shit."

I laughed at this tough ass ho and started pacing the floor. Inside I was really frustrated.

"We need to just kill this bitch," Sparkle said as she pulled out her 9mm with a suppressor on it.

"This bitch is gon' tell me somethin'." I grabbed Sparkle's cannon and placed the business end on Ms. Santos' knee. "So you ain't got nothin' to tell me?"

She just gave that same cold stare.

I pulled the trigger—and blew a piece of her knee out.

She screamed at the top of her lungs and started bouncing in the chair. Out of my peripheral I noticed Sparkle smiling. The tough cookie started crying harder.

"¡*Mi esposo te va matar*!"

"Strip this bitch naked and kill her," I said to Sparkle as I left the room.

"I got this bitch," I heard Sparkle reply as I was walking down the hallway to the back door.

I was pissed because that bitch didn't give me the info I wanted. I still had a plan B. After I got into my whip, I picked up my burnout cell phone and called Santos' number. After I dialed, I started my whip and backed out the driveway. I was pretty sure Sparkle was in that house having a ball with Santos' wife.

"Hello?" Santos answered as I was turning off the block his wife would breathe her last breath on.

I did my best Santos impersonation. "Hey, my friend."

"What do you want?"

"A million."

"You're a funny man." He laughed a little.

"Am I?"

"Yes, yes. Why would I give you a million?"

I hurried and slammed on my brakes before I crossed the intersection on Truman Road and Hardesty. Somebody in a gray new booty Monte Carlo were high speeding the police.

Whoever was in that Monte had about six cop cars trailing them. *Them niggas is hot,* I thought.

After the coast was clear I proceeded across the intersection.

"Did you hear me?" Santos asked.

"You'd give me a million if you wanna see that pretty ass wife."

He put his phone down for a second, then came back on. "Where is she?"

I gave him the address, told him he had two hours, and I hung up on him. It felt good to have one up on his bitch ass. After I hung up on him, I sent Sparkle a text telling her to get up outta there.

I eventually made it to the highway. I jumped on I-70 East and headed to the salon. Twenty minutes later I was pulling up. When I parked, my jaw clinched as I glanced at Lisa's empty parking spot. I took a deep breath, hopped out of my whip and headed in the salon.

Upon entering, it looked like it was running like a well-oiled machine. Shantel really stepped up.

"What's up, baby?" Shantel said as she washed a young lady's hair.

This bitch flirtin' in front of customers n' shit.

"What's good?" I walked back toward the office. "Let me holla at you," I told Shantel as I walked back. The other stylist spoke and gave their condolences as I passed them.

I walked in the office and I felt rage inside. I missed Lisa.

"What's up, babe?" Shantel asked, entering the office.

I turned around from Lisa's desk to face her. "Don't flirt in front of customers lil' mama." I had to put her in her place. "You hear me?"

"Umm, yeah I'm sorry." She frowned.

"Have a seat, man." I motioned for her to sit in a chair across from Lisa's desk, right next to my desk. I leaned on Lisa's desk.

"What's goin' on?" she asked.

"You think you can handle runnin' the salon?"

She smiled. "You know I can handle it."

"Do you want to?"

"Yes, Spade."

"A'ight, I'ma step up and handle the business side, and you step up and run the salon. That means your pay steps up too."

"I'm wit' it, ba—" She stopped herself. "I'm wit' it, Spade."

"Right on." I got up off the desk to make my exit. "After I get all of Lisa's shit out of here, I'll give you a key to the office."

"That'll work." She rose to her feet.

"Keep that key to the main door, that's yours. Alright?"

"I got you, Spade."

"A'ight, I'm gone." I motioned for her to step out of the office so I could look it up.

"You gon see, I'm ride or die." She winked at me as she sashayed out the door.

CHAPTER 20

Two and half hours later I was sitting in my office, downtown. I had company as well—OG Casa, Ranno and Stavi, Sparkle, and a couple of the Russian hitmen that came into town.

We were waiting on the phone call from Santos. It finally rang.

"Yeah?" I answered. I pointed to my phone to inform everybody Santos was on the horn.

"You're dead. You know that, don't you?" He was unusually cool for someone who just discovered a dead wife.

"Is that right?"

"That's right."

"Check game, homie. I got a proposition for you."

"You have a proposition for *me*?" Santos laughed like I was a peon. "I *give* propositions, you fucking mutt."

I can't wait to get my hands on this bitch ass nigga, I thought to myself.

"Sound good, my nigga." I laughed back. "Deliver Maria, or your sweet little daughter is next."

"You're a funny man."

"Try me," I said. "Call when you're ready to deliver her." I hung up on him.

"You sure you got the location for his daughter?" I asked Sparkle.

"Yep. Got a couple of guys on her every move as we speak. She has her own personal driver and everything."

"How old is she?" I thought about lil' Samantha. I had to shake that shit, though.

"She's twelve, I think," Sparkle said.

"It doesn't matter how old the lil' bitch is," OG Casa chimed in. "This shit is chess, not checkers."

"I'm wit' that," I said.

"Good," OG Casa simply stated. "A'ight, well I'm gone, son. We're ready for the next play." And with that, he, Ranno, Stavi, and the Russian hitmen left.

"Don't trip, this shit'll be over soon," Sparkle said. She got up from the chair she was sitting in and went to my mini fridge to get herself a drink.

I couldn't help but notice how thick she was as she bent down to open it.

"You want somethin'?" she asked, looking back over her shoulder.

I tried to play if off like I wasn't staring at her ass. But I knew she saw me. "Nah, I'm cool," I said, as I played like I was fucking with my phone.

She grabbed a Mike's Hard Lemonade and took a seat. "Don't let your conscience interfere when it comes to this deadly game."

"What you talkin' 'bout?"

"The daughter situation."

"I'm good."

"You're a good father. So you're apprehensive."

"I'm good," I said again.

"Okay."

"Okay," I said back.

"Well ..." She rose to her feet. "I'ma go. Call me when I need to make that move."

"I will."

***

Later that night I was at my house chilling. I had showered and I was just kicking back watching the tube. Different thoughts ran through my head as I thought about the upcoming events. Then my phone rang, pulling me out of my temporary trance.

"Yeah?" I answered.

"What's good, bro? Right on for the bond money." It was Coach Kid.

"It's all good. I still gotta holla at you, though." He had some explaining to do. I just didn't have time to get into it at that moment.

"I know, bro. But ay …"

This nigga. I just knew he was about to ask me for some money.

He went on. "… Young Dice's cousins was the ones that slid on you."

I sat up a little bit. "Straight up?"

"Straight up, bro. That's the word on the blacktop."

"Right on for the intel, my nigga."

"It's all good," he said. "You know I got you, bro."

"Fo' sho'. I'ma get up off here, though. Call Ace for any business wit' the label. He holdin' it down."

"A'ight, bro. I'm gone."

"Yep."

Them niggas gon' get it, I thought as I laid back and closed my eyes.

CHAPTER 21

"My father, Carlos. Also known as Kutz," said Maria. I looked at her like she was crazy. "You killed him."

She pulled a gun out of her purse. And pulled the trigger— BANG! BANG! BANG! *I heard screams, felt sharp pains in my chest and stomach. I was blacking out.*

She stood over me.

"The mother of your seed. Selena. She's next. See you in hell," *she said.*

I lost consciousness.

"Fuck," I uttered to myself as I woke up from that fucking dream. I looked at the clock on my nightstand and it read 10:00 a.m. I felt beads of sweat all over my frame.

I quickly got out of my bed and jumped in the shower. Had to get my day started. The shower felt relaxing. I sat in that bitch for about thirty minutes.

After I got out of the shower and got myself together, I called Army Tank. He picked up on the fifth ring.

"What's the deal?" he answered, sounding like he was sleep.

"You ain't got up yet?"

"I'm up. What's good?"

"I need you to call Coach Kid for me and get on top of that, bro. I got some other shit I gotta handle, so I need you."

"I'm 'bout to hit him right now, on mommas."

"Right on, cuzz." I loved that lil' nigga. "I got somethin' for the tummy too, bro."

"I'm rockin' regardless." He sounded offended by me offering to pay for something I knew he'd do for free. All on love.

"Still, nigga. Tell Ace to get wit' you, bro. And C-safe."

"Okay, cuzz."

I tossed my phone on my bed and ran downstairs to my kitchen. I had to put something on my stomach. I looked around my fridge but didn't find anything I felt like eating. I closed the refrigerator door and decided to go to Denny's. I had a taste for a Grand slam.

***

Twenty minutes later I was pushing down I-70 West. I was vibing to a slow jam mix as I cruised. Then I noticed a detective's car riding my ass. *Fuck*, I thought.

He hit the cherries on me quick. I thought about my cannon stashed behind my car stereo system. Even though that secret compartment hadn't been exposed, I still thought about the possibility. I slowly pulled over to the right shoulder.

As I sat on the side of the highway, I still had my foot on the brake. I thought about taking him on one. That Kremensky shit kinda had me ouked. *Nah, this just a random stop. Was I speedin'? Calm down, nigga.* All kind of shit ran through my head.

"Driver! Turn your engine off!" His voice boomed through the intercom on his pig-mobile. I was undecided, though. I sat there, losing control a little bit. "Driver! Turn you engine off, now!"

I finally did. I relaxed a little as I reached and grabbed my license and registration. When the detective got out of his car I kind of panicked. It was Kremensky's partner. I thought about starting my whip and skating off. But that would've made me look guilty, I figured.

"Step out of the car, Mr. Wright," he said when he made it to my door.

"Was I speeding?"

"Just step out of the car." He opened my door with his left hand, and had his right hand on his weapon.

"You ain't got shit better to do?" I asked as I stepped out to oncoming traffic. The highway was packed. I walked to the back of my vehicle.

"Turn around and put your hands behind your back," he said, grabbing my arm to turn me around.

"What the fuck did I do?"

He clinked one cuff on my wrist. "You're wanted for questioning."

"I need to have someone come get my vehicle," I told him.

He looked at me for a few seconds. I guess he was trying to figure out if he should let me call somebody. He cuffed my other wrist and said, "Where's your phone?"

"My right pocket."

He reached in and got my shit out. "Number?"

"Damn, I could've dialed it."

"Number?" He was getting impatient.

I reluctantly ran Ace's burnout number to him. He put the phone up to my ear, and I waited for someone to answer. Six rings later I got the answering machine. *Fuck.* I couldn't afford to have two of my whips in the impound.

"Can you call right back?" I asked.

"One more time," he said, and dialed the number and put it back on my ear.

Ace picked up on the second ring. "What's the deal?"

"Gettin' p and j'd. I need you to come grab the whip off 70 West."

"In a minute. This number will be off tonight." And he hung up.

"Let's go, muhfucka," I told the pig as I walked to the back door of his car.

CHAPTER 22

I was sitting in the KCPD headquarters waiting to get booked in. I'd been handcuffed to the waiting bench for about forty-five minutes. Sitting next to me was a smoker who kept proclaiming he was Ray Charles' nephew. Next to him was a young lady who looked to be in her early twenties. Sitting across from us on the other bench was a young nigga who looked terrified, but was trying to keep it together. Next to him were two more young ladies. I assumed them two hoes and the one on the bench I was waiting on were together.

"Bitch, I told you that was one of the secret shopper muthafuckas," the young lady across from me said to the one on my bench.

"Whatever, bitch. We was supposed to hit the other store anyway."

"This is fucked up yall," the one that looked the youngest said. "My momma gon' beat my ass."

"Yall ain't gotta worry 'bout nothin', understand me," the smoker chimed in. The young tenders screwed their faces up at him. "Yall might as well get up wit this pimpin'. Ain't gotta worry 'bout stealing clothes, just countin' dough. I'm from the bloodline of Ray Charles. My money long."

"Samuel Wright!" one of the police officers yelled my name as he was opening the gate.

"That's you, young blood," the smoker told me. Like I didn't know.

"Straight up?" I gave him a look that told him to shut the fuck up.

An officer came to uncuff me, and I was escorted back. I was instructed to stand near the wall. I started taking my shoe strings out of my shoes, flipped my pockets inside out, and took my belt off. I knew the drill. The pig took my shit to one of the counters.

"Turn around," he said when he made it back to me.

I turned and put my hands on the wall so he could frisk me. After he made sure I had nothing on me, I turned back around.

"Go over there." He pointed to the metal detector.

And the officer that was standing by it got my attention. "Come on."

After I walked through, I had to go to the fingerprint machine. An officer grabbed my right hand and scanned every part of it. Once he was satisfied with the print, he told me to sit in the cage next to it and wait.

I sat inside the cage waiting. My feet were already sweating because I didn't have any socks on. *I'm throwing these muh-fuckas away asap,* I thought as I looked down at my Nike Air Max's.

I wondered why I was down here. It could've been for a number of reasons. This shit had me hot, straight up. I had shit to handle on the blacktop, and I was stuck downtown on some bullshit.

"Just tell me how much my muthafuckin' bond is!" The smoker was at the counter going off. "My money long, god-damn it."

"Okay, honey," the female officer behind the counter said.

"Wright, this way." An officer opened the cage and motioned for me to go to a little area by the metal detectors to snap my mugshot.

After I took it, I was escorted to the same cage I was sitting in. I had to wait there until they printed out my wrist-band. About ten minutes later the same officer opened the cage, put my wristband on and escorted me to the side where they held people with state charges. Once I was safely secured in the holding tank, the officer slammed the cage door shut.

I glanced around to make sure I didn't have any prob-lems. I didn't notice any niggas I could've possibly had issues with so I relaxed a little. I walked over to a phone to make a couple of calls. I tried to call OG Casa and Ace, but I didn't get an answer. *Fuck.* I walked over to the bench in the middle of the floor and sat down.

Sitting in this muthafucka brought back memories. Last time I sat downtown I got wammied. The niggas in here were watching some movie on TNT. I tried to watch it to funnel my frustration. It wasn't working. Plus that muh-fucka was filthy. It smelled like gas, must, and old bologna sandwiches.

I got up from the bench, took to a corner and laid my Black ass down. I took one of my shoes off to use for a pillow. I laid back and closed my eyes.

***

"Wright!" an officer yelled out. I quickly sat up, put my shoe back on and got up to make my way over to him. I glanced at the clock and read five-thirty in the evening.

"Wussup?" I said once I made it to the pig.

"Detective wants you. You know which way." He moved out of the way to let me walk out.

"Fuckin' clown," I said to the nigga as I walked past him. When I made it back in the hallway, Kremensky's part-ner was standing by the bar-door that led to the elevator. I walked over to him.

Once I made it to him, he cuffed me, opened the door, led me to the elevator, and we got on. We went down a few floors and got off. He led me to an interrogation room.

"Wait here." He closed the door behind me. I took a seat and waited for his ho ass to return.

A few minutes later he was back in the room with a Miranda in hand.

"You might as well take that muhfucka back where you got it," I told him.

"I'm detective Smalls." He took a seat, ignoring my comment. "I want to ask you a few questions about Kremensky."

This muhfucka, I thought.

"Look, Mr. Smalls," I smiled. "I would love to chat, but I would like my legal representation present."

He offered a cheap grin, then rose to his feet. "Okay, Mr. Wright. We'll be in touch."

And he left. A couple minutes after that, an officer came and escorted me back upstairs.

CHAPTER 23

I was released the next morning. I was waiting on Shantel to come get me. I walked up the street to the gas station. I had to grab something to snack on. I wasn't fucking with them punk ass sandwiches in the police headquarters.

After I smashed a slice of pizza from the gas station and slammed a strawberry soda, I sat on the curb and started putting my shoelaces back in my shoes. It was going on noon, so the heat was starting to kick in.

"You need a ride, baby?" some chick asked, jumping out of an old Dodge Stratus. Petite build, pretty face.

I was good, though.

"I'm straight, lil' mama," I retorted.

"You sure?" She stood there with her hands on her hips.

I smiled at her assertiveness. "I'm good, baby girl."

She smacked her lips and walked into the gas station. I continued lacing my Max's. A few seconds later Shantel dipped into the parking lot. I rose to my feet and strolled to her car.

"You coo'?" she asked as I got in.

"Cool as I can be." I reclined in her passenger seat. "Take me to my crib."

"Show me the way, baby."

This bitch don't know when to stop, I thought to myself.

***

"Have a seat," I told Shantel as we walked through my door. She walked over to my wrap-around leather couch and sat down. "You can turn the tube on. I gotta take a shower."

"A'ight."

I walked upstairs toward my bedroom. As soon as I made it through my bedroom door I started stripping out of my clothes. I threw everything I had on in the corner of my bedroom floor. All the way down to the socks. Them muh-fuckas was getting tossed in the trash, fast.

I rushed to my bathroom and turned my shower on. I needed to get back in motion quick. Had to get that shit with Santos handled. I jumped in my shower and started washing up. While I was in there I started thinking about Kremensky's partner. I made a mental note to get up with my lawyer soon.

Fifteen minutes later I was jumping out of my shower. I grabbed my dry towel and walked into my bedroom area, drying off.

"I don't know how to work the remote," Shantel said, suddenly standing in my doorway, eyeing me down. I was still standing there drying off, dick swinging. She looked at it and licked her lips.

"I'll be ready in a minute anyway."

"Nice setup." She made her way into my room. She pretended like she was admiring my décor.

"You mind, lil' mama?"

"You act like I ain't never seen a man naked before." She walked over to me. "Let me put some lotion on your back."

She grabbed my dick instead.

Don't do it, Spade.

Shantel dropped to her knees right in front of me and shoved my dick in her mouth.

"Damn," I said, succumbing to the warmth of her mouth.

"You taste good," she said.

I looked up at my ceiling, trying to fight the urge. I wanted to pull my shit out of her mouth and tell her to get the fuck downstairs until I got dressed. But it felt too good.

The young tender started really getting into it. I grabbed the back of her head and tried to make my dick disappear in her mouth. She gagged and I smiled. *Young ass bitch*, I thought. But she got right back on it.

"Mmm," she hummed on my dick while she played with my balls. When she broke for air she made a demand. "Cum on my tongue."

She didn't have to tell me that shit because I already planned on it. A few minutes later I exploded in her jaws. And baby girl didn't stop until the last drop went down her throat.

"You got some mouthwash in here?" she asked, walking to my bathroom like a champ.

"Yeah," I simply stated. I followed behind her so I could wash my dick off with a soapy rag.

After she gargled a few times. She spit the mouthwash in the toilet and flushed it. "I'll be downstairs waitin' on you, baby."

***

"You know you was outta pocket, right?" I said to Shantel. She was taking me to meet Ace so I could get my whip.

"I couldn't help myself," she said.

Lyin' ass bitch, quit fakin'.

"I got a lot goin' on," I said. "I really ain't got time for the drama."

I thought about that crazy ass ho Tamika, how she stalked me and made me think she was having my baby. I hoped Shantel didn't have the same intentions.

We stopped at a red light and Shantel turned in her seat to face me. "That's not what I'm on," she said. "I'm tryna be your slave. I'm here to cater to you. Whatever you need …"

My dick started waking up and my ego expanded a little.

"… a slave can only serve one master. And I want my master to be you."

"I hear you, lil'—"

My phone started ringing. It was my lawyer calling me back. I had called him before me and Shantel left my house. "Hold on," I told her, and then I picked up. "Yeah?"

"Sam, what's going on?"

The light turned green and Shantel got on the gas.

"Just got out of a twenty earlier," I said into the phone. "Kremensky's partner questioning me and shit."

"Yeah, I heard about Kremensky. It is what it is. I'll look into it, so don't sweat it."

I always felt better when I talked to Puzzo.

"What else is going on?" he asked.

"Got shot at about four days ago."

"What?!"

"I'm coo'. They got my Benz on hold in the impound. I need you to call and see what's up wit' the hold."

"I'll do that when we get off the phone. You know, Sam, you've been doing good for the last year or so. Don't get yourself jammed up in some bullshit with some fucking senseless thugs. You're smarter than that."

"I got it. Call me back and let me know what's up wit' the Benz."

"Okay."

Me and Shantel were pulling up to Ace's spot as I hung up the phone.

"Alright, baby, I'ma head to the shop," Shantel said as I was opening the door to get out.

"Coo', I'll call you later." I closed the door and baby girl slid off.

"You good, my nigga?" Ace asked, walking out of his front door.

"I'm good." Me and him embraced. "Kremensky's partner questioning a nigga."

"That's silly."

"I'm hip. How the label shit goin'?" I asked, changing the subject. I didn't want to keep talking about the world collapsing around us.

"Everything good, bro. Justin's mastering Young Dice's shit as we speak."

"That's what's up." I walked over to my car parked in Ace's driveway. Ace followed. "Let me know when he gets finished," I said, opening my driver door up. I sat inside.

"You know I got you, bro," Ace said.

My phone rang again. It was Puzzo.

"Yeah?"

"You can go pick it up tomorrow morning."

"Right on, Puzzo. I appreciate ya."

"No problem. I'll be in touch." And we hung up.

"Who was that?" Ace asked.

"Puzzo. He said I can get the Benz out tomorrow."

"I got you, bro."

That nigga was a life saver. He understood I had so much going on at that time.

"Good lookin', my nigga." I started my engine. "Well, I'm 'bout to shake, my nigga. In a minute."

"C-safe," Ace said, and walked back toward his house.

I backed out of the driveway.

CHAPTER 24

The next morning I was in my spot chilling. I was a little frustrated because Santos hadn't called yet. I guess he needed an incentive. I picked up my phone and called Sparkle.

"Talk to me," she said.

"It's a go." I was telling her to make that move on Santos' daughter.

"Give me a minute," she said before hanging up.

Right after I got off the phone with Sparkle, Santos called.

"Yeah?"

"Maria's out of town. She'll be back in a couple days."

"She better be back tomorrow," I said.

"Where's your patience?"

"With my damaged lung."

"You should—"

"You got until tomorrow." I dunked on his bitch ass and tossed my phone on my bed.

I went over to my closet to find something to put on. As I was going through hangers of clothes my phone started going off again. *Santos' ho ass,* I thought as I strolled back to my bed.

I picked up my phone and looked at the screen. It was Ace. "What's good, bro?"

"I dropped the Benz off at the shop," said Ace. "They'll be done with it in three weeks."

"Right on, my nigga. What you 'bout to do?"

"Gotta meet up wit' OG Casa."

"A'ight, in a minute."

I tossed my phone back on my bed and went back to my closet and found something to put on. I tossed the clothes on my bed and jumped in the shower.

***

"I'm 'bout to pull up," I said.

"Alright, I'm 'bout to come outside."

I ended the call and tossed my phone in my passenger seat. I was sitting outside of the salon. I pulled up to give Shantel the office key. When she came out the door she sashayed to my whip. *Damn this young bitch fine,* I thought to myself. *Body bangin'.*

She made it to my passenger door and opened it. I moved my phone so she could sit down. The young tender smelled good.

"What's up, daddy?"

"Slow motion. Here's the key." I handed her the office key.

"Thank you. Are you okay?"

"I'm good. How's business?"

"Business is good. I got us."

I couldn't help but look at her juicy lips. I thought about her head game. Tremendous.

"That's what's up. Well, I'm 'bout to shake. Call me if you need somethin'."

"Okay, bye." She leaned in, kissed my cheek and got out my whip. I watched her juicy ass bounce all the way to the salon before I shook it.

***

I pulled up to my spot and I saw Sparkle's rental parked in my driveway. The dark tint concealed whoever was inside. I pulled in beside her, parked and went over to her driver side window.

"Say hello, Spade." She had a devilish grin on her face.

I looked in the back seat and seen a little Mexican girl who looked to be about twelve or thirteen. "That's what's up. So where you takin' her?"

"A safe house close by. I'ma have one of the Russian's sit with her."

"Coo'. We're going to meet up here at six. You gon' be here?"

"I'll be here." She started her engine. "This will all be over soon."

And she pulled out of my driveway.

I walked into my house and flopped on my couch. I got to contemplating about possible outcomes to all the madness that was going on. One thing was for certain—I wasn't resting until that bitch Maria was iced.

After another ten minutes of contemplating I finally turned my TV on. As I was flicking through the channels my phone rang. It was Santos.

I picked up. "Yeah?"

"You're a dead man."

"Such harsh words. What's up, my friend?"

"Where's my daughter?"

"Safe."

"What do you want?"

"Are we negotiating, my nigga?"

"I have Maria," he said. "Let's meet."

"Where's your patience?" I liked fucking with him.

"I have Maria!" he yelled. He was losing his cool. "Now let's meet, now!"

"I'll call you with the location. If you do anything outta pocket your daughter will be dead."

I hung up on him.

Then I heard three knocks on my door. I reached under my couch and pulled out one of my AK-47s. I eased over to my door.

"Who is it?!" I yelled before I made it to my door.

"It's Ace, nigga!"

I looked out of my peephole and relaxed when I saw it was him.

"What's good, cuzz?" I said after I opened my door. I moved to the side to let him come in.

"What's really good, my nigga?" he threw back, as he eyed my rifle. "Comin' to the door wit' a suey and shit." He went to my couch and took a seat.

I shut my door and went over to slide my chopstick back in its resting place. I flopped on my couch and said, "I'm a little on edge, bro. Just got off the phone with Santos."

"What's the play?"

"Supposed to be meeting him soon. Trade off wit' his bitch-ass. His daughter for Maria."

"When?"

"Don't know yet. We'll figure it out, though."

"You know I'm supposed to be rockin', bro."

I knew that was coming. I just didn't know how all that shit was going to play out. I needed Ace alive and well.

"I need you to handle the two-step, bro. Plus if somethin' happen to me, I need you to look out for lil' Samantha."

"If somethin' happen to you?" He screwed his face up. "Nigga if somethin' happen to *you*, everybody gettin' it."

My nigga.

"Nah, bro," I said. "You gotta keep a coo' head. Keep the op in rotation."

"Man, what you got to drink in this muhfucka." He rose from the couch and strolled to the kitchen. I shook my head and smiled. That nigga was a handful.

"Bring the bottle in here, bro!" I yelled out.

"Army took care of that shit, too," he informed me, as he came back into view, tugging on a bottle of Remy.

"That's what's up. You give him some snaps?"

"Yeah. I dropped off ten racks to him last night." He handed me the bottle and sat down.

"Good lookin', bro."

***

"Yall 'bout to pull up?" I asked OG Casa. I was still at my house. I had taken a power nap after Ace left earlier that day. Now it was about six in the evening.

"Yeah, we're about fifteen minutes away."

"A'ight, see yall in a minute."

While I waited for OG and the crew to pull up, I decided to call and check on Selena, Samantha, and Casey. I called Casey first. She told me she was about to walk to the beach and chill out for a little bit. She asked me when would it be safe for her to come back to Kansas City and I told her as soon as I knew, she would.

When I called Selena she said she was with her mother in her garden. Doing some feminine shit. Lil' Samantha was sleep, but she was good and that's all I cared about. Selena asked me the same thing Casey asked me. I told her the same thing I told Casey. She said some shit in Spanish I didn't understand and hung up on me. I loved that fire in her.

After those calls I looked out my front room window and I saw OG Casa and the crew coming down the block. I opened my front door and stood in the doorway. They pulled in my driveway two trucks deep, hopped out and made their way in my house.

It was OG Casa, Sparkle, Ranno, Stavi, and three Russians I didn't know.

"What's up, son?" OG Casa said as he passed me.

"Slow motion," I sad.

Ranno and Stavi just nodded their heads when they passed me. The other three Russians didn't even acknowledge me. They had their game faces on. *Rude-ass muhfuckas.* Sparkle was the last one through the door.

"What's up, cuz," she said.

"What's poppin'." I closed my door behind her.

Everybody took a seat on my wrap-around couch except the three Russians I hadn't met yet. They took positions around my living room.

331

"So has Santos called yet?" OG Casa asked.

"Yeah. He said he has Maria and he's ready to meet," I told him.

Sparkle got excited. "Let's do it."

"Where should we meet this nigga?" I asked.

"It need to be at the right location," said OG Casa.

"I'm hip. What about the Royals Stadium?"

"Too empty. There should be people around," Sparkle said.

OG Casa agreed. "She's right."

"Then we go when they have a game," I said.

"Nah, we need to get this shit over with." OG Casa rubbed his chin in deep thought.

I was getting irritated. "So whatchu suggest?"

"What's today, Friday?" OG Casa whispered to himself. Then he finally said, "We should meet him at the park Sunday."

"Swope?" I screwed my face up at him. That was the last place I wanted to meet Santos at.

"Yeah," OG Casa said.

Sparkle let out a doubtful sentiment. "I don't know …"

"I'm wit' Sparkle. Too many pigs," I said.

"That's good. That way we ensure it's a clean switch. The park will be packed so we'll blend in."

I thought about it for a brief moment. And the shit was starting to make sense to me. "That might be a good idea."

"So I have to babysit this rug rat for another day?" Sparkle asked.

"It's the best play," OG Casa said.

My phone started going off so I excused myself to answer it. Sparkle and OG Casa were still debating the play. Ranno and Stavi just listened. I made my way to my kitchen. One of the Russian hitmen was blocking my way like it was his house.

"You wanna scoot the fuck over, my nigga?" I couldn't believe this muhfucka was looking at me like I was outta pocket. He stared at me for a few seconds before he moved to the side. When I made it in my kitchen, I answered my phone. It was my lawyer. "Yeah?"

"What's up, Sam?"

"Kickin' back. What's goin' on?"

He didn't sound too happy. "You need to lay low. Detective Smalls is investigating you."

"Lay low?"

"You know what I mean. Move accordingly. No funny business."

"A'ight, right on." I really didn't feel like hearing this shit. I was on a mission.

"Alright, I'll keep you posted."

I put my phone in my pocket and walked back into my living room. OG Casa and Sparkle were still rapping.

"So when should we call him with the location?" Sparkle asked OG Casa.

"Sunday morning," I said as I sat down on the couch.

"Good idea," Stavi finally chimed in. *That fuckin' accent,* I thought to myself. "That way he can't prepare."

"Uncle's right," Sparkle smiled.

"A'ight, coo'," OG Casa said. "We'll meet back up here tomorrow night." He rose to his feet and everybody else did the same.

"A'ight, I'll holla at yall tomorrow," I told the crew. Then I eyed the Russian that had blocked my way. "You too, tough guy."

He gave me a weird look and walked out the door.

"Almost home, cuz," Sparkle said before leaving.

OG Casa stopped at the doorway. He lagged behind to get a word with me. "You talk to Casey?" he asked.

"Earlier," I replied.

"She good?"

"She coo'. Was on the way to the beach when I talked to her."

"Good, good. Men are masters of their worlds, and they put their lives on the line to protect it. See you tomorrow."

CHAPTER 25

The next morning I was riding with Ace. We were leaving one of our safe-houses in our 'hood. I had to grab some more weaponry for the next day—the day that bitch Maria would breathe her last breath.

"Slow down, cuzz," I told Ace as we were getting on the highway.

"Whatchu talkin' 'bout? I'm goin' the limit."

Maybe he was, maybe he wasn't. Either way we were too dirty to get fucked with by the pigs for something in our control.

"Just makin' sure, my nigga," I said.

"You know I got handles anyway. Take they ass on one if they jump behind me."

"Nigga, I know you got handles. I taught you. That ain't the point."

"Quit trippin', cuzz. You wouldn't even be sittin' in that passenger seat if you thought I wasn't good behind the wheel."

He was right. I didn't ride dirty with a muhfucka that didn't have handles.

"Plus," he added, "we done been on too many missions."

"What you got in the deck?" I asked, changing the subject. That Santos shit had a nigga on edge. It had me a little too paranoid.

He showed me a CD. "Bo, *Till My Casket Drops*."

"Damn right." I turned his sounds on and we let C-Bo preach the whole way to my spot.

***

"A'ight, bro, call me when you make it to the studio," I told Ace. He was sitting in my driveway about to leave. "You coo'?"

We had downed damn near a whole fifth of XO. I knew cuzz was cut; I had to make sure he was straight.

"I'm good, my nigga," he replied with a slur. As soon as we made it through my door a couple of hours prior he went straight to the freezer for the bottle.

"Sound good, nigga."

"Real talk, bro. I'm good. Ay?" He gave me that silly ass look he always gave me when he was drunk. "You know that's some bullshit, that I ain't rockin' on them gualas. I like soft tacos too, nigga." He opened his door and got out.

"We got it, bro." I laughed a little because he always had them moments.

336

"Shit ain't funny." He looked at me like I was crazy.

"You right, bro. My fault."

"Damn right it's yo fault, NIGGAAH!" He pushed my forehead with his index finger.

"Bitch-ass nigga!" I screamed as I grabbed him by his collar and slammed him on the hood of his car. I didn't want to put my fists on him because he was like a little brother to me.

"Fuck off me!" He tried to escape my grip but he was too weak. He was squirming and kicking.

"You gon' chill out, nigga!"

"Fuck you mean, nigga?" He gave me an even crazier look.

"You heard me, nigga." I tightened my grip on his collar with both of my hands. My knuckles were digging in his neck and under his chin.

"Wait 'til I get off this car," he threatened. I let him up to test his rec. He was talking too much shit.

He bounced off the hood and squared up with me. "What's poppin', nigga?"

"This ain't what you want, my nigga," I said with my hands down at my sides.

"Nigga, I ain't little no more. Square up!" He was coming closer and closer.

Drunk ass nigga.

"Chill out, bro," I warned him.

I guess he didn't give a fuck about my warning. He rushed me and caught me with a solid one to my chin. I immediately threw my hands up.

"Okay, cuzz." I jabbed him twice in his face. He tried to dodge my punches but he was too drunk. I didn't give a fuck if he was drunk or not because he touched my chin with his fist.

He tried to rush me again and threw a wild hook. I sidestepped and countered with a right hook to his head. He staggered and fell to the ground. My anger told me to stomp him out, but I was raised to never stop your homie when he's down. I was raised to let yo homie back up on his feet if he falls while yall banging. Give him a fair chance.

"Get up, nigga!"

He was on his hands and knees in my front yard, trying to get back to his feet. He took too long so I walked over to him to help him out. "Get yo bitch-ass up!" I grabbed the back of his collar and pulled him to his feet. "You good?"

"I'm good, I'm good." He acted like he was done. As soon as I let his collar go he took another wild swing at me. I ducked and he staggered to the ground again.

"Man, get yo drunk ass up." I left him there and walked in my house. I left my front door open for him to come in when he made it to his feet.

***

An hour later me and Ace were in my living room talking to each other.

"You lucky I was drunk, nigga." Ace smiled.

"You lucky you was drunk," I countered.

"Whatever, cuzz. My fuckin' head is pinging." He made an ugly face when he touched the spot on his head I hit him on.

"Should'a sat yo hyper-ass down somewhere."

"Sound good." He rose to his feet. I guess he was about to shake. "I'ma bend a couple of corners."

"A'ight, bro." I stood to embrace him. "Sorry about that shit earlier, bro."

"It's good, cuzz. I was outta pocket."

We broke our embrace and he headed for my front door.

"Call me when you get where you goin', cuzz."

"A'ight, cuzz."

I followed behind him to see him out. I watched him pull out my driveway and went back in my house and flopped down on my couch. It was going on five in the evening. I was about to pick up my remote and do a little channel surfing, but my phone started ringing.

"Yeah?" I answered with a bit of frustration. I didn't recognize the number.

"What's up, bro. You heard about Young Dice's cousins …" It was Coach Kid. "… them niggas got found slumped. Somebody bodied them."

"Ay, nigga. You wanna chill out on my fuckin' line?" I couldn't believe this little loud mouth muthafucka.

"My fault cuzz, I'm slippin'."

"Damn right you slippin'."

"I'm sayin', though. Somebody got to him before I did. You know I was about to rock on them niggas for you, bro."

Fuckin' clown.

"Straight up?" I said.

"Hell yeah, nigga. Anyway, you know I'm almost done with the project. Got 'bout three tracks left."

"Get up wit' Ace."

"I know, I just wanted to holla since I ain't talked to you in a minute."

"I'm good, young fella. I'm 'bout to bust this move, though. I'ma get wit' you in a minute."

"A'ight, cuzz. One love."

After I got off the phone I changed my mind about the channel surfing. I had to get the fuck out of the house. I ran upstairs to grab my keys. Then I walked out my house and jumped in my whip.

***

I decided to push to the Plaza. As I was on my way to the Cheese Cake Factory I sent a text to OG Casa and Sparkle. I told them to be at my house at 10:00 p.m.

Five minutes later I was parking at the restaurant. I hopped out, made my way in the restaurant, and was seated at a table on the upper level. Someone yelled my name from a couple table down. A female's voice.

"Spade, what's up!"

I couldn't see who it was at first. The restaurant was packed. Then she stood up and switched her thick ass to my table in a strapless sundress. *And baby was bustin' all out that muhfucka.* It was Tanya, Ashley's cousin. When she made it to my table she helped herself to a seat next to me.

"Wussup?" I said.

"You. Whatchu doin' here by yo'self?" She tried to put on her sexy voice.

"'Bout to put somethin' on my stomach. Who you wit'?" I glanced in the direction she came from.

"A couple of my bitches."

"That's wussup …"

My food got brought to me by a sexy ass pink toe. I thanked her and she left. Tanya rolled her eyes.

"So what yall 'bout to get into?" I figured I'd make small talk with the young tender.

"Nothin'. Why?"

"Just askin'." I started digging in my plate. A nigga was hungry.

"Mmm, I guess, boy. You—" She accidentally knocked the spoon and butter knife that was sitting on the table on the floor. "My bad, baby." She started to reach down and get it but I stopped her.

"I got it, lil' mama."

I scooted my chair out a little, and reached down to grab them. They landed right by her feet. When I got down to get them she opened her legs and exposed her meaty pussy. She didn't have any panties on under that sundress.

"It gets sooo wet. You don't know what you missin'," she said as she raised back up.

"Yeah?" My dick started to wake up. I was tempted to see what her chocolate ass was hollering about. One of her friends ended up walking to the table.

"Bitch, you just gon' leave us at the table? Rude ass." She put her hands on her hip like she was upset. She was kinda cute too. Yellow bone, 5'8", built like a brick house. Her mini skirt revealed thick thighs.

"Whatever, bitch." Tanya smiled. "Spade, this my friend Alexis. Alexis this is Spade."

"What's good?"

"High." She smiled. Then she turned her face up at Tanya. "Hurry up," she told her, before switching back to her table. I eyed that thang the whole way.

"You like what you see?" Tanya asked.

"Whatchu talkin' 'bout?"

"You can fuck us both if you want to. You know how to get in touch wit' me." And she left my table and joined her friends.

CHAPTER 26

Later that night I was sitting in my living room with OG Casa, Sparkle, Ranno, Stavi, and the same three Russians. We were going over the game plan for the next day.

"I say we let Spade ride wit' me and Santos' daughter," Sparkle said.

"Nah, Spade should ride wit' me," said OG Casa.

I asked Ranno, "How many Russians are available?"

"Seven, including me and Stavi."

"Somebody needs to already be there," I said.

"He's right," OG Casa said to Ranno and Stavi. "Have two of your guys there an hour early."

"And what time are we meeting him?" Sparkle asked.

"Two," I said.

"Too late," Sparkle countered.

"We should meet him at twelve," OG Casa said.

"I say one," Sparkle shot back. OG Casa looked her upside her head. She offered a sarcastic smile in return.

"I think twelve is coo'," I agreed with OG Casa.

"Whatever." Sparkle got up and went into the kitchen.

Bitches, I thought.

"Sparkle, in here!" Stavi said. That was the first time I'd seen him show emotion. Sparkle walked back in the living room like a little girl in trouble and sat down. She had no retort for her uncle.

"Go 'head, Casanova," Ranna said to OG Casa.

"I say have two guys at the park by eleven. The rest of us will follow each other there," OG Casa said.

"So Spade will ride with you," Ranno said to OG Casa. "Me, Stavi, and two of our hitmen will ride together. And Sparkle, Santos' daughter, and the last hitman will ride together."

"Sounds good to me. How 'bout yall?" OG Casa asked me and Sparkle.

"That's coo'," I countered.

"That's fine," Sparkle said.

"Okay," Ranno offered.

"So what time are we calling Santos?" Sparkle asked.

"In the morning," I said.

"You should call him now and tell him what time you'll call in the morning," she replied.

"She's right?" Stavi said.

"Yeah, make the call, Spade," OG Casa said.

"A'ight."

I stood up and walked toward the kitchen to make the call. The same Russian was blocking my way again. I gave him a look that told him I didn't have time to play with his bitch-ass. He moved to the side. *Muhfucka crazy*, I thought to myself.

I dialed Santos' number as I was stepping in the kitchen. He picked up on the third ring. "Talk to me, dead man," he said.

"That's funny. I'll call yo bitch-ass at ten in the morning wit' the location."

"I'll be waiting, dead man." And he hung up.

I walked back in my living room and took a seat. "Told him I'd call in the morning at ten."

"Coo'. Meet me at the dealership in the morning," OG Casa told me.

"A'ight. Who's gon' take those?" I eyed the bag of AK-47s that me and Ace picked up earlier today. They were sitting by the front door.

"We'll take 'em," Ranno said.

"You sure?" OG Casa asked him.

"Yeah, we got it," Ranno countered.

OG Casa addressed the whole room. "Alright, everybody at the dealership in the morning at ten-thirty."

Everyone started making their way out of my front door.

***

An hour later Shantel called my phone. It was going on 11:30 p.m.

"Yeah?" I answered.

"What's up?"

"Chillin'. What's the deal?"

"I have all the girls' booth fees. Whatchu want me to do wit' it?"

"Just put it up for now." I didn't have time to deal with this shit at this point in time.

"You sure? I don't mind bringin' it by."

I bet yo hot ass don't.

"Nah, you good. I gotta handle some business in the morning so I'm 'bout to lay it down."

"I hope you dream about me."

"That's cute."

"I'm fo'real, Spade."

"Sound good."

"Well, since I can't come through there, talk dirty to me while I play wit' my pussy."

I dug her aggressive nature but I was good on all that shit.

"Shantel."

"What?"

"I gotta go, baby girl."

347

"Alright. Call me tomorrow." She sounded disappointed.

"I will." And I hung up on her.

I ran upstairs to my room. Had to jump in bed and get some shut-eye.

CHAPTER 27

"You ready to make the call?" OG Casa asked me.

We were sitting in one of his trucks, parked outside of his dealership. Sparkle, Santos' daughter, and one of the hitmen were parked right beside us. And next to them, Ranno, Stavi, and two other hitmen were parked. The last two hitmen were already on the way to Swope Park. Each truck we were in was a black Tahoe. Heavy tint, heavy weaponry.

"Yeah," I answered OG. Then I picked up my phone. "… Calling his ho-ass right now."

It was going on 10:45 a.m. Santos picked up quick.

"Where?"

"Swope Park at noon," I told him.

"Swope Park?" He sounded disappointed.

In the summertime every Sunday in Swope Park was like a music video or some shit. All the hustlas, playas, pimps, and killas brought out their latest whips to show them off. I'm talking millions of dollars' worth of vehicles out there. Jam-packed. And the women showed up too. It was like a ritual in Kansas City. Fast cars, fast women. Exotic whips, exotic chicks.

"Yeah, Swope Park." And I hung up. "He'll be there," I told OG Casa.

Thanks to Sparkle each truck had walkie-talkies in them. OG Casa chirped everybody to make sure everyone was on the same channel. Once he did that he pulled out of the parking lot, and both trucks followed.

"You ready, son?" he asked me as we were driving west on Truman Road to get on 71 Highway.

"Hell yeah, I'm ready."

"Remember, Maria's gon' hop in wit' the two Russians that are already there ..." He was reminding me about the last minute preparations we came up with when we all made it to the dealership earlier. "... Don't do shit to her until we get her to the location."

"I got it, OG." I couldn't wait to kill that bitch.

"This shit'll be over soon."

He turned an O'Jays disc up and we proceeded to the park. About fifteen minutes later were all getting off on the 63rd Street exit.

"Sparkle, yall good?" OG Casa radioed her.

"Everything good," she responded.

"Ranno?"

"Yes, yes," Ranno said into the radio in his heavy accent.

"Okay, remember what I told yall at the dealership," OG Casa said. "Don't trip on the police when we pull up. They're just here to escort people in and out."

"Ten-four," Sparkle joked.

"Okay," Ranno said.

As we got closer I noticed the muthafucka was already getting packed. When we made it to the light on Swope Parkway, OG Casa turned right. The other two trucks did the same.

"That muhfucka clean," I said offhandedly when I spotted an orange Denali on 26-inch rims. Behind it was a royal blue Benz with all white leather interior. Niggas was bringing they toys out.

OG Casa made it down by Freeway Liquor and turned left; so did Sparkle and Ranno. Then OG Casa got up on the curb and hit a U-turn. So did Sparkle and Ranno. We pushed back up on Swope Parkway and made a sharp right. We headed back up toward the park entrance. There were about ten cars in front of us.

OG Casa turned his music down and checked with Sparkle and Ranno again to see if they were cool. They said they were. I looked at the time and it was 11:40 a.m.

"Almost in," I uttered. The line was moving along.

"Almost over, *shiiid*," OG Casa countered. We were about to pass the pigs and OG Casa got back on the walkie. "Be coo' yall."

We skated through the entrance with no problems. The park was already getting packed. It was about seventy-five degrees outside. It felt good. As we were driving through the park people were pulling in the grass, getting their parking spots.

"There they go over there," I said to OG Casa.

The Russians were parked next to the second shelter. OG Casa hopped the curb and headed that way. I worked the mirrors to make sure Sparkle and Ranno followed suit.

Once we all lined up with each other I looked at my phone to make sure Santos hadn't called.

"Should I call him?" I asked OG Casa.

"Nah, he'll call."

I let down my window to holla at Sparkle, who was parked right next to us on the right. The other two Russians were on the left of us. And Ranno and Stavi were parked next to Sparkle. Four black Tahoes. All heavily armed, all ready to kill something.

"What's up wit' the lil' girl?"

"She's coo'," Sparkle said after letting her window down. "Not very talkative. But at least she stopped crying."

OG Casa said out of nowhere, "Look at these young hoes. Damn shame."

I looked to the left and saw some young girls on the roof of their car popping their asses. The little bitches was thick, too.

"Broke-ass bitches!" a nigga yelled from the passenger window of a tan Benz truck riding past.

"Fuck you, pussy!" one of the bitches yelled, holding up her middle finger.

"This nigga Santos need to—" My phone rand so I stopped mid-sentence. It was him. "Yeah?"

"I'm here."

"Come by the second shelter. If you don't pull up in ten minutes we outta here."

He hung up on me.

"He 'bout to pull up," I told OG Casa.

"Get ready, yall," OG Casa said to the walkie.

"Ten-four," Sparkle said.

"Ten-four," Ranno said.

"Okay," the driver of the other truck said.

"Keep yo coo', Spade. Make the trade and let's get the fuck outta here," OG Casa said.

"A'ight," I said.

Five minutes later I noticed three black Lincoln Town Cars coming onto the grass. They parked about ten to fifteen feet away from us.

"I think that's them," OG Casa said to the walkie.

I checked my Glock to make sure I had one in the head. Then my phone rang.

"That's you?" I said into my phone.

"Yeah."

I opened the door to get out. OG Casa did the same. Once we stepped out, two Mexicans stepped out of one of the Town Cars. I didn't know which one was Santos. I eyed both of the niggas intently. I figured the older looking one was Santos. He had on a tank top, black slacks, and some slick ass loafers. He had a long scar on his face that started by his right eye and ended at his cheekbone. His hair was pulled back in a ponytail. He stood about 5'6", looked a little stocky, and had one visible tattoo on his left arm.

He reached in his pocket and pulled out a phone. He dialed a number and my phone rang.

"What's up, muhfucka?" I answered.

"Where's my daughter?"

"Where's Maria?"

He told the Mexican standing next to him something. Then the other Mexican opened the back door and pulled Maria out of the back seat.

"Be coo', son," OG Casa told me.

My blood started to boil. I thought about her trying to knock me off. She had an emotionless look on her face. She still looked the same too. She had on jeans and a halter top. I heard a door open behind me and I noticed the Russian riding with Sparkle pulling Santos' daughter out of the truck. He brought her to me and I grabbed her arm.

"Your daughter," I told Santos.

He clinched his jaw and fist and said, "Bring her to me."

"Halfway, muhfucka." And I hung up my phone.

"We got you," OG Casa said as me and Santos started walking toward each other with our gifts.

I looked around to make sure nobody was paying attention. Everybody was busy kicking it, in their own worlds. Them muhfuckas didn't have a clue that it could possibly be a blood bath right next to them.

"You know you're dead, right?" Santos said when we made it to each other.

"Tell me somethin' I ain't heard before, bitch-ass nigga." I wanted to pull my Glock from my waist and cut his ho-ass down.

I grabbed Maria as I handed him his daughter.

"Spade, I'm so sorry," Maria said to me. I ignored her.

"*Mija* ..." Santos pinched his daughter's cheek.

"Be careful," I said to Santos before I turned around and walked back to my crew.

"See you soon," I heard him say as I got further away.

Once we made it to the trucks OG Casa grabbed Maria and put her in the truck with the two Russians. I glanced at Sparkle as I went to get in the truck me and OG Casa rode in. She didn't even look my way. She had her eye on Santos and his caravan. I jumped in the truck and watched Santos pull off. I couldn't wait to get to the spot Maria would die at.

OG Casa finally got back in the truck and said, "Let's get the fuck outta here."

CHAPTER 28

"I can't wait to kill this bitch!" I said out loud.

OG Casa looked at me sideways and said, "Calm down."

We pulled out the park and headed straight on 63rd. Sparkle was behind us, the two Russians that had Maria behind her. And Ranno was behind them.

Sparkle's voice came in through the walkie. "Spade."

I picked it up out of the cup holder and replied, "What's poppin'?"

"This shit is almost over."

"Not exactly. We still gotta get Santos."

"We'll get him."

OG Casa grabbed the walkie from me. "Sparkle, yall can chat after we get where we goin'." He put the walkie back in the cup holder, turned his O'Jays up and kept pushing.

We got to 71 Highway and turned right. As we were driving down 71, I thought about how I was going to kill Maria. Would I pistol whip her first? Would I cut her fucking throat? Would I just give her a head shot and get the fuck up outta there? All kinda shit was running through my mind.

We pulled up to the red light on fifty-eighth Street and stopped. OG Casa turned his music down. He picked up the walkie.

"A'ight, Sparkle. Go 'head and turn off. Ranno, follow Sparkle. You other two stay behind me."

The light turned green and OG hit the gas.

"Ten-four," they both said.

I looked in my mirror and watched Sparkle and Ranno disappear. The truck that had Maria in it stayed behind us. We split up just in case we had a tail.

We kept zooming down the way-way. About ten minutes later we heard a loud *boom*.

"What the fuck!" I yelled.

"Shit!" OG Casa said.

I looked back and seen the truck that had Maria in it explode. OG Casa pulled to the right shoulder and we hopped out to get a better look. The truck was roasting to the frame.

"Let's go, OG." I jumped back in the truck. OG Casa did too.

He grabbed the walkie. "Sparkle and Ranno, go to Spade's house."

"What's goin' on?" Ranno asked.

"Just meet us there," OG Casa countered.

"Ain't this a bitch!" I yelled.

***

"So the truck just fucking blew up?!" Stavi shouted. He was pacing back and forth in my living room. He looked like he was more pissed-off than me.

"To the frame," I said in disbelief. I couldn't believe that shit had happened.

"Santos probably put some C-4 on her," Sparkle said.

"C-4 for what?" I asked.

"So he wouldn't have to worry about her giving him up," OG Casa said.

"Fuck!"

I got off my couch and went to my kitchen. The Remy was calling a nigga. I grabbed the bottle and returned in my living room.

"We're not leaving 'til Santos is dead," Ranno said. "Those were two of my best guys."

"Not a problem," OG Casa said.

They were sitting down making plans for the Russians to stay. I was sitting down hot as a KC summer. I was supposed to be watching that bitch beg for her life. She was supposed to be swallowing the barrel of my cannon, serious business.

"I'll be back," I told them, as I headed upstairs to my room. Had to be in solitude for a minute.

When I got in my room I sat my Remy bottle on top of my dresser. I took my shirt off and walked over to my full body mirror. I got up close to it as I observed the bullet wounds on my torso.

"Can't believe this shit," I said to myself. I sat in that fucking mirror for about five minutes. Tripping out because I wasn't responsible for Maria's demise.

I heard a soft knock at my door. It pulled me out of my trance. "Come in."

"You coo'?" Sparkle asked, coming into my room. I caught her eyes as they traveled to my bullet wounds.

"Yeah, I'm coo'." I walked over to my bed to grab my shirt. *Did she just bite her bottom lip*, I thought as I put my shirt back on. "Just wish I could'a killed the ho, that's all." I sat down on the edge of my bed.

"I feel you …" She retrieved my bottle from the dresser, brought it to me and sat down next to me. "… but at least the bitch is dead."

"I can dig it." I hit my poison.

"I just got off the phone wit' Casey too. She's catching a flight tomorrow."

"That's wussup." I thought about Selena and my daughter.

"Who is that in the picture wit' you and Ace?" She pointed to a picture I had sitting on my dresser.

"My nigga Duece."

"Never seen him before."

"He got killed about two and a half years ago." I hit my bottle again.

"Sorry to hear that."

"Yeah, I miss my nigga." I rose to my feet. "I'ma head downstairs."

"Alright. Well I was just checkin' on you, cuz." She got up too. "Where's your restroom?"

"Down the hall," I said as I walked out of my room.

CHAPTER 29

When I got back downstairs OG Casa and the Russians were still going over a game plan for Santos.

"You coo', son?" OG Casa asked me after I flopped on my couch.

"Yeah, I'm coo'."

"Just checkin'. Sparkle said Casey will be back tomorrow."

"I know." I picked up my phone to call Ace. He didn't answer.

"Since we're staying, might as well get acquainted with some American women," Ranno said with a wicked grin. Everybody busted out laughing except the other Russian hitmen. I guess them niggas were taught to show no emotions at all times.

"You a fool," I said. I needed that laugh. I sent Ace a text and told him in code Maria was dead. "You cool, OG?" I asked, holding up a Remy bottle. I knew he didn't fuck with anything but Crown Royal, but I thought I'd give it a try.

"Nooo …" he exaggerated. "… to the Royal, I'm loyal."

"Sound good."

"So what you got up for the rest of the day?" I asked O.G.

"Get them settled in, and try to get a location on Santos. Stavi already got the tag numbers to them Lincolns, so we'll start there."

"Let me know the play. I gotta at least put *one* in him. Dead or alive," I said. I thought about Lisa and Young Dice.

"I know, son," he said.

I looked at the clock on the wall and it was 2:30 p.m. *I wonder how's business at the Salon. Is Justin at the lab? I know the pigs all over the truck on the way-way.* All kinda shit was running through my head.

"We need to take them trucks back," OG Casa said.

"Yeah, let's do that. Where's Sparkle?" Ranno asked.

"I'll get her." I rose to my feet and ran upstairs.

I hung a left at the top of my steps and walked toward the bathroom at the end of the hall. When I got closer to the door I heard a moan. *What the fuck?* When I made it to the door I put my ear to it. Had to make sure I wasn't tripping.

"Aah ... mmm ... yes, yes," she moaned. She had to be playing with that pussy. "Shit," I heard her whisper.

I knocked on the door three times.

"Sparkle!" I called.

I heard some rumbling and she finally said, "Yeah ... uhm .. wussup, cuz?"

"They ready to take the trucks back," I told her.

"A'ight. Give me a minute."

"A'ight."

I walked back downstairs in disbelief. I couldn't believe she was tryna get a nut off in my bathroom.

"What is she doing?" Stavi asked when I made it back downstairs.

"Using the restroom. Here she come."

"And Spade, just 'cause Maria's dead don't mean this shit's over with. We still gotta take care of Santos," OG Casa said.

"I'm already knowing."

"Yall ready?" Sparkle asked when she made it downstairs. She tried to avoid eye contact with me.

"Yeah, let's go," Stavi said.

They all made their way out of my house. "Yall be careful," I said.

"In a minute," OG Casa offered before getting into his truck.

I watched them pull out of my driveway before I shut the door. I walked back to my couch and sat my ass down. Then I picked up my phone and called Selena.

"Hello?" she answered.

"What's up, baby?"

"Nothing, watching TV." She sounded happy to hear from me.

"You ready to come home?"

"Stop playing with me. You know I am."

I missed her voice. "You want me to drive out there to get you?" I asked.

"Yes. Is it over?"

"We'll talk about it. I'll be out there in the morning."

"Okay, *papi*. I love you."

"Love you too."

I called Casey next. "What's up, baby?"

"Chillin'. What you doin?"

"Watchin' the waves, thinkin' 'bout you."

"So what time you landin' tomorrow?"

"Sparkle told you?" I thought about Sparkle's freaky ass in my bathroom getting off.

"Yeah, she told me. Is that a problem?" she joked.

"Stop playin' wit' me. I'll be at KCI 'round five."

"I'll be there to get you."

"Okay, baby, love you."

"I love you, too."

I couldn't wait until both of my Bonnies touched down. I grabbed my remote, flopped on my couch and turned my TV on. The movie *Book of Eli* was on HBO so I kept it on that. About ten minutes in, my phone started ringing. It was Shantel.

"Yeah?" I answered.

"What's up?"

"Cold chillin'. What's good?"

"'Bout to close up the shop in a minute."

"Everything good?"

"Of course." She acted like that was a no-brainer.

"I'm proud of you, lil' mama."

"You know I got you, daddy."

"You can bring them booth fees by if you want to."

"Give me a couple hours." She sounded excited.

"A'ight."

I lounged back on my couch and closed my eyes. Figured I get a little power nap before she pulled up.

CHAPTER 30

A phone call woke me up from my sleep.

"Yeah?" I answered.

"I'll be pulling up in about twenty minutes," Shantel said. I looked at the clock on my wall and it ready 4:15 p.m.

"A'ight."

I hung up the phone. My mouth was feeling a little tangy from that cat nap so I went upstairs and hit my grill. Then I went back downstairs and headed to my kitchen. That Remy had my stomach growling.

I snatched some ham and cheese Hot Pockets out of my freezer and heated them up. Once they were done I poured me some lemonade and took my ass back to my living room and sat down. I turned to the news channel to see if anything was mentioned about the explosion. Then there was a knock at my door.

I grabbed my .38 Special I kept in my couch cushion and walked to the door. "Who is it?"

"Shantel!"

I opened the door and saw her fine ass in a mini-skirt and tank top. I moved out of the way so she could come in. She eyed my cannon. "Whatchu got that for?"

"Habit," I told her.

I closed the door, locked it and strolled back to my spot on my couch. Shantel sat across from me. I started devouring my Hot Pockets.

"The booth fees," she announced, placing an envelope on the center table in my living room.

"Right on." I bit the second Hot Pocket. "You hungry?"

"I'm good." She smiled.

I tossed the last piece of the Hot Pocket in my mouth and washed it down with the ice cold lemonade. "Be back," I said, taking my plate and cup to the kitchen. I washed them out.

When I came back in the living room Shantel had my Remy bottle turned up. She hit that muhfucka like I would.

"Damn, lil' mama," I said as I sat down.

"I can't hit yo bottle?" She turned her face up at me.

"You coo'."

My eyes went to her juicy titties and thighs. Then I eyed her juicy lips. Everything was juicy on little mama.

"I miss you," she said as she scooted next to me. She smelled good too.

"Yeah?"

"Yes." She leaned in and kissed me. I kissed her back. During our lip tease she reached down and rubbed my dick. My shit was rock hard.

I unbuckled my belt and unzipped my shorts. I lifted up and pulled my boxers and shorts down. She held my dick in her hand and started stroking my shit in her palm.

"Whatchu want me to do?" She smiled. She knew what time it was.

"That's funny."

She bent down and put her warm mouth around my dick. She got up on her knees on my couch as she sucked my dick from the side. I reached over and palmed her juicy ass cheeks. She didn't have any panties on. I penetrated her pussy with my fingers. It was wet and tight.

"*Mmm*," she hummed on my dick as she bobbed up and down. Baby started kissing the head of my shaft. Then she went down to my balls and started licking them; she jacked me off at the same time.

Baby was gettin' it!

She looked up at me and asked, "You ready to fuck me yet?"

I was tempted but I was cool. Had to go a different route with this young tender. I didn't want to fuck too fast.

"Not yet," I said.

She shoved my dick back in her mouth. I guess me declining made her more aggressive. I'm talking two hands, no hands—*gettin' it.*

"Damn," I uttered.

She let out a small laugh. "You like that, daddy?"

"Damn right."

I felt the eruption coming. The volume on my TV was tuned out in my mind until I heard, "Breaking news."

My attention was now on my TV. Shantel was still going to work. Then an image of 71 Highway popped up on the screen. They showed the burning Tahoe, engulfed in flames in the middle of the way-way. Then the reporter came back on.

"A massive explosion happened earlier today on 71 Highway. Authorities believe it happened around 12:30 or 1:00 …"

As Shantel sucked, I felt the lion trying to escape the cage.

"… we will have more information by later on tonight. But what we do know is …"

The lion escaped and I busted in Shantel's mouth. She stayed on my shit until she got the last drop. I gripped the back of her head two-handed as my body tensed up.

"… two bodies were recovered from the truck. They are believed to be males. Tune in later tonight for more information."

I quickly shoved her head off me and looked at the TV screen in disbelief. *Two male bodies? Only two? What the fuck?*

Maria …

369

Deception's
PLAYGROUND
3

Chapter 1

I was at Ace's wedding reception. Everyone was here except Sparkle; she went back to Miami a couple of months prior.

"You look good, best man," Tanya came over and said.

I was sitting at a table with Ace, OG, Casa, Justin, Cram and Coach Kid. The DJ was spinning a Jeezy record.

"Let's dance," she offered.

"I'm coo', lil' mama."

She was outta pocket. Casey *and* Selena were at this muhfucka.

"Come on, lil' mama, let me see what yo thick ass talkin' 'bout." Cram stood his drunk ass up. Him and Tanya got lost on the dance floor.

The wedding reception was jumping like a club. My nigga Ace really went through with it. I couldn't believe it. I spotted Ashley across the room with her mother and a few of her family members, laughing. Everybody seemed happy. I used it for a temporary escape from the madness.

"You think I did the right thing, cuzz?" Ace asked. He was kind of drunk.

"Don't get scared now, nigga," I countered. We all laughed.

"You good, nephew," OG Casa assured him.

My attention went to the dance floor where Tanya's thick-ass was. She still had on her bridesmaid dress—with no shoes. And baby was doing the fool on the dance floor. I thought about how fat her pussy was when she showed me at The Cheesecake Factory.

"Let me talk to you, son," OG Casa said, nodding his head toward the double doors that led to a hallway in the Rec Center we were at in North Kanas City.

We both stood up to leave. "Be right back bro," I said to Ace. He didn't pay me any attention. Him, Justin, and Coach Kid were still joking and talking shit to each other.

"I know this probably ain't the place to—" OG Casa started when we made it in the hallway.

"Anytime is the right place, OG," I interrupted.

"This Santos shit should be taken care of soon."

"And Maria?" I couldn't believe that bitches body wasn't found in that truck. We found out officially a couple of days after the explosion. The only babies found were the Russian hitmen.

"No word." He rubbed his beard. He had an irritated look on his face.

"That shit crazy."

A group of young ladies came out of the restroom. "Girl, it's all kinds of fine brothas in there," one said. They walked towards the reception.

"I'ma give somebody the pussy tonight," another young lady said. They all shared a laugh and entered the double doors.

Bitches, I thought.

"Damn right it's crazy," OG Casa said.

"So Santos is in arms reach?"

"We're on him."

"Coo'. Well let's get back in here." I patted him on the shoulder and we walked back in the reception.

When we got in I spotted Ace and Ashley on the dance floor grooving. OG Casa got lost in the crowd. Probably was about to reel something in. He kept his fishing pole on deck when women were around.

I returned to the table with Justin and Coach Kid. As I was headed that way I noticed some of the women were eyeing me seductively. *Thirsty ass females.*

"What's the deal, bro?" Justin asked when I sat down at the table.

"Yea, what's poppin', bro?" Coach Kid added.

"Chillin'." I started observing the room. As I glanced back and forth across the crowd, everybody seemed happy. Everybody except a couple of niggas standing by the bar.

For some reason they looked out of place. And they kept looking in our direction.

"Man, her thick-ass go!" Cram's drunk-ass came back to the table sweating. I smiled at his remark.

"You been dancin' wit' that ho all this time?" I asked.

"I couldn't help it. That ass *so* soft." He held both of his hands out and pretended like he was grabbing her ass as he said it.

"Sit yo' goofy ass down nigga," I laughed. I looked by the bar where those niggas were but they were gone. *Where you niggas go?* I asked myself as I glanced over the room. I didn't see them.

I got up and walked over to the bar to get me something to sip on.

"Remy," I told the gentleman behind the bar.

"Coming right up, sir," the pudgy white guy countered. Once he got done preparing my drink, he handed it to me. When I turned around, Casey and Selena were right there.

"You havin' fun?" Casey said.

"How many of them have you had?" Selena asked.

I smiled at both of them. They both were dressed to kill. Form-fitting Dolce & Gabbana dresses. Casey's was Navy and Selena's was Black. Selena had a little make-up on; not too much. Casey didn't have any on. They both had their hands on their hips, waiting for me to answer.

"What?" I asked both of their big-headed asses.

"Stop playing, Spade. Answer me," Selena said.

Casey just gave me a look. I loved fucking with their feelings. "Y'all enjoyin' the Reception?" I hit my Remy. They both rolled their eyes and walked away from me. *Where the love at?* I thought.

"I'ma get on outta here," OG Casa said, walking up with something thick. She looked like she was about forty or so. But her body was on point.

"Straight up, huh?" I raised my glass to compliment his fresh catch.

"Straight up." Him and his victim left the Reception.

I saw Ace leave the dance floor and walk back over to the table. I headed that way too.

"What you doin' later, baby?" Tanya stopped me in my tracks.

"Shit."

"Can I see you?" She touched my chest.

I peeled her hand off my Brunello Cuccinelli shirt and replied, "I'm coo', mah."

"You don't know what you missin'." And she got lost in the crowd.

I headed over to the table. The rest of the night went smooth. I stayed until Ace left. Once I knew he would make it home safe with his new wife, and Selena and Casey was cool, I went home.

Chapter 2

"So they went to the Bahamas for their honeymoon?" Selena asked. We were sitting in her living room chilling. I had been over here for about an hour.

"Yeah, they gon' be there for a week."

"Must be nice," she said with a little sarcasm.

I took my eyes off the TV and glanced at her.

"What?" She turned her face up at me.

"I ain't said nothin'," I said.

"Can't wait 'til I get married." She got off the couch and walked to the kitchen.

Ah shit, I thought.

I didn't respond to her comment. I knew that's what she wanted me to do. I turned my attention back to the flat screen. I was watching a Mike Epps stand-up.

"Daddy ..." Samantha came out of nowhere rubbing her eyes. She had on some Dora the Explorer pajamas. She had just woke up.

I held my arms out to her. "Come here, baby." I did my best baby voice. Once she made it to me I picked her chunky butt up and kissed her. "You just got up, mamy?"

She shook her head yeah and buried her face in my chest. *Daddy's little girl*, I thought to myself.

Selena came back in the living room and sat down next to me and Samantha. She had a sneaky look on her face. "You want mommy and daddy to get married?" She rubbed her daughters head. Samantha shook her head yeah.

"See," Selena said, looking at me like I was crazy.

"She don't even understand that shit," I said.

"Woman's intuition."

"You trippin'." I shook my head. I knew Ace and Ashley's wedding had her big-head-ass on the marriage kick.

"Am I?" She frowned up at me. "You remember what my mother asked me. '¿*Cuando se van a casar?* I'm tired of making excuses."

"You need to—" My phone rang so I stopped mid-sentence. *Saved by the bell.* "Yeah," I picked up. I got up off the couch and walked in the master bedroom.

"What's up, son?" It was OG Casa.

"Chillin'." I flopped on the bed.

"Where you at?"

"Selena's."

"Keep yo' phone on." And he hung up. I got off the bed and walked back out to the living room area. Selena was on the phone.

379

I walked in the kitchen to get Samantha something to snack on until her mama made something to eat. I grabbed a banana and cut it up in little pieces.

Selena came in the kitchen after she got off the phone. "My father wants us to come out there so y'all can talk"

Me and Mr. Gomez had been dialoguing over the phone for the last two months. I was ready to put some bread on some property. And he was the nigga I wanted to fuck with.

"Coo'. We can shoot there in a few days."

"Okay."

"Give this to Samantha ..." I handed her the bananas. "... I gotta bust dis move."

***

When I walked in the salon it was jammed packed. Shantel was running this muthafucka like an old school Chevy in the winter. Straight up and down. I greeted the women and walked back to my office. I took a seat behind my desk and started going over some paperwork for my Tax adviser.

After about ten minutes of observing paperwork, Shantel walked in. "What's up, baby?" She came over to me and placed a kiss on my cheek.

"Goin' over this shit real quick."

"How was the wedding?" She walked over to her desk. It was funny calling it her desk. I missed Lisa.

"It was coo'," I said.

"That's wussup."

"I ain't mad at him." I started going through the paperwork again.

"Notice anything different?" she asked with a smile.

I looked over at her and observed her. The only thing I noticed was her juicy-ass titties busting out her BeBe tank top. And wasn't shit different about them muhfuckas. Then I noticed a tattoo right above her cleavage. I couldn't see what it said from where I was sitting.

"You got a new tat?"

"Not just any tat …" She stood up and sashayed over to me. "… this is special."

I keyed-in on it and it was my government name. "You play too much," I said.

"What, you don't like it?"

"It's coo'."

Inside, though, I thought, *The bitch was trippin'*.

"I knew you'd like it." She kissed me and sashayed back to her desk.

"What if you end up gettin' a man one day?" I asked.

"I doubt if I will. I know my role. Like I told you, A slave can only serve one master."

"I hear you."

Her assertiveness kind of turned me on. I wanted to fuck her brains out in the office but I kept my desires in check.

"I start school in three months too. I'ma major in accounting."

"That's wussup. Where?"

"I'ma do the two year thing at Longview first. Get an associates."

"That's a good look, lil' mama."

"You proud of me?" she asked seductively. She had that look in her eyes, like she wanted my dick for a prize.

"I'm glad you enrolled. I'll be proud of you when you get the associates."

"Okay, baby."

"You gon' get out there and help them out?"

"Yeah." She got up and walked out the office.

Thick-ass.

I returned to what I was doing, but I was interrupted by my phone ringing. It was Casey.

"What's the deal, baby?" I answered.

"Nothin', on the way home. You comin' by?"

"I don't know. I gotta see, baby."

She let out a frustrated sigh and said, "I guess, call me later then."

"You fonkin'?" I joked.

"*You* fonkin'?" she countered. My phone beeped to let me know I had a text message. I wasn't gon' check it until I got off the phone.

"That's cute. I'ma call yo phone later."

"Make sure you do, I love you."

"Love you too." I ended the call and immediately checked my messages.

It was an anonymous text. It read: PLEASE FORGIVE ME. I unconsciously frowned at my cell-phone screen because I didn't know who the fuck sent me this message.

I shoved my phone in my pocket and continued going over my paperwork.

Chapter 3

Later that night I was with Ranno. For some reason he wanted to go to the strip club. I guess he was trying to see some American pussy. Why he wanted to go on a Sunday night was even more confusing. We were at Temptations, near downtown.

"You sure you don't want one?" Ranno asked, as he was led away by a thick white chick who wore nothing but a black thong, and some cheap black pumps. She was leading Ranno to a room where he could get a lap dance. He was asking me did I want one too.

"I'm coo', bro. Enjoy yo' self," I smiled. He went away with little mama.

The strip club was semi-packed, with a mixed crowd. I occupied a table near the bar. I had a good view of the whole club. Especially the door. Had to keep an eye on that muhfucka.

Devin the Dude's song came on, with racy lyrics—*You ain't gotta say too much / from the look in yo eyes I can tell you wanna fuck*—and a dark stallion hit center stage. The DJ introduced her as Hershey. The small crowd rushed the stage like the bitch was a superstar.

She embraced the attention with grace. True whore fashion. She came out of her outfit within seconds. As she climbed the pole men and women threw dollar bills on the stage. When she turned upside down and did the splits mid-air more money hit the stage. *That bitch gettin' it*, I thought.

"Can I get you somethin' to drink, baby?" a young lady asked as she came to my table. Her perky titties made it hard for a nigga to look at her in her eyes.

"Yeah, just bring me an Orange juice, baby girl."

Cute lil' yellow bone.

"Be right back, baby." She strutted to the bar.

She was kind of hot too. About 5'7", small waist, ass and hips just right. I eyed that demonstration all the way to the bar.

"You like?" Ranno's crazy-ass popped up out of nowhere. He startled me a little bit. If he was an enemy I could've been smoked.

"She coo'," I said. "How was yo lap dance?"

"Alright …" He did the so-so signal with his hand. "… she smelled funny, though."

I busted out laughing.

"Here you go, baby." The yellow-bone was back at my table.

"Thanks, baby girl." I grabbed the drink from her.

"No problem, honey …" she said to me. "… can I get you anything?" She turned her attention to Ranno.

"No thanks."

"Okay. Enjoy yall night," she said and she strutted off.

Work! Work! French Montana was coming through the speakers. Hershey was still on stage doing her thing. Me and Ranno looked that way.

"Amazing how her body looks," Ranno said.

"You like?"

"She coo'," he tried to mock me.

"You silly, my nigga," I laughed a little.

Ranno looked at his phone and checked the time. I mirrored his actions and checked the time too; it was 11:17 p.m.

Ranno started observing the club like he was looking for something. "I'ma get one more lap dance." He got up from the table and walked away.

"Don't go broke in dis muhfucka, bro!" I yelled as he walked away.

Hershey finally took her thick-ass off the stage.

Ten minutes later Ranno came back into view. But he was headed towards the door to exit. "Come on!" he said to me.

I glanced at the entrance and somebody was walking out in front of Ranno. I got to my feet in a hurry and caught up with Ranno. When we got outside Ranno yanked out his cannon from his waist. He had a suppressor on the barrel. I pulled my weapon too.

The nigga in front of us cut a left to the side of the strip club building. Ranno sped up, I did too. When we turned the corner the person we were following was unlocking the driver's side door to a black Lincoln Towncar. Ranno rushed him and shot him in the leg.

"Aagh!" The gentlemen grabbed his thigh and fell to the ground. I walked up on him to get a good look at him. He was a Mexican.

"Who the fuck is this?" I asked as I looked around the dark parking lot to make sure nobody was looking.

"One of Santos' men." He reached down, grabbed his collar and pulled him to his feet. I put my .40 cal to his head to get rid of his bitch-ass. "No, not now." Ranno led him to the truck we were riding in.

Chapter 4

"Where's Santos?" Ranno asked the terrified guala. He was sitting in the back seat with him. I was behind the wheel, driving nowhere in particular.

"I don't know, man," the Mexican pled. The view in my rearview mirror showed a bitch in the backseat about to piss on himself.

"You don't know, huh?" Ranno countered.

I pulled up to a red light on Truman Road and Paseo. I turned in my seat to face Ranno and our captive. Ranno pulled out a funny looking blade that was about six inches long. Probably some shit from Russia.

"That nigga know somethin'," I commented. I was ready to cut him down in the strip club parking lot. So I was kind of hot because we was riding around with his hoe-ass.

"I know he does," Ranno stated before sticking the blade in the bullet wound in his thigh. He twisted the blade inside his thigh. Ripping the muscle in his shit.

"Aagh! Aagh!"

I smiled at his pain. Out of my peripheral I noticed the light turned green. I got back on the gas and kept straight, heading East.

"Where is Santos?!" Ranno snapped.

"I don't know!"

"Pull over here, Spade," Ranno said.

Here?

"You trippin', my nigga. I'ma hit one of these back streets." I made a quick right on Prospect, then another right when I got to 23rd street. I turned inside of an alley then I parked.

"Get the door," Ranno said.

I hurried out the truck and opened the back door. Ranno got out of the other side of the truck. I grabbed the guala-guala and snatched him out. He still had the blade in his thigh. He cried out when I threw him to the ground.

"Okay, okay I'll tell you!"

"I don't believe yo' bitch-ass." I nudged his forehead with the barrel of my cannon. Ranno just looked on.

"I swear, I swear …"

"We're listening," Ranno retorted.

"Okay. He stays…."

***

"You wasn't tryna go to the strip club for the bitches, huh?" I said to Ranno. We were sitting in my living room. We had been here for about thirty minutes.

"Not a chance. But I did enjoy the entertainment," he laughed.

"How'd you know he was gon' be there?"

"Homework."

"Why didn't you let *me* kill him after he told us where Santos stayed?" I was a little pissed about that. For all I know he could have been there when they killed young Dice and Lisa. I wanted to DOA the nigga. But after he gave us a location for Santos, Ranno took the blade out of his thigh and cut his throat. He bled to death.

"Don't know, I just reacted." He rose to his feet.

"You gone?" I asked.

"Yeah, it's getting late."

"A'ight." I walked him to the door and showed him out.

Once he left I went back to my couch and sat down. Before my ass could hit the cushion my phone rung. It was Shantel.

"What's poppin'?" I answered.

"You."

"Is that right?"

"That's right. Whatchu doin'?"

"Chillin'." I grabbed my remote and turned on my TV.

"You want some company?"

"That's coo', come through."

"Be there in a minute," she said and hung up.

I looked at my cell phone screen and it was 12:51 A.M.

She tryna get into somethin'.

Not even a half hour later, my phone rang again.

"Yeah?" I picked up.

"I'm pullin' up," Shantel said.

"A'ight," I said before ending the call. The time on my cell phone screen read 1:27 A.M.

I got up and walked to my door to unlock it. When I opened the door she was walking toward my house. I left the door cracked open and went back to my couch.

"Lock that door, lil' mama," I told her when she came in.

After she locked it I noticed her eyeing my chest and core. All I had on was some jersey shorts and ankle socks. She came over and sat next to me on the couch.

"What's up, baby?" she asked, looking me up and down like I was her prey.

"Why you got that coat on?" I asked, confused. She had a khaki rain coat on.

"Why do I have it on?" She put her car keys on my marble table in front of my couch, stood up, and took the coat off. Underneath she had on a red form-fitting fishnet mini dress. No bra. No panties. I could see everything.

"That's how you feelin'?" I felt blood rush to my dick.

"Let's go."

She turned around and walked toward my steps. The bottom of her ass cheeks were busting out her dress. I noticed the Jimmy's when I got up to follow her; they had her legs looking right, from the calf muscles to the hams.

I might just have to fuck you tonight.

When we got in my room I grabbed the remote for my sound system off my dresser. After I put on a mellow mix for the occasion I went over to my king size bed. The moon light coming through my blinds allowed us to see each other.

"Let me take care of you tonight," she said softly, as she leaned in and kissed me. Then she straddled me. I gripped her ass as our tongues got familiar with each other.

Baby girl started kissing my neck, my chest, my stomach, then she pulled my boxers and jersey shorts down over my ankles and tossed them on the floor.

"Whatchu want me to do?" She smiled.

"That's funny, lil'—"

She put her warm mouth around my dick. My hand went to the back of her head.

"Don't." She moved my hand and looked at me for a second. Then she started back knockin' me down.

That's funny, I thought to myself.

She continued giving me some of the best face-game I ever had. *Baby didn't miss nothin'!* From my balls to the head, she made sure her mouth and tongue got acquainted. *It's better every time lil' mama get on dis muhfucka,* I thought.

I figured it was time I finally fucked the young tender. While she was doing wonders with her mouth, I reached in the top drawer of my nightstand sitting next to my bed and grabbed a helmet.

"It's time," I said.

"Mmm," was all she offered as she rolled her fishnet get-up off her hips.

I rolled the condom down my dick and she positioned herself to ride it.

"Thank you, Daddy," she said as she eased down my shaft. "Oooh shit! ... *Damn,*" she said as she started getting into it. She started slow at first, then she caught her rhythm and started riding proper.

Her pussy was tight, warm, and wet. I grabbed her hips and navigated the rollercoaster. She positioned her hands on my chest and started popping that pussy like a mad-woman.

"Fuck ... I'm ... I'm comin'," she uttered as I drove my dick in her every time she came down.

"Is that right, bitch?" I asked like I was possessed.

"Yeah," she cried. She collapsed on my chest when she came.

I turned her over on her back and dug into her aggressively. She wrapped her legs around my waist, inviting me to go deeper. I fucked her hard. Somehow we ended up on the floor and I was digging in that pussy from the back.

"Yes, Daddy, yes!" she screamed. I smacked her ass repetitiously as I watched my dick glide in and out of her kitchen. "I'm … co … comin' again."

"Yeah?" I sped up.

"Yeeah!" she came again.

Afterwards, I crawled out of bed and stood up naked.

In the bathroom I flushed my condom down the toilet, and it had blood on it. *Damn, lil' mama was a virgin?*

Shantel was in my bed sleep. The pussy was tight but her being a virgin didn't cross my mind. Probably because the face-game was so official. I jumped in the shower to wash the sex off of me. The whole time I was in the shower I kept thinking about her being a virgin. I couldn't believe that shit. Virgins were rare in my neck of the woods.

After I finished cleaning myself up, I dried off, applied my hygiene and joined lil' mama in bed.

Chapter 5

The next morning me and Shantel were at my dining room table eating breakfast. She kept talking about what she imagined her first time would be like.

"Damn, I didn't know yo thick-ass was a virgin," I said as I shoved a fork full of eggs in my mouth.

"I didn't tell you because I knew you wouldn't believe me," she countered.

"I hear you talkin'."

"I'm serious."

"I would've believed you, baby-girl," I lied.

She flicked her wrist at me. "Yeah right."

"Real talk."

My phone rang I got up from the table and walked over to my couch where my phone was. I picked it up and answered it.

"What's up, bro?" Coach Kid asked. Shantel took our plates to the kitchen.

"Slow motion. What's poppin'?" I sat down on my couch.

"Shit, shit, ay, who got a line on Taylor Swift?"

I took my phone away from my ear and looked at the screen appalled. *This nigga really is a clown.*

"Don't know. I think she on tour."

I couldn't believe that nigga called me about some Cavi. *He was outta pocket.*

"Damn, a'ight bro." He sounded disappointed.

"Yep," and I hung up my line.

Shantel came in the living room and said, "I'm 'bout'a get ready to go home. I gotta get to the salon."

"A'ight, lil' mama." I stood up and went over to her. I wrapped my arms around her waist and gave her a kiss.

"Call me later," she said after we broke our embrace.

"Will do."

***

At about noon that day I was down at OG Casa's dealership. We were in his office dialoguing.

"Ranno said they were gon' make sure that address is official," OG Casa shot.

"That's wussup."

"As soon as we make sure, we'll move."

"Coo'. You a'ight, OG?" He looked a little tired.

"I stay a'ight ..." He reached in his small fridge and pulled out some Crown Royal. "...Why you ask?" He poured some of the poison in his personal glass.

"Just askin'?" I shifted in my seat.

He hit his poison and said, " 'Member you was little and I was comin' down the block? And you and lil' bighead Carl was gettin' it in?"

I remembered that fight like yesterday. The first fight I had in the 'hood. I was like nine or ten years old. Carl was tripping because his little girlfriend was a little too friendly.

"Yeah ..." I smiled. "... I remember." I beat Carl's ass. But he had my eye on swolle. Caught me with a nice hook.

"I pulled over and got out and looked on. Watching yall lil' asses fight like warriors." He smiled and picked up his glass and took another sip. " 'Member what I told you after y'all fought?"

"If someone declares war on me then they don't value they life—"

"—and if you don't protect yours at all cost—"

"Then I don't value mine," I finished the words of wisdom he gave me two decades prior.

"Remember dat." He hit his Crown Royal again. I didn't know why he told me that. But I re-tucked the jewel.

***

It was going on 2:00 p.m. when I pulled into the car wash on Van Brunt. The car wash was packed. It felt good outside so I guess everybody wanted to get they whips clean. The degrees were like in the high seventies. I pulled up to the second car wash station. One car was in the station, and one truck was in front of me.

While I waited I called Selena to see what she was up to. She picked up on the third ring.

"Hi, baby," she said.

What's goin' on?"

"Just got through giving your bad-ass daughter a bath."

I laughed and replied, "My daughter ain't bad. She just adventurous."

"Whatever."

"Whatchu cookin' later on?"

To my left some chick hopped out of a pink Dodge Charger and made her way to the air freshener dispenser. *Damn that bitch thick.*

"What do you want me to cook?"

"Surprise me."

The truck in front of me pulled into the wash station. I pulled up a little bit and slapped my shit in park.

"What time are you coming by?" Selena asked.

Lil' mama from the pink Charger was walking back to her whip. I hit my horn once to get her attention. When she looked my way I waved, and she waved back. She sported just a tank top, leggings, and some pink Nike Air Max's. The sun had her dark complexion shining.

Selena pulled me out of my trance. "Spade!"

"Yeah, what's good?"

"What time are you coming by?"

"'Bout six or seven."

"See you at ten," she said before hanging up on me.

Bitch is crazy. I shook my head and turned my stereo up just enough so I could hear it.

As I was vibing to my music I was rudely interrupted by a knock on my window. It was Tanya. *Fuck you come from?*

I let my window down and said, "What's good?" I looked her up and down and noticed she was dressed down in the same thing lil' mama in the pink Charger had on. Same Max's and all.

"You," she purred, as she leaned down and placed her forearms on my driver side door. Her nipples were winking through her tank top.

"Sound good. Who you up here wit'?"

"My bitches. You just honked at one of 'em."

How many of yall is it?

"Honked at who?" I played dumb.

"My bitch Carmen …" *Carmen huh?* "… don't act like you didn't."

"Whatchu 'bout to get into?" I changed the topic. She wasn't anybody I needed to explain myself to.

"Shit. Why?" She asked eagerly.

"Just askin'."

"Hopefully you getting into me."

"You play too much." I shook my head and smiled.

"I ain't played enough. Me and my bitches 'bout' to be out bendin' corners. Call me," she said before switchin' back to the Charger. I hated bitches that ran in packs. Not my style.

A few minutes after that, the truck in the wash station pulled out and I pulled in.

***

I was back at my house an hour later talking to my lawyer. "So whatchu sayin'?"

"I'm sayin' no funny business. None!"

"Puzzo, I don't get involved wit' funny bidness."

"That's not what Detective Smalls thinks. So even if you're not, he'll try to make it seem like you are."

"So is he still investigating me?"

"I'd say you're *all he's investigating*."

I rubbed my face out of frustration. "A'ight."

"Ok, I'll keep you posted." And he hung up.

I went to my kitchen to look for something to snack on. Then I remembered Selena was cooking. I grabbed my keys and headed out the door. Figured I'd surprise her and show up a little early.

Chapter 6

One week later

"What them exotic bitches was hollin' 'bout?" I asked Ace. He'd got back from the Bahamas that morning. I went and picked him up from his house and brought him to my spot. We had been over my house chilling for a few hours.

"You know wifey wasn't havin' that shit."

"I forgot you was on the look but don't touch program now." I laughed at my own punch-line.

"It's all good nigga." He grabbed the bottle of XO off my marble table in my living room.

"Can't be nothin' *but* all good nigga. Lil' mama got you on a leash." I was playing with him too much.

"She can never have a nigga like me on a leash." He hit the XO. "Picture that."

"I just seen the pictures, I pictured it."

"Get the fuck outta here, nigga. You next." He smiled because *he* didn't even believe it.

I grabbed the XO from him and said, "Not in a million, pimpin'." I hit the bottle.

My phone beeped in my pocket so I reached in and grabbed it. I had a text message. *Who the fuck keep textin' me?*

The anonymous text read: FOR YOU I'D DIE

I shoved the phone back in my pocket and thought about who the fuck could be sending me that text.

"What's the deal, bro?" Ace must've noticed me contemplating.

"Shit." I hit the XO again. "Thinkin' 'bout somethin'."

"Thinkin' 'bout what?"

"It ain't nothin', cuzz."

"Sound good nigga." He knew I was faking.

"Serious bidness," I said, handing him the bottle.

"You ready to get in traffic?" He rose to his feet and put the bottle on the table.

"Yeah, let's push." I stood up too and we walked out my door.

***

We pulled up to the studio about forty minutes later. I spotted Crams Escalade parked outside the building when I turned down the block.

"Wonder how long big cuzz been here," Ace said after he got out of my car. I was already walking towards the back door. When I opened the door, Cram and Justin were blowing some fruity shit. It was cloudy and I could barely see they faces.

"What's up, cuzz?" Justin said putting the Backwood out. I stood in the doorway to let it air out.

"What's that, purp?" Ace asked walking right past me heading to the ashtray.

"What's up to you too nigga," Cram joked.

"What's poppin'?" Ace grabbed the Backwood and walked back out the door.

"Fuckin' crack-head." I joked wit' Ace when he walked past me.

"Whatever nigga," he countered.

After I was sure the studio was aired out good enough I walked in. I sat next to Cram and said, "What's up wit' y'all niggas?"

"Shit," Justin said.

"Kickin' back," Cram shot.

"So what we gon' do for Young Dice's album release party?" I asked.

"We should have it at Club 700," Justin said.

"I don't know," Cram said.

"It should be an all-day event," I said.

"All-day event?" Justin replied.

"Yeah, we should start it out wit' a big-ass barbeque."

"Where at?" Justin asked.

"Blue Valley Park," Ace said, walking back in the studio.

"I'm diggin' that," Cram's high-ass said.

"We can do wet t-shirt contest an' all dat," Ace offered.

"Sounds like a go," Justin agreed.

"I bet it do sound like a go, nigga," Cram said.

"Fuck you, nigga," Justin said. "You probably be the nigga puttin' up the contest money."

"I ain't fucked up about it," Cram joked.

"Trickin' ass," Ace said to Cram.

"Y'all niggas chill out. Who gon' cook?" I said.

"You know damn well Unc will cook," Ace said.

Unc was a smoker from our 'hood. All he needed was a forty-piece and he'd cook for a thousand muhfuckas.

"Coo', holla at him, bro," I said to Ace.

"I'm on it," Ace countered.

"I'll take care of the DJ. Got a bad-ass Asian bitch that do her thang," Justin said.

My phone started ringing so I excused myself. It was Casey. "Yeah?" I answered.

"What you doin', baby?"

"At the lab," I countered, walking out the back door.

"Can you come take me to get somethin' to eat? I don't feel like drivin'."

"That's funny."

"Fo'real baby."

"A'ight, give me a minute," and I hung up and walked back in the studio.

"That's dope, huh?" Ace was sayin' to Justin and Cram.

"What's that?" I asked as I took a seat in the recliner next to the couch.

"Life is a gamble," Ace said. "That's what we should call the event. Young Dice, Life is a gamble."

"I like it," I said.

"A'ight, so when we throwin' it?" Justin asked.

"Four weeks," I said.

"Coo'," Cram said.

"Let's start gettin' this shit together then," I said.

***

Me and Ace were pushing towards his house. I was about to drop him off.

"What's up wit' that ho Tanya?" I asked Ace after I turned my music down.

"Whatchu mean?"

"The bitch a lil' *too* aggressive."

"Yeah," he laughed a little. "She probably really diggin' you, bro."

I got off on the Lee Summit exit on I-70 East and said, "Sound good. It's like the bitch don't get the picture. I been tempted to test that out, but I'm coo'."

405

Ace laughed at me like I was bullshitting. "Nigga you *gon'* test that out. I would."

"Nah, I'm coo' on the headaches."

"The lil' whore be gettin' money somehow. Her and her lil' team keep somethin' goin'."

I turned on Ace's block and replied, "What that do, nigga?"

"She might be an asset." He gave me the *ching-ching* look.

"Asset my ass. I'm hella coo' on that market." I dipped in Ace's driveway. Ashley was sitting on the porch talking on her phone. I slapped my shit in park and let my window down. "What's up, Ash," I said to Ace's new wifey.

"What's up, Spade!" she yelled.

"I'm just sayin', bro…" Ace Started. "… her thick ass might be valuable."

Ace had a point.

"Might be," I said.

"Tanya said hi, Spade!" Ashley yelled. That must've been who she was talking to on the phone.

"Tell her I said what's good," I countered, shaking my head. Ace laughed.

"Fuck you laughin' at?" I asked him.

"Shit," he kept laughin'. My phone started ringing. It was Casey.

"What's good, baby?" I answered.

"You comin' or what?" She had a little snap in her delivery.

"Watch the tone, lil' mama."

"Are you coming?" She brought that shit down a little.

"Yeah, I'll be there in a minute."

"Ok, baby." She hung up the phone.

"Who dat?" Ace asked.

"Casey."

"That's where you headed?"

"Yes sir, I'll get wit' you in a minute." I extended my hand to him.

He extended his hand and said, "A'ight bro."

Chapter 7

"Damn baby," I said, holding the back of Casey's head. She was knocking me down while I drove her to get something to eat. The tinted windows on the Benz concealed her spontaneous act.

She mumbled a response while her mouth was still wrapped around my dick. I didn't understand what she said, and I didn't care. I was on my way to Burger King on Noland Road.

I finally dipped in the parking lot and pulled around to the Drive-thru. To my surprise there were no cars waiting. I pulled up to the Drive-thru menu and let my window down. What you want?" I asked Casey.

She came up off my meat and said, "Number two, witta orange pop." Then she went back on her attack.

"Welcome to Burger King, how may I help you?" It sounded like a teenage boy.

"Let me get a number two, witta orange pop."

"Hmm," Casey moaned as she kept slurping away.

"Will that be all, sir?"

"That's it."

"Okay. That'll be four-seventy-two. Pull around to the window, sir."

I let my window up and whipped around the building. One car was leaving the window in front of me. I pulled up and let my window down.

Behind the window was an overweight teenage black kid. He opened the window and looked surprised to see a woman giving a man head in the drive-thru line. That's how Casey was, though. Spontaneous. "Uh, four-seventy-two," the young kid said, trying to avoid looking at Casey.

"There you go, young fella." I handed him a ten dollar bill and pulled up to the next window.

"Here you go…" The young white lady paused. "… sir." Then she smiled like Casey was her hero.

I grabbed the food and reached back to place it in the back seat. After I grabbed the drink I said, "Have a good day."

***

After I left Burger King I went straight to Casey's spot. We had been there for a little over an hour. I was sitting on her couch fucking with my phone. Casey had moved her center table in her living room. She had a Zumba DVD in; mimicking the instructor.

Lately lil' mama had been on her work-out kick. She had her hair pulled back in a ponytail, sported some green Pumas, and had on some leggings and a green sports bra. "You talk to my daddy?" She sounded like she was out of breath.

"I holla'd at him last week."

"He coo'?" She started going into some stretches. Bending and stretching every way possible. *Damn*, I thought.

"Yeah, he coo'." I keyed in on her camel toe.

"Ah yeah?" My phone started ringing. "Hold up," I told her. I stepped outside to the evening breeze and answered my phone. "What's poppin'?"

"What's the deal, big bro?" It was Coach Kid. If I would've known it was him I wouldn't have answered the phone.

I sat on the porch steps and replied, "Shit, what's good?"

"Bendin' a couple of corners wit' my chick."

"What's good?" For some reason every time he called I got irritated.

"I need a line on that, bro."

Is this nigga serious?

"You didn't hear what the fuck I told you last time?"

"Damn bro, my fault."

"I'm sayin' my nigga, you keep hittin' my line on this hot shit. What's really good?"

"Hot shit?" He acted like he didn't know what the fuck I was talking about.

"Hot shit, lil' nigga. What, you don't understand English?"

"A'ight bro, you trippin'," and he hung up on me.

Fuckin' clown.

I got up and walked back in Casey's house. She looked at my frustrated expression and asked, "What's wrong wit' you?" She was rolling up her work-out mat.

"Shit." I walked to her kitchen. I went to the freezer and opened it. I had a half pint of Remy in there that was half full. I grabbed it and strolled back in the living room.

"Who was that on the phone?" Casey asked when I flopped on the couch.

"Coach Kid."

"What did he want?"

"*Nothin',*" I replied with emphasis.

"Hmm. Well I'm 'bout to get in the shower ..." She headed towards the steps. "... I gotta stop by the restaurant."

"A'ight," I said as she ran up the steps.

I grabbed the remote to the tube and started flicking through the channels. Then my phone started ringing again. OG Casa was hitting my line.

"What's up, OG?" I answered.

"The lil' village," he said. I got excited.

"Right now?" I looked at the clock on the wall. It was 7:15 p.m.

"Right now," and he hung up.

I turned the TV off and headed out the door. I jumped in my whip and dipped out.

Santos.

Chapter 8

When I pulled in the trailer-park homes off 40 Highway it was 7:45 p.m. I drove cautiously through the trailer park until I spotted two black Tahoes. *Bingo.*

I turned my phone off and parked next to the trucks. I killed my engine and jumped out my whip. I strolled to the door of the trailer and entered. Inside, Ranno and Stavi were beating Santos' bare feet with a hammer. Santos was trying to scream but something was tied around his mouth.

It was hot in this muhfucka too.

They had him strapped to a small metal chair. OG Casa was standing off to the side. Sitting on the floor next to his feet were two jugs with gasoline in them.

"What's good?" I said to OG Casa when I walked over to him.

"Waitin' on you," he countered.

Ranno and Stavi didn't even notice me come in. They were focused on torturing Santos.

"He have any info on Maria?" I asked OG Casa.

"He hasn't said shit. Not one word."

Ain't dis a bitch.

I walked over to the chair Santos was sitting in and yanked my metal from my waist. I pointed it to his head. Ranno and Stavi both stood up to protest.

"What are you doing?" Stavi asked, shoving my arm down. Santos winked at me.

I looked at him like he lost his fucking mind and countered, "'Bout to get this shit over with."

"Not like this," Ranno added.

"We're burning him alive," OG Casa said.

"Burnin' him alive?" I twisted my face up at OG Casa. I was ready to knock his noodles out the pack.

"Shooting him would be too easy," Stavi said. He was right too. This nigga Santos deserved to suffer.

OG Casa picked up one of the jugs of gasoline and held it out to me. "Here."

I walked over to grab it and returned to Santos. Ranno got out of the way. Stavi went and grabbed the other jug and started pouring it around the trailer. I turned my attention to Santos and smiled. OG Casa busted out the trailer windows with a crowbar. Ventilation.

"What's good, homey?" I said to him. I popped the cap on the jug and poured some on his face. And the nigga didn't budge; he knew what was coming. OG Casa and Ranno stood by the door while Stavi drenched the trailer and I drenched Santos.

When I glanced at Ranno he was smiling. OG Casa's expressions showed no emotion. My adrenaline was pumping.

"Step out y'all," OG Casa said when we were done showering Santos and the trailer with gasoline.

Me, Ranno, and Stavi stepped out of the trailer and walked to our vehicles. Ranno got in one truck, Stavi got in the other truck, and I got in my Benz. We backed each vehicle back about ten feet and got back out of them to look at the fireworks.

OG Casa came out of the trailer and stood about three feet away from the open door. Then he lit a match and threw it in the trailer. As the trailer went up in flames OG Casa strolled to the truck Ranno was driving. "Let's get the fuck outta here," he said.

We all jumped in our whips and dipped off.

***

I was at my house one hour later with OG Casa and Ranno. Stavi was at the loft OG Casa set him and Ranno up with. He had a flight out of the country scheduled for that night so he was getting his shit together.

"How long you stayin' in the town?" I asked Ranno. We were all sitting on my wrap-around couch shooting-the-shit.

He looked at OG Casa for a second then looked at me. "I'll be here for a minute."

415

"That's wussup." I countered.

"It's good you stayin'," OG Casa said.

I heard my phone ringing. It was sitting on the dining room table. I got up off the couch and went to grab it. "Yeah?" I answered.

"What's good, cuzz?" Ace said.

I paced inside my kitchen and replied, "Chillin', what's good?"

"Just seein' what was up."

"Come through in the morning. I gotta holla at you."

"What time?"

" 'Bout ten."

"A'ight, bro," and he hung up.

I strolled back in my living room with OG Casa and Ranno. They were arguing over whose idea it was to burn Santos alive. I flopped down on the couch with a big ass smile on my face. I rarely saw OG Casa have a childish moment.

"You old niggas crazy," I said after another couple of minutes of the back and forth shit.

"He know it was my idea," Ranno said,

"I know you tryna take the credit for it muhfucka," OG Casa joked.

"As long as the nigga outta here," I chimed in.

I was glad we got that nigga too. *I feel good, I ain't gon' stunt.* Even though Maria was still out there somewhere I was cool. I figured the game would catch up to that bitch. Straight up.

All I had to worry about at this time was Smalls. I knew he wouldn't rest until he found out who killed Kremensky. So I planned on staying out of his way. No hot shit.

"But he died a *horrible* death, because of me." Ranno wouldn't let it go. OG Casa didn't even respond, he just laughed at the nigga.

"Because of you," I agreed so he would leave it alone.

He looked at me with a goofy-ass expression on his face and said, "You weren't even there when we decided *how* we were going to kill him." His Russian accent was heavy. Me and OG Casa busted out laughing. That fool Ranno was a handful. I held both my hands up as if to say, "you got me."

***

It was 10:13 p.m. when I pulled up to Casey's house. OG Casa and Ranno went down to the loft.

"So is this shit over with?" she asked.

I was laying back on the bed. Casey was sitting up Indian-style.

"Some'n like dat," I said.

Casey hit her lil' shot glass of Ciroc and questioned me again. "Something like that?"

"It's over with," I stated. I didn't feel like talking about the madness that surrounded me.

"I hope so ..." She hit her Ciroc again. "...my day's been *so* long."

I sat up in the bed and removed her glass from her hand. I sat it on the dresser and instructed her to lay on her stomach. All she had on was some silk pajama pants and a see-through lace bra. She had her hair wrapped up with a silk scarf.

On the left side of her dresser she had some of her cosmetics stacked up neatly. I grabbed some oil and strolled back to the bed. I sat down on the edge of her bed next to her.

I unsnapped her bra and poured some of the oil on the middle of her back. "That feels good," she said as I slowly rubbed it on her back.

"So how was yo day long, baby?" I put the bottle of oil on the night stand next to the bed.

"This girl is always comin' in late," she whispered. The massage had her relaxing—plus that Ciroc. She closed her eyes and I felt her relax all of the muscles in her body.

"The reason legitimate?" I moved up to her shoulders. Not too strong, not too weak. I'm dope with my hands; and not just squaring up.

"She has problems finding rides. Mmm, that feels good."

"She a good employee?"

"That's the problem, baby…" She paused to let out a soft moan. "… she *is* a good employee."

I balled up my fist and went in circles down her spine. "You'll figure it out, baby."

"I know, baby."

I pulled her pajamas down and tossed them on the floor. I grabbed the bottle of oil and poured some more in my hand. I rubbed oil on both of her firm thighs. Then I went under the bottom of her see-through lace panties and rubbed her ass cheeks with oil.

"I'm getting' wet, baby," she whispered.

"Yeah?" I went to the inside of her thighs and rubbed oil there.

"Mmm," she moaned. "Yeah."

"Just relax, baby."

Instead of relaxing, she turned around and laid on her back. She spread her legs and pointed to her pussy. "Massage this."

Chapter 9

The next morning I used my key to enter Selena's house. It was about 7:20 a.m. so I knew her and Samantha were probably sleep. The house was quiet so I tippy-toed to a bedroom down the hall I kept my safes in.

The only reason I slid through here was to remove some money from my safe. I was kind of glad Selena was sleep too. Ever since Ace's wedding she'd been on some other shit.

I bent down and retrieved my small safe that was sitting behind the love-seat next to the far wall. After entering the code I heard footsteps in the living room. *Shit!*

For some reason I felt like a criminal in this muhfucka. Then my phone rang loud as hell. "Yeah?" I hurried and picked up.

"My dude runnin' the promo shit this week," Justin said.

"That's wussup." I was counting out ten grand as I talked to him. "When will the flyers be here?"

"Next week."

I stuffed the money in my pocket, locked the safe and placed it back behind the love-seat. "Coo', I'ma hit you in a minute," I said as I rose to my feet.

"A'ight, cuzz," and we ended our call.

"How long you been here?"

I turned around and Selena was standing in the door way. She was topless and only had some panties on. I could tell she just climbed out of bed.

I walked over to her to give her a hug and a kiss. "I just got here."

"You leaving?" She broke our embrace and put her hands on her hips. Her accusatory body language frustrated me.

"I gotta bust this move." I walked past her and strolled down the hallway, headed to the front door.

"Really?!" She stormed behind me.

I turned around and snapped. "Bitch, if you wake my daughter up ..."

"What?" She walked up to me and got in my face. "I'm here with her all day." She pointed to her chest for emphasis. "So miss me with that shit, Sam." She only called me Sam when she got mad.

I looked her up-and-down like she wasn't shit and walked out of the door.

***

"I'm on my way, bro." I was on the phone with Ace. He was telling me he was on the way to my house. I was pushing down Emanuel Cleaver Blvd headed to 70 East.

"Ok, bro," and I hung up.

When I reached to turn my sounds back up, my phone rang again. I didn't recognize the number but I answered anyway. "What's up?"

"What's up, Spade?" It was Tanya.

"How you get dis number?"

"Damn, like that?"

"That's yo' answer?" I said.

She let out a sigh of frustration. "Ashley."

"Is that right?" *I'ma have to check that bitch.* "What's good?"

"Was wondering if we could talk business."

I smiles as I turned onto the highway. That bitch didn't let up.

"Business huh?"

"I'm serious. We both could eat."

"I'll get wit' you," and I dunked on her.

***

"So y'all slow cooked the nigga!" Ace exclaimed. We were sitting in my living room. "Damn I wish I was there!" He smiled.

"You silly, nigga."

"Straight up, cuzz." Ace pulled out a baggy filled with Cush and a pack of Backwoods.

"That nigga didn't budge in that muhfucka though." I got up and strolled to my kitchen to grab a bottle of poison. "Took it like a champ!" I yelled from the kitchen.

"I wish I was there to help cook that Fajita!"

I walked back in my living room and Ace was twisting the Kush up in the Backwood. I sat next to him and twisted the top on the XO.

The thought of Tanya calling my phone suddenly hit me when the XO burned my throat. "Why yo bitch give Tanya my number?"

Ace gave me a confused look as the Backwood hung out the side of his mouth. He yanked the unlit Backwood out of his mouth and replied, "Whatchu talkin' 'bout?"

"The bitch hit my phone earlier …" I handed him the bottle and he took a swig. "… said Ash gave her the number."

"Wifey outta pocket…" He hit the bottle again. "… I'll holla at her."

"Yeah, nip that in the bud, my nigga."

"I'm on it."

I started talking to Ace about my potential real estate investments with Selena's pops. Told him if it was lucrative I'd bring him in. Ace was a married man *and* like my little brother. It was time for him to formulate and exit strategy. And I was going to help him.

***

"I'm sorry, Spade," Selena said. We were in the bedroom talking. I had been over here for about thirty minutes.

"Sound good." I laid back on the bed and looked up at the ceiling. "You been trippin' lately."

"I know ..." She came to the bed and laid on top of me. Her Chanel perfume teased my nostrils. "... I guess I've been filling insignificant lately." She stared in my eyes and wore a concerned expression.

"But you're not," I said to her, as I reached around and palmed her soft ass.

She kissed my lips and laid her head on my chest. "I know, baby, I know."

My hotline started ringing again. It was sitting on the dresser. Selena slid off of me so I could grab it. "Yeah?" I answered.

"What's up, baby? I'm at the mall ..." Shantel began. Selena was looking down my fuckin' throat. "...you want somethin'?"

"Grab me some kicks," I told her. "Size ten."

"That's all?"

"Yeah, that's coo'."

Selena got off the bed and left the room.

"Okay, baby," and Shantel hung up.

Immediately after the call ended I had another text message.

It read: LOVE STRANGLES RATIONALITY

Chapter 10

Later that evening I was driving nowhere in particular. The summer breeze felt good so I was out enjoying the elements. Then I decided to go to Uncle Harold's—Harold Penners—at the landing strip mall on 63rd street.

Ten minutes later I was pulling up. I grabbed my Desi out of the stash spot and jumped out my whip. Had to grab the Desi, anything was liable to jump off at The Landing.

As I was walking towards the entrance a group of young ladies in a yellow Dodge Avenger honked at me. "Hey sexy!" a couple of them yelled out.

I gave them the hand and slid in the building. Uncle Harold's was kind of packed when I walked in. I made a right to see if they had some new Rocawear summer attire.

"What's up, big bro?" someone said from behind me. I was near the wall, rumbling through some outfits.

I turned around and it was Coach Kid with a couple of niggas I hadn't seen before. I tugged my waist out of habit to make sure my cannon was there. "What's good?"

Coach Kid approached me to embrace. "Who you here wit'?"

"Solo ..." I gave him the once-over. "... who them niggas?"

He looked at the Backstreet Boys, then back at me. "My lil' cousins."

I eased down on the wall to get a word with Coach Kid alone. He followed and his back-up dancers stayed put.

"You been in the lab?" I asked him.

He rubbed his chin and gave me a pitiful look. "I been meaning to, bro. I been hurtin', though."

"Hurtin'?" I continued to ease down on the wall display.

"Yeah ..." He followed. "... plus I got that case comin' up."

When I was sure we were down far enough, I asked, "Why you been hittin' my phone on that hot shit?" I turned around and faced him. Had to let the lil' nigga know I was serious.

"I said my fault, bro." His voice was kind of shaky. I felt sorry for the little fella.

I shook my head at the nigga because his game-goofiness troubled me. "That ain't the point." I poked him in the chest with my index finger. "If you wanna holla about somethin' like that, meet me at the studio."

"A'ight, bro."

"A'ight?"

"Yeah, my fault."

"A'ight, meet there later and I'll put some change in yo pocket."

"Right on, cuzz." And he left my presence.

***

"I got you four pair. Some J's, some Barkley's, some Bo Jacksons, and some low-top Puma's," Shantel said, walking in my door with some bags in her hand. Her oval shaped D&G sunglasses concealed her eyes and half of her face. She wore a Red shoulderless mini-dress that hugged her body like it missed her. Her open-toe sandals exposed her candy red toe nails.

"Right on." I eyed her juicy ass as she sashayed to my couch.

She sat the bags down, came back to me and gave me a hug and a kiss. "I miss you, baby."

I palmed her ass and replied, "I miss you, too."

She felt my erection as we embraced. "I see."

As we stood there, sexual appetites about to get the best of us, my phone rung.

"Don't answer it, baby," Shantel said seductively.

I unwrapped my arms from around her. "I got to, lil' mama." I reached in my pocket and pulled my phone out.

"Yeah?" I answered as I walked to my couch to sit down. Shantel walked to the kitchen.

"What's up, cousin?" Sparkle said.

I was happy to hear from her. I hadn't talked to her in a while. "What's the damn deal?"

"Just lettin' you know I'll be in Kansas City tomorrow."

"That's what's up. Come through when you land."

"Will do."

"A'ight," and I hung up the phone.

Shantel came back in the living room with one of my bottles of Remy in her hand. She sat across from me and just stared at me with a sneaky smirk on her face.

"What?" I asked her.

"You think you too coo', don't you?" she joked.

"Man, I'm chillin'. Whatchu talkin' 'bout?"

She got up and came over to sit next to me. "Nothin'." She grabbed my hand and held it in hers. She tucked her feet under her ass and gave me an intense look. "I don't know what it is about you …" She rubbed the back of my head.

"Is that right?" I asked.

Then she started kissing my neck. My dick instantly came alive.

429

***

"So you got everything on deck?" I asked Cram. Me, him, and Justin were sitting in the studio. It was about 10:30 p.m. I went there shortly after I fucked Shantel's brains out.

"Yeah, everything ready, bro."

"I holla'd at Lucky too, she wit' it," Justin said.

"Who?" I asked.

"The Asian bitch."

"What the fuck kinda name is Lucky for a chick?" Cram shot.

"I'm hip," I agreed.

Justin shrugged his shoulders, implying he didn't know or give a fuck.

"This nigga don't never know nothin'," Cram joked.

"Fuck you, nigga, wit' them nappy ass dreads," Justin replied

"And I *still* get more pussy den you, nigga."

"Yall niggas stay on some bullshit," I said "Coach Kid ain't called?" I asked Justin.

"Naw."

I looked at my phone and checked the time. It was getting late, and me and Selena had to go to her people's house. "Give him this for me when he come by." I handed Justin five grand. "I gotta bust dis move."

Chapter 11
Three Weeks Later

Blue Valley Park was live. Jammed packed with fans, family, friends, and people just coming to have a good time. It was a beautiful Saturday afternoon, mid-eighties with a light breeze.

We had sexy women rocking Young Dice t-shirts. We had on Young Dice t-shirts too. The lil' Asian chick Lucky was doing her thang on the one's-and-two's. It was really live at this muhfucka. Even OG Casa showed up. And he never went to events like this. Sparkle was going to meet us at the club later tonight.

"Nephew! You want one of deese burgers!" Unc yelled out to me. He was standing over the grill with a Duece-Duece of Old English in one hand, and a spatula in the other hand. His Young Dice t-shit was ruined with barbeque sauce stains and cigarette burns.

"I'm coo'." I was standing by the DJ booth observing the crowd. I spotted Ace and Coach Kid running around spraying some young men with water guns.

"Suit ya'self, muhfucka!" Unc said to me.

Lucky was spinning Big Sean and Chris Brown's record, "My Last." *Like I, like I never had it at all all all all, all all all all* ... I started moving through the crowd.

"What's good, lil' mama?" Cram was saying to a voluptuous redbone when I walked up on him.

"Hi." She offered him a bashful smile.

"What's good?" I asked Cram.

He turned to me and introduced me to her. "What's up, bro? This is ... Sheri." He had his shirt tied over his dreads so all of his tattoos on his arms, chest, and stomach were exposed.

"I'ma move around, my nigga," I told him as I got in motion.

To my left I spotted OG Casa and Casey leaning on his car talking. I made my way over to them. "What'chall talkin' 'bout?" I joked.

"Daddy talking about lettin' Ranno run the dealership for a minute," Casey said.

I quizzically looked at OG Casa and asked, "For what?"

"Just need a break for a minute." He hit his Crown Royal bottle. "Not right away, but soon."

"That's old age," I joked.

He offered a weak smile. "Might be."

"Spade!" someone yelled. I turned around and Justin was signaling for me to come over to him. "I'll be back," I told OG Casa and Casey.

I pushed through the crowd to get to him. Out of my peripheral I noticed a detective car driving slow up the road. I stood still and focused my attention on it. As he got closer I noticed him. It was Detective Smalls. He rode past intently looking at the crowd. *Bitch-ass.*

"What's up, baby?" a female voice said as she hit me on my ass.

I turned around and it was Tanya. She had on a two-piece swim suit and some Prada heels.

"What's good?" I asked as I glanced at her assets.

"You."

"I can dig it." I kept moving towards Justin. Lil' mama followed.

"What time y'all goin' to the club later?" she asked.

"'Bout ten."

"See you then, baby." And she got lost in the crowd.

I walked up to the table Justin was at. We had a table set up with Young Dice's mixtapes, and his album. We also had Coach Kid's mixtapes out there too.

"We should've brought more," Justin said, referring to Young Dice's first mixtape we put out. Everybody loved that muhfucka. Lil' cuzz snapped on there. There were only ten left sitting on the table.

"Straight up, huh?"

Justin handed me the money he already made and said, "Straight up."

"We'll be a'ight." I stuffed the money in my pocket. "What time y'all doin' the wet t-shirt contest?"

He shrugged his shoulders. "Ask Ace."

"Where the nigga at?" I asked as I tried to spot him in the crowd.

After a couple more minutes of looking, Justin spotted him. "He over there by Lucky."

"Be back." I walked over to where Ace was at.

"Big Bro, what's poppin'?" Ace asked when I made it to him. He looked a little tipsy.

"Shit. When y'all startin' the wet t-shit contest?"

"In a min—"

Clap! Clap! Clap! Clap! Clap! Clap!

Me and Ace ducked down. Someone was firing a chopstick. The sound was too familiar. Screams came from the crowd as people scattered all over the place.

Ace crawled behind the DJ booth and pulled out an AK-47 we tucked behind there. I pulled out my Glock-17 from my waist. I tried to spot OG Casa, Casey, Justin, Cram, and Coach Kid through all of the Chaos. To my left I saw a white big-body Chevy zooming out of the park.

I ran over to where all of our cars were parked. I knew that's where OG Casa and them would eventually come if they were okay. About a second later I saw Cram helping Justin to his truck. Justin was dragging his leg.

It looked like he took one to the thigh.

"Fuck!" I yelled to myself as I ran over to help Cram carry him.

"Aagh, aagh," Justin complained when I made it to them. He wrapped his other arm around my shoulder and me and Cram carried him to the truck.

"Where's Ace?!" Cram said as we laid Justin in the backseat of Cram's Escalade.

"I don't know." Then I saw Ace's car tear out of the park to chase the big body Chevy. "There he go," I said, pointing to the rear-end of Ace's BMW.

"You coo'?" someone said to me.

I turned around and OG Casa and Casey were right there. "I'm good," I told OG. I was relieved to see them. Everybody in attendance were jumping in their cars, leaving the park in a hurry.

"I gotta get him to the hospital," Cram said, jumping in his driver's seat.

"A'ight," I countered. *Where the fuck is Coach Kid?*

"We gone, son," OG Casa said as him and Casey jumped in his whip.

"I'm right behind you."

***

Thirty minutes later I was at my house. Cram had taken Justin to the hospital. I was going to go down there but I decided not to. Smalls probably would've showed up.

I picked up my phone and called OG Casa. "Hello?"

"What's up, OG?"

"Me and Casey down at the dealership."

"Coo'. Where Casey?"

"In the restroom. You wanna talk to her?"

"Just tell her to call me when she makes it home."

"A'ight. You talk to Ace?"

"I been tryna call him. No answer."

"Let me know." And he hung up.

I tossed my phone on my couch and paced my living room floor. I was worried about Ace. And I didn't know where the fuck Coach Kid was. I picked up my phone to call Ace again. No answer. I didn't even bother calling Coach Kid because he never kept the same number for long.

When my phone started ringing I rushed to my couch to pick it up. But it wasn't Ace. "What's up?" I answered.

"You coo'?" Tanya asked.

"I'm good. You ain't heard from Ace?"

"Un-uh."

"I'm 'bout'a hit his phone." I hung up on that bitch.

KNOCK, KNOCK, KNOCK.

I went to my door and looked out the peephole. *Ace.*

I yanked the door open. I was happy to see my young nigga.

"Them niggas is cut-down, bro!" He rushed past me and walked in my house. I noticed he was driving his new-booty Buick Regal. Not his BMW he left the park in.

"Where you catch dem niggas at?" I closed my door and walked to my kitchen where Ace had walked to.

He snatched a bottle of XO out of the freezer. "Goin' down 23rd."

"Damn right." I was glad them pussies was stretched out. "Where da beemer?"

"Coach Kid got it. He 'bout'a burn it up for me." He hit the bottle and handed it to me.

"Coach Kid got it?" I asked, confused.

Ace looked at me like I was crazy. "He was drivin', bro."

That didn't sit too well with me. I didn't know if Coach Kid was solid enough for a mission.

"Yeah?" I said to be sure. I hit the bottle hard.

"Yeah, he drove," Ace confirmed. "What time we goin' to the club?"

Chapter 12

Club 700 was jammed packed later that night. Only me, Ace, and Cram stepped out. Justin was at his house chilling. The bullet had grazed the side of his thigh. The doctors stitched him up and sent his black-ass home. The niggas responsible were dead so Justin was cool. Sparkle decided not to come.

The DJ was spinning Wale's track, "Bad." The women were rushing the dance floor in an intoxicated excitement.

"It's all hoes in dis muhfucka!" Ace yelled over the music. Me and him were standing by the bar getting towback. Cram's silly-ass was all on the dance floor grooving with the women.

I shook my head, concurring with Ace's statement. I downed my Remy and told the bartender to get me another one. We rode with Cram so I was drinking a little more than I usually would. Plus I was in my feelings about Young Dice.

"Me too!" Ace said to the bartender as he sat his empty cup on the counter. The bartender put both of our drinks on the counter and slid down the bar to help the other party-goers.

"Let's push!" I told Ace as I made my way to the dance floor. Ace trailed behind me. I knew I was a little tipsy when beads of sweat started pushing out of my skin.

When we made it to the dance floor I spotted Cram right in the middle of that muhfucka. He was dancing with *two* bitches. "Look at this nigga Cram!" I yelled to Ace as I turned around to face him. But he wasn't there. *Where the fuck you go?*

I looked over and he was about five feet from Cram, dancing with a thick yellow-bone. I killed the shot of Remy I had in my hand and tossed the empty cup on the dance floor. *Damn I'm cutt,* I thought as I wiped sweat from my face.

Then Tanya popped up out of nowhere and started popping her soft ass on a nigga. She had on a tight mini-dress that had a hard time keeping her ass concealed. My dick got hard in-a-jiffy. I was so drunk I grabbed her small waist and ass. Normally you'd never catch me on a dance floor dancing.

Ace noticed us dancing together and held up his cup to commend me. I gave him a thumbs-up. Next, Tanya reached back and grabbed my dick. I reached under her dress and fingered her pussy. That's right; no panties on.

The DJ started spinning Chris Brown's "Deuces" next. Tanya turned around and wrapped her arms around my neck. I reached around and palmed her ass. Cram wasn't faking. That muhfucka *was* soft. When she leaned in and tried to kiss me I backed up. *I'm trippin'*, I thought as I made my way to Cram. Leaving Tanya there looking disappointed.

I pushed through the crowd. "Let me see yo keys!" I told Cram when I made it to him. I needed some air. He dug in his pocket and snatched his keys out. He handed them to me and I made my way outside of the club.

Damn that feel good, I thought as the fresh air hit my face when I stepped out. I spotted Cram's Escalade and made my way to it. I hit the unlock button on the car alarm and jumped in the driver's seat. I put the key in the ignition and turned the key back so I could listen to the music.

I turned the volume down to a tolerable level and pushed the button to let the seat all the way back. Once I was comfortable I rested my head on the headrest. *Drunk too mothafuckin' much!* I cracked the window.

I was cutt. Straight up.

After five minutes of chilling, the passenger door came open. Cram's Ruger was in arm's reach. I grabbed it and pointed at Tanya. *Tanya?*

"Boy, put that down." The bitch didn't even budge as she jumped in the passenger seat and shut the door behind her. I put the Ruger between the driver's seat and the floor panel.

"The fuck you doin' in here?"

She reached for my belt and unbuckled it. I let her. "This," she said as she unzipped my Rocawear shorts. I leaned up and pushed my boxers down a little bit. Letting my dick pop out like a jack-in-the-box.

She put her head down and wrapped her lips around it. I leaned my head back and palmed the back of her head simultaneously. I don't know if it was the liquor or what. But it felt like the best head I ever had in my life. I could tell she was drunk too.

She sped up, slowed down. Sped up, slowed down. After another ten minutes or so I was eager to see how that pussy felt. She continued knocking me down as I fumbled around Cram's truck for condoms.

Eventually I found them. I got her off my dick and I rolled the helmet on. She climbed over me and eased down on my shaft. Her titties were already hanging out from her drunk oral demonstration.

"Mmm!" she exclaimed as she felt me inside her. Her pussy was so wet. It felt like a river was pouring down my thighs. She was riding me aggressively.

I smacked her ass cheeks as she rode me. "Mmm," she let out. She started getting excited. "I'm comin', damn," she whispered.

Her quiet moans kind of turned me on. It's like she was moaning to herself. Lost in her own world. I started fucking her back. Driving my dick in her every time she came.

I grabbed her sweaty titties and started licking her nipples. They were salty. "Yes, yes," she whispered again.

Out of my peripheral I seen people were coming out of the club. But I didn't give a fuck. We stayed in that drunk wrestling match until I came.

Chapter 13

The next morning I rolled out of my bed with an aching stomach. I walked down to my kitchen and made me a big ass bowl of Frosted Flakes. As I sat at my table shirtless devouring my cereal I heard my phone ringing. I must've tossed it on the couch the previous night because that's where the sound was coming from.

I walked over to retrieve it. "Yeah?" I strolled back over to my bowl of cereal.

"Nigga you owe me an interior detail," Cram said.

"Get the fuck outta here nigga," I laughed. "I was ripped last night."

"So how was the pussy?"

"It was coo'." I downplayed it. Baby girl shit was fire. I regretted fucking her bighead ass.

"Sound good, nigga. I'm 'bout to bust this move, though. Hit me when you ready to pay for the detail," he joked.

"Fuck you, nigga."

"I'm just fuckin' wit' you. Hit me up, though, bro." And he hung up.

I laid my phone on the table and shook my head at the thought of me hitting Tanya in Cram's truck. *Trippin'.*

After shoving more spoonfuls of Frosted Flakes in my mouth, my phone rang again. It was Sparkle.

"What's the deal?" I answered.

"In traffic. What's goin' on?"

"Chillin'. Whatchu 'bout to get into?"

"Just riding," she said.

"Meet me at the salon."

"When?"

"Give me an hour."

"A'ight."

***

As I was unlocking the salon door, Sparkle was pulling up. I turned the key, opened the door and held it for her. She got out of her car and walked towards the salon.

"It's a beautiful Sunday, ain't it?" Sparkle said, walking in the empty salon. She had on a black thigh-length skirt, black heels, and a simple white blouse; she had her beautiful hair pulled back in a ponytail, exposing her high cheek bones.

I turned the light on and countered, "It's a'ight."

She took a seat in one of the waiting chairs. "Whatever," she smiled.

I took a seat next to her. I couldn't figure out what fragrance she had on but it smelled good. "So whatchu been up to?"

"Relaxin'." She straightened some wrinkles out of her skirt.

"I hear you. You heard about Santos?"

"I did."

"Yeah?"

"What's the problem, Spade?" She noticed a hint of frustration in my expression.

"Maria," I offered. "I been tryna chalk it up as a lost. I can't, though."

She patted my thigh. "You have to, Spade."

Bullshit. "That bitch need to die."

"So you gon' worry yo'self?"

The nerves in my left hand started twitching. "The bitch gotta go."

"I'll tell you what ..." She grabbed my hand. "... I'll see if I can handle her."

"I 'preciate it."

"No problem." She released my hand.

"So whatchu 'bout to get into?" I asked.

"I'm just chillin'. I got some work to do in a couple of weeks."

"You got a lil' boy-toy up here waitin' on you?" I probed. I'd never seen her with a man. And I never heard her talk about a man. I also thought about when I heard her playing with her pussy in my bathroom. She just seemed lonely to me.

"Oh no." She moved her index finger back and forth. "You have to earn these goodies."

"Is that right?" I smiled at her clever response.

"That's right."

"I hear you, pimpin'."

She rose to her feet, and I did too. I probably made her uncomfortable asking that personal question, but I didn't give a fuck.

She started walking towards the front door. I followed her. My eyes went to her firm ass. I couldn't help myself.

"I'll call you if I get somethin' on Maria," she said as she turned around to face me.

"Right on," she kissed my cheek and left.

***

Later that evening I decided to stop by the restaurant to see Casey. It was about 6:15 when I pulled up. When I walked in I spotted Casey behind the counter having words with two male customers. The handful of people that were at the tables eating were looking on.

"Come on, baby. A nigga can't get nothin' free?" one of the gentlemen said. He sported a blue and gray LRG outfit. He wore his blue KC fitted ball cap kind of low so I could barely see his eyes. His icey watch twinkled as he moved his arms as he was talking. His friend stood about two feet behind him. He had on a white tank top and blue sweatpants. His royal blue KC fitted ball cap matched the blue ropes in his shoes. He was bigger so I assumed he was the muscle.

"I told you, *no*. Now pay or leave," Casey said, snapping her neck. I stood back about ten feet by the soda-fountain machine. Out of sight.

"This bitch hyphy, huh, cuzz?" Mighty Mouse asked Incredible Hulk. The Hulk just smiled and nodded his head. There was a young lady standing behind Casey. I assumed she was the one working the register. She must've called Casey over when the situation got out of hand.

Casey forced a smile on her face. "Can you please … leave my establishment?"

"Bitch, this *my* city," Mighty Mouse pointed to his chest. "The fuck I look like?"

"So you're not gon' leave?"

"I leave when I feel like it. You a little too tense, baby," he smiled. "You need some dick." The Hulk chuckled at that remark. A few of the customers walked out of the door.

I finally walked up to the counter. I just wanted to see how Casey would handle the situation. But I'd heard enough. "What's up, baby?" I said to Casey.

She looked relieved to see me. "Hey, got a little situation." She flared her nose and darted her eyes at that gentlemen.

"And who the fuck is you?" Mighty Mouse asked. The Hulk stepped a little closer.

I looked at both of them niggas and smiled. "Won't y'all niggas just shake," I said.

The rest of the customers hurried out of the restaurant. They must've felt shit was about to get ugly.

Mighty Mouse started to speak. "I think you need to—"

I pulled my cannon out and pointed it at his head. His body got stiff and his jaw clinched. The Hulk pulled out his cannon too.

"I need to what?" I asked Mighty Mouse. "Tell Shaq to put his wetter down?"

He looked embarrassed. "Put it down, bro," he said to his partner.

Casey rushed around the counter and took the weapon out of The Hulk's hand. "I'll take that off yo hands, big boy." The she pointed it at his head. The young lady that was working the cash register just stood there in shock. She didn't move a muscle.

"How much was the meal, baby?" I asked Casey.

"Eighteen-seventy-three."

I reached in Mighty Mouse's pocket and pulled out a knot of cash. "Damn, you gettin' it." I joked. He looked like he wanted to make a bold move. "I wouldn't, my nigga."

"You don't know who you fuckin' wit', homey," Mighty Mouse said. Casey chuckled at his remark.

"Is that right?" I placed his money on the counter with my left hand. My right hand held a cannon focused at his head. "Count that, lil' mama," I told the cashier.

She cautiously grabbed the money and started counting it. "Twenty-five-hundred," she said when she was finished. I smiled and winked my eye at Mighty Mouse.

"Take a hunid out and give me the rest," I told her. She complied and stepped a couple of feet back from the counter.

I stuffed the rest of the money back in his pocket. "A hunid for the troubles, my nigga."

"You funny," he countered.

"I know." I fished around his pocket until I felt something that felt like an I.D. *Bingo*, I thought. I pulled it out and observed the driver's license. "Get George his food," I told the cashier. The Hulk was fuming. I could see it in his eyes.

"James, the order," she said.

James?

A young black male lifted his head from behind the cooking station. He must've been hiding. *Dis nigga.*

"Here you go," he trembled as he slid the food through the window. The cashier put the food on the counter.

I put George's I.D. back in his pocket. "Get yo' food, George." I stepped back a little but kept my cannon focused on his face.

George reluctantly reached and grabbed his order. He looked like he wanted to say something slick, but he didn't.

"Have a good day, gentlemen. Yall niggas be careful out there," I said. "Come back anytime."

They both walked out pissed.

Chapter 14

After all of Casey's employees were gone, we were in her office talking. "Where's that baby-nine I bought you?" I asked. I was sitting behind her desk like I owned the place. She was pacing back and forth.

"In the safe." She pointed behind me where the safe was located.

I shook my head in disappointment because if I hadn't showed up shit could've got out of hand. "You know what having a cow means, don't you?"

She stopped in her tracks and darted her eyes at me. "Don't play wit' me."

"Don't play witchu my ass; you got a license to carry, so *carry.*"

"I don't wanna scare my customers, *or* my employees." She started pacing her office again.

"They wouldn't see dat baby-nina."

"What if them niggas come back?" she said.

So you just gon' change the subject?

"They won't."

She put her hands on her hips. "And how you know, Spade?"

"Trust me," I assured her.

She walked over to me and sat on my lap. "Thank you for earlier, baby." She kissed me hard, gave me a lot of tongue.

"It's good." I gently slapped her ass.

"I want you right now," she said seductively in my ear.

"I thought you said not in yo office no more."

"I'm willing to make an exception."

**

I was pulling up to my house at about 9:45 p.m. Selena's car was sitting in my driveway when I pulled in. *The fuck she doin' here?*

When I parked and hopped out, she got out of her car too. "What's up, baby?" I said to her.

She walked up to me and gave me a hug. "Hey," she whispered.

After we broke our embrace and walked to my front door, I asked, "Everything a'ight?"

"Just wanted to see you. I miss you." I unlocked my door and went in.

She went to the couch and sat down. I closed the door and observed her demeanor. After I locked the door I went over and sat by her.

"I miss you too." I gave her a kiss. "You been drinkin'?" I tasted vodka on her tongue.

She grabbed my hand and squeezed it. "Do you love me?"

I looked at her like she was crazy. "You know I love you."

She leaned in and kissed me aggressively. "I love you too," she said after our lips unlocked.

"Where's Samantha?"

"With my mother. She got in town yesterday. She's at the house."

"You hungry?"

"Not really." She started looking around my house like she was a tourist or some shit.

I could tell she just wanted to chill with a nigga. I grabbed my remote off my table and turned my T.V on. She leaned her head on my shoulder and started rubbing my chest.

It was something going on with her. Maybe she was tired of the program. The multiple women program. Maybe all of the madness in the underworld was getting to her. I rubbed her back and just sat there with her. No words, no nothing. Sometimes silence is better than noise any fucking way.

Me and Selena were just sitting there holding each other. Then my fucking hotline rang. *Shit,* I thought to myself. I hated upsetting Selena.

"Yeah?" I answered.

"Bro, come to the lab!" Justin said. His tone was urgent.

"What's up?" I leaned up, inadvertently pushing Selena off of me. She smacked her lips out of frustration.

"It's Ace and Coach Kid!"

"A'ight," and I dunked on him.

"I gotta go, baby." I turned to Selena.

"Go where?"

"To the lab." I stood up. "It's Ace and Coach Kid. Stay here, I'll be right back."

***

I hurried up and jumped out of my whip when I pulled up to the lab. I heard a lot of commotion when I walked up to the door.

"Bitch-ass nigga!" I walked in as Ace was pistol whipping Coach Kid. Coach Kid was on the ground with a bloody face, begging Ace to stop. *SMACK!* "You plottin' on me, nigga?" *SMACK!*

I ran over and pulled Ace off of Coach Kid. Coach Kid struggled to get to his feet. "Ain't nobody plottin' on you, nigga. You trippin'," Coach Kid said.

Justin was leaning on his crutches in the corner smoking a blunt. "Deese niggas been goin' at it for 'bout twenty minutes."

I looked at Ace. "What the fuck is up, cuzz?"

454

Ace had his eyes locked on Coach Kid. He didn't even pay me any attention. He had tunnel vision, straight up.

"Ace!" I grabbed his shoulders and shook him.

He finally blinked a couple of times and looked at me. "What's up?"

"What the fuck is goin' on, my nigga?" I dropped my hands off of his shoulders.

He pointed his gun in Coach Kid's direction. "Dis bitch-ass nigga tryna get me."

I looked back at Coach Kid to hear his retort, but he didn't offer it. He just shook his head while he held his bloody face.

"How you know?" I asked Ace.

"The niggas he was plottin' on me wit' ..." He wiped the sweat from his forehead with his free hand. "... One of them niggas told me."

"I turned to Coach Kid. "Straight up, Coach?"

"Fuck nah, cuzz," Coach Kid pleaded. Justin shook his head at Coach Kid's reply. He didn't believe him. And I didn't either. *I hope this shit ain't true.*

"You lucky I didn't cut yo bitch-ass down!" Ace yelled.

"Coach ..." I gave Coach Kid an intense look. Looked him in his eyes. "Is this shit true?"

His eyes went to the floor. "Nah, bro."

Lyin' ass nigga.

I turned to Ace. "He said he didn't, cuzz. We gotta take his word for it."

"Yeah, a'ight."

"Clean yo'self up, bro," I told Coach Kid.

Chapter 15

Me and Ace walked in my house at about 10:15 p.m. He followed me from the studio.

"That nigga fakin'," Ace said as he strolled to my kitchen. I flopped on my couch and let out a tired sigh. Not a sleepy tired. But a tired of the never-ending bullshit tired.

"I already know."

Ace came back in the living room with a bottle of Remy in his hand. "Lil' Bobby told me the whole scoop." Ace flopped down on the couch next to me.

"So what you wanna do?"

He passed me the poison. "I don't know yet."

"This shit crazy." I hit the bottle hard. It was always some bullshit in the game.

"I was kinda feelin' the lil' nigga after he took me to rock-out on them suckas." He reached for the bottle. I handed it to him.

"Shit crazy," was all I could say.

"What's up, Ace," Selena said when she got to the bottom of the steps. She had on one of my t-shirts that went to her knees. She walked to the kitchen.

"What's good?" Ace retorted.

I eyed her intently as she walked to the kitchen. *She need some dick.*

"Let me know when you figure it out," I told Ace.

He hit the bottle. "I will."

Selena headed back upstairs with a bottle of Grey Goose in her hand. She must've gone to the store when I was gone.

"I gotta tell—" Ace's comment was interrupted by my ringing.

"Hold up, bro," I told Ace. "Yeah?" I answered.

"What's up, sexy?" It was Tanya.

"Chillin'."

"You miss me?"

"That's funny."

Ace looked at me with curiosity in his eyes.

"Damn, like that?" Tanya countered. "I miss you."

"I hear you." I thought about how wet that pussy was.

"When is round two?"

"Let me hit you back." I hung up on her and put my phone back in my pocket.

"Who was dat?" Ace asked.

"Tanya," I said, and he laughed. "Whatchu have to tell me?"

He hit the bottle again. "Ashley's pregnant."

I smiled. "Straight up?"

"Straight up," he confirmed.

"Congratulations, my nigga." I extended my hand to him. He grabbed it with aggression. "Right on."

"I'ma be an uncle."

***

"*¡Ayi, papi, i Duro!*" Selena screamed. We were damn near an hour in on an aggressive fucking-match. I had her face down, ass up as I slammed her from behind.

The sweat from my face dripped on the small of her sweaty back. "You still fonkin?"

I asked like she was an enemy of mine.

"No baby!" she exclaimed.

"You sure?" I smacked her ass. We were in my upstairs hallway. I don't know how we ended up there. It started out on some halfway romantic shit in my bedroom.

"I'm … I'm sure!"

I pulled out of her and laid back on the hallway floor. My knees were burning from my hallway carpet. Selena turned around and wrapped her warm mouth around my dick. I stared up at the ceiling as she got lost on my meat. Sucking and smacking her lips on my pipe.

"Damn," was all I could say. She went down and took my sweaty balls in her mouth. She stroked my dick with her hand as she did it. *Damn.*

Chapter 16

The next morning I was sitting on my couch watching Sports Center. Selena was in the kitchen cooking breakfast.

"How many pieces of sausage do you want?" She came into view—titties bouncing, just panties on.

"Just put a few on there."

"Okay." She smiled and walked back in the kitchen.

It felt good chilling with her. And the sex the previous night was on point. We needed that shit. It was definitely some tension between us prior to me penetrating that pussy.

"Come eat, baby," she said, bringing our plates to the table. I got up and went to the table. I grabbed a fork and started to dig in one of my French toast. "Say grace first." She grabbed my hand.

Grace?

"Go 'head," I told her. She closed her eyes and started saying grace. I kept opening and shutting my eyes. Her prayer was a little too long for my appetite.

"Amen," she finally said.

We had small talk as we dug in our food. The next month I was going to invest in my first property with her pops. Selena was happy that me and Mr. Gomez were going to be working together. Then she went left on me.

"What do you think about marriage?" Her facial expression was a serious one.

"I guess I haven't—" My phone started ringing. *Yes.*

She stabbed one of her French toast aggressively and said, "It's on the table."

I went over to grab it and I answered. "Yeah?"

"Whatchu doin', son?" OG Casa said.

"Eatin' breakfast wit' Selena."

"I need you to come by the dealership and holla at me."

"Give me a minute," and I hung up. I went over to Selena and gave her a kiss. "I gotta bust this move, baby."

"Whatever."

"Lock up when you leave," I said as I headed upstairs to get dressed.

***

I walked in the dealership an hour and a half later. Ranno was talking to a few customers when I walked by. "Spade," he smiled. "What's going on?"

"Chillin'. OG in his office?"

He shook his head yes and I headed that way. When I walked in the office OG Casa was lookin' over some paperwork.

"What's good, OG?" I took a seat in one of the chairs across from his desk.

"Nothin' much. How you doin'?" He looked tired, like he'd been up all night.

"I'm coo'."

"How's Samantha doin'?"

"Her little bad-ass coo'. She wit' her grandma right now."

"That's good, that's good." He reached in his mini-fridge and pulled out his Crown Royal.

"What's goin' on, OG?" Something was up.

He paused for a second and hit the bottle. "I'ma be goin' to Ohio."

Ohio?

"For what?" I asked.

"I have cancer."

That floored me. "What?!"

"Yeah. I'm goin' to Ohio tomorrow." He hit his bottle again. "Start chemo."

"This some bullshit." My jaw and fists clinched.

"Don't trip, Spade. I'll be coo', Casey's goin' with me."

She knew?

"Yeah?" I didn't know what the fuck to say.

"I didn't want her to tell you. I wanted to tell you myself."

"How long you gon' be there?"

"Don't know yet. But Ranno's going to run this shit while I'm gone."

Damn, everybody knew but me.

"You sure you gon' be coo'?"

"I'ma conquer dis shit. Trust me."

***

On the way to Selena's I rode in silence. I couldn't believe OG Casa had cancer. *What if he don't survive? If he does, what if it comes back?* All sorts of shit was running through my head.

OG Casa was my big-homey. The thought of that nigga not surviving cancer was bothering me. I planned on cracking a bottle of XO as soon as I got to Selena's. I wasn't worried about shit but being around my daughter.

As I was pulling in Selena's driveway my fucking phone beeped, alerting me of a new message.

I'M SO SORRY, the text read.

I shoved my phone in my pocket and killed my engine. I hopped out and walked towards Selena's front door.

I gotta change my number ASAP.

Chapter 17

"Where's Samantha?" I asked Selena as I tossed my keys on the kitchen counter.

"She went back to my parents' house with my mother." Selena was sitting in the living room watching a rerun of *Fashion Police.*

"You didn't think I needed to know dat." I yanked the freezer door open and grabbed one of the three bottles of XO I had on chill.

"She's with my *mother,*" she countered like I was tripping.

I cracked the bottle of XO and replied, "And what the fuck that mean?" I hit the bottle hard. Made an ugly face as the liquor burned my throat.

"You need to calm down."

I walked in the living room and sat on the love seat to the right of the couch she was sitting on. I hit the bottle again and sat it on the glass table in front of me. "Calm down, huh?"

"Yes ..." She snapped her neck like a sistah. "... calm down."

"Bitch, you need to calm down."

Her eyes got wide because she was surprised I called her a bitch. She jumped to her feet, rushed over to me and stood over me with her hands on her hips. "Who do you think you're talkin' to?"

I looked at her like she was crazy. "Who the fuck you think I'm talking too?" I tried to reach for my bottle but she pushed my forehead with her hand, and that changed my mind about grabbing it.

"I don't know who you think you're talking to, but you better check that shit. Okay?" Her Spanish accent always came through heavy when she was mad.

I rose to my feet and pointed my index finger at her forehead. "Bitch, you betta keep yo hands off me."

Her eyes got even wider and she tried to hit me but I caught her by the wrist. Then I twisted her arm and tossed her ass on the couch. Tears started coming down her face as she cussed me out in Spanish.

Seeing her cry made me realize I was tripping. I was taking my frustration over OG Casa having cancer out on her.

"My fault," I offered weakly.

She bounced back on her feet and started hitting me in my chest with her fists. She slapped me a couple of times too. I grabbed her and hugged her tight, let her get all of the pain out. Not just the pain from me disrespecting her right then, but the frustration she was holding in since Ace's wedding.

"My fault, man," I said as I held her.

***

"Do you think he'll make it?" Selena asked as we were lying naked in her bed. After we argued for minutes, we fucked for hours. The room smelled like pussy and alcohol. After we fucked I told her the reason I was tripping.

"I hope so." I traced her spine with my index and middle finger. Her head rested on my chest and her leg laid over my waist.

"Me too. I like OG Casa."

I smiled. It was funny hearing her say his name. "He should be coo'."

She reached down and grabbed my limp dick. Cuzz-cuzz was out for the count. She slid down and kissed the head. "¿*Como estas?*"

"He sleep, lil' mama."

"I know how to get him up."

***

Later that evening I was at Casey's house. We were sitting in her living room talking about OG Casa. "You still could've told me that," I said.

"How many times do I have to tell you, he said don't say nothin'."

"Sound good," I responded coldly.

"You tryna fake a fallout?" She grabbed my hand.

"That's funny," I smiled. "So you goin' wit' him?"

"He needs me. Plus I don't want none of them hoes goin' with him."

"I'm takin' yall to the airport. A'ight?"

"Fine with me," she said.

I felt my phone vibrating in my pocket. I grabbed it out and answered. "Yeah?"

"One of yo lil' bitches?" Casey asked as she got up and ran upstairs.

Whatever.

"What's up, baby?" Shantel said.

"Kickin' back. What's up?"

"Just checkin' on you. Everything ok?"

"I'm good. You at the salon?"

"Mm-hmm. Can I come by later?"

"That's coo'. What time?"

"'Round nine or ten, baby."

Casey came into view, ass naked in some four inch heels. "A'ight, call me." And I hung up.

I looked Casey up and down like a restaurant menu. "That's how you feelin'?" I asked as she posed for me.

"You know I need some dick before I go." And she turned around and seductively walked back to the steps.

***

It was going on ten o'clock when I pulled up to my house later that night. As soon as I walked in my door I went upstairs and laid down on my bed. I was exhausted. Too much fucking earlier in the day.

I laid in the dark and let my thoughts run wild. Thinking about the past, present, and the future. Life was like the dopest pitcher on the mound, with an arsenal of different pitches. And I'd swung at damn near all of them.

When I started to doze off, my phone rang. I let it go to the voicemail because I was too tired to talk. It rang again. *Fuck.*

"What's up?" I answered.

"Come to Truman, bro," Justin said.

I sat up in my bed, now alert. "What?"

"Come to Truman, we all down here. It's Coach Kid."

"I'm on my way."

Chapter 18

I pulled up to Truman Medical Center and parked in the underground garage by the emergency entrance. I saw Cram, Ace, Justin, and a small crowd of people through the hospital window when I was pulling in.

I hurried and parked and hopped out. "What's good, bro?" Justin and Cram said simultaneously when they walked up to me.

"Chillin'," I said. We walked through the emergency doors. "What's up wit' Coach?"

"He on life support, bro," Justin said.

Life support?

A small crowd was sitting in the waiting room crying. The niggas that were at Harold Penners with Coach Kid were pacing the floor with tears running down their faces. *This shit crazy.*

"Where he get caught at?"

"He was at Fast Stop on Eastwood Trafficway," Cram offered.

Ace was talking to a nurse by the counter. I assumed he was trying to get the scoop on Coach Kid's condition. Make sure he was cool.

"Who the fuck did it?" I asked, pissed off.

Cram and Justin shrugged their shoulders. They didn't have a clue who did it. Ace finally walked over to us. "What's up, bro?" he said to me as he leaned in to embrace me.

"Shit. What the nurse talkin' 'bout?" I asked.

"It ain't lookin' too good, bro." He shook his head like he was disappointed.

"Where his moms at?" I asked.

"Back there with him. I think she thinkin' 'bout pullin the plug," Ace said.

I excused myself and stepped outside for some fresh air. I went through the potential perpetrators in my head. *Is some more of Santos' men around?* I walked to my car, confused.

"Ay, cuzz," Ace called out as I was walking to my car. I turned around and leaned on my trunk. Ace strolled over to me.

"What's the deal?"

He leaned on my trunk next to me. "You know that nigga had to go."

I looked at him upside his head. "What?"

"Come on, bro…" He pulled some pre-rolled Backwoods out of his pocket. He pulled one out of the pack. "… I couldn't let cuzz shake and bake around dis muhfucka like shit was sweet."

Dis nigga.

I shook my head and smiled. Ace probably didn't tell me because I probably would've told him to relax. I was relieved because that eliminated any thoughts of Santos having more goons gunning for my circle.

"So you didn't wanna tell me you was gon' rock on him?" I asked.

"It slipped my mind, bro," he lied. Ace couldn't lie straight to save his life.

"Get the fuck outta here." I nudged him with my elbow.

"Come on, bro ..." He smiled as he looked at the Backwood in his hand. "... you almost made me drop the stogey."

"Fuck that stogey," I joked. "I'ma head back in there." I walked back towards the hospital. Ace stayed by my car and lit his Backwood. I walked through the hospital doors.

"His moms said she don't want him to suffer," Justin said. "They 'bout to pull the plug."

***

"Guess what he was in when I caught him," Ace said. We were sitting on my back patio. The moon bullied the sky, and the breeze was just right.

"What?"

"The Beemer."

What the fuck? Coach Kid was supposed to get rid of it. He was definitely in violation.

"Straight up?"

"That muhfucka swiss-cheesed now." Ace laughed at his own dirty work.

"You didn't have to do him like that, though. Nigga got hit eleven times."

"Oh well. He shouldn't have crossed game."

I couldn't get mad at him. I was the reason he was the way he was.

"Sound good." My phone started ringing. "Hold up, bro." I got up from the lawn chair I was sitting on and walked in my house. "Yeah?"

"You busy?" Shantel asked.

"Hollerin' at Ace."

"You still want me to come by?"

"That's coo'."

"I'll be there in about an hour."

"A'ight." I hung up and went back outside with Ace.

When I stepped on the patio Ace had a 'wood burning. I covered my nose with my hand. "My fault, bro." He put the cherry out on the balcony.

"Crackhead-ass always smokin'," I joked.

"Nigga, if you didn't have just one good lung you'd be hittin' dis purp too," he said with conviction.

"Whatever, nigga." I flopped in the lawn chair. Him mentioning my one lung made me think of Maria. *This punk ass bitch still breathin'.*

"Where you think that bitch at?" He read my mind.

"Wish I knew, my nigga. Wish I knew." I stared in space as I thought about that evening at the Peachtree.

"Wish I knew too, cuzz."

***

At about 12:40 a.m., I was jumping out of my shower. Shantel was in my bed ass naked, stretched out. As she slept I went downstairs to call Sparkle. I needed to know if she had a location on Maria. I couldn't let it go.

"Hello?" she answered as I sat down on my couch.

"You sleep?"

"I'm up."

"The fuck you doin' up at this time'a night?"

"None of your business," she joked.

"Sound good, ay?" I said. "What's up wit' Chica?"

"Still looking."

"What are the chances?"

"Don't know, but I'm on top of it."

"A'ight, let me know."

"Will do." And she hung up.

I got up off of my couch, frustrated. I ran up my stairs and headed for my bedroom. I needed to get some shut-eye. I had to take OG Casa and Casey to the airport at nine in the morning.

Chapter 19

"So when y'all gon' be back?" I asked OG Casa and Casey as I snatched their luggage out of my trunk. We were standing in front of the terminal at KCI Airport.

"I'll probably be back in a couple of weeks," Casey said. "I'm just making sure he gets settled in."

"I told her she didn't have to come," OG Casa said.

"*So.*" Casey screwed her face up at him.

OG Casa laughed at her. "Calm down."

"Whatever …" She flicked her wrist. "… I'm 'bout to take these tickets in here." She walked in the airport.

"You coo'?" I asked OG Casa seriously.

"I'm straight." He placed his hand on my shoulder. "Ready to get this shit over wit'."

"I feel you."

He took his hand off my shoulder and turned to walk in the airport. I grabbed him and Casey's bags and followed behind him.

***

I was pushing towards the salon about an hour after I dropped OG Casa and Casey off at the airport. As I was pulling up to the salon I received another text.

It read: MY LOVE IS INFINITE

Selena, I thought. *It gotta be.*

I parked in my parking spot and called Selena.

"Hey, baby," she answered.

"Chillin', what's good?" I played it cool.

"'Bout to make breakfast."

Breakfast my ass.

"Yo love is infinite, huh?" I asked knowingly.

"What do you mean, baby?"

"That's cute."

"What?" She laughed.

"Stop playin' wit' me, man." I laughed too. "You know what I'm talkin' 'bout."

"What?"

"You didn't send me that text?"

"Text? What text?" she asked seriously.

"Nothin', man."

"What text, Spade?" Her curiosity increased.

"I keep gettin' these text messages on my phone."

To my right I saw Shantel making her way to the passenger side of my car. She was dressed down in a Rocawear t-shirt and sweatpants.

"What are the messages saying?"

Ah shit, here we go.

"Just random shit, baby." I tried to blow it off. Shantel opened my door, sat down in the passenger seat and kept quiet. She knew what was up when I was on my horn.

"Hmm," Selena countered. "Where you at?"

"At the Salon."

"Okay baby, call me later."

"A'ight, I love you."

"Love you too."

I pushed my phone in my pocket and turned to Shantel. "What's up, baby?"

She leaned in and kissed my cheek. "Hey."

"We packed in there?" I asked her.

"A little. Nothin' I can't handle."

"That's how you feelin'?" I smiled at her cockiness.

"That's what I'm knowin'," she quipped. "What you doin' later, baby?"

"Ain't no tellin'."

"Ok, I'ma call you later. I gotta talk to you."

"About?"

She smiled and replied, "Later." She kissed my lips and jumped out the car.

Bitches.

I reached for my door handle and opened my door. I had to run in the salon and grab some paperwork. When I shut my door a detective car quickly pulled up. It was Smalls. *What the fuck you want?*

I leaned on my car and waited for him to hop out.

"Samuel, how you doin'?" He was dressed like a gang-unit officer. He had on some blue jeans, Kansas City Royals t-shirt, black Nike Air-Max's, and a pig-issued 40-cal sitting comfortably in his shoulder holster. His sunglasses concealed his eyes.

"Coo' till you showed up," I said as he walked up to me.

"Kremensky was right. You are funny," he smiled.

So was watchin' Kremensky beg for his life.

"What's up, man?" I had no patience with his hoe-ass.

"Oh nothin'." He put his hands on his hips and took a deep breath. "Just thought I'd stop by to say hello." He took his sunglasses off of his face.

"That's funny," I smiled.

"How's Mr. Walker doin'?" He was talking about Justin.

"He good. How's he supposed to be doin'?"

"His leg cool?"

"Why wouldn't it be?" I kept my cool.

Smalls walked up on me and his smile was replaced by a look of contempt. "I hope you're enjoying your freedom while you can. Unlike Kremensky, I don't play both sides of the fence."

"I ain't tryna hear dat shit."

"You're going to hear this." He walked up a little closer to me. "I *bleed* blue. I *breathe* blue. I have a reason to believe you killed my partner. I don't give a fuck if he was dirty or not. I'm comin' for your ass." He put his sunglasses back on and strolled to his car.

Chapter 20

I was sitting in my house later that night. Smalls had a nigga on edge. I went over that morning I killed Kremensky in my head. Thought about any possible slip-ups. I didn't think of any.

"That nigga ain't got nothin' on me," I said to myself.

As I sat up for a few minutes convincing myself that my tracks were covered, my phone rang. It was Tanya so I ignored it. After I sent her to voicemail I looked at the time on my phone.

It was 8:25 p.m.

She called right back. "Yeah?" I answered on the fourth ring.

"Spade, where you at?" She sounded like something was wrong.

"Chillin'."

"I need your help, please."

"What's up?"

"I'm stranded by the Boys and Girls Club on 43rd."

"Stranded?"

"My tire caught a flat and I can't get in touch wit' nobody." She sounded sincere but I didn't feel like going to help her out.

"A flat? You hot, man."

"Please, Spade. You know how these young niggas are if they see me by myself they might try to rob me or some-thin'." She had a point.

"Where you at?" I asked like I didn't remember.

"Spade, stop playin'."

"A'ight, give me a minute."

"Thank you, sweetie."

***

When I pulled in the Boys and Girls club parking lot I saw a white Lexus leaning on the curb. *Damn, lil' mama got a Lexo.* I'd never seen her car before.

I called her phone.

"Hello?" she answered.

"That's you?"

"Yeah." She opened her driver door and got out. I ended the call and pulled up behind her.

Before I got out I checked my waist to make sure my hammer was there. I got out and approached her. *Damn she lookin' good tonight,* I thought as I watched her mini-dress hug her body.

"Ain't nobody ever teach you how to change a tire?"

She put her hand on her hip and tilted her head to the side. "I wouldn't have called if I could." She sounded relieved that I was there.

"Sound good. Pop the trunk."

She opened her driver door and bent down to hit the trunk button. I eyed that ass as she bent down. She stayed bent over a little longer intentionally. *Play too much.*

I walked to her trunk and opened it. Inside were a lot of brand new outfits for men. All kind of shit: Rocawear, Black Label, Polo, Coogi, you name it. And they still had the security tags on them. Ace wasn't faking. Them bitches kept something going.

I shoved all of that shit to the back of the trunk and went for the spare tire and carjack. I snatched them out and sat them on the ground, as Tanya watched close like she was trying to learn.

I walked to my car and opened my passenger door, peeled off my shirt and threw it on the seat. I removed my Cartier watch and put it in the seat too. Tanya eyed my bare chest and licked her lips. I took my cannon off my waist and secured it under my passenger seat. Then I thought about it and retrieved it. *Fuck that,* I thought.

I walked back over to her car. I laid my cannon on her rear tire. That was the one that was flat. I grabbed the jack and put it under the frame of her car, then put the four-way on the lug nuts and started loosening them.

Tanya's phone rang. "Yeah, bitch," she answered. "… Spade's helping me … okay, bye."

"Who was that?" I asked as I picked the car up.

"My bitch, Carmen, dang," she responded sarcastically.

"Sound good."

I finally got the car up far enough to remove the tire. I unscrewed the lug-nuts and snatched the tire off. I reached over and grabbed the spare. As I was putting it on Tanya picked up my cannon.

"What kind of gun is this?"

"Put that down, lil' mama. It ain't a toy."

"Sorry." She placed it on the hood of my car.

When I got the tire on, I started twisting the lug-nuts on. Then a van pulled into the parking lot. *Who the fuck?* Two niggas hopped out masked down, with weapons in-hand.

I got up to go look for my cannon but Tanya beat me to it. I thought she was going to aim it at the niggas but she aimed it at me.

"Don't move, nigga," she said.

What the fuck, dis bitch.

The two niggas rushed over to me with their biscuits aimed at me. One of them smacked me upside my head. *SMACK!*

"Aagh!" I exclaimed as I held the side of my head and went to one knee. They both grabbed me and dragged me to the sliding door of their van. "You niggas better kill me," I told them.

"Shut the fuck up, nigga," one of them said. The other gentlemen grabbed some rope out of the van and tied my wrists together. Then they tied my feet and ankles together.

"Hurry up and get him in the van," I heard Tanya say.

They put a bag over my head and tossed me in the van.

Chapter 21

I was tied to a chair in a furnished bedroom. I looked around and noticed a queen-sized bed covered with a solid tan comforter. There was a 42-inch plasma TV hanging on the wall, and posters of Nicki Minaj, Jessica Rabbit, and Deelishis on the wall also.

This gotta be a bitch's room, I thought as I spotted some female cosmetics in front of the dresser mirror. The side of my head homeboy hit me on was pinging.

"You need anything to drink?" Tanya asked ,stepping into the room. She was accompanied by two gentlemen. I assumed they were the same niggas that pulled up to the Boys and Girls Club.

Tanya sat on the bed. The two niggas stood by the doorway. They had their masks off.

"Nah, I'm coo! What the fuck y'all want?" My eyes bounced to each one of them. Then my attention stayed on the two niggas. *Hold up.*

"You sure?" Tanya said.

"What's up?" I countered, not looking in her direction. I was still sizing up Owen and Kevin Hart. *Bingo,* I thought. They were the same niggas from Ace's wedding reception.

"Somethin' to drink?" she said.

"Bitch, do I look thirsty?" I turned my attention to her.

"Watch yo mouth, fam," one of the gentlemen said. I smiled at his tough guy act.

"Once again, what the fuck do you want?" I asked Tanya.

"Well ..." She stood up and came over to sit on my lap. My arms were tied behind the chair, and my ankles were tied to the legs of the chair. So I couldn't throw the bitch off me. "... How does five-hundred-thousand sound?" she whispered in my ear and kissed my cheek.

"Sound like you don' lost yo' muhfuckin' mind."

She got up off my lap and walked back over to the bed. The gentlemen that had his game face on came over to me and punched me in the face "Chill out, funny guy," he said, walking back to hold his post.

"What you think, you gon' get this shit off, Tanya?" I asked, trying to conceal the pain I felt from homeboy's punch. I had a tingling sensation where he punched me at.

"You know how long I been waitin' for this?" Tanya asked. It looked like her eyes were watering up.

"I don't know what for," I countered.

"So you thought you wouldn't pay for what you did to my family?" she said seriously.

I twisted my face up out of confusion. *Yo family?*

"Bitch, what the fuck are you talkin' 'bout?" I asked.

The same gentlemen extracted his pistol and approached me. *SMACK!* I spit out a mouth full of blood on the floor. *I better not get free.*

"This the last time I'ma tell you to watch yo mouth." He walked back over to his timid side-kick.

"I'm talkin' 'bout my brothers." Tanya stood up and came over to me. "First you killed my brother in that car wreck back in the day." She put her hands on her hips. "And I don't know for sure, but I have a strong feeling you killed my brother, Duece, too."

Ain't dis a bitch.

"Don't be surprised, honey …" She rubbed my cheek. "I've always stayed in Kansas, that's why you never seen me. We all have the same daddy."

"Is that right?" *This shit crazy.*

She walked back to the bed, sat down, and crossed her legs seductively. "That's right. But you know what?" She pointed her finger at me. "I might let you live if you get me the money today."

"And if I don't?"

"Do I really have to answer that, baby?"

All kind of thoughts were running through my mind. I started questioning my ability to avoid deception. Why didn't I see this coming? Why didn't Ace know his wife's cousin was Duece's sister? Was Ace's wife in on it? Would they kill me?

I thought about my daughter and what she was probably doing at that moment. Would I see her again? I looked at Tanya.

"Let me make a call?"

She smiled and nodded at Kid and Play. The timid one pulled a phone out of his pocket.

Hoe-ass nigga, I thought.

He handed the phone to Tanya. "Who you callin'?" she asked me.

"Does it matter, bitch?"

The nigga that got a kick out of hitting me started to approach me. "He coo'," Tanya said to him. He returned to his post. "He's just upset."

"I'm not upset, I'm sad," I retorted.

"About what, baby?"

"Sad that today you three muhfuckas made death wishes," I smiled.

The tough guy rushed over to me. What I said must've pissed the timid one off too, because he hurried over to me as well. They took turns beating and smacking me. I tried to struggle free to no avail. In seconds I felt my right eye swelling up. Blood leaked out of my nose and mouth.

"That's enough!" Tanya yelled. I felt dizzy and my vision was blurry. My head hung down like my neck could no longer support it.

***

What seemed like an hour or two later Tanya walked back into the room. My right eye was swollen shut, and I had a severe headache.

"Here you go, baby." She came over to me with a cup of water. "You look thirsty."

I didn't want shit that bitch was offering but I needed it. My throat was dry and my stomach was empty. I lifted my head up and let her pour the water down my mouth. I looked down at my shirt and it was filthy. Sweat and blood got comfortable on that muhfucka.

"You gon' let me make that call or not?" I looked up at Tanya.

"Sure, baby." She tried to rub my cheek but I moved my head and looked at that bitch like she was crazy.

She chuckled at my action and walked to the dresser. She opened the top drawer and pulled out a pair of scissors. *What the fuck is up wit' dis bitch?*

She walked over to me with a devilish grin. "What you think you 'bout to do wit' those?" I asked.

She didn't reply. She put the scissors to the bottom of my Etro shirt and started cutting it up the middle. I hoped she wouldn't cut my torso on accident. After she cut the middle she moved behind me and cut my sleeves down the middle too. Then she snatched the shirt off me and threw it on the floor.

"You gon' let me get that call or what?"

"Soon." She rubbed her index finger down the middle of my chest. My jaw clinched out of frustration. I couldn't believe I was tied to a chair with a swollen, bloody face.

She walked back out of the room.

Chapter 22

Tanya and the Doublemint Twins walked back in the room together. Tanya sat back on the bed and the two clowns held their previous post.

"What time is it?" I asked Tanya.

"Ten-forty-five," she countered. I knew it was getting late due to the darkness outside.

"You gon' give me that call or what?"

She held out her hand, signaling for one of the niggas to give her the phone. "The number?" she asked me.

I gave her Sparkle's number. She dialed it and walked over to me. She put the phone to my ear and I listened to the phone ring. *Pick up, pick up.*

"Hello, Ms. Ohio speaking." Sparkle played a role because she didn't know the number.

"This Spade."

"What's up, cousin?" She got back on the range.

"I'm in a jam. Got caught slippin'."

"I'm tracing the call now."

"They want 500k," I played on.

"Really?"

"Yeah, where we at, third street?" I asked Tanya.

"No, I'll call her with the location." Tanya's dumb ass didn't know I was letting Sparkle know it was three of them.

"They gon' call you wit' the location," I told Sparkle.

"No need," and Sparkle hung up.

"She ready," I told Tanya as I moved my head back from the phone.

"Good, I'll be right back, yall watch him," she told the two niggas.

"How much yall niggas gettin'?" I asked when Tanya was out of the room.

"Nigga, we gettin' half. Two-hunid and fifty thou-wow," the timid one bragged. He looked young. Probably in his late teens. The other one looked a little older.

"Shut up, nigga," the tough guy told him.

He frowned at the tough guy. "What? We gon' kill him anyway."

Really?

"Straight up, huh?" I countered. "I'll give you niggas the whole five-hunid if yall untie me right now."

The younger one looked like he was considering it.

"What the fuck we look like?" the older one said.

"Yeah, what we look like?" the younger one followed.

I laughed at them niggas and shook my head. "Yall sure?"

"We good," the tough guy retorted.

"Yeah, a'ight. I guess you niggas will die tonight then."

They didn't like that. They both rushed and proceeded to beat me. I let out loud sighs as they took turns beating me in the face and body. I felt like I was about to die in this muhfucka. I tried to struggle free but they had my wrists and ankles tied like they were professional kidnappers.

After what seemed like forever, Tanya came into the room. "What the fuck are yall doin'?" They stopped their attack. *Thank God this bitch came in.*

I felt like my world was over. I felt like giving up. They had a nigga in a jam. *Sparkle need to hurry her ass up.*

"He keep running his fuckin' mouth," the older one countered.

"Get the fuck out!" She pointed outside the doorway for emphasis.

Chapter 23

"You know I wish we could've met under different circumstances," Tanya said as she sat on the bed.

I didn't respond because I couldn't. I didn't have the energy to. It felt like my left eye was about to swell up too. My breathing was heavy and it felt like my shoulders were about to pop out of their sockets from my arms being tied behind my back so long.

"You hear me?" she asked. I couldn't see out of my right eye. And my left eye allowed little vision.

"What time is it?" I said, losing consciousness.

"Time to get paid. My cousins went to meet yo girl."

Cousins, huh?

"Yeah?" I shook my head, trying to stay alert.

"The sad thing is, I'ma have to let my cousins kill you."

"Yeah?"

"Afraid so." She got up off the bed. I turned my head in the direction she walked so I could see her out of my left eye. "My brothers are in the ground, so in the ground *you* go."

"Yeah?"

"I got a surprise for you first." She walked out of the room.

Again I tried to wiggle free to no avail. I didn't know what that bitch was going to get.

I just knew I couldn't take any more torture. Seconds later Tanya and the bitch from the carwash walked in the room ass naked. *Carmen?*

"Figured I'd let you go out with some good thoughts. 'Member you was honkin' at her. It's a shame you'll never get *any* pussy again."

"Damn, girl, why yall do his fine-ass like that?" Carmen said.

"Shut up, bitch," Tanya said.

Where the fuck you at, Sparkle?

Carmen laid on the bed and opened her legs, exposing her meaty pussy. Tanya got on her knees on the floor and pulled Carmen's pussy to her face. My vision blurred a little.

"Damn, bitch." Carmen started to moan.

I closed my left eye and started to nod off. I could still hear Tanya and Carmen.

"Oooh ... shit."

Sparkle, where the fuck you at, I thought. Carmen cried and moaned for another ten minutes or so. "Let me taste you."

I heard bodies moving so I forced my left eye open. Them raunchy hoes were in the sixty-nine position. Their bodies were a blur but I tried to stay focused on them. I didn't need any surprises.

They were "mming" and "awwing" as they tasted each other. I wasn't turned on, though. Them psycho hoes were probably gon' poison a nigga after their twisted-asses got done fucking each other.

"You like this, Spade?" Tanya asked as Carmen stuck something in and out of her pussy. I assumed it was a dildo but I could barely see. And my head was hurting even more.

"Let's … suck … his … dick."

I gotta get the fuck outta here.

After a short pause, Tanya concurred. They both got off the bed and came over to me. Carmen went for my belt and unbuckled it. Tanya unbuttoned my shorts and unzipped them. I wanted to fight them off but I didn't have the energy. I couldn't move. They both forced my boxers and shorts down to my ankles.

I started slipping out of consciousness again as one of them wrapped her mouth around my limp dick. I shook my head and forced my left eye back open. My dick started to harden as Carmen sucked my dick and Tanya tongued my balls.

"That's right. Get hard for mama," Carmen said.

Tanya came up and wrestled for my meat. Carmen took Tanya's previous position. My whole being was exhausted. I just wanted all that shit to be a bad dream. I dream I could wake up from.

"Mmm," Tanya moaned as she continued her oral attack.

"Girl, let me get some more," Carmen said.

Tanya raised up and let Carmen get back on my pipe. I needed to get the fuck out of here.

"It's a shame this good dick will go to waste," I heard Tanya say.

My mind and body couldn't hang on anymore and I dozed off.

Chapter 24

"Spade." Somebody slapped my face. "Spade!"

Sparkle, I thought as I came to. She had on all black like a ninja, and her hair was pulled back in a ponytail. After she made eye contact with my left eye she hurried behind me and untied me. I was glad to see her.

My arms felt like concrete slabs when they swung free. I looked down and my shorts were still down to my ankles. I felt violated and embarrassed. After Sparkle untied my ankles, she helped me to my feet. I still had strength in my legs but my upper body felt like I got jumped by a thousand men.

Sparkle led me to the dresser and leaned me up against it to support my body.

"No! No!" a female screamed.

SMACK!

"Shut the fuck up, bitch!" *Ace.* He must've had one of them hoes in another room, slapping the dog shit out of her.

Sparkle bent down to pull my shorts up to my waist. She moved my dick to pull my shorts all the way up. When she zipped and buckled my shorts up she walked me out of the room.

In the living room the two tough guys lay dead on the floor. Brain fragments rested next to their cracked skulls.

"What's up, bro?" Ace looked over at me and a tear rolled down his cheek.

In front of him, Carmen and Tanya were tied to two chairs. Carmen's dead weight was slumped over in her chair. It looked like her throat was hanging out of her neck. Tanya's face was bloody and more swollen than mine. Ace was pistol-whipping her. His cannon and the hand that gripped the cannon were covered in Tanya's blood.

"I left her for you," Ace said.

Sparkle led me over to them. I grabbed the gun out of Ace's hand and shot Tanya four times in the face. Then I handed the gun to Sparkle.

"Come on, bro, let's go." Ace put my arm over his shoulder and led me to the door. Sparkle opened the door for us and we walked out. "We in that truck," Ace said, referring to a black GMC Envoy. It was still dark outside. But I was unaware of the time.

As we were walking down the porch steps, Ranno jumped out of the driver's side of the truck. He had two gasoline cans in his hands. He walked right past us and headed in the house.

Ace helped me in the back seat when we made it to the truck. Sparkle and Ranno were inside of the house. I knew they were decorating the house with gasoline.

"I can't believe that bitch!" Ace exclaimed.

"It's good," I countered with a dry throat. I glanced at the digital clock on the dashboard and it was 2:21 a.m.

"Nah, it ain't good." Ace was beyond pissed. "Justin got yo whip down at the studio," he said, frustrated.

"Right on."

"Yo phone and shit in the glove box."

Sparkle and Ranno finally came out of the house. They rushed to the truck as the house got brighter with flames.

***

I was in one of Sparkle's hideouts, laying in a king-size bed. Ranno said he was heading down to the loft. Ace was in the living room making a few calls for me. I told him to call Selena, Casey, and Shantel to let them know what's going on.

"Here's another ice pack," Sparkle said, walking into the room with an ice pack in one hand, and a glass of water in the other hand. She sat both items on the night stand right next to the bed I was laying in. My head was feeling a lot better after I swallowed the pain pills she gave me.

"Right on, Sparkle," I told her. If it wasn't for her, then them muhfuckas probably would've cut me down.

"I got you." She sat on the bed next to me and removed the first ice pack I had on my eye. It was melting anyway. She put the new ice pack on my eye and got up to leave. "I'ma put this back in the freezer." I couldn't refrain from looking at her figure in that tight black body suit as she left.

"I told everybody you coo', bro," Ace said, walking into the room. He tried to avoid looking at me. I know it hurt him to see me like this.

"Right on, bro," I countered.

"I'ma get on out of here. I'll come check on you tomorrow."

"A'ight, C-safe."

He left in a hurry.

I grabbed the remote to the plasma TV hanging on the wall and turned it on. It was on CNN so I left it there. They were talking about war. How many forms war presented itself in. The variety of deceitful maneuvers in the game. The playground is deadly. One slip up and you can lose your life.

Sparkle stuck her head in the door. "I'm right in the other room if you need anything."

"Coo'," was all I offered.

I can't believe Tanya was Duece's sister.

That explained her aggressiveness. Her cunning. Her sexual advances. If greed didn't outweigh revenge, that bitch would've had me knocked.

After another ten to fifteen minutes of pondering, the TV started watching me as I dozed off and went to sleep.

Chapter 25

Two weeks later I was back to normal. I was on the way to my house on a Wednesday morning. I had just left a gas station near my home. When I pulled in my driveway my phone started ringing.

"Yeah," I answered as I put my whip in park.

"Sam, what's going on?" Puzzo said.

"Chillin'." I hopped out my car and walked toward my house.

"How's everything?" he asked. I unlocked my door and entered my spot.

"Coo', I guess." I walked over to my couch and sat down. "Just tryna focus on my businesses."

"I know you might be upset, but I have some bad news."

I frowned and countered, "Bad news?"

"The DA has issued a warrant for your arrest."

I sat up on the edge of my couch with a confused expression on my face. "What the fuck you mean a warrant, Puzzo?"

"Don't worry. They—"

"*Don't worry?*"

"Sam, I'll tear this case apart. You know that?"

"What's the warrant for?"

"Murder."

"The shit Smalls been on my ass about?" I went to my kitchen to retrieve my poison.

"Yes."

"So what now?" I asked after I hit the bottle.

"They're going to let me turn you in."

No good.

"How much is the bond?"

"No bond, yet."

I hit the bottle again as I walked over to my couch and sat down. "You know I can't do that."

"Don't be stupid, Sam."

"Let me think about it and call you back." I hung up the fucking phone and tossed it on my couch.

Ain't dis a bitch!

I needed to figure some shit out. I knew the case was weak but I wasn't trying to turn myself in. Them muhfuckas would have to catch me.

What about my daughter? What about my op?

I reached for my phone to call Ace, but it rang when I grabbed it.

"Yeah?" I answered it.

"Open the door." It was Casey. *When she get back?*

"A'ight." I got up and opened the door for her. I left my door ajar and walked back to the couch.

"What's up, baby?" Casey said when she walked in. She had on a yellow sundress and some open-toe sandals.

"Chillin'."

She put her Coach bag on my living room table and sat on my lap. "You miss me?"

"You know I missed you." I kissed her.

"What's wrong?"

"Shit."

"You sure?" she inquired.

"Positive," I countered. "How's OG doin'?"

"He's doin' cool. He keeps complaining about his beard being gone, but he's alright." I smiled at the thought of OG Casa. I wondered if he would suggest I turn myself in.

"That's what's up."

"I got back this morning. One of his little hoes came to see him, so I left."

"Yeah?" I palmed her ass. I missed her.

"You heal well." She rubbed my face.

"I guess."

"Come on." She got off my lap and walked toward my stairs. "Let me take care of you."

I got up and followed her to the steps.

***

Two hours later I was in traffic driving with extreme caution. I was working the shit out of my mirrors. Casey went to her house after we fucked. I was on my way to meet Ace at the studio.

As I was pulling up, Ace and Justin were standing outside smoking. I parked behind Justin's Jaguar and hopped out.

"What's good, bro?" Justin asked as I approached them.

"Chillin'," I countered.

"You good?" Ace asked me, throwing the remainder of the Backwood.

"As good as I can be." When I made it to them we embraced and walked in the studio.

"What's up wit' OG Casa?" Ace asked as we all sat down.

"Casey said he coo'. I ain't talked to him yet," I replied. "What yall niggas been doin'?"

"Kickin' back," Justin said.

"I got a little situation," I said seriously.

"Situation?" Ace frowned.

"Whatchu talkin' 'bout, bro?" Justin countered.

"The DA issued a warrant for my arrest." My eyes bounced from Ace to Justin.

"A warrant?" Justin replied. Ace just shook his head in disbelief.

"They chargin' me wit' Kremensky's murder."

"This some bullshit," Ace offered.

"I'm hip," Justin said to himself.

"Puzzo said they gon' let me turn myself in, but I'm coo'. They gon' have to catch me."

"Damn right," Ace smiled.

"I don't know, bro. That probably won't look too good," Justin said. Ace looked at Justin like he had some shit on his face.

"I'ma need y'all niggas to hold some shit down," I told both of them, disregarding Justin's opinion.

"Whatever you need, bro," Ace responded seriously.

"Yeah, whatever," Justin complied.

"Coo', I'ma figure this shit out and let yall know."

"You know we got you," Ace said.

I couldn't believe the position I was in. I had been out of the joint for damn near seven years and now I was wanted for murder of a cop. I know the District Attorney would try to come at me with everything they could. I also know me going on the run would make me look guilty but I didn't give a fuck.

"I 'preciate you niggas steppin' up, bro," I countered.

"It's all good," they both said.

***

"Yo daughter misses you," Selena said through the phone. I was sitting in my bedroom going over a game plan in my head.

"I miss her too. Where she at?"

"Hold on," Selena said. Say hi to Daddy," I heard her tell our daughter.

"Hi, Daddy," Samantha said through the phone.

I smiled and my eyes watered at the thought of me trying to raise her from the big yard. "Hey, baby," I said, trying to stay strong.

"I miss you," she said.

"Miss you too, baby," I countered as a tear rolled down my cheek.

She chuckled and said, "Love you."

"I love you too."

"She so silly," Selena said as she got back on the phone. I pressed my eyelids with my index finger and thumb to prevent any more tears. "You comin' by?" she asked.

"Yeah, I gotta talk to you anyway."

"About what?"

"I'ma holla at you."

"So you're not going to tell me?" Selena asked.

"I'ma holla at you about it."

"Alright, I love you."

"Love you too."

I tossed my phone to the side, laid back and stared at the ceiling. I had so much shit going for me. Sitting down for a murder is something I didn't want to do willingly. They'd have to catch me. And if they did catch me, I hoped Puzzo would do his thing and get me acquitted.

As I continued to ponder on my issues, my phone started ringing. "Yeah," I answered.

"What's good, cuzz?" Ace asked.

"Slow motion."

"I'm 'bout to swing through."

"A'ight."

Chapter 26

"I'ma get up outta there, bro," Ace said. We were sitting in my living room shooting-the-shit over a bottle of XO. He was talking about leaving Ashley.

"You sure 'bout that?"

"I can't be around a bitch I can't trust." He took a swig from the bottle.

"And she said she didn't know Tanya was Duece's sister?"

"That's what she say," he said weakly.

"You believe her?" I grabbed the bottle from him and took a swig.

"No good."

I shook my head as if I was saying no. I didn't know what to say, but I felt him. Even if she didn't know Tanya was Duece's sister. If Ace couldn't trust her, the relationship was no good. I thought Ashley knew, to keep it a hunid. And I wanted to kill that bitch but she was carrying Ace's seed.

"What about the baby?" I passed him the bottle.

"That's why I'm so fucked up about leaving."

"This shit crazy, cuzz. A nigga don't know who to trust."

"I'm hip," Ace agreed. "This shit is never-ending."

"Welcome to deception's playground, my nigga."

"I done wore my welcome out."

We both shared a short laugh. An evasive laugh to tell the truth. Because wasn't shit funny about what me and Ace had been through. We just played the hand we were dealt to the best of our ability. That's the only way I can justify the madness.

"So where you talkin' 'bout shakin' to, bro?" I asked.

"Probably grab a lil' loft or somethin'."

"You can hold the spot down," I suggested.

He screwed his face up at me. "I ain't thinkin' like that, my nigga, where you goin'?"

I broke down my game plan to him. Told him it was a possibility I could be sitting down for a while. But them muhfuckas would have to catch me. I let him know that I planned on shooting to Miami. Squat at Sparkles beach house for a minute. I let him know I needed him and Justin to hold the entertainment company down and look out for Samantha.

After a short verbal battle he said he'd hold it down.

***

"How you feel about helping me out at the salon?" I asked Casey over the phone. She was still at her restaurant doing last minute paperwork.

"Whatchu mean?"

"I'ma be shootin' to Miami for a minute," I reluctantly stated.

"Miami?"

I started pacing my living room floor because I knew the conversation wouldn't go as smooth as I wanted it to. "Yeah, Miami. I'm going down there to check on some new locations for another salon," I lied.

"Hmm," she offered. "What do you need me to do?"

"I'ma have Shantel call you and go over everything with you."

"Shantel?" There was a knock at my door and my heart dropped. *Fuck, the boys.* I thought the police were at my door.

I tippy-toed to my door and looked out of the peephole. *Shantel?* I was relieved because it wasn't the police. But I didn't dig lil' mama popping up at my house.

"Who is Shantel?" Casey asked.

"She replaced Lisa," I said as I opened the door for Shantel. Shantel walked right past me and took a seat on my couch. She put her phone on the table and crossed her legs.

"Whatever boy, have her call me."

"Boy?"

"Bye." She hung up on me.

I turned my attention to Shantel. "What's good?" She looked like something was on her mind. I went over and took a seat next to her.

She responded nervously. "Whatchu been doin' all day?"

"Chillin'. What's up?" I knew something was on her mind.

"I can't just stop by?"

"Yeah, but I know somethin' is up." I looked at her seriously.

She looked down at the floor and started fiddling with her fingers. "I'm ... I'm pregnant."

Get the fuck outta here.

"You what?"

"I'm pregnant." A tear rolled down her cheek.

I wasn't ready for this shit. But I knew it was a possibility. "How you know?" was all I could say.

She looked at me like I was crazy. "Spade, stop playin'."

"I'm sayin' ..." I rose to my feet and walked to my kitchen. I grabbed a bottle of Remy and walked back in the living room. "You sure you ready for a kid?" I tried to hold the responsibility of a child over her head.

"Are *you*?" she asked defensively as I sat back down.

I didn't want to tell her she could possibly be a single mother if I got slammed on that Kremensky case. She didn't even know I was going on the run.

"I gotta tell you somethin'." I tried to pass her the bottle after I hit it. Not even thinking about her being pregnant.

"Boy, stop playin'." She turned her face up and touched her stomach. *I'm trippin'*, I thought. "What do you have to tell me?"

"I gotta shoot outta town for a while," I said.

"What happened?"

"I'm lookin' for a Miami location for the salon."

She looked at me quizzically. "Miami location?"

I took a swig of the poison. "Is that hard to believe?"

"Are you in trouble?"

This bitch won't let up.

"I'm coo', baby." I leaned in and gave her a kiss. "I'm just tryna expand the business."

"So I'm supposed to run the salon by myself?"

"Casey gon' help you."

"Who's Casey?"

"Someone close to me." I grabbed Shantel's phone off the table and put Casey's number in there. "Call her next Monday."

"Somethin' don't feel right." She moved over to me and wrapped her arms around me. She smelled like Chanel perfume.

"Everything coo', lil' mama," I assured her, rubbing her back.

"You promise?"

515

"Yeah. And the baby gon' be coo'."

She leaned up and gave me her tongue. "I hope so," she said after our lips unlocked.

"I got you." I picked her up and carried her upstairs to my bedroom.

***

While Shantel slept, I sat on my back patio. Drink in hand, mentally preparing to go on the run. *And* Shantel was pregnant. That was the worst timing ever.

"Fuck!" I exclaimed to myself.

I looked up at the night sky and wondered was there a God out there somewhere. Was he punishing me? Would he get me out of this jam? Why now? Why this?

Kremensky was a pig who deserved to get killed. Maybe I was getting punished for something else and it just came in the form of a murder charge on a pig. Now I had to go on the run and leave everything behind. My operation, my daughter, my team, and my soon-to-be child.

I felt like the world was against me. I felt like God was against me. And the Remy wasn't making it any better.

"Why you sittin' out here?" Shantel asked from behind me. She sounded exhausted.

"Thinkin'," I countered. She came over and sat on my lap.

"You know you can tell me anything," she said softly.

"I know." I hit my bottle again. "It ain't nothin'."

"Well come back to bed." She got up and grabbed my hand.

Chapter 27

"Bye, baby." Shantel gave me a kiss before she walked out my door the next morning.

"Be careful," I told her.

"I will." She closed my door behind her.

I looked at my clock on the wall and it read 9:42 A.M. I still had to go see my daughter and talk to Selena. As I sat and pondered on my day, my phone rang. It was OG Casa.

"OG," I answered.

"What's up, son?" He sounded good.

"Tryna figure it out. How you feelin'?" I slouched down in my couch.

"Ah man, I'm good. Can't believe I'm beardless but it'll grow back," he laughed.

"I hear you."

"So what's goin' on witchu?"

"Man, got some bad news."

"What?"

"Puzzo said the DA charged me for that Kremensky shit."

"That's not good. What's yo plan?"

"Hit the way-way."

After a short pause, he said, "You sure?"

"Can't turn myself in, OG, I'm good."

"I know you're man enough to live wit' yo decision."

"Damn right."

"Let me know where you're headed and I'll get some money down there to you."

"No need, OG. You know I'm good. I just need you to make sure everything coo' when you get back to the town.

"I got you."

I couldn't believe that I was having this conversation with OG Casa. I wouldn't even get to see him before I headed out. That hurt.

"Right on, OG," I said. "So when you headin' this way?"

"In a few weeks."

"Coo'. I'll hit you from the burn-out soon as I land."

"A'ight, be careful," and we hung up.

Damn.

I picked up my phone and called my lawyer. The secretary put me straight through. "Sam," Puzzo said.

"What's goin' on?"

"They said you have until tonight to turn yourself in."

"Can't do it."

"Sam, I'll make sure you get a bond."

"That's coo'. But I can't do it. Fuck them pigs."

"So what are you going to do?"

"I'll call you wit' the details." I hung up on him.

Dem muhfuckas talkin' 'bout tonight.

I ran upstairs and packed some money in a duffle bag—$200,000 to be exact. Then I got on the phone and called Ace.

"What's up, cuzz?" Ace answered.

"I need you to come through."

***

"Take that to Ranno's loft, bro."

Ace was sitting in his car in my garage with the duffle bag. "He know I'm on the way?"

"He waitin' on you."

"A'ight."

I hit the wall push-button to let the garage up. Ace backed out and slid off. I jumped in my Benz and backed out too, tapping my programmed visor remote to let the garage back down. Then I headed to Selena's.

I pulled up to Selena's twenty minutes later. I used my key to enter as usual.

When I walked in, Selena and our daughter were in the kitchen while Selena cooked.

"Daddy, Daddy!" Samantha ran to me with her arms out.

I reached down and picked her up. "Hey, baby." I kissed her on the cheek. I walked over to Selena and kissed her neck. She had sausages laying on a plate next to the stove. Inside the skillet she had three French Toasts cooking. It smelled good in this muhfucka.

"Hey?" Selena said.

"What's up?" I said, nibbling on Samantha's hand.

"Just makin' breakfast."

"I hope you makin' enough."

I walked out of the kitchen with my daughter still in my arms, took her to Selena's room and sat on the bed. I laid back and laid Samantha on my chest.

"You miss me?" I asked her.

She gave me a serious look because she was really trying to understand what I was saying. "I *mishu*," she said.

I stared into her big eyes, instantly regretting all the dirt I had done in my life. All the shit that led up to this present moment. "Miss you too, baby." I patted her butt and tickled her.

She laughed uncontrollably and buried her face in my chest. I leaned up and sat her on my lap. "Daddy gotta go for a while." She looked up in my eyes and just listened so I continued. "I'ma still see you baby, just not as much. I made some choices and I have to accept what's comin'. You hear me?"

"Breakfast is finished." Selena stood in the doorway.

I wiped the water from my eyes. "A'ight." I picked up Samantha and walked to the kitchen.

***

"What were you saying to Samantha?" Selena asked. We were sitting on the bed talking. Samantha was in her room taking a nap.

"I gotta shoot to Miami for a while."

"Why?"

"I got charged for a crime I didn't commit," I lied.

Selena stood up and started pacing the floor. "What?" She was about to start crying.

"Don't trip, baby. It'll get handled."

"What crime?" she asked as tears rolled down her face.

I went to her and held her in my arms. "Some bullshit, baby."

"*Por favor no me dejes,*" she sobbed.

"Trust me, baby." I grabbed her shoulders and held her out in front of me. "I need you to be strong for our daughter."

She wiped the tears from her face. "Okay."

I pulled her back in my embrace. "I'm just leaving for a little while. Till I figure this shit out."

"What do you need me to do?" she asked softly.

"Nothin' yet, baby." I rubbed her back. "I'll let you know."

"Okay." She kissed my neck.

Damn, I'ma miss y'all, I thought.

Selena kissed my lips and I palmed her ass. Then we fed each other our tongues and kissed like we would never see each other again.

A few seconds later we were stripping out of our clothes.

Chapter 28

Later that evening I was still at Selena's. We were sitting in the living room watching TV—me, Selena, and Samantha. I needed to spend that time with them. I didn't know what the future held for me.

As we chilled in the living room on family time, my phone rang. It was Sparkle.

"What's up?" I answered.

"I'm ready when you are," she said.

"I'ma shoot down there Saturday."

"Okay, bye."

I shoved my phone in my pocket.

"You're leaving in two days?" Selena asked.

"Yeah."

It looked like her eyes were starting to water up. "Everything gon' be coo'. Trust me." I put my arm around her.

"*Trust me*," Samantha tried to mock me.

That put a smile on me and Selena's faces.

"I hope so," Selena said.

***

"You know, one day you will get caught," Ranno said. We were sitting in OG Casa's office at his dealership.

"I'll deal with that when the day comes," I responded confidently.

"You think you'll beat it?"

"I'm sure I will. But they gon' have to work to get me." I thought about my last seven-year bid. How stressful it was at times.

"I hear you. So when are you leaving?"

"Saturday," I said. "I'll come get the money that mornin'."

"Two days?"

"Yep."

"If you run out of money don't hesitate to call."

"Right on, but I think I'll be good."

***

"I been thinkin', bro ..." I was riding with Ace. We were driving nowhere in particular. Just pushing, trying to get a little time in before I shook it. "... maybe you *should* get a loft," I told him.

"I was thinking the same thing. Even if I told them I didn't know where you was. Yo spot will still be hot."

"Scorching," I added.

"I found a loft earlier today downtown."

"I can dig it," I said as I gazed out of the passenger window. I paid close attention to everything we passed. The liquor stores, barber shops, strip malls, restaurants. Everything.

The 'hood babies playing in the streets. The smokers and drunks hanging on the corners. The exotic cars, the candy-painted Retro's. The fast women, even the relentless pigs.

I would miss it all. The heartbeat of Kansas City, Missouri. The culture, the hustle, the swag. *Damn*, I thought to myself as various thoughts paraded my brain.

"… You hear me, nigga?" Ace asked, tapping my shoulder, pulling me out of my trance.

"What's up, bro?"

"I said Casey called me asking me all kind of questions."

"Questions?"

"Yeah. You didn't tell her you was goin' on the run?"

"Not yet," I said weakly.

"She sounded kinda hot, my nigga."

She don't miss a beep.

"I'ma holla at her."

"You better, nigga." Ace laughed. "So when you headin' out?"

"Two days," I told him. "Matter' fact …" I picked up my phone and sent a text to Puzzo's personal phone. I told him to tell the DA he would bring me in next Monday. *Damn near forgot.*

"What's up?" Ace asked.

"Had to text Puzzo. But yeah, bro, I'm outta here in two days."

***

"So when was you gon' tell me?" Casey asked. We were sitting in my living room. We had been there for about ten minutes. She was waiting in my driveway when Ace dropped me off.

"Today," I lied. I didn't know how to tell her.

"Nigga quit lyin'." She bounced to her feet and stood over me. "What you thought I couldn't handle the news?" She put her hands on her hips. "I'm not a kid no more, Spade."

Her frustration was sexy to me. "I know you ain't."

"So don't keep nothin' like that from me."

"How'd you know anyway?"

"Daddy. He thought you told me."

"Because I was."

"Whatever." She covered her face with her hands and started crying. I pulled her down on my lap and wrapped my arms around her.

"Don't trip, man. I'ma take care of dis shit."

"What if you don't?" She looked deep in my eyes.

"I will."

"You better." She stood back up and walked to my kitchen. "'Cause I'm not gon' be raising no baby by myself!"

Baby?

"What?" I stood up and walked towards the kitchen.

"You heard me." She stormed past me with a bottle of water in her hand. She sat down on the couch.

I turned around and went over to her. "Whatchu talkin' 'bout?" I sat down next to her.

She took a swig of the bottled water. "I'm pregnant, Spade."

This is too much for a nigga to handle.

"When was you gon' tell me?"

"Now you know."

Chapter 29

Saturday, day of departure

I was in my kitchen grabbing a pint of Remy out of my freezer. Selena was on her way over. Our daughter was at my mother's house. I had my day planned out. I would see Selena this morning, catch Casey and Shantel after that, and meet Ace and Sparkle at Ranno's. Sparkle would drive me to Miami later in the evening.

As I walked out of my kitchen my phone rang. "Yeah?" I answered.

"What's goin' on?" It was OG Casa.

I sat down at my dining room table. "Chillin'." I hit the Remy one time.

"Everything lined up?"

"Yeah, shit in order."

"When you get down there, call me. And understand that I don't agree wit' yo decision, but I support it."

"I know, OG."

"A'ight, I'm gone," and he hung up.

As soon as I sat my phone on my marble table, it rang again. "Yeah?"

"I'm outside," Selena said before hanging up. I put my phone back on the table.

I jumped to my feet and opened the door for her. She hopped out of her black Acura in a tight shoulderless mini dress. Her long hair moved with the mild wind as she walked to my front door. She looked like a runway model.

She play too much.

"What's up, baby?" she said when she made it to me. She kissed my lips and walked to my kitchen. I noticed her walk was a little nastier than usual. She must've wanted some dick before I left.

I shut my door and followed her. "What's up?"

When I got in my kitchen she was looking in my freezer. She pulled out one of my Remy bottles. "Open this," she said, holding the bottle out to me.

I chuckled because she didn't drink for real. "It's one open on the table." I grabbed the bottle from her and put it back in the freezer.

She sashayed to my dining room. I followed behind her and had a seat at my table.

"What time are you leaving?" She took a sip straight from the bottle. She damn near coughed it back up.

"Slow down." I smiled at the ugly face she made. "'Bout six."

She looked at the clock on my wall. "It's nine in the morning," she said quietly to herself.

She grabbed the bottle and took another swig. She handled that gulp a little better.

"It's gon' be a'ight, baby." I grabbed her hand.

"You promise?"

"Yeah," I responded, even though I didn't have a fucking clue. I grabbed the bottle and took a swig myself.

"My father said if you're having *any* doubts about your lawyer's competence he'll hire the best team for you." She gently rubbed my hand.

"Tell him I appreciate it."

My phone started ringing again. "Don't answer it, baby," Selena said.

"I got to." I went over to my table to get it. "Yeah?" I said as I flopped on my couch.

"What's good, cuzz?" It was Ace.

"Hollerin' at Selena."

He said, "Just tryna see what time you want me to meet you at Ranno's."

"Meet me there at five."

"You sure you don't need me to do nothin' else?"

Selena hit the bottle of Remy again and stripped out of her mini dress. She didn't have anything on underneath it.

"Nah, you good," I responded, not taking my eyes off of Selena's amazing figure.

531

"A'ight, bro."

Selena walked over to me.

"A'ight," I said, as I hung up and put my phone back on the table. "That's how you feelin'?"

"Come on." She headed for the stairs to go up to my bedroom. I jumped up and followed.

As soon as we got in my bedroom I started coming out of my clothes. Selena helped me with my shoes and sweat-pants. As soon as my dick was free she wrapped her wet mouth around it. I laid back in my bed and watched her work.

"Do yo thang then," I said to her.

She "mmmed" and "awwed" while she fed on my package. She was going all out too. Sucking my balls and everything. I grabbed the back of her head as she went to work.

A few minutes later I got her up off my dick. I laid her down and spread her legs. I tasted her meaty entrance.

"Damn, daddy," she cried.

I licked her clit and put a couple fingers in and out of her pussy. She gyrated her hips and moaned from the pleasure. Her pussy was dripping wet. After I sucked her pussy for a while longer I decided to penetrate her.

"Mmm," she moaned when I entered her.

***

An hour later me and Selena were in my bedroom having a small disagreement.

"Why do I need those?" she asked, looking at two handguns that I laid on my bed.

"Because I want you to have 'em for protection."

She sat on the edge of my bed and shook her head. "I don't like guns, Spade."

"I understand that. But I want you to go to the range wit' Casey."

"What are they?"

"A baby forty, and a baby nine." I picked the baby forty up and put one in the head. "It's ready, but the safety is on. This is the safety." I showed her where the safety was. "Safety on, safety off," I demonstrated for her.

"You really think I need those?"

"You never know."

"I guess." She shook her head like she was appalled. *Women.*

My phone started beeping. Notifying me of a text message. I picked it up and it was an anonymous text.

It read: I'M DOWNSTAIRS BABY

What the fuck?

I grabbed the baby nine and walked out of my bedroom.

Chapter 30

I walked down my steps cautiously. I didn't know who the fuck was in my house. I held my hammer out in front of me when I got to the bottom of my steps. My living room was empty as I slowly crept through.

Somebody playin' too fuckin' much.

I walked down the hallway that led to my kitchen. Nobody was there. I listened closely for any movement, I didn't hear anything.

When I walked towards my dining room I felt something hard touch the back of my head. "Put the gun down, baby," a familiar voice said.

Ain't dis a bitch.

I slowly put the gun on my dining room table.

"Go over there and have a seat," said the voice.

I strolled to my couch and sat down. *What the fuck*, I thought as I looked at the perpetrator. It was Maria.

"What the fuck are you doin'?" I asked.

She walked over and stood about three feet from in front of me. "I miss you," she said.

I looked her up and down, assessing her frame. She had her hair pulled back in a ponytail. She sported a tank-top, some cotton shorts, and some blue new balances. All in all, the bitch still looked good.

"You don't miss me, bitch," I countered as I reasoned with myself. I tried to figure out how I could get that gun out of her hand and blow her fucking brains out.

"I do, I do." A tear rolled down her cheek. "You ruined my family."

How the fuck she know where I stay?

That bitch was the one sending the text messages the whole time. How did she get my fucking number?

"Yo pops tried to have me killed," I said.

"And I told him not to." Her voice was shaky.

"I thought you loved me, baby girl."

"I do, I do."

"So why you got that gun pointed at me?" *I gotta get that biscuit out of her hand.*

"I don't know what else to do." She tightened her grip on the gun. I clinched my jaw because I thought she was going to squeeze the trigger. "My father's dead, my uncle is dead. I have no one."

"Listen ..." I tried to reason with her. "We can work this shit out, baby. We both lost people we love. Let's put that shit behind us and go back to how it used to be."

"My life has been miserable without you," she responded.

"Mine too," I lied.

"Really?" she asked, lowering the gun a little bit.

"Yeah, baby."

She shook her head no and raised her cannon back up. "Stop lying to me, Spade!" she exclaimed.

I shifted on my couch. Nervous reaction, I guess. "I'm keepin' it a hunid, baby."

"No! ...you're not!"

"I am, I am."

"Fuck you!"

"Calm down, lil' mama."

"You calm—"

BANG!

Blood squirted out of Maria's forehead. Her body fell to the floor hard. Behind her Selena was standing with the baby forty I gave her. Her arms were shaky and she dropped the gun on the floor.

I rushed over to her and hugged her. "Go upstairs, baby. Go!" I told her. She ran upstairs crying.

I turned around and looked at Maria's dead body lying on my living room floor.

"Bitch," I said to her dead body. I bent down and picked up the baby forty Selena dropped. Blood poured out of Maria's forehead and settled on my living room floor.

I hurried and grabbed the gun Maria had and ran in my kitchen. I grabbed a trash bag out of my kitchen closet and put both guns in there.

I'ma have Ace get rid of these.

I ran upstairs and shot to my bedroom. Selena was balled up in the corner crying. I tossed the trash bag on my bed and went over to her. "Stand up, baby." I pulled her to her feet.

She was crying uncontrollably. I shook her hard to get her attention. "Listen! Calm down!"

"I ... I just killed ... killed her."

"I know, I know." I pulled her to me. "Don't trip, baby. Go home and wait for me to call. I got you."

"You promise?"

"Yeah, baby, now go." I pointed to the doorway.

She rushed out of my room and left. I hurried behind her. I caught up with her going down the steps and wrapped my arm around her. I tried to prevent her from seeing Maria's dead body. Once she made it in her car and pulled off, I closed my door. *Shit,* I thought to myself when I looked at Maria's dead body lying on my floor.

I had to think fast.

Ranno and Ace.

***

"You're lucky you have hardwood floors," Ranno said, closing the trunk on a new booty Buick Lacrosse. Inside that trunk was Maria's corpse in a body bag. We were standing in my garage.

Ace walked into the garage with the trash bag that had the guns in it. "Here you go," he said, handing the bag to Ranno.

"These never existed," Ranno said after he grabbed the bag.

I reached my hand out and gave Ranno a gentleman's handshake. "'Preciate it."

"No problem. Sparkle's at the loft waiting on you," Ranno said.

"Coo'. You ready, Ace?" I asked.

Ace was going to take me to meet Sparkle. Ranno was going to make Maria and those cannons disappear.

"Yeah, let's shake," Ace said.

I hit the garage door opener to let Ranno out. Once he pulled out, I closed it. Me and Ace went back through my house to make sure there wasn't any traces of Maria anywhere.

Once everything was in the clear we headed out.

We jumped in Ace's rental and pulled away from my spot. "Sparkle got my money down there?"

"Yeah, bro. Er'thing in order," Ace countered.

"Coo'."

When we got to the end of the block I lived on, Ace took a left turn. As soon as he did, two police cars got behind him and hit their cherries.

"Fuck!" I exclaimed.

"Don't trip, bro," Ace said, pulling over to the side of the road.

He kept the car in drive and held the brake. One of my old moves. I worked the mirrors to see what the uniforms would do. The officer in the car directly behind us got out of his vehicle and approached the car cautiously. As soon as he made it to the trunk, Ace took off.

As we gained distance I looked back and noticed the pig running back to his car. The car behind him peeled off and tried to catch up with us.

"You betta shake 'em, cuzz," I told Ace.

"I got dis, nigga," Ace said, making a hard right.

We fishtailed a little, then Ace whipped it back in control. We were all the way down the block when the police car finally turned on the block.

"Go nigga, go!"

Ace smiled as he hit a left turn, then a right. Up the road was the highway.

"Hit the way-way," I said.

I looked back again and both police cars were still pursuing us. Ace had them beat, though. He jumped on the I-70 west highway entrance and floored it.

Epilogue
One year later

"I'll be out there in a minute," I told Casey.

She wrapped a beach towel around her and walked out of the door. Her, Sparkle, Selena, lil' Courtney, and lil' Samantha were going down to the beach. I was the last one in the beach house. Ah yeah, lil' Courtney was me and Casey's baby girl. Courtney Lashay Wright.

Where did I put them fuckin' flip flops?

I searched around until I found them. I was cold chilling in Miami. When me and Ace took the pigs on one a year ago it was a close call. But we got away clean. Sparkle was waiting on a nigga like she was supposed to, I hopped in her whip, and we skated off like normal civilians.

We made it to Miami with no run-ins with the authorities. Smooth sailing, straight up. Ace and Ashley got a divorce. He said he couldn't trust no bitch no matter how hard he tried. They still shared parenting duties. They had a little girl.

OG Casa was back in the town moving and grooving like old times. His beard grew back and he still had a thing for Crown Royal and women. He kept the maintenance up on my house despite the fact that the pigs popped up from time to time.

Ranno went back to Russia when OG Casa was good enough to handle business on his own. Me and Ranno still talked periodically.

Shantel had my son a few months ago. Samual Lendall Wright Jr., my lil' nigga. She was supposed to bring him down here next month. I couldn't wait to see them.

My phone started going off as I walked out of the bathroom I occupied. "Yeah?"

"You coming or what?" Selena asked.

"I'm on my way." I hung up the phone.

Fuck you think you rushin'?

When I walked in the living room to leave the beach house there was an unusual silence. Then …

Boom!

"FBI! Get Down! Get Down!" It seemed like twenty FBI agents rushed in that muhfucka. *Fuck!*

My heart dropped as I stood frozen with my hands in the air. A few agents rushed me and slammed me on the ground.

"Aagh!" I screamed as one of them twisted my arm behind my back and slapped some zip-lock ties on my wrist.

"Get the fuck up." Two of the agents lifted me up to my feet.

"Mr. Wright ..." A different agent approached me. "We've been waiting for this day. I hope you told your loved ones you love them," he smiled. "Get his ass outta here," he told the two agents that held my arms.

They followed his command and escorted me out of the beach house. It seemed like everything was moving in slow motion. I saw different agents scattered throughout the beach house tearing that muhfucka up, but I didn't hear anything.

I thought about Samantha, Courtney, and Lil' Sam. How long would it be before I could see them as a free man? I didn't know what the feds had on me. But I knew they didn't come for you unless they had something concrete. And I still had to fight the murder case I had for Kremensky.

Oh well, I figured. It is what it is. I played the game and I had to accept what came with it. Damn, the game is a bitch.

I'll see the streets again.

Text **JORDAN** to **77948**

And stay updated on all of Jordan Belcher Presents' *newest releases, free giveaways,* and *special promotions!*

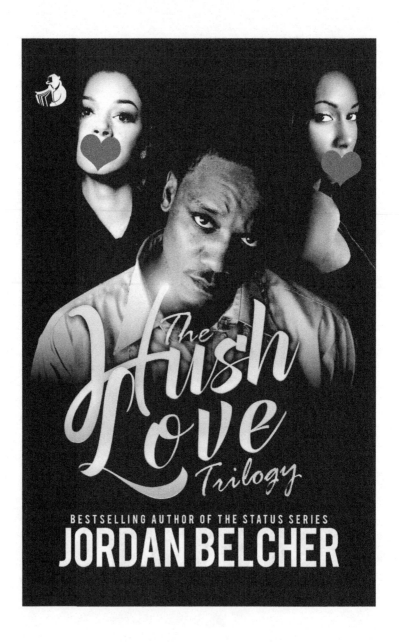

Made in the USA
Monee, IL
01 August 2021